A MURDER BY ANY NAME

ALSO AVAILABLE BY SUZANNE M. WOLFE

Unveiling

The Confessions of X

A MURDER BY ANY NAME

AN ELIZABETHAN SPY MYSTERY

Suzanne M. Wolfe

CROOKED
LANE

NEW YORK

Published in the United States by Crooked Lane Books, an imprint of The Quick Brown Fox & Company LLC.

Crooked Lane Books and its logo are trademarks of The Quick Brown Fox & Company LLC.

Library of Congress Catalog-in-Publication data available upon request.

ISBN (hardcover): 978-1-68331-714-2
ISBN (ePub): 978-1-68331-715-9
ISBN (ePDF): 978-1-68331-716-6

Cover design by Andy Ruggirello
Book design by Jennifer Canzone

Printed in the United States.

www.crookedlanebooks.com

Crooked Lane Books
34 West 27th St., 10th Floor
New York, NY 10001

First Edition: October 2018

10 9 8 7 6 5 4 3 2 1

For Magdalen, Helena, Charles, and Benedict

Confusion now hath made his masterpiece!
Most sacrilegious murder hath broke ope
The Lord's anointed temple, and stole thence
The life o' the building!
—Macbeth

PROLOGUE

The Palace of Whitehall

"God's bollocks, girl! I'm freezing my tits off!"

Lady Cecily Carew murmured an apology while she fumbled with the last of the bodice hooks. Finally, the bodice came undone, and she stepped back, her head lowered so the Queen could not see her expression. She had only been a lady-in-waiting a few weeks, but she despaired of ever getting used to the Queen's way of speaking. She swore like Dicken, the irascible and wizened stable hand on her father's manor, who addressed his four-legged charges and sometimes his two-legged betters in language liberally laced with the dung he shoveled all day. It was unseemly for the great Virgin Queen, Elizabeth the First, ruler of the greatest nation on earth, to use such language, Cecily thought. When her father told her she had been chosen to wait on the Queen, she had been overjoyed, envisioning a monarch who surrounded herself with poets and musicians, a court which echoed to the sweet notes of madrigals and the honeyed words of sonnets, the court her grandmother had known in the early days of Henry VIII, before the king got fat and ugly and homicidal.

Eleanor, the prune-faced Countess of Berwick, dug Cecily sharply in the ribs and thrust at her the bodice she had just removed from the Queen's bony shoulders. Heavy with embroidery and studded with pearls that shimmered in the candlelight, the sour smell of sweat coming off it and its greasy feel made Cecily want to wrinkle her nose, although she was careful not to do so in the royal presence. A week ago she had helped fill the Queen's bath with hot water, sprinkling rosemary, lavender, and rose petals in the water, then carefully testing it before the sagging, skeletal royal body lowered itself stiffly beneath the surface. Cecily had been horrified to discover that the Queen's body was not milk-white as she had imagined, but gray like unbleached fustian, fingernails rimed with black, like her teeth. Used as Cecily was to frequent summer dips in the river that cut through their land at home, or daily ablutions from the ancient well that stood in their courtyard and had been giving the sweetest water in all of England since the time of the Conqueror, or so Cecily's father claimed, she was appalled. Naked and stripped of the white paste she wore thickly smeared on her face, throat, and hands to cover up the small pox scars she had received in her youth, the Queen's grimy, ill-smelling body reminded Cecily of an old woman she had seen begging outside the palace.

But the Queen was adamant: only once a month would she endure the perilous and foolhardy ritual of bathing. Even a numbskull, she was fond of saying, knew that the hale and hearty were carried off after bathing by rheums and catarrhs and God knew what other poxy ailments of the lungs. So once a month, her ladies-in-waiting cleaned the cobwebs and rat-droppings from the great copper bath in the storeroom, dragged it to the Queen's inner chamber, set it before the fire, and began the laborious and tedious task of filling it with buckets of boiling water hauled up the myriad palace stairs by the scullery maids from the cavernous kitchens below.

Cecily draped the Queen's nightgown over a stool before the fire to warm, careful not to scorch it as she had done the previous week, and then picked up a silver bowl and linen towel from the hearth and carried them over to the countess.

"Stand here," the countess ordered, indicating Cecily should hold the bowl directly in front of the Queen. "And don't spill it. You're all fingers and thumbs tonight."

Cecily kept her eyes lowered as she had been instructed, relieved she would not witness the uncovering of the royal flesh as the countess dipped the towel in the water and stroked it carefully over the Queen's face and throat, rinsing it out in the basin, the water swirling gray grit as the chalk and lead cosmetic dissolved.

"What ails you, girl?"

It took Cecily a moment to realize the Queen was speaking. Glancing up, she saw the royal eyes, brown as two old pennies, assessing her with shrewdness and not a little kindness.

"I am quite well, thank you, Your Majesty." She gave a little bob, careful not to splash water onto the Queen's chemise.

"Bollocks," the Queen replied. "She's either homesick or dreaming of a lusty suitor, mark my words." This last accompanied by a lewd wink directed at the countess who tut-tutted priggishly.

"Up the spout, up the spout," a voice chirruped from the four-poster bed in the corner where Codpiece, the Queen's diminutive Fool, was insolently stretched, with his stubby arms folded behind his head on the pillow, his short legs crossed at the ankles.

"Don't be cheeky," the Queen admonished, but not before Cecily saw the corner of her mouth twitch.

Codpiece was a constant irritant in Cecily's life and, she suspected, in the lives of all the ladies-in-waiting and the entire court. Of indeterminate age and four feet high in thick-soled boots, he followed at the Queen's heels like an undisciplined puppy, making verbal messes wherever he went and gnawing on subjects best left alone. Seldom checked and outrageously spoiled, he thought nothing of interrupting the Queen in the middle of an audience with the Dutch or French ambassador, freely giving his opinion on matters of state, but couched in puns and euphemisms so convoluted and paradoxical they made Cecily's eyes cross. Just the other day, Cecily had been horrified when he had suggested to the Queen in the middle of an audience that she need do nothing about the French, as the pox would soon decimate their population and give her a bloodless coup. The Queen guffawed, and the ambassador walked out in a huff. In vain did Baron Burghley and her other advisors complain that the Fool's bawdy and only marginally witty interjections during crucial negotiations put the realm—not to mention the Queen's dignity—at risk and made her the laughing stock of Europe.

"Are you a traitor then, Codpiece?" the Queen had said. "Shall I cut off your head?"

"If you wish, Your Majesty," the Fool replied, giving a low, mocking bow, the absurdly long feather in his velvet cap wafting perilously close to the royal nose. "But then where would you be without a cod in a piece?"

"I am already cod-less, Imp," the Queen replied, rapping him on the head with her knuckles.

"So you are, O wise Virgin," he retorted. "Less cod and more peace. Precisely my advice about France."

The Queen snorted and threw him a sweetmeat, which he caught in his mouth like a dog. Cecily and the rest of the court had tried not to look appalled.

"Well, child," the Queen was saying, "have you a suitor?"

Cecily felt her cheeks flame as she remembered, too late, the advice given her by her friend, Mary, also one of the ladies-in-waiting, only a year older but already wise to the Queen's eccentricities and the raucous life of the court.

"Never look the old bat directly in the eyes," she had told Cecily on her second day at court. "She once said the eyes are the windows to the soul. Too bloody right. And she's got a front row seat."

Cecily was, in fact, dreaming of a suitor, but her virginal and romantic mind would never have characterized him as *lusty*. She barely knew what the word meant. Never once, in all her sixteen years, had she equated the goings-on of the animals in the fields in spring and Dicken's anatomically rich invective—not to mention the Queen's—with what a man and a woman got up to in the privacy of a bedchamber. When she thought of suitors, she envisioned a lovesick gallant plucking at a lute while he stared soulfully into her eyes, or rose-scented missives declaring undying love, chastely slipped down the front of her bodice.

Her mind wandering, she recalled the one event in her brief sojourn at court that had fulfilled all her romantic expectations: the lavish ball given annually by the Queen at Hampton Court to celebrate the anniversary of her accession to the throne on November 17, 1558. The sumptuous ballroom had blazed with the flames of a thousand beeswax candles shimmering off the gorgeous rainbow of jewels worn by the ladies and, most of all, by the Queen herself. Cecily had been dazzled, so much so that Mary had had to give her an elbow to remind her to lift the Queen's cloth of gold train from under her feet so that Gloriana Regina did not face-plant on the gleaming floor in front of the entire court. Once safely settled on her throne, Elizabeth had dismissed the ladies-in-waiting to dance. Only the countess remained by the Queen's side, scowling in disapproval as the women ran joyously into the whirling, stamping fray.

"Just look at the old battle-ax," Mary hissed into Cecily's ear as she dragged her onto the dance floor. "She looks like she just sat on one of those monstrous long hairpins she wears. She can't bear anyone to have any fun. Bah!"

Cecily giggled, then blushed to the roots of her hair as a young man gave her a low bow. Mary blew him a kiss but moved on, dragging her friend with her.

"That's Sir Hugh," Mary said. "You need to watch out for him. He thinks he's God's gift."

Cecily glimpsed a humpbacked man standing in the shadows. His face was pale and his clothes dark. The deformity of his back made his head twist up at an angle so that he appeared to be craning his neck forward. His dark eyes were fixed on Cecily, an enigmatic smile on his lips. "Who's that?" she asked, shivering despite the tremendous heat of the room.

"The Spider," Mary said. "Cecil. He runs the spy network for Sir Francis Walsingham."

"Isn't he a bit young?" Cecily asked. Despite the deformity which made the Spider's body look old, his face was that of a young man in his early twenties.

"Baron Burghley is his father," Mary explained, "and pulled strings to get him appointed. Sir Robert's supposed to be studying at Cambridge but he's being groomed to succeed Sir Francis. Stay away from him. He's dangerous."

It was a chilling reminder that beneath the glitter and pomp of the court moved dark, dangerous currents. Currents, Cecily knew, that could kill. She looked hastily away and saw a dark-haired man leaning nonchalantly against a wall, with his arms folded and a sardonic expression on his face. He seemed to be watching the Spider. When he caught her looking at him, he winked. Cecily smiled back, the threat of the spymaster forgotten.

The rest of the night passed in a frenzy of dancing. Cecily lost track of how many courtiers she danced with, but when Sir Walter Raleigh took her hand to lead her into a galliard, she was so overcome with awe that her legs almost refused to hold her up, until a stocky man in plain attire, a soldier by the look of him, cut in and whirled her away from the dashing explorer. Only one partner displeased her—a man dressed in sulfurous yellow who ogled and smirked at her the whole time and whose hands felt like dead fish.

The love note she had longed to receive at the ball had indeed finally appeared that very morning, but in the most unlikely of places, and it smelled more of tallow than of roses.

As the most junior of the ladies-in-waiting, she had taken up the rear of the little procession following the Queen as she swept out of the chapel after matins like a blazing comet at the head of a rainbow-hued tail of velvet and silk that rustled like a summer's breeze over the tiled floor. Eager to catch the ear of the Queen before her never-ending round of audiences with foreign ambassadors and meetings closeted with Baron Burghley and the Privy Council in the Star Chamber, the ladies and gentlemen of the court pressed thickly into the aisle behind Cecily, pushing and shoving, occasionally stepping on the back of her gown, causing her to stumble. It was in the crush at the door, when the Queen stopped to speak to someone and her ladies milled about waiting for her to proceed, the countess moving irritably among them to chivy them into some order, that Cecily felt someone slip something into the pocket of her skirts. Fishing it out, she saw a tiny rolled piece of parchment. Heart fluttering like a trapped bird, she scanned the faces around her, but no eyes were fixed on her with veiled yearning, no lips discreetly kissed the tips of fingers. Courtiers began to fall back as the Queen moved on, her ladies following. Tucking the note back into her pocket for safekeeping, Cecily hurried after them.

Cecily had to wait until the Queen had broken her fast and stomped off to her first audience before she had a chance to read the note. She asked the countess permission to go to the privy, set in an alcove off the staircase leading to the royal apartments.

"If you must," the countess replied, as if a call of nature were a deplorable flaw of character.

Once she had drawn the curtain across the doorway, Cecily extracted the scrap of paper from her sleeve and, with trembling fingers, unfurled it. There was just enough light from the barred casement window, set high in the wall for ventilation, for her to read the words written there:

Meet me in the chapel after compline at midnight. Come alone. Tell no one.
  Signed, A heartsick admirer

Suppressing a tiny stab of disappointment that the note was so brief and not more flowery—*O Diana, Chaste Huntress of my Heart* or even the less exalted and more shopworn *Sweetheart* would not have gone amiss—Cecily focused on the word *heartsick*, reasoning that if the note were penned in haste, there would be no time for a more effusive and elaborate salutation. She was also a little miffed that her secret admirer, although "heartsick" (she kept returning to that), did not think she had the wit to come alone or keep their assignation secret, feeling it necessary to instruct her accordingly.

If Cecily's innocent head were not so peopled with lovelorn swains and shepherdesses, pining poets cruelly separated from their Beatrices and Lauras, she would have noticed the note's rather chilly, schoolmasterly tone.

As it was, she could hardly keep her mind on the endless tasks of the day, a day that somehow must be got through before she could discover the identity of her "heartsick" (it was growing on her) admirer. She had been set to repairing a billowing mountain of the Queen's petticoats. She worked at it until her fingers ached and she thought she would go blind, the countess insisting on tiny, precise stitches. This was followed by rubbing stinking animal fat into the soft leather of the Queen's shoes—another huge pile. Rich as her father might be, she had never in her life seen so many pairs of shoes, petticoats, stomachers, sleeves (individually sewn onto the Queen's dress each morning), stockings of wool and finest linen, lawn handkerchiefs and belts and vests and . . . It made Cecily's head spin to think of it all. She was certain the contents of the royal wardrobe could have clothed the women of an entire village, if not the whole of London.

But the job she hated most—absolutely loathed, she guiltily confided to Mary—was when she was set to combing and curling the royal wigs, a task she equated with currying a dead sheep. Yet another cherished illusion brutally done to death on her arrival at court. She had thought the Queen's fiery red locks were her own, a miracle of longevity deservedly bestowed by Mother Nature on such an august monarch. Ravished by the piles of intricate curls, frizzes, top-knots, and braids crowned with pearl, amethyst, emerald, carbuncle, and sapphire headdresses or smothered with tiny diamond stars as if they had been sprinkled with heavenly dust, Cecily was initially dazzled. Yet the hair itself, though brilliant of hue and adornment, was as wiry and coarse to the touch as the fur of her father's favorite brindled hound, Nellie, woven as it was onto a linen cap that, astonishingly and horrifyingly on her first night, had been tenderly lifted off the Queen's head by the countess to reveal a flaking scalp barely furred with white stubble. It took all of Cecily's training and good breeding not to shriek aloud with shock.

"Bald as a coot," was how Mary had put it later when they were cozily tucked up in their shared truckle bed, the attic filled with the soft feminine snores of their fellow ladies-in-waiting and the occasional porcine grunt. "And scurvy too," Mary added with relish.

"Shh," Cecily whispered. "Someone will hear."

"Like I give a toss."

As always, she was both scandalized and titillated by Mary's derisive manner when speaking of the Queen. She couldn't help but think it a little treasonous but would find herself dissolving into giggles nonetheless. Healthy as horses and blessed with strong teeth; shining, cascading tresses; supple limbs; and cast-iron constitutions, neither girl could imagine herself at twenty-five, let alone fifty-two.

As she stitched at the clothing and rubbed at the shoes, Cecily's mind had continually circled around then landed on likely candidates for her secret admirer. Like a bee drowsing among the gillyflowers in her mother's walled garden, her thoughts bumbled happily from one face to another: the handsome page of the Duke of Sussex, said to be a distant cousin, whom she had caught staring at her across the banquet hall as he stood behind his lord, ready to carve his meat; or the young tenor, second row, third from the left, in the Chapel Royal, whose golden voice sent shivers of delight running up and down Cecily's spine, the purity of his voice more than compensating for the impurity of his complexion. Perhaps it was someone she had danced with at the Accession Day Ball, she wondered, although she sincerely hoped it wasn't the man in yellow with the clammy hands.

At last the long day was over. Gloriana Regina was put to bed with much ceremony and a soothing tisane for wind, now a staple of the bedchamber since the menu at court reflected the fasting season of Advent and was comprised extensively of a volcanic combination of lentils, beans, and dried peas. Cecily was dismissed from the royal bedchamber, thanking God it wasn't her turn to bed down on the straw-stuffed bolster before the fire in case the Queen should want something in the night. But just as Cecily was leaving, the countess called her back and instructed her to mend the torn lace on a stack of royal handkerchiefs. Trying to hurry in the dim light of a solitary candle, Cecily fretted that she would miss her assignation. The tower clock chimed the quarter hour after midnight just as she was biting off the thread on her last stitch. The countess herself had long since taken herself off, no doubt to get her feet up before the fire in her private rooms across the hall. Feeling guilty for lying to her friend about sneaking off to the chapel before bed, Cecily tiptoed out of the room, closing the door quietly. But Mary had been laid up with a cold all day. Looking in earlier to see if she needed anything, Mary had raised a bleary, red-nosed face from the pillow and, in a voice very like that of a frog in the pond back home, croaked that she needed nothing, thank you very much. The politeness with which she said this convinced Cecily that Mary must surely be at death's door.

★   ★   ★

Worried that she was too late, Cecily made her way swiftly down the stone steps leading to the chapel. Except for the occasional eruption of male laughter from one of the public rooms where the Royal Guard nightly gathered to drink and play dice when they weren't patrolling the palace, it was quiet. A dog barked outside, followed by an angry shout and a yelp as if the dog had been kicked; then all fell silent again. Nights in the palace were given over to men—soldiers mostly, but also clerks, pale with hunger, fingers stained with ink, clutching their masters' eleventh-hour missives, or young pages drooping against doorways, unshaven chins sunk on hollow chests, put there to guard their masters from the sudden intrusion of an irate wife while they tumbled a serving maid in the marital bed.

If the nights were the province of men, the days were ruled by women, with Elizabeth Regina the sun that shone above them all, a source of light as well as blistering heat that seared and shriveled any who were foolish enough to incur her wrath. But despite the dominance of the female sex at Elizabeth's court, Cecily had once overheard Sir Walter Raleigh—Cecily had a tremendous crush on the dashing explorer, especially since dancing with him at the ball—mutter to his neighbor that "Her Majesty has bigger balls than a Brahmin bull." Ignorant as to the meaning of *Brahmin*,

Cecily knew by painful experience that *bollocks* featured often in her royal mistress's speech.

The torches in the wall sconces flickered as an icy draft gusted from the arrow slits in the stairwell, causing shadows to writhe on the walls like tormented souls. Cecily shivered and pulled her fur-lined cloak more tightly around her, praying she didn't trip on the hem and break her neck. Her feet felt numb, the thin kid-skin slippers feeble protection against the icy slabs. At last she reached the bottom and, peeping into the corridor to make sure no one was about, ran silently toward the chapel, clutching the note tightly in her fist like a talisman.

CHAPTER 1

The Black Sheep Tavern, Bankside

The Honorable Nicholas Holt, younger brother of Robert, Earl of Blackwell, lately returned from spying for the Queen on the Continent, was dreaming of white, willing female flesh, his lips grazing over smooth pearlescent thighs, lute-flaring hips and upward to what he confidently anticipated to be pillowy and perfectly rounded breasts; murmuring endearments, if not of love, then those guaranteed to induce enthusiastic cooperation—*sweetheart, my Venus*, even the low and surprising moan *Mouse*. The only fly in the ointment was an inhumanly pitched shrieking that kept putting him off his amatory stride.

"Rise and shine, rise and shine, rise and shine . . ."

"I'm risen," he growled.

"Evidently," a voice said.

Nick blearily became aware that the voice was male and could not possibly have emanated from the lips of his dream goddess. At the same time, her flesh began to melt, oozing unpleasantly through his fingers like marchpane on a hot summer's day at the fair, until she was gone. In its place a horde of blacksmiths set up shop inside his skull and started clanging away.

"John," Nick said without opening his eyes, "be a pal and sod off." And as an afterthought: "And shut that bloody parrot up before I stuff it up your arse."

The shrieking subsided to low avian grumblings as John Stockton, Nick's friend and companion in arms, threw a cloak over the stand where Bess, said parrot, was chained. Next he shook Nick, who was sprawled on a bench in a corner of the taproom of The Black Sheep, the tavern Nick owned and John ran. A raspy, wet tongue began to slaver Nick's face.

"Cut it out, Hector," he muttered, pushing the big canine muzzle away.

"Nick," John said, "there's an urgent message from your brother."

"He can sod off too." But something in John's voice made Nick open his eyes. "What's wrong?"

"It's Sir Edward Carew's daughter."

"Which one?"

"Cecily."

Nick sat up quickly, then regretted it as the room tilted and his stomach lurched. Hector, his enormous Irish wolfhound, so massive the shaggy head was on a level with his own, was regarding him with reproachful eyes. Nick had fought beside Sir Edward, visiting his manor in Herefordshire many times. He recalled Cecily as a shy, dreamy girl with long, fair hair and guileless cornflower-blue eyes. As he grew accustomed to the shuttered gloom of the taproom, he recognized an adolescent boy in the livery of his brother, standing near the door, face taut, eyes black holes in a white face.

"What's amiss, Alan?" he asked, pulling on his boots and buckling on his sword belt. Black wings began to beat inside his chest.

"It's Lady Cecily," the lad replied. "She's been murdered." Then he burst into tears.

*   *   *

The corridor outside the chapel was in an uproar, a seething mass of plush taffeta brocade and the humbler fustian as nobles, pages, and servants jostled one another and craned their necks to see through the crossed pikes of the two stony-faced Royal Guards positioned at the door. Nick pushed his way through the crowd, the page boy, Alan, at his heels. Hector padded silently behind, a path magically opening up around him like Moses parting the Red Sea as people shied away from this canine monster.

Nick had questioned Alan closely as they were being rowed across the river in the wherry Robert had sent to fetch him, a river crossing being quicker than attempting London Bridge on foot, or even on horseback, with its throngs of pedestrians and lumbering carts. All the boy could tell him was that at first light, when the Queen and her ladies had gone to the chapel for morning prayers, they had discovered Lady Cecily's body.

*   *   *

"Let me pass," Nick said.

The guards' expressions did not change, the wickedly sharp pikes remaining resolutely crossed. Nick sighed.

"Robert," he shouted. "Tell these trained monkeys to stand aside."

"Let him pass," a voice ordered. Wood clashed on stone as the guards came to attention, pikes smartly brought into the upright position.

"Majesty," Nick said, belatedly catching sight of a froth of red curls just inside the door. He gave a small bow, all he could manage in the cramped space, then entered the chapel.

"Thank you, Alan," Nick said, touching the boy gently on the shoulder. "Tell the earl I will speak with him later." Nick saw his brother, Robert, with an arm awkwardly about the shoulders of Sir Edward Carew, who was sitting on the altar steps, face buried in his hands, shoulders heaving, although not a sound escaped. Alan nodded and went to stand beside them.

The Queen was striding up and down the center aisle, her inner circle watching from the pews with pale, strained faces. Off to one side, the white-haired Baron Burghley, the Queen's chief advisor and Lord Treasurer, was whispering urgently in the ear of Sir Francis Walsingham, Secretary of State. A young boy in a white surplice, one of the choristers, was throwing up in the corner. Even the Queen's Fool was silent, standing forlornly off to one side like a forgotten child. As Nick approached, the Queen abruptly stopped and whirled around. Two bright spots of color burned on her cheeks, and her brown eyes bore into him like gimlets. He recognized the signs: the Queen was afraid and because she was afraid, enraged.

"Disperse those ghouls," she bellowed. "It's not a goddamned cockfight."

A tremor passed through the crowd outside the chapel, like a chill wind. The guards stepped forward, and reluctantly, with many a backward glance and low muttering, people began to drift away.

"Come with me," the Queen said, turning on her heel and making for the altar.

The chapel was brightly lit with candles and torches held by guards in a circle around the altar, but the acrid smell of pitch and beeswax could not mask the faint odor of the onset of decay. Nick briefly closed his eyes; he was all too familiar with that smell. Here, however, in this place of worship, it seemed doubly obscene. Here should be safety and hush, not the scrape of steel on bone, the clash of metal on metal, the banshee screams of the dying; here should be peace.

Nick spotted Cecil, the Queen's spymaster under Sir Francis Walsingham, standing behind the altar, with his back to the rood screen. His nickname at court was the Spider, for he favored black and preferred dark corners, the better to observe without being seen.

At the absurdly young age of twenty two, Cecil was a prodigy. Officially still a student at Cambridge, his father, Baron Burghley, had persuaded Sir Francis Walsingham to take him on as an assistant. Cecil had proved to be a master at uncovering traitors and plots, soon becoming invaluable to the Queen's chief spymaster, especially since Sir Francis was in failing health. Now Cecil virtually ran Walsingham's spy network and was rumored to be poised to succeed him. Affectionately called "Pygmy" by the Queen on account of his short stature, Nick preferred the much more popular nickname of "Spider."

Nick now knew who had summoned him. Coerced into working for Cecil a year ago, he had spent the past six months traveling around Europe as a dissolute nobleman out to see the world, in reality spying on the Spanish navy yards. The look Cecil gave him from under hooded lids told him he should have reported in by now. He had been back in London for over a fortnight. Only Walsingham, the Spider, the Queen and—unbeknownst to Nick's masters—the faithful John Stockton, knew he was a spy and a man who ferreted out the truth. To the rest of the world, he was a sot and the rapscallion younger brother of a great lord, a blight on his aristocratic house, and the envied master of the biggest dog they had ever seen. It was a perfect, though frequently tiresome, cover.

Nick saw the Queen briefly lay a be-ringed hand on Edward's bowed head as she climbed the steps. At her approach, the guards parted to reveal the altar.

Cecily was laid out with her hands crossed over her breast in a terrible parody of tranquility, her face a beautiful alabaster effigy, her eyes mercifully closed. *Arranged,* Nick thought at once. A low rumbling emerged from Hector's throat, his hackles standing up along his back.

"Easy, boy," Nick said.

Behind him he heard the Queen ordering everyone out of the chapel except for Cecil and Nick, whom she motioned to remain with a flick of her hand.

"Take my ladies back to the royal apartments," she instructed the countess, who was standing motionless with a blank expression, oblivious to her women who were clustered around her, weeping. "*Now*, Eleanor," she added gently when the countess did not move. The countess gave a start, as if awakening from a trance, and began to usher the ladies-in-waiting down the aisle, forgetting to curtsey to the Queen, an unprecedented lapse in protocol and as eloquent an expression of shock as Nick had ever seen.

The Queen turned to Nick's brother. "Escort Sir Edward there too, Robert," she said. "Comfort him as best you can. I shall join you anon."

When the chapel had emptied and all but the Queen, Cecil, and the Royal Guard remained, Nick leaned over the body, forcing himself to look dispassionately.

Below Cecily's neck, the effect of peaceful repose was cruelly mocked by a tiny hole in the fabric of her dress beneath the left breast. Sending up a silent apology to the dead girl for such a violation of her modesty, Nick gently unhooked her bodice and moved the material aside so that her breast was exposed. As he expected, a corresponding hole obscenely marred the alabaster white of her skin. An upward thrust to the heart with a stiletto, Nick realized. An assassin's blade as long and slender as a needle, made to slide between the ribs before the victim even knew she had been stabbed, it was an elegant and deadly weapon, easily concealed. He gently pushed on the flesh around the wound with his finger, and dark, viscous blood emerged. Heart blood. A treacherous way to kill, and silent, but a quick way to die. Mercifully, Cecily would not have known what was happening, would have had no chance to cry out. Nick would not be surprised if no one had heard anything last night.

He reached out and gently manipulated Cecily's crossed arms, then her legs. Out of the corner of his eye, he saw the Queen flinch. Cecil looked at him over the corpse. *Do what you have to do,* his look said. *As long as you get results.* Nick shrugged. Everyone knew that a body went rigid not long after death and then relaxed again a few hours later. What was not commonly known was what his friend, Eli, a Jewish physician of great skill, had told him: that a corpse could often tell the careful examiner how it had died and even, approximately, the time of death. The problem, Nick knew, was not how and when, but who and why.

"Cover her up, for pity's sake," the Queen exclaimed, turning away.

"I'm sorry, Majesty," Nick said, "but I need a friend to examine her just as she is." Then added: "A Jewish doctor."

The Queen looked sharply at him. "I overheard a fool muttering that this is a murder perpetrated by the Jews. A sacrifice of an innocent to mock the Eucharist." Before Nick could speak, she waved him silent. "Utter folly, I know. Whoever did this is a member of the court. *My* court." Her eyes flashed dangerously, and Nick was suddenly reminded of her father, Henry VIII, the Tudor Lion. "But the mood of the city will turn ugly if these rumors spread, as they are bound to do. Londoners have been known to riot for less." She was silent for a moment, then nodded. "I will have him escorted here in secret. He may examine the body." She turned to one of the guards. "See to it," she ordered.

"Thank you, Majesty," Nick said.

His gaze moved farther down the body. There was no other damage. A mercy. A brief vision of Cecily, alive and laughing, came to him: He had been strolling by the river on the Carew estate one evening at dusk when he heard a splash. Thinking he had disturbed a waterfowl from its nest in the reeds, he'd scanned the river and seen a lithe white body emerge above the surface and then dive down again like a sleek albino otter. He had crouched in the long grass watching, entranced by the girl's innocent play, a river naiad straight out of the tales of Ovid. When she began to swim toward the bank, he stole silently away, not wanting to frighten or shame her. Her innocence had stayed with him and provided a kind of solace in a world neck-deep in lust, greed, treachery, and death.

Now that loveliness had been callously snuffed out. Nick vowed to find the monster responsible and hand him over to the executioner to be hung, drawn, and quartered, for surely only a low-born varlet's death could atone for such a sin.

"Find the one who did this, Holt," the Queen said, as if reading his thoughts. "And bring him to me for, by Christ, I will not suffer such a man to live." She looked down at Cecily for a long moment, then leaned over and kissed her tenderly on the forehead as a mother might kiss a sleeping child. Then she turned and swept out of the chapel, ordering the guards to permit no one access except Nick, Cecil, and Eli the physician.

"Here," Nick said, thrusting a flaming torch at Cecil. "Hold this."

If Cecil minded being ordered around by one of his spies, he didn't show it. The son of a commoner and Baron Burghley, the former Sir William Cecil and the Queen's most trusted advisor, perhaps he considered it politic to comply with an order given by the son and brother of an earl, an aristocratic heritage bred in the blood and not merely bestowed by a grateful monarch like his own father's title. In fact, he rarely showed emotion of any kind, his voice always pitched low, face bland, his prodigious intellect and love of cruelty apparent only to those who knew him very well indeed. Like Nick.

Born with a deformed spine and consequently hunchbacked, he was short in stature and walked with a pronounced limp. It was easy to underestimate him, to treat him as an object of derision. He used long used this to his advantage, squatting like a black spider in the dark corners of chambers, listening and recording, always recording, filing away names and injudiciously spoken words in the great ledger of his remarkable memory, constructing webs in which to snare the traitor and the assassin. Although only in his early twenties, he had swiftly made himself invaluable to the Queen, with his network of spies at home and abroad, with his lists of traitors, his suspicions of plots. Cannily exploiting the Queen's very real fear of assassination (she had survived several attempts), he had convinced her that he and his network were the only bulwark between her and the assassin's knife or musket ball and gunpowder.

Nick noticed that one of Cecily's hands was tightly closed into a fist. Gently he pried open her fingers one by one and extracted a tiny roll of parchment. When he read it, he was assailed by a terrible anger that the girl had been so heartlessly tricked to her death. He imagined her anticipation during the day, her girlish romantic fantasies, her excitement as the time for the assignation approached. Perhaps she even knew her killer.

Nick also felt a small flicker of hope, for now he had a letter written by the murderer himself. If he could match the handwriting, then he would have his man. And the specification of the time—midnight—made Nick suspect that Cecily had received the note yesterday morning. In view of the fact that the Queen's ladies were kept busy throughout the day tending to the needs of their royal charge, Nick thought it likely that the only opportunity the killer would have had to freely approach Cecily in a crowd would have been after morning chapel the day before. Before chapel, the Queen would have processed down the aisle, her ladies following in her train, the pews already packed with courtiers. After the service, the Queen was well known to stop and hear petitions, giving her ladies a brief opportunity to fraternize. Anyone could have brushed against Cecily in the crush and slipped her a note.

Nick decided to proceed on the assumption that the killer must have attended morning chapel. This, at least, had the virtue of narrowing down his suspect pool.

He held the parchment to Hector's nose. "Seek," he commanded.

CHAPTER 2

The Palace of Whitehall

Nick and Cecil followed a few steps behind as the dog nosed around the floor of the chapel, up the aisle, back again, in and out of the pews, then suddenly made a beeline to one of the choir stalls, where he stood, tail wagging.

Nick peered over the front of the stall and saw something white protruding from under the seat.

"What is it?" Cecil asked.

"Not sure." Leaning over, Nick extended his arm as far as it would reach and picked it up. A bleached linen handkerchief, reasonably clean. No embroidery or lace or helpful initials sewn into the corner—it could belong to either a man or a woman. But one thing he did know: it belonged to someone at court. Only a courtier could have picked up the French fashion for handkerchiefs; the common folk outside the walls of the palace still used their sleeves.

Nick put the square of linen to his nose and inhaled: no flowery perfume such as a woman might use, but a strong odor of garlic and something else he couldn't identify but which made his eyes water. Now all he had to do was find someone with a bad cold, he thought ruefully, which included just about everyone from the Queen down to the lowest scullion who cleaned the jakes. He could safely rule out the Queen and illiterate servants. And probably women. Not only did it take strength to lift a dead body, and he could detect no sign of drag marks on the chapel floor, but the selection of the victim—a beautiful, virginal girl—bespoke a lust for desecration that, in his opinion, only a man could harbor. The killing was motivated, at the very least, by a kind of twisted hatred, and Nick made a mental note to ask Kat, the madam of a Bankside brothel and a friend, if she had ever heard of such a thing before. Crimes of passion were not uncommon, especially against women, but this was different. In the absence of any sign of the victim's struggle—torn fingernails, scratches or bruises to the body, disheveled clothing—this crime did not burn hot and fierce with the fires of any passion Nick recognized, but burned blue like ice. Dante had been right to bury Satan up to his chest in ice in his *Inferno*, rather than having him writhe in the flames of torment the way so many medieval painters had depicted him. Ice immobilized, numbed, held you in an unbreakable grip, and turned the heart to stone. Most disturbing of all, Dante's Satan wept frozen tears as if he grieved for paradise lost, morally aware of his evil, yet utterly unable to change. A recent friend of Nick, a young man called Will Shakespeare, mad for acting, who kept body and soul together stabling horses for a local theater, had once shyly confided during a late night drinking session at The Black Sheep that he hoped one day to write a play with a hero modeled on Dante's Satan. Nick had almost fallen off the bench laughing. He couldn't imagine such a man being called a hero and said as much. More like a monster.

"But that's the point," Will said, excitedly waving his beaker about so that ale slopped onto his doublet. "A monster is a beast and thus has no conscience. It takes a man to do unspeakable things while knowing they are evil. He can even suffer remorse and still go on."

"Then it is not remorse," Nick said, "for he would stop."

"Ah, my innocent friend," Will said, "have you never regretted a sin you could not stop committing?"

At that Nick had gone quiet. He thought of Kat and all the times he had vowed never to see her again and all the times he had failed. He thought of his work for Cecil and how he hated the lies and deception it involved—a life from which he was powerless to break free.

★   ★   ★

Nick folded the handkerchief and put it with the scrap of paper in his pocket. It would be useless now to give the handkerchief to Hector, as the trail of the killer would have been long since destroyed by the crowd milling about the corridor outside the chapel. He would give him a good whiff of it later and pray that Hector would recognize its owner as Nick hunted the killer. He moved the torch back and forth above the choir stall, carefully scanning for more evidence that the killer, and perhaps Cecily, had sat here. He almost missed it: winking like a small ruby in the light of the torch was a single spot of blood on the armrest that separated two stalls. He rubbed at it and studied his finger. Definitely blood. She had been stabbed here and then carried to the altar, where she had been posed. Stiletto thrusts bled very little; most likely the spot of blood was made when the dagger was withdrawn and a drop fell from its tip.

Nick beckoned one of the guards over. "Who discovered the body?"

"One of the choir boys," the man replied.

That would have been the lad he saw being sick, Nick thought. "Bring him to me," he instructed. "Not here," he added. "Can you find me another chamber?"

The guard nodded and went off.

"Any ideas?" Cecil asked.

Nick shook his head. "Not yet. But I'll have to interview everyone who was in the chapel this morning." He ticked them off on his fingers. "Choristers, altar boys, chaplain—whoever accompanied the Queen."

Cecil nodded. "I'll see to it." He left the chapel.

Nick looked after him thoughtfully, marveling anew at how calm Cecil was. Even Nick was shaken by the staged nature of the crime, despite having seen many a body on the battlefield and in the alleys and stews of Bankside, a notoriously dangerous place to roam after dark. Cecil, however, had spent his life safely indoors, shuffling paper, far from the dangerous world of espionage. Like a grandmaster, he moved his pieces on a chessboard as if each move were an academic problem and not the life—and frequently death—of a man. There was something missing inside him, Nick concluded. If Eli cut him open, he would find a great gap where the man's heart should be.

At that moment, he saw Eli enter the chapel. A small, slight man, dressed in the long black robe and skullcap of a physician, his attire having nothing to do with his religion, but rather, as he had told Nick, affording a perfect disguise. Carrying a leather satchel over his shoulder, Eli moved quickly and gracefully, his shoulder-length black hair tied back with a leather thong, his dark eyes already riveted on the body on the altar, with never a glance at Nick.

Nick joined Eli at the altar and watched as his friend began a close examination of the body. Gently opening her mouth, Eli leaned over and sniffed several times.

"No wine or potions," he said softly, as if to himself. Next he examined the wound below her left breast. Like Nick, he prodded the opening. "The killer had to be close," he said.

"Someone she trusted," Nick agreed.

"It takes a steady hand to insert a stiletto," Eli said. "The placement has to be just right. There was no hesitation."

"Not drunk then."

"Ice-cold sober," Eli agreed. "This is as neat a murder as I have seen." This lack of passion disturbed Nick the most. Most murders were fueled by lust or liquor, envy, greed, or anger. Occasionally fear. But this murder was strangely dispassionate, impersonal, as if Cecily had simply been in the wrong place at the wrong time. Yet the note proved she had been carefully selected. It didn't make sense. And then there was the placement of the body, almost as if laid out as a sacrifice. It reminded Nick of the religious rites in ancient times, when virgins were offered to the gods.

"Can you tell if she was raped?" Nick asked.

Eli lifted her skirts. "Not that I can see," he said. "Her underclothes are undisturbed. Any chance I can examine her more closely?"

He meant, Nick knew, cut her up. A practice that was illegal but, he admitted, often yielded valuable results. Eli had told him that the doctors in Salamanca *dissected* corpses, as he called it, and made highly detailed sketches of human organs, veins, and bones. Thirty years before, Eli said, the great physician Andreas Vesalius had been investigated, at the command of the Holy Roman Emperor Charles V, for being a great proponent and practitioner of dissection. Acquitted of moral turpitude and of being in violation of the teachings of Holy Mother Church, stipulations had since been made that only the corpses of beggars and whores could be "abominated" in this way. Nick had to admit that he found dissection repellant but could not deny its usefulness in determining how someone had died, especially if the person had been poisoned. Eli's religion, like the Christian faith, forbade such a practice, but his curiosity about the human body and his bitter hatred of ignorance were greater than his fear of Jehovah's wrath.

"No," Nick replied. "The Queen has taken a personal interest in this."

Eli nodded. The body would be washed and laid out before traveling in a funeral procession to her home in Herefordshire, where she would be given a lavish Christian burial service in the family chapel before being interred beneath its stones. The few corpses Eli had dissected had been those of paupers. The rich took care of their own—living or dead.

Eli drew down Cecily's skirts and stood back. "At least she died quickly," he murmured. "She would have known no fear."

Nick crouched down to where Hector was stretched out, nose between his paws, and ruffled the dog's head. The warmth of the fur and the way the dog's sides rose and fell like a great bellows, helped the sorrow pass. But the relative painlessness of her death was scant comfort. It was as if the cold, everlasting stillness of the girl's body and her manner of dying had laid an icy finger on his heart, and he must touch something living or else die a little himself. It was as he expected when he first examined her body:

somehow this was a type of lust killing, but not a sex killing. Another thing that didn't make sense.

"She was as chaste as the goddess Diana," Nick murmured to himself, thinking of his glimpse of her swimming in the river.

"Any idea when she was killed?" he asked out loud.

"Six to eight hours is my guess," Eli replied. "Around midnight." He lifted her skirts again, rolled her over on her side, and pointed to a dark discoloration on the back of her thighs and buttocks. "The blood sinks to its lowest point," he explained. "The longer the body lies, the darker the stain." He turned and smiled for the first time since he had entered the chapel. "Which is why Rivkah insisted you sit up all night after you were wounded. To prevent bleeding from your neck."

Grateful for this reminder that friendship and hospitality existed in a world where young, innocent girls were butchered, Nick laughed, the sound a little thready. "She could have explained that at the time," he said. "I'm not as stupid as she thinks."

"Or look," Eli said. Then suddenly serious: "I'm finished here. I'll write down a few notes. Come by later?"

Nick nodded and clasped his friend's shoulder. "Take care. Some are already saying your people are to blame for this."

Sorrow darkened Eli's eyes. "So it has always been," he said. "We are ever history's scapegoats."

"Go with God, my friend."

"Shalom."

CHAPTER 3

The Palace of Whitehall

While he waited for the first witness in the room the Queen had ordered to be at his disposal for the duration of the investigation, Nick pondered the implications of the rumor that the Jews were responsible for Cecily's murder. As Eli had said, the Jews were always convenient scapegoats. He recalled that in times of plague—a common occurrence in the summer months—people muttered that the Jews had brought a curse on London. Nick had once thrown a customer out of The Black Sheep—not a local, but a sailor from one of the ships moored at Bankside—for his hateful diatribe against the Jews. In his cups, the sailor had ranted they were "limbs of Satan" and had many colorful and brutal suggestions for what he would do to them were he in charge. The local patrons trooped after Nick as he hauled the sailor out of the tavern by the hair and tossed him into the stinking water of the Thames. Then they applauded and trooped back, cheerfully leaving the man to sink or swim. Many of them were patients of Eli and Rivkah, who were well known in Bankside not only for being excellent physicians but also for refusing to take payment from the poor.

Nick smiled to himself, remembering what Rivkah, Eli's sister, had said: "Unless you're sick or dead, Eli has no time for you."

"Not true, Mouse," Eli had replied, pulling on her braid.

"Hah," she had said, flouncing off, then ruining the effect by sticking her tongue out.

Nick sometimes felt a pang when he watched Eli and Rivkah together. Nick had no sisters, two having died in infancy, and sometimes longed for that easy and affectionate familiarity with the opposite sex. His relationships with women were always complicated.

Eli and Rivkah had a closeness he envied, one that had been forged in adversity. Forced to flee Salamanca in northeastern Spain four years earlier, after their parents and younger siblings had been burned to death in their home by a rioting populace, they had fled to England and sought anonymity in the teeming backstreets of Bankside. Never again would they live in a ghetto, Eli vowed. They were too easy a target for persecution, clustered all together. The Christians always knew where to find them.

London was a place of relative safety, but also one of exile. Eli had attended the University of Salamanca's renowned medical school, practicing at the *Hospital del Estudio* on the *Patio de Escuelas* where the Doctors of the Queen lived, famous in all of Europe for their healing arts. Now Eli practiced in the stews and alleys of Bankside, delivering babies to whores and cleaning and stitching the wounds of criminals, pimps, and those travelers unlucky enough to wander unsuspecting into the fetid warren that lined the south bank of the Thames. He never complained, saying that a sick or wounded body was the same in England as in Spain, highborn or low; man, woman, or child, but Nick came to see that Eli's skill far surpassed the needs of his patients. Rivkah herself was as skilled and knowledgeable in medicine as her brother, but as a woman, she had been barred from formal training. The way her mouth would quirk up in a tiny bitter smile when Eli spoke of the greatness of Salamanca's medical school told Nick how much she grieved for her exclusion.

"I studied at the University of Eli," Rivkah would say, smiling at her brother. "The best in the world."

Nick had met them by chance over a year ago when he was wounded in an alley near a tavern. Nick had been careless. He had witnessed a meeting between a court clerk and a Spanish captain and had seen documents change hands. When he left the tavern to follow the captain back to his ship, he had been jumped by two men waiting in an alley nearby. He had managed to fight them off, but was discovered, bleeding profusely, by Eli as the doctor made his way home after delivering a baby in the one of the neighborhood hovels. The wound was a serious one, as one of his assailants had intended to cut Nick's throat (Nick had managed to stab the other man in the shoulder of his sword arm, disabling him). As he swerved aside just in time, the blade had caught Nick under the right side of his chin and glanced upward over his jawbone and cheek, barely missing his eye. But it had nicked an artery, and he was in danger of bleeding to death.

Eli helped him into a tiny two-up two-down timber house, sat him on a rickety stool, lit some candles, then ran up a ladder to what Nick assumed were sleeping chambers above. Through a haze of pain and blood, he heard a low conversation, then Eli's steps on the ladder, followed by feet in emerald felt slippers, carefully descending rung by rung.

"Can you heat some water, Mouse?" the man said. The girl nodded, her face hidden by a curtain of black hair. Under a hastily thrown-on cloak, Nick glimpsed a linen nightgown. She had been sleeping, but her movements were calm and precise, as if her husband brought back bleeding strangers every night of the week. "And I'll need a needle and thread." Then Eli folded a square of clean linen into a thick pad and, placing it in Nick's hand, said, "I suggest you press this as hard as you can against your neck if you don't want to bleed to death all over my sister's nice clean floor."

Nick's heart did a little flip when he realized the girl was not Eli's wife, then gave a giant lurch when he caught sight of her face as she carried a bowl of steaming water to the table. She looked just like Eli—dark eyes below thick brows, small straight nose, jutting cheekbones, wide mouth. The only difference he could see was her hair, as dark as her brother's but falling in waves over her shoulders down to her waist. He knew there were other, more interesting, differences, but these were hidden by a billowing dark-colored cloak she must have hastily slung around her shoulders when Eli awakened her and which she now held protectively about her body. As if resentful of his astonished gaze, she gathered up her mass of hair in both hands, twisted it into a knot at the back of her neck and secured it with a quill pen she picked up from the table. He caught a glimpse of the lace on the plunging neckline of her gown before she wrapped the cloak around herself again.

"We're twins," she explained unnecessarily.

"I can see that," Nick replied, in a voice that sounded surprisingly croaky. He saw again the small twin mounds pushing out the front of her shift.

The girl scowled. Nick thought this made her look even more beautiful. Tendrils of hair had escaped her makeshift knot and were wafting against her smooth pale cheeks as she moved around the table, setting out clean napkins, a jar of some ointment, and a needle and thread, which she first dunked in boiling water with tongs and then set carefully on a clean strip of linen. A strand of hair had caught in the corner of her mouth, and he longed to lift it away with his finger and hook it over her ear.

"He's obviously delirious," the girl said, addressing her brother. "Not enough blood to the brain. Perhaps we should purge him, relieve the pressure on his . . . *extremities*." Nick blanched as she lifted a razor from the table and smiled sweetly.

Calmly Eli rolled up his sleeves and began to wash his hands. "My sister has a, shall we say, *narcotic* effect on men," he said conversationally. "Which is a good thing, as what I'm about to do is going to hurt like the dickens. But I should watch it if I were you. She's handles a mean scalpel."

Nick remembered feeling a little resentful at this apparent lack of sympathy for his agony, then marveled at the sureness and rapidity with which Eli sewed up the wound and stanched the bleeding. He was right: it did hurt. A lot. But Nick clamped his lips firmly together and did not utter a sound, hoping the girl would notice his bravery. The rest of the night he spent sitting bolt upright before the fire, and when he asked if he could lie down, the girl shook her head.

"A drink?"

She clapped a beaker of water down by his elbow.

"I was thinking more of wine."

She snorted. "Call if the wound reopens," she said, a little callously Nick thought, given his ordeal. Then she and Eli took themselves off up the ladder to bed. Though dizzy with blood loss, something that would soon pass the girl informed him in the morning, Nick was quite certain he owed them his life. He returned to the house a few days later with a small bag of gold. Eli refused payment, but the girl, who he learned was named Rivkah, took the purse from him.

"My brother believes in a utopia where medicine is free to all. I, however, know that utopia means No Place and that even doctors must eat." He noticed her use of the plural as she slipped the purse down the front of her bodice. She didn't offer him a drink then either.

After that, he found himself dropping by almost every week to sit at their scarred kitchen table, drinking wine (she had smiled when she poured him his first beaker), talking with Eli, and watching Rivkah's graceful movements around their tiny kitchen, listening to her comments—astonishingly learned—and her quick bursts of laughter, slightly disconcerting as she did this even when Nick didn't think he had been funny. He even celebrated Shabbat with them one Friday at sundown, feeling a kind of hunger that had nothing to do with lust as he watched Rivkah light the candles and, with upturned palms, chant a low, melodious blessing in a language he didn't understand. During the meal of lamb and bread, Eli raised his goblet.

"To Nick, the sacrificial lamb who daubed his blood above our lintel so the Angel of Death passed by."

"Shalom Shabbat," responded Rivkah solemnly, then spoiled it by crossing her eyes and singing the opening bars to the nursery rhyme "Baa, Baa, Black Sheep." The next day, Nick changed the

name of his tavern from "Ye Olde Cock" to "The Black Sheep."
John clearly thought Nick off his rocker. Rivkah and Eli thought
it hysterical.

After the meal, he had leaned forward to blow out the candle,
but she stopped him with an urgent hand on his arm.

"No, Nick," she said. "God alone is Lord of Light."

He sat back, uncertain of what she meant but feeling he had
done a great wrong. Eli grinned but did not explain.

★ ★ ★

A knock on the door roused him from his reverie. It was soft,
tentative, and Nick might have missed it if Hector hadn't raised
his head and looked at Nick as if to say, *Aren't you going to answer
that already?*

"Enter," Nick called.

A diminutive figure appeared in the doorway.

"Come closer, where I can see you."

It was a boy, clearly reluctant to enter. He was shooting terrified glances at Hector. "Don't worry," Nick joked. "He's had his
breakfast." Then he immediately regretted it when the boy turned
pale and swayed on his feet. "Sit down," Nick said, gently guid-
ing the boy to a stool and pressing him down on it, his body
unresisting, the bones in his shoulders thin and brittle as a skinned
rabbit's. Nick poured a goblet of wine from a flagon on a side
table and handed it to him. "Drink this," he said. "You'll feel
better."

The boy took the goblet and held it to his lips, his hands shaking so badly half of it spilled down the front of his white surplice.
Nick looked away. The red stain looked like blood.

He sat facing the boy, leaning back in the chair and crossing his legs to give the impression of ease. Hector put his head on Nick's knee, and he played with the dog's ears. The lad continued to stare at Hector as if expecting him to leap on him and devour him at any moment.

"What's your name?" Nick asked gently.

"Robin," the boy replied, his voice unbroken, pure as spun glass. When he sang, his voice must soar like a bird in the vaulted ceiling of the chapel. He couldn't be much more than ten, Nick thought. A child.

"What kind of dog is it?"

"Irish Wolfhound," Nick replied.

"Did you breed him?" the boy asked. "My father breeds dogs—greyhounds—but not as big as yours. My pony, Bob, is the same size." Then he added, "I call him that because that's what I do when I ride him. Bob up and down." He gave a tiny smile at the memory. A little color had come back into his cheeks, whether from the wine or the mention of his family, Nick didn't know, but he was relieved. He had thought the poor lad was going to faint dead away when he first saw him. The boy was the chorister Nick had seen being sick in the chapel when he'd first arrived there—the one who had found the body.

Nick was not averse to taking his time. Although he knew most children were well acquainted with death by the age of ten, most having lost younger siblings to disease, or a mother in childbirth, he was quite certain the boy had never encountered anything as brutal as what he had seen in the chapel that morning. "He was starving in an alley in Spain. I adopted him. Isn't that so, Hector?" At his name, the dog lifted his head and regarded his master with a look of great sagacity.

Almost tripping over him near the docks in Valencia, Nick

had found Hector emaciated and covered in sores, with a broken front paw and three cracked ribs. He had obviously been savagely kicked and beaten, but whether he had been abandoned or had run away, Nick did not know. What he did know was that he wanted to kill the man who had brutalized such a noble beast. Still a puppy but huge nonetheless, the dog had calmly regarded Nick when he hunkered down and spoke softly to him for a long time, eventually putting out his hand for the dog to sniff. At first, the dog had growled from deep within his chest, a sound not unlike that of a ship's hull scraping against a stone jetty, but Nick could tell he didn't have the heart for it. He was too battered, too hungry, too close to death. Carefully and speaking softly to him all the while, Nick lifted him, the dog whimpering in pain but otherwise acquiescent, a dead weight in his arms. Nick thought his back would break as he staggered to the inn where he was stay-ing. He ordered meat and water and a bowl of hot water, splints, and bandages. Then he set about trying to save the life of the dog that he had already christened Hector for his courage and his refusal to die. Ever since that night, Hector had been his shadow, refusing to leave the man he clearly regarded as his savior.

At first when Nick had to leave him back at the inn, the whole neighborhood had complained of the dog's doleful baying.

"Like a tormented soul in hell," Mistress Baker, who else but the baker's wife, had informed Nick, her arms, beefy as a man's from hauling great trays of bread out of the oven, folded primly over her capacious bosom. "Fit to wake the dead, it were. Give me quite a turn."

Eventually, as Hector understood that Nick had not aban-doned him and would always come back, he took to lying in the corner of the tavern, his head toward the door, watching for his master's return. Maggie, John's wife, told him that she always knew when Nick's wherry landed at the dock because Hector would give a low whine of excitement, his tail sweeping rapidly back and forth like a demented broom, his eyes locked on the door. Maggie was very fond of Hector, as his quiet, massive presence in the tavern inhibited even the most pugnacious and ale-soaked neighborhood bullyboys. Unlike the other tavern owners in the area, Maggie never had to mop up blood, send for the bonesetter, or have John throw someone out. At the first sign of trouble—a harsh word, a hand snaking toward a dagger—Hector would lumber to his feet; the troublemaking patrons would take the hint and leave.

"Do you want to pet him?"

The boy gulped.

"Hector," Nick said, "go and make friends."

The dog padded over to the boy and lifted a great paw. When Robin tentatively took it, Hector, as if recognizing a wounded soul akin to his own a year ago, began to slaver the boy's face with his great raspy tongue until the boy giggled and fended him off.

"You found the body," Nick said while the boy was distracted. He had often found that people answered more truthfully and with greater accuracy when their minds were on something else.

The boy nodded. "Yes, sir."

"Tell me," Nick said. Hector nuzzled the boy's cheek as if in encouragement.

"It was dark," Robin said. "It's my job to light the candles. I'm the youngest, you see. The others get to sleep in. It's not fair." Then he brightened. "But I'll be eleven after Christmas."

Nick hid a smile. "Go on," he said.

"I had a candle I lit from the brazier in the courtyard. I'm too short to reach the torches on the wall. So I could find my way, you see," he explained as if that weren't perfectly obvious. From his intent, inward-looking expression, his half-closed eyes, Nick could tell he was reliving the events of the morning, almost talking to himself.

"First I lit the sconces in the choir stall, as I always do, and then I went to the altar." He stopped, and the skin around his mouth stretched thin, his eyes widening at the memory.

"It's alright, Robin," Nick said. "Take your time."

"I didn't notice anything amiss at first," he said. "I was trying not to let my candle go out. It's very drafty in the chapel, you know." He swallowed. "It was only as I was reaching up to light the first candle that I noticed . . . *it*." He was twisting his fingers together now, Hector forgotten, his eyes beginning to swim. "*Her*. The Lady Cecily." He looked up, his face crumpling like gold foil. "She used to smile at me, gave me a sweetmeat once. Said I sang like an angel. She was so *pretty*." He buried his face in his arms and cried as if his heart were breaking. As it probably was, Nick thought. Another innocent victim, one more reason, if he had needed it, to bring the killer to justice.

He waited. In his experience, grief was better let out than kept in. Eli agreed with him, saying that people who never showed emotion were prone to all sorts of stomach ailments, disorders of the bowel. At last Robin's sobs turned to hiccups and then to a sad, intermittent snuffling as he wiped his nose on the sleeve of his once-white surplice. When at last he raised his eyes to Nick's, he looked as if he would never be happy again.

"Did anything seem out of place?" Nick asked.

"What do you mean?"

"Something out of the ordinary," Nick explained. "Something

missing that should have been there or something that was there that shouldn't have been."

Robin sat quietly, his hand absently rubbing the top of Hector's head, all fear of the dog forgotten.

"Not really," he said after a long pause. "Only . . ."

Nick leaned forward, careful not to startle him. "Yes?"

"There was a funny smell."

"What kind of smell?" Perfume? Tallow? Urine from a terror-loosened bladder? Nick did not suggest any of these, wanting Robin's memory to be untainted, clear.

"Like medicine," he said eventually. "Like when I had a cough and Mama put stuff on my chest. It made my nose tickle."

Liniment, Nick thought. It was used as a kind of rub or poultice for all kinds of ailments, including strained tendons in horses, chest colds, bruises, and sprains. He would ask Eli and Rivkah about its ingredients and pray they weren't so common as to be useless as a clue. He recalled the handkerchief and wondered if his killer had a cold. Not much use to him as half the court was snuffling and sneezing with winter colds.

After questioning Robin further, it became clear that he had no more to tell.

"Why did you call him Hector?" the boy asked as he was leaving.

"It's the name of a great soldier," Nick replied, not feeling it necessary to burden the child with the plot of the *Iliad*.

"Are you a soldier?" he asked, pointing to Nick's scar, which ran from his temple down the right side of his face, not raw and lumpy like so many scars, but straight, clean, and white thanks to Eli's expert stitches.

"Yes," Nick said, thinking, *If a spy can be called a soldier.*

"I love your dog," Robin replied, impulsively kissing Hector on the nose. The dog reciprocated enthusiastically. "Oh, I almost forgot." He withdrew a hand from deep within the folds of his surplice and handed something to Nick. "I found this on the floor by the choir." Then he was gone, immeasurably happier than when he had arrived, his face glistening with dog saliva.

In his palm, Nick saw a pea-sized yellow stone, topaz by the looks of it, and small enough to have fallen from the inlaid pommel of a dagger. Nick would have said a woman's earring, except he had already decided that the killer was a man. He would have to ask the Queen to order all men at court to surrender their personal daggers so he could examine them, a time-consuming task and one he was certain would yield no results. The knife used to kill had been a stiletto—an assassin's blade—and no courtier in his right mind would carry such a thing openly about his person in the Queen's presence. It would have been tantamount to treason.

★ ★ ★

Nick spent the rest of the afternoon and early evening questioning most of those who had been in the chapel or had known Cecily at court. He learned little of value except that he could now construct a fairly accurate timeline for the day and evening of her death. Mary, her friend, was inconsolable.

"If only I hadn't been ill," she wailed, her noisy lamentation interspersed with violent sneezes, her face puffy from weeping. "I was in bed all day," she said. "I was even excused from chapel that morning."

So that meant she would not have seen anyone pass the note to Cecily, Nick thought with regret.

"Otherwise, she would have told me she was going to meet someone. We told each other everything," Mary said sadly.

"You didn't see her at all?" Nick asked.

"Only once." Mary burst into a fresh fit of weeping, and Nick passed her his handkerchief. Her own was a grubby, sodden mess. "I was mean to her when she asked if I needed anything. I said, 'Thank you very much.'"

Nick didn't think that a particularly sarcastic thing to say, but eyeing the girl shrewdly, he surmised she was a bit of a mouthy one. A right goer, as John would have put it (out of earshot of his wife, of course). He comforted her as best he could and dismissed her. There were several people he had yet to see: the Countess of Berwick was so stunned, she had been sent home to her nephew's London house by the Queen and ordered to rest, and then there was Codpiece the Fool.

He got up and stretched. The small chamber they had given him was comfortable, part of a suite kept for visiting dignitaries. The walls were covered in tapestries to keep out the chill, and there was a roaring fire in the grate. A pewter flagon and matching goblets stood on a side table inlaid with tortoise-shell, along with a silver bowl of fruit. Cold chicken and a loaf of bread had been carried in on a tray just as darkness fell. He had shared his meal with Hector, who had gulped the meat in two bites, then coveted the bones with his eyes.

"Forget it, pal," Nick said. "Rivkah says they're bad for you." She had told him that, unlike beef bones, the bones of poultry splintered easily and could pierce the stomach like sharp needles.

Hector flopped down before the fire with a long-suffering sigh only partly feigned. He had a huge appetite, and Nick knew he needed more food. But before he left the palace, he needed to see the Queen and report in.

As if on cue, a royal page knocked on the door.

* * *

Nick was led to the royal apartments and shown into a book-lined room that was obviously the Queen's private study. A large table next to the window was littered with papers, and an enormous ring, carved with the Tudor rose, lay next to an embossed seal as if it had just been pressed into warm wax. Otherwise the room was plain, functional, its only concession to luxury a fortune in beeswax candles that bathed the room in a golden glow and the sweet scent of honey. Elizabeth was alone, sitting in an armchair in front of a crackling fire, with her feet up on a low stool. On a table beside her, two long-stemmed goblets of Venetian glass stood to hand along with a matching crystal flagon glowing a rich ruby red. Draped over her bony shoulders, she wore a heavy, loose garment of deep-pile tawny velvet over a fine linen under-dress. He had never seen her without her armor of stiff brocade and jewels, intended to dazzle and, more to the point, distract the eye that would otherwise have noticed the aging flesh and webbing of fine wrinkles around her eyes and mouth. He made a low obeisance.

"Yes, yes," the Queen said, waving him to a seat opposite. "Sit down for God's sake before you give me a crick in the neck. And tell your monster to guard the door."

Nick signaled to Hector and then sat down opposite her, waiting for her to speak while enduring the royal scrutiny for what seemed an age. He was careful to look calmly back, showing neither insolence nor fear nor a craven obsequiousness. A man was a fool to underestimate Elizabeth just because she was a woman. Plenty had made that mistake and had paid for it with their heads on Tower Green. But Elizabeth was not only a canny Machiavelli—over the years she had successfully strung along countless suitors seeking her hand in marriage, not to mention the French and Spanish ambassadors—she was reputed to be one of the most learned women in Christendom. She rode to hunt, won at chess, spoke several languages and read Latin, Hebrew, and ancient Greek fluently. She also swore like a dosshouse toper. All in all, Nick was quite fond of her and thought her a great improvement on her sister, Bloody Mary, and her syphilis-crazed father, Henry VIII, who solved his marital problems by lopping off heads. But Nick never made the mistake of letting down his guard.

"I hear you named your parrot after me," said the Queen at last.

Nick blinked. This was the last thing he'd thought she would say, but he had heard her opening gambits in chess were tricky.

"I won the bird in a card game, Majesty. She was already named."

"By whom?" the Queen asked, regarding him slyly.

"I forget. I was rather drunk." He would not betray his friend Kit, who had named the parrot in a fit of pique after the Queen had read one of his poems and said it was rubbish. He was always in trouble, ranting and raving against the authorities—"purblind, lily-livered, three-inch, dribbling, doltish, and babbling sons of whores" was one of his more moderate rants for the men who comprised the government of the realm—and he didn't need Nick to dig him in any deeper. Kit's influence on the parrot's execrable vocabulary was plain to all who set foot in The Black Sheep.

"Horseshit," the Queen said. "It was Christopher Marlowe. Now there's a dark horse for you, to continue the equine theme. But clever, very clever."

Takes one to know one, Nick thought.

He and Marlowe had become friends when Kit had started frequenting The Black Sheep a year ago. Snooping through Cecil's desk the last time he had been called in to report and Cecil had briefly left the room, Nick found out that Marlowe was also a spy. They had never talked about it, nor had their paths ever crossed on missions; Nick did not even know if Kit was aware he was also in the espionage business, but he suspected he did. With his quick dark eyes, sarcastic tongue, and fearsome intellect, nothing got past Kit Marlowe. He was obsessed with characters who were convinced they were either demigods or demons. One day, Kit swore, he would pen bloody dramas that would break upon the literary world like the Trump of Doom. So far he was still working on a play about a monomaniacal tyrant called Tamburlaine. As far as Nick knew, this seesawing from impossible heights to unimaginable depths matched Kit's temperament perfectly. He was either flying high as a kite or sunk in deepest melancholy. In either state, he drank more than Nick had ever seen anyone drink—more than he himself drank, and that was saying something. As Kit always seemed to have plenty of gold, he was one of The Black Sheep's best customers, so John and Maggie put up with his drunken soliloquies, often letting him sleep it off on a bench in the corner, as Nick himself had done the previous night, too inebriated to climb the stairs to his chamber above the taproom. But he had a soft spot for Kit, sensing a sensitive and tortured soul beneath the bravado. The parrot, Bess, referred to her former owner as "Mephistopheles."

The Queen picked up the flagon and poured the wine. She handed him a glass and sat back, cradling hers, but not drinking.

"You're loyal to your friends, I'll say that for you." Then, in one of her famous mercurial changes of mood: "This is a terrible business, Nick. I'm relying on you to get to the bottom of it." She looked at the fire and shook her head. "Poor, poor girl," she murmured. "Her parents are beyond grief." She looked back at him. "You realize the implications, do you not? The *political* implications."

"I do, Majesty," he said.

The Queen had spent her reign skillfully balancing between religious extremists—not only Protestants versus Catholics but also various Protestant sects, the Puritans' chief among them—that denounced the Church of England her father had established as being closet Papist. They sought to establish their own "pure" version of the Christian faith based on a literal interpretation of the Bible unmediated by clergy. Nick knew Elizabeth privately regarded the Eucharist as no more than a symbolic commemoration of the Last Supper, rather than a sacrament of the actual body and blood of Christ, but she strictly maintained the outward observance of all the pomp and ceremony of the Church of England, the official religion of the land. Publically she attended morning and evening services, took the Host once a week, maintained a choir that performed the masses of Byrd and Tallis, and read the Book of Common Prayer. Privately, she was rumored to pour over the writings of Luther, Zwingli, and Calvin, an activity that would have sent her to the block in her father and sister's time. Her younger half-brother, the sickly Edward VI, was said to have shared his sister's interest in the new religion sweeping the Continent, but he died of consumption, at the age of sixteen, before he could legislate comprehensive religious change.

As a young woman, Elizabeth had seen just how destructive religious mania could be: her half-sister, Mary, a fanatical Catholic besotted with her husband, Philip II of Spain, had sought to bring back the Popish religion with fire and the sword. Elizabeth had chosen a middle way, stating that she did not intend to make windows into men's souls, something the populace correctly took to mean that as long as their bodies observed the rituals of the Church of England and they refrained from sedition, their souls were free to believe whatever they wanted. It was a brilliant stroke of statecraft, but there were those who murmured against Elizabeth and questioned the integrity of her faith. In short, she walked a fine line between opposing factions. A very fine line indeed. This murder could tip the balance if either her Catholic or Puritan enemies could make the case that the blasphemous nature of the murder somehow indicated her reign was spiritually corrupt and thus illegitimate. As the daughter of an anointed Queen executed for witchcraft, Elizabeth knew from harsh experience that a smear of holy oil on the forehead in Westminster Abbey did not guarantee the throne.

"Any progress?" the Queen asked.

"Not much," Nick replied and proceeded to fill her in on Eli's findings. When he came to the manner of Cecily's death, the Queen slammed her glass down on the table so violently, Nick was sure it would shatter. She did not speak, but her face was stony, her lips a thin line, her eyes obsidian in the firelight. He explained his theory about the killing: that it was not from sexual lust but from something infinitely cold and calculated.

"A premeditated assassination," Nick said, "as if the killer is sending a message."

"And what might that be?"

Without breaking eye contact, he said, "That your reign is a blasphemy."

"And, by extension, so am I," the Queen said.

Nick nodded. "I would guess that the placement of the body is in some way a stab"—he winced inwardly at the word—"an *attack* aimed at you personally or the church."

"Same thing," the Queen snapped. "My father, God rest his soul, saw to that."

Whether this was said with irony or not, Nick did not know, but he acknowledged the truth of it. When Henry VIII had broken with Rome, he had appointed himself Supreme Head of the Church in England.

Nick laid out the objects he had found in the chapel: the note, handkerchief, and the stone discovered by Robin.

The Queen took the note, read it quickly, then handed it back. "He must have known her," she said after a short silence. "This would not have worked on one of the older girls. It's too brief, for one thing, and the tone is all wrong. Not a declaration of love so much as a command."

Nick nodded, surprised at the Queen's perceptiveness. Perhaps she had received love letters in her youth. For years there had been rumors that she and her favorite, Robert Dudley, Earl of Leicester, had been lovers. Childhood friends and less than a year apart in age, only the suspicious death of Robert's first wife, Amy, from a fall down the stairs at their home, had kept them from marrying. The Queen, it was said, would never choose a prince consort who was suspected of murder. Perhaps this was one of the reasons Cecily's death had affected her so deeply. Once again the taint of murder clung to her court. She had recently appointed Dudley Commander of English forces in the Netherlands since that country's revolt against Spain, to get him out of the way, it was rumored, because he was now old and paunchy, a mere shadow of his dashing former self. But Nick knew such talk was mere jealousy because of his long and close relationship with the Queen. Truth be told, she trusted no one as completely as she trusted Dudley. His appointment was, in part, a cover for the establishment of an espionage network. Marlowe had just returned from Holland, and Nick surmised that he and Dudley had been in close contact, meeting in out-of-the-way inns to exchange information. Despite the tittle-tattling, or maybe because of it, Nick had nothing against him. His own mother, Agnes, the Dowager Countess of Blackwell, was Dudley's friend and neighbor, as he kept a great estate in Oxfordshire near their family seat of Binsey. Dudley was fiercely loyal and, like the Queen, Nick too prized that quality above all others. In the shifting sands of court and the world of espionage, trust was a rare commodity indeed.

"He exploited her youth and naïvety," the Queen said. "Anyone could see her head was filled with romantic rubbish. She was so *innocent*." This last was said with such sorrow that Nick thought for one panicky moment the Queen would cry, a thing unheard of except perhaps by the women who attended her in her private chambers. Even in the dicey years of her sister's reign, when her life hung by a thread due to the deep animosity Mary bore her for the supplanting of her mother, Katherine of Aragon, in favor of Elizabeth's mother, Anne Boleyn, Elizabeth had not shed a single tear, but held her head high, or so Nick's mother reported with something akin to wonder. Only the fact that Mary failed to produce an heir and that even she had apparently balked at shedding royal blood, albeit only a half-sister's, had saved Elizabeth. All those who had stuck by her in those perilous times had been rewarded with high office and titles when she ascended the throne in 1558: Dudley had been appointed Master of Horse and became the Earl of Leicester, Sir William Cecil was given the title Baron Burghley and the post of Secretary of State, which he held until, fourteen years ago, he was made Lord Treasurer.

Nick sometimes wondered if the Queen's tolerance of his own outwardly disreputable and rather seedy life at The Black Sheep was due more to her friendship with his mother than his work for the Crown. Certainly she had never lectured him on his duty to uphold the glory of an ancient and noble house by marrying appropriately nor, God forbid, upbraided him for his questionable morals (she must be aware of his "friendship" with Kat, the wildly successful and notorious madam of a Bankside brothel). Elizabeth might be changeable by temperament, but she was loyal to her friends—to a fault, some whispered. Eight years before, she had forgiven Dudley for secretly marrying her cousin, Lettice Devereux, Countess of Essex, without her permission, perhaps because Lettice gave birth a suspicious five months after the nuptials, clearly a marriage of convenience rather than a love match. Nick suspected Dudley's posting to the Netherlands was, in part, to keep him from the undeniable charms of Lettice, much younger than the Queen and blessed with a glorious auburn mane of her own hair. The Queen was a woman after all.

"I want this devil caught," the Queen said, her eyes glittering with anger. "I want his head rotting on London Bridge. I want to see ravens feasting on his eyes." Then, as if suddenly exhausted by her desire for vengeance, she raised a hand in weary dismissal, the merest flick of the fingertips. "Give my best to your mother when you next see her."

Nick rose and bowed.

"And Nick?"

"Majesty?"

"Nice scar."

CHAPTER 4

Kat's Brothel, Bankside

Despite the lateness of the hour and the peril of a river cross-ing at night, Nick decided to return to The Black Sheep after leaving the Queen's study. It would have made more sense to stay the night in the rooms made available to him, but he was suddenly overcome by a powerful urge to flee the palace, that lab-yrinth of corridors echoing with footfalls and whispers and suspi-cions. He had always hated court life with its intrigues and power plays, the artificially courteous manners concealing the burning ambition, the petty jealousies and rivalries, the backbiting. Not for the first time, he was profoundly glad he had been born a younger son. Let Robert, older than Nick by ten years and stolid as a Flemish burgher, negotiate those treacherous waters.

Sitting in the boat, the sound of the oars rising and dipping, the occasional grunt of the oarsman as the boat caught the current and had to be kept steady, its prow resolutely pointed at the farther shore, Nick gazed into the blackness all around him, and it seemed to him that this void, this nothingness, was where the case was leading him. Into the soul of a man who had premeditated the murder of an innocent girl, who had lured her and murdered her and posed her, all for some as yet unknown purpose. He felt adrift in this blackness, cast off from solid ground, where motives and desires were plain, understandable—jealousy, ambition, lust, greed, anger, those he recognized. The lantern hanging on an iron stanchion at the prow of the boat cast a lurid glow on the straining face of the oarsman, a ghostly Charon ferrying the souls of the dead across the River Styx. Nick shivered and wrapped his cloak more tightly about him, comforted by the warm weight of his dog leaning against his legs. He was being fanciful, he knew. As Will had said, a murderer was not a demon but a man of flesh and blood. As such, his motives, however torturous, must surely be decipherable. All Nick had to do was find the beginning of the thread, the motive, and follow it step by step to its source.

Fetching up at St. Mary's Queen Dock, a little upstream from the Great Stone Gate connecting London Bridge with Southwark Street, Nick alighted and paid the boatman. He fixed a leather leash to Hector's collar, not to restrain him but to use as a guide through the dark warren of Bankside, where the Watch did not venture; where no lights shone above the doorways of wealthy merchants; no liveried page stood at the doors to welcome late-night revelers. Turning west along the bank, he passed the dark outline of the church of St. Mary Overie on his left, the river on his right, careful to keep his gaze straight ahead, his steps purposeful. His cloak was thrown back over his left shoulder, his right hand on the hilt of his sword by his hip, and he was aware of being observed by myriad eyes from alleys and dark recesses, assessing him with expert, criminal intelligence for signs of weakness, the merest hint he was unarmed, lost, unprepared.

Hector padded noiselessly ahead, making a left and then a

right on Clink Street, unerringly nosing toward home, a huge black shape more effective as a deterrent than any blade or skill with which Nick could wield it. As he drew closer to home, Hector uttered a low deep-throated growl, a vibration of the air, a sign he had caught the wild, sharp scent of the bearbaiting ring, the distant belling of the dogs as they circled their prey, snapping and snarling, yipping as they were hurled against the wooden barricades that ringed the blood-soaked arena. Although hugely popular as a sport, Nick had no stomach for either bearbaiting or bullbaiting; the sight of a noble beast, chained to a stake, unable to defend itself, sickened him; the faces of men contorted by cruelty and bloodlust even more so. But situated a mere block west of the bearbaiting ring with the bullbaiting ring to the east, The Black Sheep was the tavern of choice for many of these spectators, and Nick could little afford to alienate them by revealing his revulsion for their sport.

Suddenly unable to stomach the sea of drunken, if amiable, faces, the slaps on the back, and the inevitable questioning by John he knew would greet him as soon as he set foot in The Black Sheep, Nick abruptly changed his mind. He had promised Eli he would drop in on him, but he couldn't face even that. He would stop by in the morning.

"Kat's," he murmured, and Hector obediently turned to the left.

Kat had been Nick's first friend in Bankside. He had met her five years before when he had visited her premises after a long stint on the Continent. An accident, really, that he had fetched up there. His ship had moored at St. Mary's Queen Dock, and he had been in need more of a tankard of ale than a swift roll in the hay. He had walked into Kat's brothel thinking it was a tavern.

One look at Kat—statuesque, lush of body, and with a mass of shining dark hair that tumbled over creamy shoulders, he had quickly forgotten his thirst. She had flashed him a smile, nodded to the big bruiser stationed at the door (Joseph, as Nick later learned) and, taking his hand, led him through a back door and up some stairs. Nick went meekly as a lamb, his eyes riveted on the hypnotic sway of her hips beneath scarlet velvet as she preceded him up the narrow stairs. Later he was to learn that he was the exception to the rule, that Kat had long since "retired."

"I suppose I should feel flattered," Nick said, lying exhausted but deeply contented on her bed some time later.

Kat shrugged a naked shoulder. "I have needs too," she said.

Nick looked at her and noticed her quick, ironic gaze and the strong set of her mouth and chin. He grinned. "Maybe you should pay me," he said, running an exploratory finger down the column of her neck, over her shoulder and around the curve of one breast.

"Maybe I should," Kat murmured. "But first you have to earn it."

Afterward, Kat told Nick something of her life. Orphaned at twelve, she had been taken in as a scullery maid in a great house, where she was repeatedly molested by the master. When she went to the cook for help, that worthy lady told her it was the master's right to use her so in return for a roof over her head and food in her belly. The next morning, before dawn, she tied her meager belongings in a handkerchief—a shift, cap, and five pennies she filched from the cook—and fled, instinctively making for London, where she knew she could disappear. Even the theft of a penny or a single handkerchief was a hanging offense, and she had no intention of swinging from the gallows. Once there, she soon ran out of money and had to sell the only thing of value she owned—ironically, the same body she had sought to protect. Naively thinking she was working for herself, she was soon disabused of this when she was kidnapped off the street, held against her will in a house of ill repute in Southwark, and repeatedly beaten and raped. There she was told, in no uncertain terms, that if she did not want to end up floating in the Thames, she would have to go to work for Gorgeous George, a notorious pimp who ran prostitutes for Black Jack Sims, the local area crime boss.

Once Joseph had put paid to Gorgeous George, Kat went into business for herself; eventually she bought herself out of the brothel and rented a room, where she plied her trade, gradually building up a clientele of better quality from across the river—young toffs and wealthy merchants from the city, rather than the sailors and low-life scum that lived and worked in Bankside. Building on a reputation for cleanliness, wit, astonishing technique, and guaranteed customer satisfaction or their money back, Kat eventually saved up enough to buy the house in Dead Man's Place, where her brothel was currently located. When Nick asked her why she had chosen that particular house, she replied, "Location, location, location. I raise men from the dead."

"That you do," Nick had replied.

Kat had laughed and set about putting her words into deeds.

Black Jack Sims, so-called for the color of his teeth as well as his heart, recognizing a gold mine when he saw one, left Kat in peace, only demanding a cut of her earnings in return for the protection of his bullyboys. Local legend had it that when he visited her for the first time and attempted to strong-arm a swingeing sixty percent, Kat had cajoled, charmed, and bullied him into settling for twenty percent with occasional perks thrown in when the mood took her. He left with a smile on his face that some uncharitable souls claimed was the only apocryphal part of the story.

★　★　★

"Are you awake?"

"Why does everyone keep asking me that?" Nick grumbled. Still conscious, but only just, he was enjoying the sensation of complete blankness, a kind of floating, limbless ennui after his recent exertions with Kat in her massive four-poster bed. *La petite mort* as the French, those self-proclaimed experts in love, called it. When she opened the door, he had fallen on her like a ravening wolf, hands tearing at her clothes, desperate for the touch of her warm, fragrant flesh, the hot gust of her breath in his mouth, the feel of her strong white legs locked around him. Afterward, she cradled his head against her breast, where he lay like a beached fish, gasping for air.

"Better?" she murmured.

"Mmm."

★　★　★

They were in her luxurious apartment on the top floor of the three-story building that housed her knocking shop. Only the faint sound of drunken singing and the occasional slamming of doors could be heard beneath them; Kat had had a double floor put down to insulate against noise. Retired at thirty-five, she devoted herself to the business of running a brothel, taking an almost motherly care of the girls who worked for her, making sure they were healthy and that they were not molested by the clients. Downstairs in the ground-floor taproom, she employed a hulking behemoth of a man called Joseph, formerly The Terror of

Lambeth, a wrestler fallen on hard times after a series of humiliating defeats in the local fairs. He had accosted her in a dark alley one night when she was fifteen and at the height of her trade, but in thrall to a brutal pimp. With the quick wit of a born survivor, she had made him a business proposal: work for her and eat for a lifetime or have a knee-trembler up against the wall and starve tomorrow. He had chosen the former, proving that brawn was not mutually exclusive to brains. He immediately set about demonstrating his loyalty by beating Kat's pimp so severely that he left the area as soon as he could walk again, thus sending a powerful message to the criminal underclass that Kat was not to be touched except when sufficient money had changed hands. Joseph had been with Kat for twenty years, as much her guardian angel as Hector was Nick's. He favored gamey leather jerkins over a shirtless torso, all the better to show off his still impressively bulging biceps. With his broken nose and one eye half-closed from an illegal jab from an opponent's elbow, he was fearsomely ugly to behold, but Nick had seen the softness in his eyes when he looked at Kat, the surprising delicacy with which he handed her into a carriage. If she had allowed it, he would gladly have slept on the floor outside her door each night, the better to guard her; instead, he had grudgingly settled for a room next to Kat's, on condition that the connecting door would never be locked.

Joseph and Hector shared a deep understanding and mutual respect. As soon as Nick entered the brothel, Joseph appeared, as if by magic, with a great, dripping shank of beef, which he silently gave to the dog. Now replete, Hector was crashed out on the rug before the fire, faintly snoring, having shown not the slightest interest in the strenuous activities of the previous hour.

Nick felt Kat shift as she reached across him, then smelled the acrid tang of smoke. He cracked open an eye. Propped on the pillows, her still thick brown hair spread out against the white linen, her splendid breasts on full display, she was holding a long-stemmed pipe between her lips, contentedly puffing away. He levered himself up onto one elbow, reached for the pipe and took a long drag, letting the smoke out slowly before handing it back.

"Thief," she said.

Brought back to London by Sir Walter Raleigh after his voyage to the New World, the court and gradually the whole of London, or at least those who could afford the expensive import, had been swept up by the tobacco craze. Smoked by the indigenous peoples of the Americas for centuries, the leaves of the tobacco plant were widely praised for their health-giving properties—sharper mental faculties and a convenient way to retain one's youthful figure among them. Nick thought it a wonderful drug, even more so since the Puritans vociferously decried it, stating that belching smoke from the mouth was unnatural and devilish, the first step on the slippery slope to hell, where they would get their fill of fire and brimstone for all eternity and serve them jolly well right. Eli too had misgivings, worried about long-term damage to the lungs, but Nick had only laughed.

"Life's too short," he said.

"Then why make it shorter?" Eli replied.

Not for the first time, Nick had found himself without a ready answer.

★ ★ ★

"Tell me about the girl who was murdered," Kat said.

Nick obliged. Kat, he knew, was no shrinking violet, having

witnessed and been victim to the worst of human nature, but neither was she callous.

Kat was silent after Nick finished telling her, the pipe long since
extinguished, held loosely in her fingers, forgotten. The rosy flush
that had suffused her face after their lovemaking was gone; now
her skin was alabaster white, her mouth tight with revulsion.

At last she spoke: "Posed on the altar, you say?"

"With her hands crossed over her chest like an effigy."

"And she was a maid? No lovers?"

"Innocent as Eve before the fall."

"Perhaps it was her innocence that drew her killer?" Kat
murmured.

Nick reached for a goblet of wine next to the bed, taking a
hefty swig as if he could wash away the taste of death. When he
offered it to Kat, she shook her head. Before the fire, Hector gave
a great sigh as if, even in sleep, he was attuned to his master's
moods. In that room, lit dimly by the orange glow of the fire, the
candle burning beside the bed, gold and silver thread glinting in
the arras hung on the wall, thick curtains over the window ban-
ishing the darkness outside, it was easy to feel safe, immune from
evil. As if their lovemaking was innocent play in an innocent world.
Now Nick's words had introduced a serpent. Cecily's death lay
between them, clamoring for redress.

"It's not a sex killing," Kat said. "Too cold." She laid the pipe
down and slid down under the covers, molding herself into Nick's
side as if she suddenly felt a chill. He put his arm around her, his
fingers playing with her hair. "Men are usually stupid, more brut-
ish and impulsive. Present company excepted," she added as an
afterthought. Nick felt her mouth quirk up at the corners.

"I appreciate that," he replied, grateful for her slight attempt at humor. His grim narrative had momentarily quenched her spirit as surely as if he had snuffed out the candle. Now she was rallying. He kissed the top of her head.

She raised a troubled face to his. "He's going to do it again, Nick," she said. "You know that, right?"

CHAPTER 5

London Bridge and the City of London

Despite getting very little sleep, Nick rose early, reluctantly disengaging from Kat's warm body, carefully sliding out from her out-flung arm, her leg resting tantalizingly against his groin. It took a huge effort of will not to rouse her as he himself was aroused. She murmured in her sleep but did not awaken. He stood for a moment looking down at her, her face partly obscured by a tangle of hair, mouth slightly parted, a fist curled beneath her chin. Her breathing shallow, almost imperceptible, so deeply did she slumber. In the deep relaxation of her face, the lines of age and experience were smoothed out, and he glimpsed the girl she had once been. He suddenly wished, with all his heart, he had known her then, had somehow been able to save her from the men who had used and abused her, then discarded her when they were done. He wondered fleetingly if that was what he himself was doing. After all, he came to her when his need became too much to bear, when he was sad and lonely. She received him into her inner sanctum with generosity of spirit, amused affection, and not a little passion, he flattered himself. He loved her as a trusted friend, and he would have died to protect her. In her company, he felt more truly himself than with any other woman he had ever met. Even Rivkah.

The thought of Rivkah made him reach for his clothes. He dressed quickly and left.

★   ★   ★

When he arrived at their house, Eli and Rivkah were seated at the kitchen table, eating a simple breakfast of bread and honey washed down by small beer. Wordlessly, Rivkah got up and brought another cup, which Eli filled with ale. Nick reached for the bread. He was ravenous.

"Sorry I didn't come by last night," he said between mouthfuls. "I was"—he searched for the right word, conscious of Rivkah's eyes on him—"busy."

"I bet," she said, taking back the loaf and savagely sawing at it.

Nick flushed. "The Queen kept me late," he said, then was instantly annoyed at himself for explaining. "She liked my scar," he added, addressing Eli.

Eli raised his cup. "Nice bit of stitching, if I do say so myself. *Salud!*"

"Cheers." They clinked and drank deeply. Rivkah pointedly turned to Hector, who was sitting hopefully by her chair, and fed him a slice of bread as if to say: *I am now turning my attention to the only other rational being in this room beside myself.* Laughing at the slobber he left on her hand, she impulsively grabbed his great shaggy head and planted a resounding kiss on his nose. "Master Messy," she rebuked fondly. Hector looked at her with adoration; Nick looked away.

Once they had finished eating, Nick brushed the crumbs off the table and laid out the note, handkerchief, and topaz.

"Smell this," he said, pointing to the square of linen.

Warily, as if it were tainted by plague, Rivkah picked it up between finger and thumb, sniffed it, then handed it to Eli, who did the same. They looked at each other.

Nick waited, always intrigued by the way they silently conversed, as if so attuned to each other's thoughts, words were superfluous.

"Ginger and linseed oil," Rivkah said.

Eli nodded. "And garlic."

"Liniment," they said together.

Nick hid a smile. They often spoke simultaneously but seemed completely unaware of it. Eli had told him that their mother reported that when they were babies, they had crawled over each other as matter-of-factly as if the other's body were an extension of their own, as natural as people crossing their legs when they sat down.

"And there's a trace of capsicum," Rivkah added, looking at Eli again.

"Are you sure?" Eli sniffed again and smiled. "She's got a better nose than me," he explained.

"What's capsicum when it's at home?" Nick asked.

"Guinea spice," they said. Then, when he still looked nonplussed, "a kind of pepper. It's thought to loosen catarrh in the chest."

"Is that significant?"

"Could be," Eli replied, slowly. "It's extremely rare in England. Rare enough in Spain. Very costly. I saw it once in an apothecary's shop in Lisbon. The herbalist told me he'd gotten it from a Portuguese sailor in exchange for a remedy for scurvy. Mouse?"

"I know of only one place it could have come from in London," she said. "A shop on Candlewick Street not far from the Bridge. Master Hogg is the apothecary." She frowned.

"What?" Nick asked.

"Well, the mix is a bit unusual as well as being expensive. The most common ingredients for a chest liniment or poultice are licorice and comfrey. Don't you agree, Eli?"

Her brother nodded.

"What does that mean?" Nick asked.

"That whoever purchased it is well off and well read," Rivkah replied. "Or knows someone who's just come back from abroad."

Fired up by this possible link to the killer, Nick decided to make a visit to this Master Hogg right away. When he asked if Eli wanted to accompany him, Eli shook his head.

"Can't," he said. "I'm due at St. Mary's."

"Getting baptized?" Nick teased.

"An infirmary for the poor," Eli said without offense. He got up and slung his satchel over his shoulder.

"A *free* infirmary," Rivkah muttered, but Nick saw the pride in her eyes as she looked at her brother.

Eli bent to kiss her cheek. Then turning to Nick, "Mouse can go with you." He grinned at her and left.

Nick and Rivkah eyed each other across the table. The house suddenly felt very quiet. Nick could hear sparrows chirping insolently in the solitary apple tree in the back garden, even the faint screech of the knife sharpener's grindstone two blocks away.

"You don't . . ." they said together, then laughed awkwardly.

"You first," Nick said.

"You don't *have* to take me," Rivkah said, getting up and moving randomly about the tiny kitchen, straightening things.

"You don't have to come. I mean, aren't there things you need to do?" Nick vaguely nodded at the room, then was puzzled when spots of color appeared on her cheeks.

"Like what?" she said angrily. "Sweeping? Sewing a button on your shirt? Women's work?"

Appalled, Nick held up his hands, palms outward. "No, no. I didn't mean that. I meant: don't you have any patients to see today?"

Rivkah looked narrowly at him. As he had done with the Queen, Nick held her gaze, trying to make his expression as guileless as possible. For the first time, he was grateful to the Spider for making him a spy skilled in the art of deceit. Truthfully, he had meant housework. He had seen the local matrons scrubbing their front steps, sluicing them down, opening shutters to air out their homes, other things involving water and polish and rags. Then in the afternoon, the smell of cooking, of suppers being prepared. He did not despise these women; on the contrary, it gave him a warm feeling to think that womenfolk all over London and the world were tending the hearth, making it ready for their lord and master's return after a long day at work. He only felt a little wistful he had no one to do that for him. Maggie didn't count, as she was John's wife, although a marvelous housekeeper—none better; and it was ridiculous to think of Kat lifting a domestic finger. He knew Rivkah was a skilled healer and visited patients in the neighborhood as well as ministering to them in her kitchen and the infirmary at St. Mary's, but their home was always spotless, their meals well prepared, so she must be a good housekeeper too, he reasoned. Unless Eli pitched in. Nick immediately dismissed that idea as being too outlandish by half.

He became aware that Rivkah had spoken. "Pardon?"

"I said, I'll come with you." She flung on a fur-lined cloak and picked up a large basket.

Nick grinned.

"I'm almost out of lavender and arrowroot."

"Oh."

Instead of taking a wherry across the river—a bitter easterly wind coming in off the Fens and the Wash beyond was sloshing water against the wharves, and the boats moored there were rocking alarmingly from side to side, their boatmen hunkered in the bottom, miserably blowing on chapped hands—they decided to walk across London Bridge. Nick offered Rivkah his arm. She hesitated for a moment, then took it. In the night, a hard frost had turned waterlogged potholes to ice; piles of ordure and rubbish, frozen into ruts, made walking difficult, but at least they didn't have to wade through mud, and the stench from the riverbank was moderate. Rivkah picked up her skirts with one hand, and Nick noticed she was wearing thick woolen stockings and ankle boots with nail-studded soles. He nodded to himself in approval. He'd expected a laborious progress across the bridge, with Rivkah teetering on the inadequate cork-soled shoes most women wore. Now they could stride out—relatively speaking, considering the slippery condition of the roads. But at least Nick didn't have to worry about Rivkah turning an ankle. They picked their way carefully east toward the Great Stone Gate, the ancient entrance to the bridge where Southwark Street, the main thoroughfare of Bankside, began and continued due south to the coast.

Two blocks from the bridge, they began to hear the rumbling of carts, the shouts of drovers and stall owners selling their wares, the fretful bleating of sheep and mournful lowing of cattle, the hum and buzz of a multitude of voices gossiping, haggling, berating children or husbands, giving orders, calling out to friends—the deafening, intoxicating, hubbub of the busiest road in London.

Above their heads, like so many candy apples on sticks, traitors' heads gazed sightlessly over the teeming streets of Bankside and beyond, stoic philosophers disdaining the world. It was a chilling reminder to foreign travelers newly landed at the southern seaports that treason and sedition were punished to the fullest extent of the law. Londoners were used to them and even gave them cheeky names—Baldy, His Nibs—but Nick had seen Spaniards, Dutchmen, Turks, Norsemen, and the French pointing and chattering to one another in their tongues, clearly unnerved by this grim English greeting.

Hector went ahead, clearing a path, Nick and Rivkah following close behind. As they turned left onto the Bridge proper, Rivkah glanced at him, her look questioning. Most people had to proceed single file, so crowded was the street, so clogged with vehicles and animals being driven to market. Nick shook his head slightly, trapping her arm against his side; he had no intention of surrendering the warm closeness of her, the happy illusion they were a couple out for a morning jaunt. This was the first time they had been alone in public together. He glanced sideways, but Rivkah was looking straight ahead again, the hood of her cloak hiding her face except for the tip of her nose, pink in the raw December air, her breath a feathery plume as she walked, surprisingly fast for a woman surrounded by merchandise. Nick had mentally prepared himself for a leisurely, meandering journey to the apothecary's in Candlewick Street, expecting Rivkah, like any normal woman, to want to browse in the stalls along the bridge. Near Nonesuch House, an extravagant wooden house with turrets and gilded accents, an architectural folly if ever Nick saw one, they passed a draper's with bolts of thick-piled, many-hued cloths—wools, felts, velvets—laid out on a trestle table hinged below the front window of the shop. An underfed and under-dressed draper's apprentice was bawling the merits of his master's cloth into the street, his adolescent voice wobbling precariously from bass to soprano and back again.

"Finest wool in all of Merry England," he shouted. "Feel it, mistress," he implored Rivkah. "Lovely nap."

"You should be wearing a scarf and mittens," Rivkah told him severely. "You'll catch your death standing out here all day." Then she kept going with not so much as a glance at his wares.

His mouth agape, the boy looked at Nick who gave him a sympathetic grin over his shoulder as Rivkah towed him along, momentary allies in their shared bewilderment about the female sex.

Rivkah did stop once at a grocer's, where she purchased a handful of rather wizened apples after inspecting them minutely for worm holes and bruising. She refused to pay the tuppence the grocer demanded, claiming that out-of-season apples, doubtless moldering in a barrel for two months, were only worth a penny, and even that was outrageous. Again, Nick looked sympathetic, but the grocer, unlike the draper's boy, was philosophical, clearly used to the discriminating tastes of his predominantly female clientele.

"Mayhap get better ones tomorrow, mistress," he said, pocketing the coin in a flash. "Expecting a delivery any day if the lazy buggers can get a move on."

"I'll be sure to check back with you, Master Grocer," she replied, giving him a dazzling smile. "Many thanks."

The grocer doffed his cap, and they moved on.

"This way," Rivkah said, turning left along Thames Street, past Fishmonger's Hall, then right on Dowgate. They were in the heart of the great Guild Hall district, those sumptuous edifices of timber and lathe erected in the Middle Ages as gathering places, in truth "showcases," for the proud members of wealthy guilds— Tallow Chandlers' Hall, Skinners Hall, Merchant Taylors' Hall, and—Nick's personal favorite—Innholders' Hall, although he had been miffed to learn he was not eligible for membership in the latter since The Black Sheep was not considered an inn as it had no stables attached nor rooms to let. Informed of this by a snooty clerk in the front office of the guild, Nick was briefly tempted to inform the odious little quill pusher of his illustrious pedigree and how much wine and ale his forbears had drunk in their time— enough to float a small galleon—but he refrained, merely turning on his heel and stalking away.

At the intersection of Walbrook and Budge, they turned right onto Candlewick Street. Rivkah stopped at a shop occupying the ground floor of a black and white timber house, its third story listing drunkenly over the street, creating a natural porch and blessed shelter from the wind. A painted wooden sign depicting a pestle and mortar swung creakily on its hinges above the door. A bell tinkled as they entered.

The inside of the shop was so dim that it took a few moments for Nick to spot a pimply youth with his elbows on a counter by the far wall. To his left, through a doorway, Nick could see Master Hogg, a short, rotund man with a fleshy face in which button eyes seemed to disappear in the folds, busily grinding something in a mortar.

Aptly named, was Nick's first thought.

Arranged on the table about the apothecary were various jars, bottled concoctions, and bunches of dried herbs. Hogg was whistling tunelessly between his teeth and seemed unaware of their presence, despite the herald of the bell.

"I'd like a word with your master," Rivkah told the youth.

"Oh yeah?" he drawled, absently picking his teeth with a dirty fingernail, eyes lustfully raking Rivkah's body, even though she was tightly swaddled in her cloak.

"Hector," Nick said softly.

The dog stepped out of the shadows by the window and laid his chin on the counter so his eyes were on a level with the youth's. The apprentice gave a strangled yelp and jumped back, flattening himself against the wall and dislodging a jar that crashed to the ground in a great puff of white dust.

At the commotion, the apothecary bustled out of the back room, wiping his hands on an apron. "What's all this then?" he demanded. The boy gibbered, pointing. Master Hogg turned around and blanched.

"Master Hogg?" Rivkah said pleasantly, as if she were a local housewife come to purchase a remedy for her husband's piles. "A word, if you please."

"Get that *thing* off my counter," the apothecary spluttered, his jowls trembling.

"He's resting," Nick said. "It's been a long walk."

"A word?" Rivkah repeated, steel creeping into her voice.

The apothecary reluctantly took his eyes off the giant head on his counter and looked at Rivkah. Nick could see he was thinking that the quicker he answered their questions, the quicker they would leave and take the monster with them.

"I believe you stock Guinea spice?" Rivkah said.

Master Hogg nodded. "When I can," he said. "It's hard to come by, and there's not much call for it. Too expensive."

"So you would remember who you sold some to," Rivkah said. "It being rare and not much sought after."

The man nodded again.

"Do you keep records?" Nick asked.

"Only of orders," the man said. "When people want something special."

"Like Guinea spice?"

"That would be correct."

"Names would be helpful."

"Can't do that," the apothecary said smugly. "Client confidentiality."

"Come now, Master Hogg," Rivkah said. "You are not a physician."

The apothecary folded his arms across his chest. "Even so."

Nick sauntered over to a shelf by the window and picked up an enormous glass jar filled with murky liquid with a nameless something floating in it. Holding it up to the light, he could just about make out a jellied abomination of nature—a lamb with two heads.

"Look at this," he said to Rivkah, holding out the jar. "Twins."

She frowned, whether from his tasteless joke or, more likely, because she was wondering what he was up to. Behind her, Nick could see beads of sweat pop out on the greasy forehead of the apothecary, even though the room was cold.

Nick tipped the jar slightly, sloshing some of the liquid onto the floor. "Oops!"

"Butterfingers," Rivkah said.

Master Hogg bolted around the counter, paying no heed to Hector, and tried to wrest the jar from Nick, who held onto it.

"Have you any idea how rare that is?" the apothecary said.

"Just a few more questions."

Master Hogg sighed, then nodded, his eyes never leaving the jar, as if Nick had kidnapped his firstborn son and heir.

"Can we see your order book?" Rivkah asked.

"Wat!"

Rivkah opened her mouth to repeat the question, then realized the apothecary was addressing his apprentice. The boy unfolded himself from the floor, where he had been crouching as far away from Hector as possible; took a giant book from a shelf under the counter; and banged it on the table.

Rivkah leafed through it, her finger swiftly running down entries. She stopped halfway down the second to last page.

"'Guinea spice, three ounces; one order; six shillings, three pence; two days after All Saints,'" she read.

"Name?" Nick asked. A name would give him a starting point, perhaps lead him directly to the killer. The murder had happened a month later, on December 4th.

"'Boy,'" Rivkah read.

Nick's heart sank. "Boy?" he almost shouted.

"What's wrong with that?" the apothecary said, his eyes darting nervously from Nick's face back to his beloved jar. "You don't think I ask the name of every servant who comes in here, do you?"

"What was his master's name?" Nick asked, forcing patience.

"Wouldn't say."

"And that didn't bother you?"

"He had money, didn't he?" the apothecary whined. "It's

not like he wanted arsenic or ground foxglove to off the mother-in-law."

"Livery?"

"None."

Nick sighed. He was tempted to drop the jar and dump its loathsome contents all over the apothecary's fine woolen gown.

"I paid a fortune for this," Master Hogg said when Nick returned the jar to him. He stroked its sides lovingly. "Siamese twins," he informed them. "Born every thousand years when Gemini is in ascendance."

"You've been diddled," Nick said, opening the door to let Rivkah and Hector precede him. "Check out the stitches joining the heads."

Closing the door behind him, Nick saw the apothecary anxiously inspecting his treasure, his eyes huge and bug-like through the glass. The pimply youth was sniggering.

★   ★   ★

"That was a waste of time," Nick said when they were back on the street.

"At least we have a date," Rivkah said. "November third."

Nick noted the "we." He also noted how her cheeks were glowing, whether from the cold or the excitement of the chase he didn't know, but he appreciated the effect.

"You didn't get your lavender and . . . what was the other stuff?"

"Arrowroot. It doesn't matter," Rivkah said, pulling a face. "I'm not buying from that defective numbskull. Gemini indeed! He ought to bottle himself so people can stare at him!" She muttered something under her breath about superstitious nonsense and living in the Dark Ages before saying, "Where to now?"

"Whitehall," Nick said. "I have to see Codpiece and the Countess of Berwick. They were the only ones I didn't interview yesterday."

"In that case," Rivkah replied, "I'll give it a miss. You know how I hate all those court toadies."

Nick suppressed his disappointment, but he understood. As a Jew, Rivkah was wary of drawing attention to herself, preferring to stay close to her neighborhood, where people knew her and were indebted to her for curing them of one ailment or another. It was not fear exactly—Nick knew Rivkah was courageous; Eli had told him she had tried to rescue their infant sister from their burning home in Salamanca—just an overabundance of caution. Given her tragic past, he couldn't blame her.

She was even more at risk as a Spaniard. Earlier that year, England had unofficially declared war on Spain, siding with their ally, the Dutch; long brewing, the hostilities between the two nations had been inadvertently made inevitable when, in 1570, fifteen years before, Pope Pius V issued a bull excommunicating Elizabeth for heresy, thereby deposing her and making it open season for assassination attempts. With one stroke of a pen, regicide was elevated to a holy act. He had former Catholic friends, now fled abroad, who felt that their highest act of patriotism for England would be to put a dagger through Elizabeth's heart. Nick had never understood the torturous morality behind this kind of reasoning, nor the frightening self-righteousness it implied. He had spent the last year making frequent trips to Spain, trying to discover the war footing of the Spanish. A letter he had intercepted in Barcelona had identified a Catholic agent named Gilbert Gifford, who was subsequently arrested in Rye, Sussex. Under threat of torture, he was turned into a double agent working for Sir

Francis Walsingham and the Spider. Nick knew that Gifford was somehow involved in a high-level plot to indict Mary, Queen of Scots, for treason and force her cousin, the Queen, to sign her death warrant. Mary still languished in prison, but the Queen and the rest of the country, especially Londoners, were twitchy. Nick had nightmares of an anti-Catholic mob cornering Rivkah in the streets and tearing her limb from limb. With her dark hair, brown eyes, and accented English, she stood out as a foreigner. Sometimes that was all a mob needed—to vent their fears on someone who looked different.

"Hector can go with you," he said. When she looked as if she might argue, he added, "You can protect him."

She called to the dog, and she and Nick parted, Rivkah walking east toward London Bridge; Nick heading toward Old Swan Stairs, where he caught a ferry to Whitehall, a long pull west against the tide.

CHAPTER 6

The Palace of Whitehall

On arriving at the palace at the Privy Stairs, a more central place to alight from the river than Whitehall Stairs, Nick paid the sweating boatman and told him to wait. He didn't know how long he would be, but wanted to make sure he had a ride home, a short row east across the river to Lambeth Stairs, then a brisk walk along the riverbank by Paris Gardens to Bankside. On entering the palace, he inquired as to the whereabouts of the Queen, knowing she seldom went anywhere without her Fool. He was told by a surly usher with reeky breath that she was closeted with her Privy Council—that meant she was without the Fool, the usher informed him with malicious glee, as the usually mild-tempered Baron Burghley had recently threatened to have Codpiece hung, drawn, and quartered after he had upset an inkpot over some papers waiting to be signed.

"Serve him bloody well right, and all," the man cackled, blowing pickled herring at Nick. "He's a right menace, that one."

Without bothering to reply, Nick made straight for the Queen's private apartments, hoping to catch the countess as well—two birds with one stone. *More like one and a half birds,* he mused as he negotiated the maze of corridors, *unless the fat pullet of a countess makes up the half missing from the Fool.* Vastly entertained by this idea, he emerged at the top of the stairs to the main hallway leading to the royal apartments.

"Psst!"

Nick looked around but could only see the Royal Guards positioned one on each side of the door to the Royal Suite, pikes crossed. They might have well have been carved out of stone for all the notice they took of him.

"Psst!"

The curtain twitched over the entrance to the privy set in the stairwell. A face peered out. At first Nick thought it was a small boy; then he realized it was Codpiece.

"Just the person I wanted to see," Nick said. "I was told you were not in the Privy Chamber, but I see that I was wrong."

"Ha ha," Codpiece said sourly. When Nick would have replied, he held a stubby finger to his lips. "Not here," he hissed. "Follow me."

Nick followed him back down the staircase into a small room at the bottom. A storage room by the looks of the barrels and stacked crates with straw spilling out of them. A scuttling in the corner told Nick they weren't alone, and he wished Hector was with him. He shuddered. He hated rats. Carriers of disease, Eli said. Which was why he and Rivkah had no rushes on their floors but plain slabs of stone, washed daily. No sense providing a nest for them to breed, Eli said. Both he and Rivkah couldn't understand why the poor still strewed rushes on their floors—an ancient practice from the days of the Plantagenets, long abandoned by the gentry—the noisome mess changed only twice a year.

Codpiece stuck his hand into one of the crates and removed a candle and tinderbox. Nick got the impression he had stowed them there beforehand. His movements were fluid and sure, and he struck a spark on the first try, blowing on the lint until a small flame appeared. He lit the candle, dripped wax onto the top of a barrel, and stuck the candle down on it. It gave off a feeble light, just enough to make out the Fool's features when the door was closed. Then Codpiece replaced the lid on the crate and hopped up on it, legs sticking straight out like a child's. Nick leaned in the doorway, arms crossed.

"Why the secrecy?" he asked.

"That's a foolish question," the Fool said. "I thought better of you."

Nick regarded him thoughtfully. Not only had Codpiece refrained from making a feeble pun on the word *foolish* in relation to himself, but his voice sounded different—deeper, more serious, without the singsong cadences he usually employed. Nick got the uncomfortable feeling he had underestimated him.

Codpiece watched the change in Nick's expression and smiled. "No need to get your hose in a twist. Most people think because my body is small, so are my wits. Ergo: A monster must be a simpleton. My parents certainly thought so. That's why they sold me to a traveling acting troupe." Briefly a shadow passed over his face, then he brightened. "Such foolishness serves me well." He was back to double meanings—a flicker of his usual self.

"I'm beginning to see that," Nick said with a twinge of guilt. Before he had reluctantly agreed to spy for Cecil and been sent on his first mission to the Continent, Nick had avoided the court like the plague, despising the jockeying for favor, the blatant smarming, and the incessant backbiting. Like most people, he had assumed that Codpiece was simple, although he had to admit, his repartee was so pointed that Nick suspected there was more going on inside the dwarf's head than people gave him credit for. And more going on inside his heart. Nick had picked up on the Fool's bitterness, his underlying grief. Nick couldn't imagine how he would have felt if his parents had sold him like the two-headed lamb Master Hogg kept in a jar, a freak of nature to be gawped and shuddered at. The court was like the jar where Codpiece was displayed for all to see, his origin as fantastical as the one related by the apothecary. Generally, Nick knew, people saw only what they wanted to see, a two-headed sheep, a Fool, or a monster, seldom looking closely enough to see the sleight of hand, the stitches, the shining intelligence in Codpiece's eyes and realize they were being duped. Himself included. Nick wondered if the Queen kept the Fool by her as a kind of joke on her court; she was certainly canny enough to be capable of such a thing.

"What's your name?" Nick asked.

The Fool blinked as if he hadn't expected such a question. "Richard."

Nick stepped forward and held out his hand. "Pleased to meet you, Richard. Nick."

After a moment's hesitation, the Fool took it. His hand was small, but the grip strong. "Better stick to Codpiece in public," he said with a wry smile. "Don't want to blow my cover."

Nick sat down on a crate next to him. "Why are you telling me this?"

"Because I can help you find whoever murdered that poor child," the Fool said. "I can be your spy."

Nick laughed out loud. He couldn't help it. The irony was too great. "Sorry," he said at last, recovering himself. "I'm not laughing at you, Richard. I swear."

"I know," the Fool said. "You're laughing because you work for the Spider, and you hate him, and now here you are being offered a spy of your own."

Appalled, Nick looked at him. "How the hell do you know that?"

"I told you: people underestimate me, say things they shouldn't, leave incriminating documents around. They pay me as much mind as they would their dog." He said this remarkably cheerfully. And well he might, Nick thought. It gave him access to enormous power. It was also a dangerous game to play without a protector. "Anyway," Codpiece said. "I picked the Spider's pocket when he wasn't looking and had a gander at a document he was carrying: instructions for the "Black Sheep." Wasn't hard to figure out that was your code name." The Fool tried unsuccessfully not to look smug.

"Who's a clever dick then," Nick said, miffed at the Fool's obvious hilarity at his code name, one he hadn't known until this moment. But he had to own that he was impressed by the Fool's sleight of hand. And his courage. Codpiece grinned.

"Does the Queen know?" Nick asked. "I mean, does she know the difference between Codpiece the Fool and Richard the Spy?"

The Fool eyed him. "You're really quite bright," he said. "All things considered."

"What things?" Nick asked, still irritated at being laughed at. By a court jester to boot.

"Your ancestry, for one. All that inbreeding over the centuries tends to dull the mind. Robert's not the sharpest knife in the drawer, I notice."

Nick was aware that the Fool was watching him, interested to see how he would react to a slur on his family name. "Robert may be a bit slow," he admitted, "but he's honest and kind. Qualities I, alas, do not possess. Robert takes after our father; I take after my mother."

"Agnes, Dowager Countess of Blackwell." The Fool nodded. "The Queen is very fond of her. Plus, you are a recusant Catholic. That puts you in an awkward situation, I imagine. One where you are keen to prove your loyalty."

Nick blinked, astonished at how well informed the Fool was and deeply disturbed at this mention of his recusant status. It seemed that however much he proved his loyalty to the Crown, there would always be doubt as to where his allegiance lay. This was the nightmare that he lived with, that at any given moment Elizabeth could decide to have him and his family arrested on a charge of treason. To be a Catholic, even a secret one, was enough to send someone to the block. He wondered if finding Cecily's killer was yet another test of his loyalty.

Slapping his palms on the tops of his thighs, Codpiece seemed to come to a decision. "To answer your question," he said, "the Queen does know. Why do you think she keeps me by her all the time? Not merely for my charm and good looks, surely? I imagine the same applies to you. We are both outsiders with something to lose. That keeps us loyal."

"Why the cunning, old—"

"Now, now," said Codpiece, holding up his hand. "That's treason."

Nick was surprised to see the Fool was serious. Then he

remembered that just five years before, an Act of Parliament had been passed stating that any derogatory remark about the Queen, no matter how trivial, was illegal. Many had found themselves hauled up before the magistrate in the assizes after a ribald comment about the Queen's vaunted virginity or the absurdity of her wigs, remarks usually made in their cups. If they were lucky, they got away with a hefty fine; if unlucky, a public whipping followed by a hefty fine. People muttered about tyrants, but it was surprising, or perhaps not so surprising given human nature, that informers out for a reward were ten a penny.

"I'm very loyal," Codpiece said, eyeing him. "Best to keep that in mind. The Queen told me you were loyal too."

Nick thought back to his conversation with the Queen about Kit Marlowe. She must have talked to Codpiece right after he left, or perhaps the jester had been in the room, hiding behind the arras. A stage cliché, but an effective hiding place especially for someone as diminutive as the Fool. That meant the Queen herself had set up this meeting. Codpiece was her spy at court as Nick had been the Spider's abroad. Now he was back in England, Nick wondered if the Queen had her eye on him as an adjunct to the Fool; after all, Richard had to stick close by the Queen's side, whereas Nick was free to roam. Nick wondered if the Spider knew of Codpiece's real purpose other than entertainment.

"The Spider knows nothing of my true role at court," Codpiece said, reading Nick's mind again; like his royal mistress, it was an unsettling knack he had. "Nor does the Big Cheese."

Nick suddenly became very thoughtful indeed. If Cecil and the "Big Cheese," as Codpiece put it—the great spymaster himself, Sir Francis Walsingham, Secretary of State and architect of her state spy network—knew nothing of Codpiece's true identity, what did that say about how much the Queen trusted them? Or perhaps she trusted them but still needed an alternative source of information, one she could count on absolutely when it came to the shifting loyalties and machinations of her court. Utterly dependent on her largesse and forever barred from high honors, even an advantageous marriage—not to mention someone who, by his very role as court jester, was never taken seriously, the Fool was the ideal choice. He was the Queen's eyes and ears. And it seemed that the Queen was using Nick in the same way. Who better than a recusant Catholic to investigate her court? Clever, clever Bess.

"How can you help me?" Nick asked.

"I can keep my eyes peeled," the Fool said. "My ears open. You are much too conspicuous. That dog you have, he's like a herald announcing your presence: 'Hey everyone, Nicholas Holt's coming!'"

Nick flushed. "The Queen's not the only one who appreciates loyalty," he growled. "I'd kindly ask you not to abuse my dog."

"Sorry," the Fool said, although he didn't look very penitent. "This murder is aimed directly at the Queen," he said in a more serious voice. "It's clear Cecily was not the true target. That child never harmed anyone." His voice became husky, and he cleared his throat. "She was killed," he went on in a steadier voice, "not because of *who* she was but *what* she was—a lady-in-waiting."

"Thank you, Richard," Nick said dryly. "That much I managed to work out for myself."

"Never hurts to summarize and clarify, Nick," the Fool replied airily. "Where was I? Oh yes: So who is trying to discredit the Queen? That's the question that must be answered."

"Her enemies are legion," Nick said, ticking them off on his fingers: "Catholics at home and abroad; the Spanish, obviously; supporters of Mary, Queen of Scots, in Scotland, France, and Spain, not to mention the ancient Catholic nobility at home, mostly in the north; the Calvinist Scottish government; the Puritans; Anabaptist extremists; disgruntled courtiers."

"Not the last," the Fool said emphatically. "This is not a personal crime; this is political. I can feel it in my water."

"It's also religious," Nick said. "The placement of the body tells us that. The Chapel Royal. The altar. Which means it's also political. Whoever killed Cecily left her there for the Queen and the court to find. It's clearly an attempt to destabilize the Crown and the government."

"Correct," Codpiece said approvingly, like a schoolmaster to his brightest pupil.

Nick knew he was taking a risk, but he also knew that, even in the spy game, he had to trust someone sometimes. Still, he had to remember never to let his guard down completely in front of the Fool. There was plenty Nick didn't want passed on to the Queen.

Nick told Codpiece of the clues he had found at the scene, of his fruitless follow-up at the apothecary's.

"November third. That's something."

"Not much," Nick said. "I doubt you're going to come across a diary saying: "November third—purchased Guinea spice; December fourth—murdered sweet young girl in the Chapel Royal.""

The Fool's mouth twisted with distaste, and Nick regretted his flippancy. Who was the Fool now? He told Richard about the topaz. "But no one's going to be wearing a stiletto in their belt," he said. "So that's a bust too. Still, I'll have to check all the daggers."

"Topaz as a charm against anger," Codpiece mused. "Interesting." He jumped down from the crate. "Must be off. The Queen will be back shortly. No doubt in a fury after having to deal with those loggerheaded dunces for an eternity of blah, blah, blah." He grinned and swept into a low bow, his crimson velvet cap brushing the floor. "Splendid to make your acquaintance, Nick. So looking forward to working with you."

Fascinated, Nick watched as he reverted from Richard, the Queen's clever spy, back to Codpiece the Fool. Not only had his voice taken on a higher, more singsong register, but his mannerisms had changed, were jauntier, more devil-may-care.

"Likewise," he said, opening the storeroom door. "You should be on the stage."

"I was," the Fool said, blowing out the candle and stowing it back in the crate, careful to first pinch off the wick so it wouldn't smolder. "That's where I met the Queen for the first time. I was in a play at Greenwich."

He did not elucidate further but, as Nick stepped out of the storeroom, took hold of Nick's sleeve.

"There is one good thing to come of this tragedy," Codpiece said, grinning. "It's put a stopper on the countess. She's gone quiet. She approved of Cecily when she first came to court." He grunted. "Well, she would, of course. Cecily was as green as they come, not a scrap worldly." He looked thoughtful. "But she seemed to have taken against her recently." He shrugged. "Probably due to the girl's friendship with Mary, who—let's be honest—was a bit of a bad influence. Anyway, she seems to be shocked by Cecily's untimely death. Seems the miserable old bag has a heart after all."

"Is the countess in the royal apartments?" Nick asked.

The Fool shook his head. "She's still at her nephew's house in the city." Then he darted through the door, and Nick watched as he skipped off down the corridor, singing, "Hey nonny, nonny" in a ridiculous falsetto.

CHAPTER 7

House of Sir Christopher Stokes, Cheapside

When he emerged from the palace at the Privy Stairs, Nick discovered the boatman had abandoned him in favor of another fare—always plenty to be had when the court was in residence. Cursing himself for forgetting to encourage the ferryman's loyalty with the promise of a generous tip, he doubled back into the palace complex, emerging through the Court Gate onto King Street. A small crowd had gathered near the gate, mostly farmers from the outlying districts, but also a few tradesmen and carters.

"Filthy Jews," Nick heard one man mutter, a bricklayer, judging by the hod he carried over his shoulder.

The man, a big burly fellow with currant eyes set in an expanse of puffy flesh like buttons sewn too tightly to an overstuffed pillow, his breath hot and yeasty from the ale that appeared to be his main sustenance, bellied up to him. "Filthy, pox-ridden, plaguey Jews. String 'em up and good riddance."

"Aye," the crowed chorused. The two soldiers standing, pikes crossed, before the gate shifted uneasily.

"There's no problem, I trust," Nick said to him, keeping his voice friendly. Despite the Queen's attempt to keep Cecily's murder a secret, word of it had already gotten out and was clearly spreading. It wouldn't do to provoke these men into outright panic. Like a contagion, rumor would spread until it crossed the river and inflamed Bankside. If that happened, he was fearful harm would come to Rivkah and Eli.

"We heard the Jews had killed an innocent lass," the bricklayer said. "One of the Queen's ladies. Cut her up on the altar like a side of beef."

"Aye," the crowd intoned again, the sound darker, more menacing.

"There's absolutely no evidence to suggest it was the Jews," Nick said, but he could see from the skeptical faces around him that they didn't believe him. "Go about your business," he said. "I can assure you, in the Queen's name, that she has the matter well in hand. She thanks you for your concern."

At the mention of the Queen, the bricklayer stepped back a pace. Perhaps he was reassured, or perhaps he was reminded that large gatherings outside the royal palaces were regarded as seditious and could result in imprisonment and even death if violence broke out. Either way, the bricklayer gave a sign to the others, and the crowd began to melt away.

"Ta for that," one of the soldiers muttered. "For a moment there, I thought things were going to go tits up."

"They still may," Nick said. "So keep your eyes peeled and get reinforcements if you need them. But no heavy stuff," he warned. "It will only make matters worse." Confident he had managed to diffuse the situation, at least temporarily, he set off north to Charing Cross. At the intersection of King Street and the Strand, he turned right toward St. Paul's. Despite his casual demeanor to the crowd and guards, Nick was profoundly disturbed by what he had just witnessed. Cecily's body was barely cold, and news had begun to spread that the Jews were responsible. By tonight, the whole of London would be inflamed by the ugly rumor. By tomorrow, so would Bankside. Like the plague, bigotry was no respecter of rank, trade, or distance. The bridge that he and Rivkah had so lightheart-edly traversed that morning, reveling in the bustle and hum, would carry the disease of fear and hatred just as easily as it did commerce. He must warn Eli and Rivkah to keep a low profile until Cecily's murderer was caught.

Nick also pondered his conversation with the Fool, or Richard as he now thought of him. Still rattled by the fact that Richard knew he was a spy, Nick realized he was also relieved. It was a lonely business pretending to be someone else—the wanton will-o'-the-wisp noble who, inexplicably, had turned his back on his family to run a tavern in the shadiest district of London. No matter. The Black Sheep was the perfect place to receive infor-mation straight from the wharves, the boats and ships that docked there carrying secret information that was slipped into his hand as he sat in the taproom pretending to be more drunk than he actually was. Sometimes, like the other night, he was precisely as drunk as he seemed.

The Fool's sudden transformation reminded him of the pro-cessions he had seen in Spain on Holy Days, a strangely disturbing yet exhilarating experience. A statue of the Virgin, pale, serene, eyes cast modestly down, bobbing shoulder-high through a seeth-ing mass of humanity. What did she see as she looked down with that enigmatic half smile? The innocent babes held aloft for her to bless, the leering faces of the drunks, the crazed eyes of the ecstatic, the calculating eyes of the cutpurses moving through the crowd, identifying easy marks, eyes averted in guilt like Nick's own eyes because the gentle gaze of this lovely woman was more than he could bear, knowing he had just taken the life of a man who had tried to kill him in one of Madrid's backstreets.

And the masks—devils and angels, apostles, martyrs. An assassin's eyes looking through the mask of an angel, an innocent's behind a devil's. Presumably, the Queen of Heaven could tell the difference, could see the true nature of her subjects, the heart of flesh beneath the velvet and sequins and lace, all that beguiling glitter of earthly pomp. Nick wondered if his own Virgin Queen was so adept. Elizabeth's precarious position at court when she was a young woman had made her a shrewd judge of character. But she was only human, despite the divine attributes bestowed on her by a largely adoring populace, a status she assiduously cultivated with her white face paint and dazzling jewels. She might abhor all things Popish, but she had freely borrowed from the Catholic Church's rituals and superstitions when it came to how she presented herself to her people. The Virgin Mother, a paradox she exploited for all it was worth. Despite pulling off this theatrical coup—and it was a brilliant piece of theater, Nick had to own—she must know her limitations. Why else instruct her Fool to spy on her own court?

Where the Strand became Fleet Street, Nick continued east toward Whitefriars. He crossed the bridge over the Fleet Ditch, London's main sewer, which emptied into the Thames a few blocks south, instinctively holding his breath and refraining from looking down. If he had, he would have seen hundreds of rats swarming over human and animal waste, burrowing and rooting in refuse of all kinds, including the occasional corpse.

★　★　★

Approaching St. Paul's Cross, his eye was caught by a young beggar girl, crouched on its steps, selling nosegays—in truth, mostly dried grasses and dead twigs in December. Digging out a shilling, he walked over and gave it to her. Her eyes widened at the amount, twelve times too much—a penny would have been too much for her sad wares.

"Thank you, sir," she said, biting the coin in a disturbingly professional way to check it wasn't clipped or counterfeit. Apparently satisfied, it disappeared into the bundle of rags she called clothes. Greasy strands of hair straggled out of a dirty bonnet; her face was smeared with dirt, her nose red and lips chapped from the cold. Her thin frame shook as if afflicted by the palsy. She could not have been more than six or seven.

Nick took the pathetic little bunch of twigs and weeds, pretended to smell them appreciatively, then made a small bow and quickly turned away before she saw the raw pity on his face. Newgate Prison was not far away; he wondered if her mother or father were locked up and she had gone out to Spittal or Moor Fields early that morning to gather whatever was growing in order to make enough pennies to pay their miserable fine. He thought of Kat and how perilous it was for young girls on the streets of the capital. It was a miracle Kat had survived. He wondered what this girl's chances of survival were. If starvation and cold didn't get her, a pimp or pervert with a predilection for young flesh would.

Most of the prisons were filled with vagrants rather than criminals. And there were plenty of them to choose from: Newgate, the Fleet, Bridewell, the King's Bench, the Hole at the Counters, all within or near the city walls; and south of the river in Southwark, the Clink and the Marshalsea. And these were just the public jails. Many private stately homes had dungeons deep below their cellars where malefactors could languish for weeks without a hearing.

It seemed that everywhere he looked there were beggars— former soldiers with legs or arms missing, desperate-eyed women clutching scrawny infants too weakened by hunger to cry; scores of children running in packs like wild dogs, some as young as three or four; men and women too old to work—an endless panoply of misery and despair. Some beggars were obviously tricksters, concealing bladders of pig's blood with which they daubed themselves so passersby would pity them and open their purses, or mothers who pinched their children to make them cry. Most were simply destitute, and it was common to find a stiffened corpse lying in an alley after a hard freeze the previous night. Before Henry VIII had grabbed up the monasteries and convents when he declared himself Head of the Church in England, these great monasteries, which abounded in the city of London, had fed, clothed, employed, and healed the poor: Black- and Whitefriars, Clerkenwell and the Crutched Friars Priories; the hospitals founded by religious orders—St. Bartholomew's; Bethlehem or Bedlam for the insane; St. Katherine's Hospital near the Tower; St. Thomas in Bankside, close to where Nick lived. By snaffling up the lot, Henry VIII, that most covetous of kings, had ripped the guts out of the institutions of Catholic charity that for centuries had been the last hope of the poor, the sick, the old, and the very young. Nick wondered how long Elizabeth could go on ignoring the problem; not until there was a riot, he'd wager, and one of the sumptuous houses of a member of the Star Chamber was burned to the ground. Self-interest was always a good motivator.

Bankside was an anomaly. Unlike the rest of London, it was openly criminal and catered exclusively to the entertainment needs of the larger metropolis on the north side of the river—theaters, bear- and bullbaiting rings, cock fights, prostitutes. Out of sight, out of mind was how the beadles, magistrates, and Queen's Justices thought of it. As long as the cutpurses, harlots, smugglers, rapists, murderers, gamblers, and—especially beloved of the Puritans' self-righteous ire—those suspiciously itinerant masters of disguise and deceit, actors, stayed on the south side of the Thames, they were left in relative peace. Stray over London Bridge to infect the rest of London, like rats bringing the plague, and that was another matter entirely. Whipping, branding, and mutilation were the least of the punishments that awaited them; more commonly, death by hanging; being hung in cages to slowly starve; or, if the crime were especially heinous, drawn on a hurdle, hanged by the neck, and then quartered while still alive.

The severity of the punishment for capital crimes did not bother Nick; it was the harshness of punishment for crimes committed out of desperation, hunger, and poverty that he considered inhuman. Perhaps it was his friendship with Kat that had made him more aware of the law's frightening blindness when it came to intent and motive: if she had been caught after stealing from the cook at the great house, she would have swung from the gallows or, at the very least, been mutilated by having her nose slit or cheek branded.

As Justice of the Peace for the county, Nick's father had held monthly assizes in the great hall, mostly handing out punishments in kind—a dozen eggs in compensation for stealing a chicken, a bolster of duck down for filching bedding from someone's clothesline or window, a fortnight shoveling horse manure for the theft of oats. How could he punish people harshly for being hungry? he said. The old earl handed out humiliating but non-lethal punishments for more serious crimes: a day in the stocks for a fraudulent baker, pelted by his customers with stale bread—misery for him, great fun for them; a week wearing the Drunkard's Cloak (an ale barrel with holes cut out for the head and arms) for a notorious drunk who beat his wife. His father once told the story of a woman who had been so incensed by her husband's abuse, she had deliberately pushed him down a hill when he was wearing the Drunkard's Cloak, and watched him roll into a muddy ditch, almost suffocating in the process. Her neighbors had stood by and applauded. The earl had refused to prosecute the wife when her husband brought suit against her for battery.

"He didn't lay hands on her again," Nick's father said.

Nick had been largely oblivious to the harsher laws of the land, but since taking up residence in Bankside and coming to know Kat, Eli, and Rivkah, not to mention the denizens of his district, those criminals he greeted by name in the taproom of The Black Sheep or in the street—Pip, Black Jack, Henry, Joe, Will, Kit—he had come to put a human face on a whole class of undesirables. Kat had taught him what it meant to be despised as a profession; Eli and Rivkah, what it meant to be persecuted as a race. No longer insulated by the privilege of birth, he was more aware of the misery around him, more prone to anger at the great gulf between the haves and the much more numerous have-nots. Nick was convinced that poverty was the chief reason most turned to crime. For those who committed the worst crimes of all—murder, treason, sedition, rape—he had no mercy and considered no punishment too cruel. Determined to seek out the man who had murdered Cecily, he would be there to witness his terrible end. This he vowed.

The face of the beggar girl rose in his mind's eye. If Rivkah had been with him, she would have taken the girl home with her and gently questioned her until she got her whole sorry story. Unlike him, she would not have been content to merely hand over a coin—money he could well afford—and stroll on, conscience salved.

He smiled briefly at the memory of their morning walk across the bridge, of her mental nimbleness in their confrontation with the apothecary, and of her small figure, absurdly dwarfed by his huge dog, striding purposefully down the road. Then he grew somber again. Despite their deep friendship, there remained an unbridgeable divide between them that was not merely one of class: she was a woman, he a man; she was a Jew, he a Christian, at least nominally; she was a Spaniard, a citizen of his country's mortal enemy. He despaired of ever crossing that gap. That he yearned to do so was something he had long admitted to himself. His greatest fear was that she would learn he was spying on her country, her people, perhaps even believe he was spying on her and Eli, feigning friendship in order to get close to them. He couldn't bear to think of her eyes clouding with mistrust, her prickly sense of humor becoming muted, her friendship withdrawn. And Eli? After John, he was Nick's closest friend; Nick owed him his life. To lose brother or sister would be a kind of death.

★ ★ ★

Nick arrived in Cheapside and easily found the house of Sir Christopher Stokes, a four-story black and white timber and

plaster construction with expensive mullioned windows on the
upper floors—a sign of great wealth, as glass was exorbitantly
taxed. It was situated just past Milk Street and before St. Mary le
Bow, wedged between a goldsmith's and a wig shop specializing in
wigs made from human hair rather than horsehair. Although the
wig shop had no royal emblem emblazoned across its lintel to indicate royal patronage, Nick thought it unlikely the Queen would
advertise her baldness to the public at large. The frothy, red-curled
confection perched on the head of a mannequin in the front window certainly reminded him of one he had recently seen the
Queen wearing. But no one in their right senses would be foolhardy enough to indicate by word or deed they knew the Queen's
hair was not her own. Nick wondered how such an offense would
be punished: hanging, boiling in oil, stretching on the rack? Having
to wear one of those ridiculous things on his head for a month would
be punishment enough, he concluded with a grin. Like wearing one
of his mother's obnoxious lapdogs.

Nick had never formally met Sir Christopher, only glimpsed
him from time to time among the sycophants fawning over the
Queen at court. Hard to miss with his expensive canary-yellow
doublets (the cloth dyed with saffron, one of the costliest imported
dyes on the market), slashed and double-slashed to reveal crimson
and sky-blue silk underneath; his fashionably short cloak cut too
far above the waist to be warm, and fussily thrown back over one
shoulder; his immaculately trimmed beard pomaded to a point
in the latest aspiring Sir Francis Drake fashion; his single drop
earring. Nick thought him a popinjay, a mere flapdragon. He
was constantly amazed at the torturous routes of family blood-
lines, how they veered and shifted over time like errant rivers,
sometimes snaking back on themselves to throw up a present-day

copy of an ancient, worthless ancestor the family would have loved nothing better than to forget. Who would have thought that the fat, domineering, perpetually sour Countess of Berwick could have had such a lightweight for a nephew and heir? Nick was certain it was only his aunt's patronage that had secured the man his post.

The door to the town residence of Sir Christopher Stokes was made of solid, pitch-blackened English oak, banded with brass for security. Every house in this wealthy, predominantly mercantile neighborhood was similarly fitted. A brass knocker in the shape of a dolphin hung in the middle. Nick knocked loudly three times. A furious yapping, slightly muffled by the thickness of the door, ensued. Thinking of his mother's lap dogs again, he prepared to have his ankles savaged by an absurd ball of fluff. For the second time that morning, he wished he'd brought Hector along.

"Yeah?" a voice drawled through the crack in the door, managing to sound both bored and insolent. "We don't want any, whatever it is." The barking became hysterical.

"I'm here on the Queen's business," Nick said, trying to hold his temper in check.

"Bugger off!"

Nevertheless, the door opened. Nick saw a white streak dart around the boy's legs. "Sit," he commanded, pointing a finger at it. The small dog abruptly sat, blinking up at him with a look very like astonishment. Nick stepped past it into the house. The boy's look of insolence was replaced by one of profound admiration.

"Who is it, Perkin?" a voice called querulously.

Nick followed the voice, taking the stairs two at a time. Perkin, who should have been trying to pass him so he could announce him formally, followed behind. At the sound of his master's voice, the dog left his place by the door and raced up the stairs giving Nick and Perkin a wide berth.

"How did you do that?" Perkin asked, his voice filled with admiration. "He never obeys anyone."

"Practice."

The room Nick entered was richer by far than the Queen's own study. A bonfire roared in an enormous stone fireplace, making the room stifling. A gray pall of smoke hung just beneath the ceiling, an ornate job of molded plaster and gilded heraldic shields that made the room claustrophobic and caused Nick to duck involuntarily. Thick tapestries in dark, funereal colors adorned the wall—a pity, Nick thought, as what he could see of them were made of rather fine linen-fold oak paneling. A thick layer of dust coated every surface, as if the room was hardly ever used.

Reclining on a chaise longue lay the countess, a fur rug tucked around her legs, her ample bosoms rising like twin mounds of sweating dough. Perched on a chair opposite was her nephew, Sir Christopher, resplendent in bilious yellow, holding the tiny dog in the air and crooning to it. The dog hung listlessly between his hands, front paws drooping, but its moist, cataract-ridden eyes held a deeply malevolent glint, as if it were contemplating sinking its teeth into its master's lily-white throat. And Sir Christopher was indisputably its master, as the countess wore an expression of deep disgust when her gaze fell on both nephew and dog alike. Sir Christopher kissed it tenderly on the nose and then gave a violent sneeze. Not surprising considering the dust. Nick could have written his name—nay, an entire sonnet—in the thick layer coating the sideboard. Nick felt sorry for the dog.

"You've upset him," Sir Christopher said, shooting Nick a malevolent look.

"Oh, put a sock in it, Christopher," his aunt barked. "And put that loathsome animal down." She turned a minatory eye on Nick. "The Honorable Nicholas Holt," she said. "To what do we owe the pleasure?"

At the mention of Nick's title, Sir Christopher leapt to his feet, indicating Nick should take his chair. "Most honored," he murmured, bowing obsequiously, the dog tucked beneath his arm like a fur muff.

Nick eyed the dog hair liberally coating the chair Sir Christopher had just vacated, and took a stool. "Countess," he said, ignoring her nephew, "I've been commanded by Her Majesty to investigate Cecily's death."

At her beloved Queen's name, the countess sat up straighter, but her face drained of color. Nick was surprised; he hadn't known the old battle-ax was so filled with the milk of human kindness as to care so much about a junior lady-in-waiting who had only been at court a few weeks. But then again, Richard had told him she was overcome by grief, although, looking at her now, it seemed as if she were more out of sorts than grief-stricken. Notorious for her insistence on etiquette, she was probably more upset about the disruption caused by Cecily's death than the actual fact of it.

"That poor, poor child," the countess murmured, unknowingly echoing the Queen's words the night before. "Was she . . . ?" Her fingers plucked at the rug fretfully as she searched for the right word. Her eyes fixed on Nick's imploringly.

"*Interfered* with?" he said, using a euphemism he hated, but choosing to take pity on her.

She nodded.

"No," he replied. *Not in the way you mean,* he thought, blinking to remove the image of the wicked hole over Cecily's heart.

"Thank God." The countess began to make the sign of the cross, then froze. Nick pretended he hadn't seen. It was common for people the countess's age to remember the time when the Catholic faith was freely practiced—the only difference then, that the king styled himself Head of the Church. Everything else had been the same: the Mass, the sacraments, incense, vespers, matins, the Latin liturgy. It wasn't until Edward, his sickly son, mounted the throne under the radically Protestant sway of his uncles, the Seymours, that the changes in ritual began—the introduction of the Book of Common Prayer in the vernacular, the banning of the rosary and feast days of saints and other "Popish practices." As a contemporary of the Queen, the countess would have been raised in the old faith, and those childhood habits were hard— nay, impossible—to break. Nick's own mother, Agnes, was the same. He had often seen her fingers unconsciously moving in her lap, as if she were telling her beads. He had once asked her if she actively practiced the old faith.

"That would be treason," Agnes had replied.

Only afterward did Nick realize that she hadn't answered his question.

"You saw her on the day she died, did you not?" Nick asked the countess gently.

She nodded. "Yes. I did. She was on duty as usual. We were a bit shorthanded with Mary off sick and two others . . . *indisposed*."

Nick took her to mean something to do with female physiology such as menstruation or even pregnancy, a state not unheard of with ladies-in-waiting in a court surrounded by men. He steeled himself for a spate of euphemisms. His mother's sister, Lady Herbert, was a great one for them. As boys, he and Robert had often been reprimanded for laughing and rolling their eyes when she was in full cry: "late" for deceased, as if the person had overslept and missed an appointment with his barber; or—Nick's personal favorite and one that his aunt repeatedly used to describe her dead husband—as having "joined the Choir eternal."

"Rubbish," his mother had once snapped. "Reginald was tone deaf."

"Did you notice anything unusual about her behavior that day?" Nick asked the countess.

She frowned. "What do you mean?"

"Anything out of the ordinary. Did she receive a message from anyone? Did her mood change at all?" He was trying to confirm his suspicion that Cecily had received the note on the morning she died.

The countess looked down, the folds of her double chin bunching up over her lace ruff. Nick noticed her fingers were still plucking at the rug. At last she raised her head.

"Cecily was a shy girl," she said. "She hadn't been with us for long."

Nick waited patiently.

"She seemed as usual in the morning when we dressed the Queen. Before chapel," she explained. "But after we returned from chapel to the royal apartments she seemed . . ."

"Yes?"

The countess frowned. "Well, *different* somehow."

Nick tried to remain patient at the slow trickle of information. Few civilians thought like spies, paying attention to peoples' moods, the way they said things, noticing small changes in routine or behavior. "In what way?" he prodded.

"She seemed happier, excited even. And she asked to go to the privy right after we returned." The countess frowned again, and Nick briefly felt sorry for the ladies-in-waiting under her dominion if a simple request to relieve themselves was considered a crime.

"No," she said, as if reading his mind, "you don't understand. She had gone right *before* chapel and it wasn't her—" She broke off abruptly and flushed. "Monthly course," she said finally. The countess glared at Nick for making her speak of such matters.

The note, Nick thought. He felt a brief flicker of triumph that his suspicions had been confirmed. Someone passed it to her in chapel that morning, and she had later excused herself so she could read it. Deliberately making his voice casual, he asked if the countess had seen anything out of the ordinary before, during, or after the service. He was particularly concerned with the time after the service.

"What do you mean?" she said. "It was just chapel. Same every morning."

An honest answer. Habit was hard to remember, the sequence of routine actions blurred. Unless something out of the ordinary happened, one merely assumed something had happened as it always had, rather than actually remembering it. Given enough time, the assumption would take on the guise of an actual memory. Nick had interrogated enough people to be familiar with this strange phenomenon of the human mind.

Nick tried another tack. "Who was sitting near Cecily in the pew?" This should be easier for her to answer as there was a strict rule of precedence, which would be engraved on the countess's mind. She was known to be a great stickler for rules.

"As the youngest and most recent of the ladies," the countess said, "she was at the end near the center aisle on the right side of the chapel."

That meant another lady-in-waiting would be sitting on her right, and the center aisle of the chapel would be on her immediate left. No one sitting next to her had slipped her a note. Nick did not think it could have happened during the service, but he had to check. That left afterward, when people were hurrying to breakfast or jostling to be the first to importune the Queen for some favor.

"Who was sitting behind her?"

A log spat in the fire, and an ember landed on the floor. Sir Christopher jumped up and stamped it out. He had been so quiet up to now that if it hadn't been for his occasional sneezing, Nick would have forgotten he was there.

"It could have been anyone," the countess said, looking at Nick as if he were an idiot. "I was sitting next to the Queen in the front pew."

"Of course." According to court precedence, Cecily would be seated behind the Queen, the countess, and the most senior ladies-in-waiting. The countess would have had her back to her.

"What about when you were leaving the chapel?"

"She was still behind me," the countess said, moving restlessly under the rug. Nick could see she was losing patience. But now he knew that she would not have seen anything. Her only use was in nailing down the approximate time when the note could have been passed.

Stifling his disappointment, he gave her his most winning smile. "Bear with me, if you would," he said.

She snorted, obviously immune to his masculine charms. A widow for many years, Nick was amazed she had even deigned to marry in the first place, so great was her disdain for the male sex. No wonder her nephew was terrified of her. "Can we get this over with?" the countess said. "I'm not well." As if to prove it, she sneezed. "Bloody dog," she muttered, eyeing it malevolently. Her nephew looked apologetic but made no attempt to put the dog out of the room.

"But when you returned to the royal apartments, you noticed her mood was different?"

"As I said before," the countess replied. She looked at her nephew. "Christopher, all these questions are making me thirsty. Get some wine."

Nick hid his surprise at her giving orders as if Sir Christopher were her servant. No doubt used to her imperiousness, he meekly got up and went to the door.

"Perkin," he bawled. "Wine."

The countess blinked in surprise, then looked irritated. "Must you shout?" she complained. "My head's splitting."

"Sorry," he mumbled and sat down again.

"In what way different?" Nick pressed.

"Happier."

"And then she asked to go to the privy?"

The countess nodded.

"How did she appear when she returned?"

"Secretive."

An interesting word, Nick thought. And unexpectedly astute of the countess. "But she said nothing?"

She shook her head.

"And later that night, when the Queen was going to bed?"

"She was distracted. Kept forgetting things." She glared at Sir Christopher. "Like the wine."

At that moment, Perkin sauntered in, carrying a silver tray with matching flagon and goblets. Nick was a little taken aback by how wealthy Sir Christopher appeared to be. Everything was of the best—woven, not painted, tapestries from either the Gobelins Royal Factory in Paris or the most famous tapestry district in France, Arras, judging by the quality of thread and color. Thick glass on the casement window; embroidered cushions on the window seat; silver candlesticks on the mantelpiece. He wondered if Sir Christopher were involved in the luxury trade. There was the dolphin knocker on the door—a maritime symbol—and he had heard somewhere that Sir Christopher often traveled abroad.

Setting the tray down on a large oak press against the wall, Perkin poured and handed around the cups, serving the countess first, Nick second, Sir Christopher last. *Pecking order,* Nick thought, concealing a grin. Servants always revealed more about their masters than people thought. From the time of ancient Rome, comedy was replete with the stock characters of uppity servants running the lives of dullard masters, cuckolding and fleecing them with impunity. Nick always liked to question servants if he could. That was why he had made a mental note to return to the apothecary's at closing time. He hoped to have a quiet word with Wat, the assistant. And now that he had established his credentials with Perkin vis-à-vis the lad's mortal enemy, the hideous ball of fluff, he had no doubt he would be forthcoming if only Nick could get him alone.

He was often amazed at how eager most servants were to spill the beans about the most intimate and embarrassing details of their masters' and mistresses' lives, without money changing hands. At first he had been surprised, expecting discretion, but then he had quickly come to realize that revenge for innumerable slights, real or imagined, was usually the motive behind such loquacity. Whatever the reason, he usually profited by it. He could also learn a great deal just by watching the body language of servants; when Perkin placed his master's goblet on a table beside him, Nick saw him shoot Sir Christopher a contemptuous look and then ostentatiously brush at nonexistent dog hair on his doublet. Nick noticed that Perkin's left hose near his ankle had been torn and inexpertly sewn up. His doublet was stained, and his linen shirt yellow with age and gossamer thin with wear. For a household as rich as this one clearly was, Nick thought it strange the servant should be so shabbily dressed. Sir Christopher struck him as a person whose vanity demanded that his servants do him credit, but Perkin wore no livery and seemed to be the only servant in the household.

Sir Christopher seemed fastidious in all other respects—the way he dressed, for example: matching hose and slippers, jewels chosen to complement the color of his doublet. Nick had an instinctive mistrust for a man who took such care with his dress and toilette; he thought it womanish. He himself was dressed in whatever clothes lay on top of the heap on his bedchamber floor. Today it was a padded leather jerkin with a reasonably clean shirt underneath and a workaday doublet cut unfashionably low and loose in the leg, like breeches. His stint as a soldier had taught him to choose comfort, durability, and freedom of movement over fashion. Sir Christopher's yellow doublet was cut so high on the thigh and was so voluminous he looked like an obscene squash.

Perkin's shabby appearance was an odd anomaly; one more thing Nick added to his list of why he couldn't stand Sir Christopher.

"Thank you, Perkin," the countess snapped. "That will be all." It seemed she too had witnessed this dumb show, and however much she herself despised her nephew, inferiors slighting their betters was clearly not to be tolerated.

The lad sketched a perfunctory bow and withdrew. Nick could imagine him listening outside the door.

Nick sipped his wine, wishing they would offer him some food. He hadn't eaten since he had broken his fast with Eli and Rivkah that morning, and it was long past midday. Outside the window, the brief daylight of winter was already fading, the room becoming dim. Soon it would be the shortest day of the year. Christmas would be upon them, and the court would move to Hampton Court for the festivities. He must hurry to solve this case before then, before people scattered to their own estates. And he must hurry if he were to catch Wat at the apothecary's before dark, even if it was only a brief walk from Cheapside. He rose and set his goblet down.

"Just one more question," he said.

Sir Christopher had also risen and was hovering near the door as if he couldn't wait to see Nick out. The countess gave a great sigh—pure theater—a clear message that her patience had been sorely taxed, but she was willing to put up with it for the moment. Nick had saved his most difficult question for last.

"Why were you so upset by Cecily's murder, Countess? I'm told you didn't like her very much." He deliberately hardened his voice and phrased it as bluntly as possible for maximum shock, hinting that others had been gossiping about her behind her back. He was heartily sick of the countess's air of superiority and wanted her rattled, off balance.

She opened her mouth, then snapped it closed again like a trap. Her eyes bulged and spots of color suddenly flamed in her cheeks.

"I say," Sir Christopher objected.

Nick ignored him and waited, his eyes on the countess.

"How dare you?" she said, but her heart wasn't in it. She looked more flustered than indignant once the initial shock of his rudeness had worn off. Nick saw her glance quickly at her nephew as if drawing strength from a relationship where she was clearly dominant and never on the receiving end of impertinent questions. Nick guessed the only person she considered her superior was the Queen herself. An earl's younger son was a nothing.

"It was—it *is* a terrible thing," she said at last. "I would not wish such a death on my worst enemy." Before Nick could reply, she added, "And Cecily was not my enemy, young man. A bit flighty, perhaps, especially after she took up with Mary, but a good girl at heart. Although," she added, "she was useless as a lady-in-waiting."

Nick suppressed a flicker of anger. He would have described her friend Mary as flighty, but not Cecily. Cecily was sweet and innocent, almost ethereal with her long golden hair and guileless blue eyes. It was her very innocence that had made her such a perfect victim, someone easily taken in by that cold note. She was so much a child that she would have thought nothing of the note's prescriptive tone, not being long out of the schoolroom herself. And to describe Cecily as useless was unkind; she had only been at court a few weeks and was still learning the ropes. It was inevitable that she should make mistakes. The countess's harsh judgment was clearly based on envy, Nick thought. Envy of Cecily's youth and innocence, perhaps even envy of the Queen's affection for her youngest lady-in-waiting. He knew he had outstayed his welcome. Concealing his dislike, he gave a small bow. "Thank you, Countess. You've been most helpful."

Sir Christopher was hovering near the door.

"Did you know Cecily?" Nick asked.

"I danced with her once," he replied. He flushed at the memory.

Now Nick remembered seeing them dancing at the Accession Day Ball. His impression was that Cecily had agreed to dance with him out of politeness and perhaps because she was too inexperienced with men to know how to refuse. Certainly, he recollected, she had made sure to disengage her hand quickly after the dance was over and glide away into the crowd so Sir Christopher could not ask her again.

Nick started to leave, then swung back. "Where were you at midnight last night?"

"At the Custom House," Sir Christopher said.

"At midnight?" Nick said incredulously.

"My nephew works all hours," the countess said proudly. "He is a highly successful merchant."

Nick glanced at Sir Christopher for confirmation. "A shipment of Venetian glass," he explained. "Very costly. Seems it was 'lost.' I was called in to sort it out."

"Did you find it?" Nick asked.

"Turns out it was unloaded onto the wrong wharf."

Nick knew that business on the busy docks and quays of the Thames went on around the clock. London was, after all, one of the biggest centers of commerce in all of Europe. Still, it was unusual for a man of Sir Christopher's wealth and status to be required to take himself to the docks in the middle of the night, even if a costly import had been misplaced. He wondered if Sir Christopher was the kind of man who found it impossible to leave his underlings to get on with a job, who was constantly fussing over their every move. He certainly looked the type. Still, something was fishy about his alibi, and it would have to be checked.

As Nick turned to go, he thought he saw the flash of something in Sir Christopher's eyes, quickly gone. *The worm turns,* he thought. *Well, well.*

Nick left the room and descended the stairs. Perkin was loitering in the hallway by the front door, but Sir Christopher was still standing on the upstairs landing, so Nick decided to postpone his talk with the lad. He could return when he was sure Sir Christopher was out.

When Nick dropped by the apothecary's on his way back from Sir Christopher's, he found the shop closed. A chink of light showed through the shutters on the second floor, but he had no way of knowing if Master Hogg lived above his shop or merely rented out the space. Besides, he preferred to talk to Wat alone. He would have to come back later and watch for him to leave; apprentices spent half their lives delivering goods, so he was certain he would catch Wat at some point. With night falling, Nick gave up for the day and continued back to Bankside along London Bridge.

CHAPTER 8

The Palace of Whitehall

He returned to Whitehall the next day with Hector and John. Maggie, John's wife, had not been happy when Nick asked if he could borrow her husband for a couple of days. John stood silently by and let Nick do all the talking. A brave man in a fight, he was a complete coward when it came to the wife he adored.

He had known John, the son of his father's steward, all his life. As boys they had fished in the streams on the estate and hunted rabbits together; as teens they had taken it in turn bedding wenches in the barn, the other acting as lookout in case they were discovered. When he went off to Oxford at fifteen Nick had begged his father to let John come with him as his manservant—in truth, his companion. His father, with characteristic fairness, had deferred to his steward, John's father, who had reluctantly agreed. He had known for years that his eldest son wasn't cut out for facts and figures, the tally books and records of a steward's life. His younger son, Simon, being naturally bookish, showed more aptitude, and he had long been training him to take over his position. The long and short of it was that Master Stockton gave

John his blessing; the earl gave him a horse—a much more practical gift, but no less loving for that—and a small purse of gold.

Two years ago they had met Maggie when he and John had stopped by the tavern, then named Ye Olde Cock, after having disembarked at Bankside after a trip to the Continent. Seated before the fire in the taproom, Nick had gradually become aware that his friend kept looking at the woman behind the bar. A boy was helping her, obviously her son by the strong resemblance and the way she smiled at him and occasionally ruffled his hair.

"See something you like?" Nick had quipped, digging John in the ribs. John had ignored him and kept staring.

"Don't blame you," Nick had said. "She's a looker all right." The woman had a heart-shaped face and flashing green eyes. Curly auburn hair tumbled out of the kerchief she wore tied around her head, and she kept blowing at a strand that was tickling her cheek—a very fetching sight, Nick had to admit. She moved quickly and efficiently about the bar, chatting with customers and occasionally good-naturedly shoving them away if they got too friendly. Interestingly, Nick noticed that few customers molested her, tipsy as they were. A rough lot, mostly sailors and men of less definable professions that Nick suspected landed squarely on the wrong side of the law, they seemed content to lean their elbows on the bar and feast their bleary eyes on her. Much the same way John was doing.

Except that John was watching one man in particular more than he was looking at the woman, Nick realized. Squat, wide, and with a once powerful torso now running to fat, the man was leaning across the bar saying something to the woman. She frowned, shook her head, and tried to move away, but the man grabbed her arm and yanked her forward, upsetting the tankard of ale she was carrying. Her son tried to intervene but was brushed off as if he were a troublesome gnat, and fell back behind the counter. John leapt to his feet and was almost to the bar before Nick realized what he was doing. The sound of the punch John delivered was drowned out by the shouts of the crowd, but Nick saw it in dumb show as the man's head snapped back on impact. The man stood his ground, and as he launched himself at John, they began to grapple. At the first sign of trouble, the other patrons had drawn back to the edges of the room, part entertained, part fearful. Nick saw another man detach himself from the crowd and move toward John. In his hand, Nick caught the glint of a knife.

"Behind you, John," Nick yelled and flung himself at the man. There wasn't enough room to draw his sword, so Nick went for the man's knife hand, grasping his wrist and twisting until the weapon clattered to the floor; then he swung him around and delivered a straight-handed chop to the throat followed by a knee to the groin. Not very sporting, but effective. Fighting for his life in Spanish alleys and dockyards had led Nick to believe that the notion of fair play was overrated. The man toppled like a felled oak and lay there making peculiar retching noises. By the time Nick looked up, he saw that John had the squat man in an armlock and was repeatedly bashing his head against a post. Nick watched admiringly. The man's head was hard—he'd give him that. It took five blows before his eyes rolled back and he went slack. John let go, and the man joined his companion in a crumpled heap. Immediately, the other patrons stepped over the bodies, bellied up to the bar, and demanded more ale.

After closing, Nick and John sat on in the tavern while Maggie, the tavern's owner, explained who the men were and why they had been strong-arming her. Distant cousins of her deceased husband, they were demanding she sell the tavern to them for a pittance. They had been harassing her for months, and there was nothing she or her twelve-year-old son, Henry, could do.

"Tell you what," Nick said. "I'll buy the place at full price, and you run it." He had been looking for a home base and already had his eye on Bankside for its wharves and jetties, its constantly shifting population, and the fact that people didn't ask too many questions. A much better place to meet with informants and receive letters from abroad than in the more settled neighborhoods of the city, where families had known one another for generations and everyone's business was an open topic of conversation.

Maggie looked doubtful and glanced at John, who nodded. "Do it," he said. "Nick won't cheat you—I promise you that."

"We'll do it legally," Nick said. "That way you'll be protected. I'll sell it back to you for a token price when Henry comes of age."

"Why would you do this?" Maggie asked. "You don't know me."

Nick glanced at John, who was looking at Maggie with a silly grin on his face. Henry was looking at John as if he were the Second Coming.

"No," Nick said, "but I know John."

"We'll think about it," she said, taking Henry's hand.

In the end, Maggie decided that Nick's plan was the only way to prevent her husband's relatives from taking the tavern. A few weeks after the fight, a lawyer from the Inns of Court across the river showed up, a thin, dyspeptic man in a dusty, rust-colored doublet, claiming a woman couldn't inherit property in her own right unless there was no other male relation, however distant, and said he had been retained by her husband's family to sue her in the courts. When she retorted that Henry was his father's heir, the lawyer told her the cousins also contested the legitimacy of Henry's birth, claiming he was not his father's true son and citing her well-known sluttishness. He had witnesses to swear as much, he said. Maggie had flown into a rage and all but thrown the man into the street herself. Later, John found her weeping in a back room. That same night Maggie sold the tavern to Nick, signing her name with an X witnessed by John and a priest from St. Mary Overie. A few months later, she and John were married. Jane, named for John's mother, was born a year later.

★ ★ ★

"How am I supposed to take a delivery of ale?" Maggie asked, shifting Jane on her hip and glaring at Nick. He had just informed her that he was kidnapping John for an indefinite period. "You know I can't lift those casks myself."

"Get Henry to do it," he replied. "It'll at least get him out of bed." Henry was Maggie's fourteen-year-old son, John's stepson, much given to bunking off when any work was to be done.

"Bone idle" was how his mother less charitably put it.

Nick sympathized with the lad. He remembered how he had been at that age, feet too big for the rest of his body, with a stomach perpetually on fire with ravenous hunger, a face marred by pimples, and a desperate and guilty urge to tumble any woman who crossed his path, irrespective of her age or looks. Sex, food, and sleep were his Holy Trinity—in that order. Henry spent most evenings sitting moodily in the corner of the tavern, scribbling on a piece of parchment and ogling the tavern's few female customers, mostly old bawds who were finding business a bit thin on the ground and needed the johns to be more than a little drunk to even consider a quick shag. Gunpowder wouldn't rouse him in the morning. The only effective wake-up call, one that made his eyes fly open in panic, was the sound of his mother yelling his name. He and Bess, the parrot, got on famously, in part because, as he had confided to Nick one night after sneaking too many tankards of ale, he found her less intimidating than his mother, and he was compiling a list of the bird's astonishing command of invective. Nick suspected this was a cover for writing soppy poetry, but didn't let on. Hector regarded Henry with the same tolerant affection he would an endearing but imperfectly trained puppy.

⋆　⋆　⋆

Nick and John spent two largely fruitless days camped out in the room made available to them in the palace. The first evening they spent drinking with the Royal Guard, questioning them about the night Cecily died and whether anyone had seen anything. No luck.

The second day, slightly the worse for wear, Nick continued interviewing those who habitually attended morning chapel, as well as those who had been present in chapel the morning Cecily's body was found. He couldn't rule out the fact that, in addition to passing the note to Cecily the day before, the murderer had wanted to be present when the body was found in order to gloat at the horrified reaction of the court. Meanwhile John rounded up all the men's knives and examined them. Most of them were of plain design, and of those that were jeweled, not one had lost a stone, let alone a topaz. Nick's efforts were also a bust. All he discovered was that the majority of those present, if not directly involved with court duties like the Queen's ladies-in-waiting, pageboys, choir, and clergy, were the worst of the court toadies eager to impress Elizabeth with their early morning piety. Nick doubted she was so easily taken in, but suspected she would make a pretense of being so just to see their sleep-raddled faces and stifled yawns. The only thing of interest he did find out was that Sir Christopher Stokes, in accordance with what his aunt had said, had indeed been called to the Custom House the night that Cecily was killed, but the man Nick had talked to, a Master Summers, told him that Sir Christopher arrived around nine and left again an hour or so later, after the shipment of glass had been located. That left him plenty of time to get to Whitehall by midnight. According to Codpiece, who had supplied him with a list of all those he remembered being there, Sir Christopher was in chapel both the morning of Cecily's death and the day her body was found.

"Never misses," Richard told Nick.

"Religious, is he?"

"Nah. Just can't pass up the chance to lick the countess's arse," Richard sneered. "Has to keep his aunt sweet because she keeps threatening to leave everything to the Queen when she pops her clogs. She's fabulously rich, with houses and land all over the place."

That's why she treats him like dirt and he takes it, Nick thought. It seemed Sir Christopher's only act of rebellion was his refusal to give up his dog.

★   ★   ★

Nick and John sat sprawled in front of the fire. One of the pageboys was taking Hector for a walk in the grounds; Nick hoped the poor lad was not being dragged headlong through too many hedges and midden heaps.

Nick was thinking it through. Why had Sir Christopher lied about the time? The only reason could be that he was eager to remove himself from the frame for Cecily's murder. A stupid lie that automatically moved him to the top of Nick's suspect list. Nick knew Sir Christopher had been in the chapel on both mornings: he had glimpsed him there himself when he examined Cecily's body—the yellows Sir Christopher favored proclaimed his presence as effectively as the sun breaking through the clouds on an overcast day. Thanks to Codpiece, Nick also knew that Sir Christopher had been in the chapel the day before, when someone had slipped Cecily the note.

So far everything pointed to Sir Christopher's guilt, but Nick could not get over the trivial nature of the lie. Admittedly, Sir Christopher was timid by nature and browbeaten by the countess, but that did not make him stupid. Judging by the opulence of his house, he was a highly successful businessman, and that meant he must be well able to track imports and exports, broker sales, sign customs dockets, pay his taxes, and organize a complex delivery schedule—all the myriad details his occupation demanded. In Nick's experience, most detection work consisted of unraveling small lies, making sense of odd discrepancies in people's routines, and interpreting behaviors that seemed out of character, but he had come to realize that most of them meant nothing more than that human nature was a changeable and contradictory beast. Sometimes people lied for the hell of it or simply out of habit or even from an overabundance of imagination, embellishing what would otherwise be dull stuff. Whatever the reason, Nick was determined to get to the bottom of it. He had sent for Sir Christopher.

"You're in for a treat," he told John.

"Can't wait."

* * *

Sir Christopher arrived wafting clouds of cloying cologne, the lace ruff encircling his throat so wide it made him look like John the Baptist after Salome had gotten her wish.

"Come in," Nick said.

Gingerly lowering himself into the chair deliberately positioned in the middle of the room facing Nick, as if he were the accused and Nick his judge, Sir Christopher fussed with his doublet, arranging the folds just so. John was pacing behind his chair, a technique they had perfected, designed to keep the interviewee unsettled.

"What's this about?" Sir Christopher asked, craning to look at John, frowning slightly. Nick could tell he was trying to figure out the relationship between them, whether John was a servant or perhaps a poor relation. The plainness of John's clothes seemed to suggest the latter, but then again, Nick himself was also dressed plainly, especially for an earl's son, certainly in comparison to the dandy before him. Sir Christopher was bound to be confused, and that was fine by Nick.

Nick sat sphinxlike. Silence, he found, was an invaluable tool in questioning. It made people uncomfortable, and they invariably blurted out things they had no intention of saying just to fill the void. He watched as Sir Christopher tried to wait him out, fidgeting in his seat, picking nonexistent fluff off his hose before finally bursting out with "You may have been misinformed yesterday."

Nick remained silent.

"I was called to the Custom House a mite earlier than I said."

Only three hours earlier, thought Nick.

Sir Christopher looked first at Nick, then at John, hoping, perhaps, for some expression of understanding. Receiving only blank stares, he went on: "Er, yes, well. I now recall that the boy from the docks came for me at nine."

"And when did you leave the Custom House?" Nick asked.

"I don't really remember," Sir Christopher said, squirming in his chair. "Certainly it was late."

"The exact time, if you please," Nick said.

"Ten thirty," he admitted.

"Good," Nick said. "Now we're getting somewhere. And where did you go after you left the docks?"

"I came here."

"To the palace?" John exclaimed, shooting Nick a look. "At that time of night?"

"My aunt had sent a message during the afternoon that she wanted to see me. I was going to go earlier, but then I got called to the docks." Sir Christopher gave them the kind of smile one man gives another when the vagaries of women are the topic of conversation. "You've seen my aunt," he said. "She brooks no contradiction. It's more than my life's worth to go against her in anything."

More than your inheritance is worth, you mean, Nick thought.

"What time did you arrive, and how long were you with your aunt?" Nick asked.

Sir Christopher gazed out the window as if he were trying to remember, but Nick got the impression that he had his answer ready. "It must have been eleven or so," he said. "Yes, eleven. And

I was with my aunt until well past midnight. I have a room in the palace, you know," he added smugly, as if that were an impressive sign of his prestige. Nick suspected it was a squalid little cupboard tucked behind some stairs.

"So your aunt can vouch you were with her?" said John.

"Oh yes," Sir Christopher replied. "She always tells the truth."

"I'm surprised the countess keeps such late hours," Nick said.

"She takes her position very seriously," her nephew boasted. "She's up at all hours in case the Queen should need anything in the night."

Fetching mulled wine and simnel cake from the kitchens for the royal midnight snack was the job of the more junior ladies-in-waiting, Nick was sure. But he could imagine the bossy countess supervising every tiny detail: making sure the wine was hot, but not too hot—it wouldn't do to scald the royal mouth—the cake fresh and free of weevils, the fur rug tucked just so about the bony royal knees. In some ways, Nick could see that her nephew took after her; it was obvious in the way he was willing to go out to the docks on a cold December night. Neither aunt nor nephew seemed able or willing to delegate.

Nick went over the timeline in his head: Sir Christopher left the Custom House at ten thirty (verified by Master Summers); he maintained he arrived at Whitehall by eleven and was with the countess through midnight (which the countess would verify, Nick had no doubt). Cecily's body could not tell them precisely what time she met her death, but the note could: midnight or shortly thereafter. So Sir Christopher was in the clear. Nick owned that he was disappointed. There was something about Sir Christopher that made his flesh crawl, and arresting him would have given the Carew family a quick resolution. It would have afforded them at least some comfort to know that their daughter's killer had been caught.

The fact remained, however, that Sir Christopher had initially lied about the time he was at the Custom House, and Nick couldn't figure out why. To hide his bafflement, he decided to engage Sir Christopher in aimless chat and see if he could get a better handle on the man. Sometimes people let things slip when their guard was down.

"How did you get to Whitehall?" Nick asked.

"Wherry," Sir Christopher replied.

That was the nearest form of transport from the Custom House, Nick knew. He mentally constructed a map of London in his head: the Custom House and Legal Quays were situated on the river east of London Bridge, between Billingsgate fish market and the Tower. That particular stretch of river was deep enough for merchant ships to dock and consequently was dotted with quays specializing in imported goods, each quay dedicated to a particular commodity: Old Wool Quay for wools and felts; Sabbes Quay for pitch, tar, and soap; Gibson's for lead and tin, mostly shipped from Cornish mines; Somers for Flemish merchants. The quays bristled with cranes, the docks swarming with stevedores and traders day and night, endlessly feeding the voracious maw of London with imported goods.

"A bit dangerous in the dark, wouldn't you say?" John put in. "Shooting the bridge is risky enough in daylight. And the tide was coming in, if I recall."

Sir Christopher looked startled, as if he had assumed John would hold his tongue when his betters were speaking. "I'm not afraid of shooting the bridge," he said, picking a piece of fluff off his jerkin and dropping it fastidiously to the floor. "Even at night."

Nick glanced at John.

Once past the bridge, rowing upstream on the western side of the bridge was relatively safe if the tide was coming in, as it pushed the boat well beyond the danger of the bridge's arches. When the tide was going out, rowing upstream was impossible, so strong was the surge in the opposite direction toward the Wash; a boat would be inexorably drawn toward the arches, no matter how fast or powerfully the ferryman rowed. Coming from the Custom House east of the bridge, Stokes' boat would have had to pass under the bridge in the same direction the tide was flowing. Shooting the bridge was something only a boatman who had been working on the river all his life, who knew its moods and ways more intimately than he did a lover's, would attempt, and even then scores of boats capsized each year, their passengers found floating white-faced and bloated as far downstream as Greenwich, a look of grotesque surprise on their drowned faces. "You're a braver man than me," Nick said.

Sir Christopher looked smug. This habitual expression was getting on Nick's nerves, and he had to resist the urge to throw the simpering fop out the window.

"Did you know Cecily well?" he asked suddenly.

The change in subject startled Sir Christopher. "Er, no," he said. "I didn't." When Nick looked skeptical, he added: "I *knew* her, of course, but not well. Not well at all."

"But well enough to ask her to dance at the Accession Day Ball," Nick said. He had watched as Sir Christopher had sidled up to Cecily and whispered in her ear. The girl had shrunk away, looking embarrassed. She had desperately looked around for her friend Mary, but Mary had been flirting with someone else, a handsome, fair-haired young man called Sir Hugh. Cecily had been too inexperienced to know how to refuse Sir Christopher's request, so Nick watched as, forcing a smile to her lips, she reluctantly gave him her hand and allowed him to lead her into the dance. As soon as it was over, Nick saw her duck into the crush on the sidelines and disappear, leaving Sir Christopher standing awkwardly alone, looking crestfallen.

Perhaps remembering how he had been abandoned by Cecily after only the first dance, two spots of color appeared on Sir Christopher's cheeks. "I took pity on her," he said. "It was her first dance, and she was shy. She needed someone to break her in."

Sir Christopher's choice of words revolted Nick; as if Cecily was a fractious filly who needed to be tamed. And trust Sir Christopher to make himself out to be the knight in shining armor galloping to the rescue of the fair maiden in distress. In reality, it was Sir Christopher who had been the awkward one, skulking on the sidelines and ogling the women in their low-cut dresses. Cecily would have quickly learned how to comport herself more confidently in social situations; Sir Christopher never would.

"Did you want to sleep with her?" Nick asked. All during the dance, Sir Christopher had stared at Cecily with a hunger that, judging by the way she held her body as far away from him as she could, the girl felt but did not understand. Cecily had mostly kept her eyes on the floor, praying, Nick was certain, for the dance to end.

The spots of color on Sir Christopher's cheeks deepened from pink to crimson. "Certainly not," he sputtered indignantly. "That would have been"—he searched for a word—"*unseemly!*"

But human, Nick thought.

Suddenly weary of this strange little man, Nick looked at John. "I think that's all. Anything else?"

John shook his head. "You can go," he told Sir Christopher, who looked more than a little put out to be dismissed by an underling. He hesitated as if he were going to refuse to budge, but then, glancing at Nick, who gave him a bored stare, changed his mind.

"Right. I'll be off then." He scuttled to the door, then turned. "If you want my opinion," he said, "it's the Jews."

"I beg your pardon?" Nick said.

"The Jews," Sir Christopher repeated as if explaining to a particularly dull schoolboy. "That's what everyone's saying." He was gone before Nick or John could respond.

★ ★ ★

"Bigoted git!" John said. He spat eloquently into the fire before moving the chair Sir Christopher had been sitting on back to its original position near the fire. He sat down in it and stretched out his legs.

"Bigoted *rich* git," Nick said.

"Can't buy balls."

"True."

"He's right about one thing," Nick said. "Everyone *is* saying the Jews are to blame." He told John about the crowd at the gate. "I'm worried about Eli and Rivkah."

"Want me to go back to Bankside and warn them?" John asked.

"Maybe later." Nick got up and started pacing the floor. "We'll have to check with the countess, of course, but it looks like Sir Christopher has an alibi."

"Looks like," John agreed morosely.

"But why lie about the time?"

John shrugged. "Who knows? Most people lie by instinct."

"You're probably right," Nick said, "but it bothers me."

"Want me to ask the countess about her nevvie?" John said, an evil glint in his eye.

"Tempting," Nick said, grinning. They were both imagining the countess's outrage at being interrogated by a steward's son. Then he sighed. "I'd better do it."

"Take Hector along to protect you," John advised.

"Good idea," Nick replied. "She hates dogs."

CHAPTER 9

The Palace of Whitehall

It turned out the countess was still at her nephew's house in Cheapside, so Nick decided to go in search of his brother, Robert. He hadn't had a chance to speak to him since that morning in the chapel five days ago, and he felt guilty about his friend Sir Edward, Cecily's father. He had briefly sought him out the day of the murder to give him his condolences, but he felt he should have done more. The fact that he was trying to find the person who had murdered the man's daughter did not assuage his conscience. He decided to go for a stroll around the palace, looking for them. After being cooped up indoors for so long, he needed to stretch his legs.

"I'll stay here," John had volunteered, "in case someone comes looking for you."

"So you can take a nap, more like," replied Nick.

John gave him an innocent look.

Nick met the hapless page, coming in from outside with Hector, as he was leaving. As he feared, the boy's clothes and face were sadly besmirched with mud, and there were leaves and twigs in his hair. But both boy and dog looked happy, the one beaming, the other with a silly doggy grin on his face.

"Thanks, mister," the boy said, reluctantly handing Nick the leash. "Your dog's magic." He gave his new best friend a parting pat on the head and vanished down a corridor.

Nick and Hector wandered in the direction of the tilting ground, the dog bounding joyously ahead as if he had not just been out for a run. Frost rimed the grass, and the frozen stalks crunched under his feet. If it continued as bitter as this, Nick thought, the Thames would ice over, and children would strap beef shin bones to their shoes for skates. It didn't happen often, but when it did, river trade would come to a temporary halt, the dockworkers and ferrymen taking full advantage of Mother Nature's holiday, the rest of London cursing as they broke the ice in their water pitchers in the morning or resigned themselves to walking instead of taking a boat.

The huge rectangular expanse of the tiltyard, the center divided by a scarred wooden barrier, tiered stands rising on the eastern side so as not to impede the view from a long row of windows in the palace where the Queen and her ladies viewed the jousting, was empty and eerily silent. A flock of seagulls blown inland from the coast huddled miserably at the far end, white specks against the brown of the recently churned up, now frozen earth. Hector lolloped toward them, and they rose as one, giving their mournful cries, then slowly flapped toward St. James's Park, the Queen's private hunting grounds. A bare three weeks ago, Nick had been here for the festivities of Accession Day on November 17th, the most elaborate public celebration of the year. Usually he gave it a miss, having no patience with fake fighting, but this year he had come to cheer on Robert, who, to the surprise and consternation of the family, and citing his namesake, their great-grandfather, had entered his name in the jousting lists, styling himself Sir Trusty. Stopping by Robert's tent to wish him luck before his bout, he had been amused to find his brother dressed in armor that looked as if it hadn't been out of mothballs since the time of the War of the Roses.

"Where did you get that piece of junk?" Nick asked.

"Found it in the attic above the brew house," Robert replied. "According to mother, it used to belong to Sir Robert the Doughty, our great-great-grandfather." Robert flexed an arm, the joints screeching hideously. "It needs oiling," he said apologetically.

Nick knew the roof in the brew house leaked. Their ancestral home, Binsey House in Oxfordshire, was perpetually falling down; when it wasn't the tiles on the roof blowing off, it was the well silting up or the stone flags in the kitchen sagging due to the slow subsidence of the foundations. A veritable money pit was how Robert glumly described it. Nick loved its hodgepodge of ramshackle buildings, the original core of the medieval manor haphazardly added to over the centuries by various ancestors with no eye for architectural harmony or planning. A wing here, a new stable block there, a solar with a balcony that gave onto the picturesque view of the laundry wall.

Still, he sympathized. As the eldest son, it fell to Robert to maintain it so it could be passed down to Pip, his nine-year-old son and heir, who that day was standing proudly beside his father as his squire. Nick winked at his nephew and then scooped up his youngest niece, Meg, who had toddled toward him and was gripping his leg for support, in danger of bringing down his hose. Placing his lips against her blond, duck-down curls and breathing in her baby scent, he surveyed his brother affectionately.

Ten years older than Nick, Robert was more solid in build and, to his own everlasting chagrin, three inches shorter than his little brother. He compensated for his thinning brown hair by wearing a luxurious spade-shaped beard of which he was inordinately proud. His wife, Elise, Nick's sister-in-law and mother of his five nephews and nieces, was always nagging her husband to shave it off.

"Why can't you go clean-shaven like Nick?" she would ask. "It looks like a dead badger."

Robert would say nothing, but neither did he shave. He knew how to keep the peace and go his own way. Not for the first time, Nick saw that a wise man lurked beneath his brother's placid exterior. Sir Trusty indeed.

Robert was the reason Nick was a spy, although his brother didn't know it. Nick had received a summons from Cecil, Walsingham's newly appointed spymaster. Surprised and more than a little curious, Nick had showed up at Cecil's offices in Whitehall. While at Oxford, he had been approached by one of Sir Francis Walsingham's lackeys and asked if he would spy for his country. Nick had sent the man away with a flea in his ear, and he and John had gone out to The Spotted Cow in an alley behind New College and got rip-roaringly drunk. This was the first time he had met The Spider, the man who ran the day-to-day business of Walsingham's spy network, and his first impression when he saw him hunched behind a large desk, with a soft April dusk falling outside the windows and the candles not yet lit, was that the spymaster's nickname was well deserved: he did indeed look like a spider, one of those seemingly innocuous brown ones that like to hide in dark corners of kitchens and potting sheds, but whose bite is deadly.

"Ah, the Honorable Nicholas Holt," Cecil said. "Do come in." He didn't stand, nor did he offer Nick a chair. Nor, Nick soon learned, did he believe in beating around the bush.

"Do you recognize this?" Cecil said, pushing a sheet of parchment across the desk. Puzzled, Nick picked it up and immediately recognized his brother's handwriting and seal. He quickly scanned the contents: a newsy letter of the sort that friends would exchange. Glancing at the salutation at the top of the letter, Nick felt his legs go weak. It was addressed to an old Oxford friend of Robert's, a Francis Vaux, who had fled to France and had since become a Jesuit priest. The letter was dated only two months before. He threw the document back on the table as if it had scorched his fingers. "There is nothing treasonous here," Nick said. "It is merely news about the county. Francis used to live near Oxford." He pointed to a sentence. "Here Robert is telling him that a parcel of land along the Windrush River has been sold. What of it?"

"Nothing," Cecil said, "On the surface, it is all very innocent, boring even. Very like your brother, in fact." He smiled nastily. "But what if this is code? How better to hide a treasonous plot than in something as seemingly innocent as a discussion of farmland or who has married whom? I'm sure Phelippes would be interested." Cecil was referring to Thomas Phelippes, Sir Francis Walsingham's crack code breaker. "At the very least," Cecil murmured, "it is treasonous to even correspond with a Jesuit. Especially if one is from a famous recusant family. Perhaps I should have a little chat with your brother?"

Nick went very still. The not-so-veiled threat of torture hung in the air like noxious smoke, making it hard to breathe. He badly needed to sit down but somehow managed to remain standing.

"My brother is entirely blameless," Nick said, trying to master his rising panic and keep his voice even. "His only fault is that he is too innocent, too trusting." He tapped the letter. "This proves it. If he were plotting with Jesuits, do you really think he would be so stupid as to write this?"

Cecil's eyes crinkled with amusement. "Calm yourself," he said. "I am merely discussing what *might* be construed. Your brother is probably guilty of no more than a misguided sense of loyalty to former friends. Dangerous friends, I might add. However . . ." Cecil let the word hang in the air for a moment in order to allow Nick to hear Robert's screams as the winch was turned on the rack and the ropes tightened. "It might be as well to be sure." If Nick could have saved Robert by plunging a dagger into Cecil's heart, he would not have hesitated even if it had meant the ax. But that was not how The Spider worked; if Cecil had seriously thought Robert were conspiring with the Jesuits, he would already have ordered his brother's arrest. Cecil had merely threatened the castle in order to take the knight. Walsingham's attempt to recruit Nick when he was at Oxford had merely been the opening gambit in a long, intricate game. Nick should have known that, as the younger son of a prominent recusant family, he was ideal spy material. His mother's friendship with the Queen notwithstanding, Walsingham and Cecil would always be able to coerce him to do whatever they required merely by the threat of treason.

"What do you want?" Nick said, although he already knew the answer.

In exchange for burning the letter and forgoing an investigation of Robert and his contact with Francis Vaux—"For now," Cecil warned, making it clear that this would be held over Nick's head forever—Nick was to work for him.

He was by no means a coward, but Nick knew that he was putting his head in a noose. London was crawling with Spanish and French spies—most commonly merchants who had easy access to ships and could smuggle letters in and out of the country in casks of butter; bales of velvet, rolls of tapestry; tubs of rice, millet, and peppercorns. But there were other, more dangerous, types walking the streets—landless men on the make who had no loyalty other than to their purses, who would work for any master if the price was right, and slip a blade between someone's ribs if the price was even better. In a backstreet or seedy tavern, Nick's noble blood would not save him from the assassin's knife: if anything, his lineage would make him more identifiable, at least in London. On the Continent, he would have a better chance of blending in.

"For how long?" Nick asked.

"For as long as I need you," Cecil replied blandly.

Nick didn't even need to think about it. "On one condition," he said. "My brother is never to know."

"Agreed."

★   ★   ★

It would break Robert's heart to know that he had become a spy in order to protect him, Nick thought, watching his brother affectionately as he tramped up and down testing his armor. He creaked with every step.

"I think you should call yourself Sir Rusty," Nick said. "Much more appropriate."

Elise laughed. She was sitting on a stool in the corner of the tent, surrounded by her children and Constance, their overworked, frazzled nursery maid. Thirteen-month-old Meg finished exploring

Nick's face and pulling on his ears with her chubby hands, and held out her arms to her mother. Nick deposited the child in Elise's lap and kissed his sister-in-law on the cheek. Agnes, his seven-year-old niece and mother's namesake, was sitting beside her mother with her arm around Bess, just turned three. Nick made an elaborate bow.

"Ladies," he said. They giggled and Bess put her thumb in her mouth.

Five-year-old Nicky, his own namesake, was sitting by himself in a corner of the tent, disconsolately throwing walnuts at his mother's lapdog, Tarquin, who had one eye shut and one open in a vain attempt to sleep and simultaneously look out for missiles.

Nick squatted beside him. "What's up, little man?" he asked.

"I'm not a squire," Nicky said. His face was streaked with dirt where he had rubbed his grubby knuckles in his eyes.

"Want to be my squire?" Nick said. The little boy's face brightened and then immediately fell when he saw his uncle wasn't wearing armor or carrying a lance.

"You're not a knight," he said.

"Good point," Nick replied. "But I do need a page."

"No thanks." Nicky glumly resumed tormenting the dog.

Nick gave up. He knew when he'd been bested in a joust of logic by his small nephew.

"Forget Sir Sulky," Elise said. She cocked an eyebrow in her husband's direction. "Will you be the children's guardian when their father kills himself later today?"

"I'll do my best," Nick replied.

"I'm not proposing to kill myself," Robert grumbled, his voice echoing strangely behind the visor of his antique helmet as if emanating from a deep well.

"You will if you wear that thing down," his wife retorted. "You're blind as a bat."

Nick was fond of his sister-in-law. Some thought her shrewish, but Nick correctly identified her sharpness as a desire to see Robert succeed in his manorial responsibilities. Her sometimes acerbic comments concealed a deep love and fierce protectiveness. Nick admired her unflagging devotion and, for the most part, good humor. It couldn't be easy birthing five children in nine years, and they had lost a newborn son to whooping cough just the previous spring. He could see by the shadows in Elise's eyes that she still grieved.

As it turned out, Robert was not killed. Knocked off his horse in the first bout before he even had a chance to level his lance, he limped off the field with nothing more serious than injured pride. Afterward, in the tent, he and Nick had toasted the bruised family honor with a keg of ale.

★ ★ ★

Nick slowly walked the perimeter of the tilting ground, thinking how strange it was that a place could be so desolate when only a few weeks before it had been teeming with life. That was the way with death—a sudden, incomprehensible, and permanent cessation. Just days ago, Cecily had been pulsing with life. He kept seeing her at the Accession Day Ball: late in the evening when only the young still had the energy to keep on dancing, he had seen a youth grab her hand and swing her into the dance, an elaborate chain that circled and wove, faster and faster, until there was only the bright kaleidoscope of whirling skirts, the flash of jewels warmed by perspiring flesh, the stamping of feet and rhythmic clapping of the older onlookers gathered, as Nick was, on the periphery. Then her cheeks had been flushed, not ashen; her breast heaving, not still; her eyes sparkling, not closed in permanent sleep.

Suddenly cold, Nick called to Hector and turned back to the palace. As he neared, he heard the tolling of the chapel bell and saw a funeral cortege emerge from beneath the Court Gate, Sir Edward and Robert leading, the chief pallbearers shouldering a pathetically small coffin. A priest, an open prayer book in his hands, intoned a prayer that, on the crisp winter air, came cleanly to Nick's ears:

We brought nothing into this world; neither may we carry anything out of this world. The Lord giveth, and The Lord taketh away . . .

The rest of the words were drowned out by the keening of a woman, Cecily's mother, supported bodily by her ladies. Near them stood a cart with two ebony horses at its head, black-liveried groomsmen holding their bridles as they stepped nervously and tossed their heads, spooked by the sound of such desolation.

Nick turned away. Cecily's murderer had wiped out her future as casually as someone smudging an insect crawling on a page. She should have known love, held a newborn baby in her arms, watched grandchildren romping at her feet, died in her own bed with her family about her. And God had allowed it to happen. For a brief moment, he was tempted to shout his fury aloud, drown out the prating priest, who thought the words written by Archbishop Cranmer could smooth the lines of grief etched on the faces of Cecily's parents, aging them a decade in a few days; could shore up the ruin of their hearts. Instead, Nick stepped forward as the coffin was slid gently onto the back of the cart and covered with a black cloth. Mounds of winter greens were spread over the top.

"I'm so sorry," he said.

Lady Carew turned to Nick, eyes unfocused, hair disheveled, completely changed from the beautiful woman he had known. "She loved flowers," she said. "But there are no flowers in winter." Suddenly, hideously, she began to laugh.

Her ladies led her to a carriage with drawn curtains, half-carrying her up the steps, the sound of that terrible laughter muted but still audible from within. Nick turned to his friend and grasped his hand with both his own. "Edward," he said. "What can I do?"

Sir Edward looked at him a long time and then gave a strange smile, mirthless and cruel—a silent echo of his wife's despair. "Do what the Queen commanded you to do, Nick. Find her killer," he said. "And bring him to me. Alive." Then he turned and mounted a black-caparisoned horse, his movements stiff like those of an old man.

"Do you hear, Nick?" he shouted. *"Alive!"* Then he spurred his horse, and the procession set off, bridles and hooves muffled so no jingle, no jolly clash of metal on metal disturbed the still, cold air. Only the low rumble of the wheels as the cart bore Cecily on her last journey home.

From a window in the palace, Nick saw the Queen watching, her presence a silent valediction to the girl who had served her so briefly. Beside her, the small plump figure of Cecily's friend, Mary, the white flash of a handkerchief as she dabbed her eyes. Not much of a send-off, Nick thought, but the Queen had ordered that the manner of death and obsequies be kept quiet.

CHAPTER 10

The Palace of Whitehall

Once the cart had passed under the Court Gate and turned down King's Street, Nick turned to Robert, who was dressed for travel in thigh-high boots, with a sword buckled to his belt and a thick cloak, long enough to drape over the horse's withers, slit down the sides to allow easy access to his weapon. The roads were plagued by roving bands of beggars who attacked strangers passing through. Usually armed with cudgels, occasionally primitive bows and arrows, they would think twice if they saw a sword and a man who looked as if he could use it, especially a man on horseback who could easily run them down. Nick thought it unlikely a funeral cortege would be attacked: even thieves respected the dead or, if not respected, at least feared the fires of hell. Nearby a groom was holding the bridle of a large bay, Robert's stallion, Neptune, its flanks steaming in the cold air.

"I'll catch up with them on the way," Robert said.

Nick nodded. The cart, with its sad burden, would move at a snail's pace, taking more than a fortnight to reach the Carew estate in Herefordshire, longer if the weather turned to rain and the roads became muddy.

"I'll go home after the funeral," Robert added.

Nick could tell Cecily's death and the grief of her parents had deeply disturbed Robert, who had recently lost a child himself that spring. Usually present at court during Advent and the Christmas festivities, Nick knew his brother needed to be with Elise and the children at this time, to reassure himself they were safe and in good health. Both were aware that death could strike suddenly and without warning: one day a person could be hale and hearty; the next, sweating with fever and being prayed over by a priest. That was one reason why this murder was so terrible. There was death aplenty in the world through disease and mishap, so a deliberate snuffing out of the young and healthy seemed particularly heinous.

The brothers embraced. Robert mounted his horse, lifted a gloved hand in farewell, and rode off. Nick watched him go with a heavy heart before turning back to the palace. He didn't envy Robert the bitter, endless miles, with plenty of time to meditate on the brevity of life, the arbitrariness of death, the possibility that justice would never be served. Nick much preferred to be up and doing, seeking out the man who had ruined so many lives, not least that of an innocent young girl. The fact that this death was not arbitrary, but planned, gave him a small hope that justice would prevail, but only if he could uncover the killer's mind, walk that labyrinth of tortured logic that had made the killing of a young girl a rational act; only then would Nick discover his identity. He passed the guard on duty at the gate. The man said nothing, perhaps out of respect for Nick's sadness, perhaps out of indifference.

★　★　★

On his way back to the room, Nick reflected that he was going about this all wrong. Instead of looking for the suspect among the court, he decided to start interviewing servants, who were the most likely to have noticed something unusual, the ones whose duties consisted of working long after the rest of the court had gone to bed, people like the night watchmen, pages, kitchen maids, pot boys—those at the lowest level of the palace food chain. If that drew a blank, the only thing he could do—and he shuddered at the thought—was to wait for another murder.

When Nick entered the room, he found John talking to a thin, waiflike girl perched on the very edge of one of the chairs, as if she feared it would collapse beneath her at any moment; or perhaps she had never sat on one before, knowing only stools and the floor. She jumped up when Nick entered, her eyes wide with terror, as if he had caught her filching the family silver. Nick waved her back down and, crossing the room, took a platter of bread and cheese off a sideboard and handed it to her. She looked up at him as if he had offered her the Crown Jewels.

"Go on," he said. "Tuck in."

He watched as she carefully placed the platter in her lap and picked up a hunk of bread, tearing into it with small pointed teeth like a woodland animal famished from the long winter months. She hunched over the food, sticklike arms encircling the plate, in the way of the starving, as though she feared Nick would change his mind and snatch it away.

"This is Matty," John said. "Her job is to light the fires."

Nick had already figured out that Matty was a cinders; her skin had the corpse-like pallor of an underfed, overworked indoor servant. Aptly named, her hair was matted and looked as if it had never been introduced to water and lye. The charcoal smudges on her hands, face, and clothes proclaimed her a cinders, the lowest of the low and precisely the type of person he should have interviewed in the first place. Her task was to light the fires in the small hours of the night before dawn, so the bedchambers lucky enough to have a fireplace would at least be tolerable for those who were fortunate enough to sleep until the sun nudged over the horizon or even as late as when it reached its zenith. The name of her lowly station came from raking out the burned remnants of fires all day long and hauling the cinders to the midden heap. Judging from the twigs and wood shavings in her hair, Nick suspected Matty slept curled in the woodpile next to the kitchen fire. It hurt his heart to look at her. She looked the same age as Agnes but had none of the apple-cheeked radiance of his well-fed niece. Instead, she had more in common with the beggar girl on the steps of St. Paul's Cross the day before. It was even possible Matty and the beggar girl were as old as eleven or twelve but looked younger due to the malnutrition that had stunted their growth. As far as Nick could see, the only advantage Matty had over the beggar was that she worked indoors out of the bitter winter cold.

"Hello, Matty," Nick said. He perched on the edge of a table a few feet away, deliberately making his movements casual, less intimidating. He ordered Hector to lie down under the same table: he had seen how her eyes had danced with terror when she saw the dog.

Both men waited until she had cleared the bread and started in on the cheese. Nick was pleased to see a little color had come to her cheeks. He looked at John to signal he should take the lead, as he seemed to have built up a rapport with the girl.

"Matty," John said. "Tell my friend Nick what you told me."
She gulped down a last mouthful. "I heard him."
"Who?"
"Him."
Nick sighed inwardly.
"The gent what offed the lady," Matty explained.
"Tell us," John encouraged. He passed the girl a cup of ale so she could wash down her food and, hopefully, speak a little more clearly. Up to now she had mumbled as if unused to speaking in complete sentences, as no doubt she was, Nick reflected. It was unlikely that anyone in the palace would be interested in the opinions of a lowly, illiterate, and inarticulate cinders. Perhaps this was the first proper conversation she had ever had in her young life.

"I was passing by the chapel, and I heard voices."
"What kind of voices?" Nick asked.
"Ghosts, that's what." She shivered and hugged herself with her sticklike arms. "The chapel's haunted," she whispered. "They sleep in them graves and come out when the bell tolls midnight."
Nick realized Matty was referring to the gravestones set flush with the floor in the central aisle.

"Everybody knows that," she said, looking a little stunned at the delivery of this long sentence.
Because servants such as Matty were invisible, Nick knew. People assumed their fires, food, and their neatly brushed and folded clothes laid out in readiness on the chest in the morning all occurred as if by magic, as if invisible spirits attended them. They seldom saw the human faces behind such ministrations, unless the servant became ill and their bath water was cold or their porridge burnt. Not everyone treated their servants this way; Robert and Elise certainly did not, nor did the Carews. But Robert and

Edward ran country estates where servants had been with families time out of mind and were treated almost as if they were extended family themselves. Witness his brother's steward, Simon Stockton, trained by his father the old earl's steward. But here in London, and especially at court, servants were anonymous, rootless, mere tools of convenience for those who could afford them. He thought of how shabbily Perkin had been dressed in comparison to his master, Sir Christopher.

Keeping his voice patient, Nick asked: "Ghosts of men? Women?" No response. "One of each?" he tried again, a little desperately.

"Yeah," Matty said, eyes lighting up. "That's it. A gent and a maid. Must have been sweethearts before they croaked."

Matty must have overheard the killer and Cecily talking. Finally, a witness.

"Why do you say that?" John put in. "Why sweethearts, Matty?"

Now it was John's turn to be subjected to a pitying look. "They was whispering is why."

Nick suspected that Matty's notion of love between the sexes was comprised solely of witnessing secret assignations where adulterous husbands and faithless wives met their lovers in deserted corridors and corners to whisper, snatch passionate kisses, and more. God only knew what she had seen on her nightly rounds of the palace. Creeping silently down the endless hallways, turning her little white face to the furtive sights of the bedchamber, Matty was far more of a ghost than the spirits she imagined haunted the chapel.

"So you couldn't hear what they were saying?" Nick tried to keep the disappointment out of his voice.

Matty shook her head. "Nay."

During the next half hour, John and Nick patiently and gently extracted all that Matty was capable of telling them: that a "gent" (gruff voice) and a "maid" (higher voice) were whispering together in the chapel at midnight. Matty was quite precise about the time, as the signal for her night shift to begin was the chapel bell tolling twelve times. She counted the chimes carefully, she said, as it was more than her life was worth to leave any fire unlit, the "house-keeper being a right stickler." Raking and laying out the fires in all the bedchambers of the "toffs," in readiness for lighting just before dawn, took her all night. Nick had a vision of her as a little mouse scurrying down corridors and tiptoeing into bedchambers while the occupants were sleeping, her mousy hair and slight stature only serving to reinforce this impression. When asked what she was doing in the passageway outside the chapel on the ground floor, when all the best bedchambers were located on upper floors, she explained it was a shortcut from the kitchens she always took, that it was the quickest way to the rooms next to "the pretty garden" where she always started—she meant the royal apartments that were located in the east wing across from the Privy Garden. Nick had no reason to doubt her. In her way, Matty was the perfect witness. Not only did she have no reason to lie, but she possessed a simplicity of soul that gave her a kind of unimpeachable integrity. Nick was sure that it would not have occurred to her to make up a story, nor did he think she had the necessary imagination even if she had wanted to.

When asked if she had seen the "ghosts" leave the chapel, she grew wide-eyed, and Nick realized at once he had asked a foolish question. It wasn't likely that someone as timid as Matty would wait for the ghosts to emerge. She would have been terrified enough just hearing them, and according to her, she was fearful of getting behind in her tasks.

After painstakingly going through her story and extracting nothing new, Matty's eyelids were beginning to droop in the relative warmth of the room and from the novelty of a chair to sit on. Nick chided himself for not remembering that she was accustomed to sleeping during the day so she could work through the night.

"Is there anything else you can tell us before you go?" he asked.

"The gent ghost had a cold."

"How do you know?"

"He sneezed."

Nick thanked her, telling her quite truthfully that she had given them better information than anyone else.

Her wan face lit up. "You think so?"

"No question."

She lifted her rancid skirts between thumb and forefinger and gave an awkward curtsey, the courtesy of her gesture strangely moving.

"And Matty?" Nick said as she was leaving.

"Yeah?"

"Don't tell anyone you've spoken to us, all right?"

She studied Nick for a moment as if she hadn't heard him correctly. Then her bladelike shoulders lifted up and down in a shrug. "Who am I going to tell?" Casting one last longing look at the empty platter and the fire crackling merrily in the grate, she was gone.

Nick paced restlessly about the room, then sat in the chair Matty had vacated and stared into the fire, the fire Matty had no doubt laid for him while he had slept, oblivious, in his nice warm bed that morning. He was no better than anyone else; he took servants for granted, didn't even notice their existence half the time. It was disturbing to think that Matty and others like her would spend their whole lives drifting around a palace filled with laughing, striving, luxuriously dressed people while they themselves went hungry and were clothed in rags. The thought made him profoundly depressed. Rivkah had once said that what was needed was a home for street children, most of them orphans, where they would be clothed and fed and taught useful and respectable trades. Oddly enough, Kat agreed with her, and the two women had huddled together discussing it at The Black Sheep. Nick didn't know if anything would come of their idea of a home for orphans, but it was a novel idea. Hitherto, the monasteries and convents had provided food and shelter to vagabond children, but now that they had been shut down and sold up by Henry VIII, there was no place for children to go except into servitude, prostitution, or criminal gangs. He supposed Matty was more fortunate than most; at least she had somewhere to sleep at night and regular food, even though it consisted of scraps from the kitchens.

"You should go back to Maggie," he told John. "She'll have our guts for garters if you don't put in an appearance."

"She'll understand," John said. "She's horrified about what happened to Lady Cecily." But he stood up and began to gather his things.

"And John?" Nick said. "Be sure to warn Eli and Rivkah to keep their heads down until this is over."

"I will," John replied. "Never fear."

"I'll stay and talk to a few more people and perhaps go and see if I can talk to Hogg's apprentice, Wat, and Sir Christopher's servant, Perkin." He looked out of the window and saw that the day was already waning, the shadows getting long, the sharp outlines of the buildings blurring. Too late to wander through the streets of London. "The truth is, John," he said, "I haven't got much to go on."

John put a hand on his shoulder. "You will," he said.

CHAPTER 11

The Palace of Whitehall

Nick spent the night walking the palace, hoping to pick up clues, to see if there was something he had missed. At the very least, to get the feel of the place as the killer must have experienced it.

After the clamor and frenzy of the day, the corridors and narrow passageways were dark and eerily silent, his footsteps on stone and wood unnaturally loud, as if the palace had been stricken by the Black Death and he was the only survivor. Before midnight, he saw the faint glow of candlelight from beneath doors, heard voices whispering and laughing; cries of passion; a disheveled page hurrying by on some errand or other; maids running to and fro, carrying jugs of hot water and spiced wine. But after midnight the palace lay wholly silent and dark, as if a giant hand had thrown a black muffling coverlet over it. Only the hard glitter of a quicksilver moon in a cloudless sky conjured a ghostly world of half-perceived forms. Nick would not have been surprised to see the headless figure of the Queen's mother, Anne Boleyn, drifting mournfully through the rooms where once she had danced, where once she had reigned supreme in King Harry's heart, her laughter echoing in the rafters—gay, brittle, and not a little fearful, knowing, as her daughter Elizabeth knew, as Nick knew, as poor Cecily now knew, that the ceremony of life was soon done, that after the bright sunlit day came darkest night.

Nick shivered and told himself not to be fanciful. The lantern he carried was smoky and foul smelling, and he breathed in deeply to clear his head. He would have preferred not to have advertised his presence by carrying a light, but there was no other way to see where he was going, and he had no intention of breaking his neck by falling down the numerous winding stairs.

The palace kitchens were deserted, the fire banked down to a dull glow, a faint snoring emerging from the pantry's half-open door. The royal reception rooms were equally abandoned. His footsteps were loud in the vacant air; the dais with the great, carved throne was denuded of awe without the dazzling majesty of the Queen seated there; and the room, hushed and a little melancholy without the discreet murmur of advisors, the whispers of sycophants, and the entreaties of loyal subjects high and low. When all the pomp and ceremony was done, it was just a room like any other.

Except for their eyes, which tracked him whenever he passed, the guards paid him no heed. Hector kept close as if he too were affected by this dreamlike state, padding noiselessly at his master's side.

At four in the morning, Nick gave up and returned to his room. Chilled to the bone, he was overjoyed to see the fire in his room had been lit.

"Bless you, Matty," he said softly.

Perhaps this was her way of thanking him for the bread and

cheese or, more likely, the way he and John had talked with her as if she were a human being capable of thinking and feeling, of experiencing sorrow and joy.

Undressing, he crawled under the icy, clammy sheets. Although he didn't make a habit of it, for Hector took up too much room for Nick to sleep comfortably, this night he patted the bed for Hector to jump up. Lifting up the covers, Nick allowed the dog to burrow under and settle by his side. Soon the bed was warm, the sound of Hector's breathing the last thing Nick knew.

★ ★ ★

He was running down a corridor blazing with thousands of torches set in sconces on the walls. The stones radiated heat like an oven; his breath was stifling in his chest; and sweat ran down his back and face, stinging his eyes. He wasn't running away from something, but toward it, trying to stop something from happening at the end of the corridor, but the corridor never seemed to end, twisting and turning, stretching on and on and on without end. Just when he felt he could run no more, his breath coming in great heaving gasps, his heart pounding as if it would fly from his chest, the corridor straightened, and in the distance he saw a pale, shimmering figure of a woman hovering above the ground. Nearing her, he saw that her hair was golden and floated nimbus-like around her head, as if she were suspended in water. She was dressed in crimson brocade, and he thought her the most beautiful woman he had ever beheld. Cecily, but not Cecily. Or rather, Cecily as she would have become if she had lived—a ravishing, alluring woman. She was holding out her arms invitingly. With a groan, he reached for her and bent to kiss her mouth but instantly recoiled. Her lips were cold as marble, her body not warm and pliant, but freezing to the touch, as if he had plunged his hands into a snowdrift. Looking down, he saw his palms were red. At first he thought the dye from her dress was running, that she had been out in the snow. Except that it was too cold for snow. His mind labored to understand.

"I'm yours," she whispered.

Raising his eyes, Nick saw that she was changing, her face melting, rearranging itself until she resembled Rivkah, her hair no longer fair, but black; her eyes brown, not blue. He opened his mouth to speak, to ask her what she was doing wandering all alone in the palace at night.

"Shh," she said, putting a finger to her lips.

He looked down again at his hands and realized that the stain was not dye, but blood, and that it was gushing from a great hole over her heart. And now he could hear sounds other than his labored breathing, voices hissing, murmuring, building to a roar that hurt his ears.

"Dirty Jew. Dirty Jew. Dirty Jew." Nick tried to close Rivkah's wound with his hands, but the blood just spurted faster, squirting between his fingers into his face, his hair, his mouth, until it was shooting out like water between the starlings of London Bridge, a torrent of blood coursing down the corridor, swirling at his feet, mounting higher and higher, to his ankles, then his knees, then his thighs. He was going to drown in blood, he thought. Rivkah's blood. And all the while she was looking at him as if he were a stranger.

"No, no, no, no," he sobbed.

Then a great scream tore the air, a woman's, although Rivkah's finger was still pressed against her lips, her mouth closed.

From somewhere far off, he heard Hector barking, and Nick

awoke, writhing and clawing at the covers, chest laboring, his face wet with tears. "Mother of God!"

He sat up. A faint lightening in the room, the merest outline of furniture beginning to emerge from the darkness, told him dawn was not far off. Hector was not lying next to him, but pawing at the door, barking. From the corridor outside, he heard running, then someone was hammering on his door.

Nick leapt out of bed and started pulling on his clothes. "Enter," he yelled.

A guard burst in, the lantern he was holding swinging crazily from his hand and throwing writhing shadows on the walls of the room. "You have to come," he panted. "There's been another one."

With Hector coursing ahead of them as if he knew exactly where to go, Nick followed the guard. As he ran, Nick felt he was still trapped in his dream, his stomach twisting with dread, his mouth filling with the bitter taste of iron. Irrationally, he thought Rivkah had come to the palace looking for him and that something terrible had happened to her. He followed the guard along the corridor, past the chapel, to the door leading to the royal wine cellar. At the steps leading down into the cellar, the guard stopped.

"Down there," he said, pointing a shaking finger.

A knot of servants were crowding the corridor outside the cellar door, talking in hushed voices. As Nick shouldered his way through, he recognized the royal cook, resplendent in a snowy apron, surrounded by his kitchen staff. This early in the day, only the kitchens would be busy, the bakehouse ovens long since lit, the first batch of loaves already cooling on the great stone hearth in preparation for the royal breakfast.

Mixed in among the kitchen staff were men muffled against the cold in scarves and cloaks, tradesmen making early morning deliveries to the great kitchens, mostly country folk from outlying areas, on their way to the London markets along Cornhill and Cheapside for flowers and vegetables, or Newgate Street for meat. Their carts would have entered the palace through the Court Gate and drawn up beside the entrance to the vast pantry that opened onto the palace's inner court. Nick could hear the horse harnesses jingling and chickens clucking miserably in the freezing air. By the sound of it, one cart was full of squealing piglets. Women with cloth-covered baskets over their arms were sobbing, and men who looked like farmers muttered gruffly among themselves; used though they were to the harshness of life, they were visibly shaken, their usually ruddy faces drained of color. Nick saw a few make the sign of the cross on their breasts, heedless of the Royal Guards standing nearby. Nobody cared about forbidden religious practices that morning.

"Let me through," Nick ordered as some, presumably in shock, refused to move aside.

Nick descended into the cellar. He came out into a cavernous stone room stretching far under the palace, and stacked between the stone pillars holding up the vast stone ceiling stretched row upon row of casks of wine, barrels of ale, and firkins of small beer, as far as the eye could see. A guard was standing at the base of the steps, holding a lantern; another stood beside a large cask set against a pillar opposite the stairs. At his feet was a crumpled form. The cellar reeked of spilt wine and blood. Steeling himself, a muttered prayer that it not be Rivkah rising unbidden to his lips, Nick stepped forward and looked down. Lying on her back, hands crossed on her breast in the now familiar pose, lay Mary, Cecily's best friend. The first thing he noticed was that she was not fully dressed as Cecily had been, but was lying only in her shift. On her feet were soft kid slippers of the kind that ladies wore indoors. Judging from her state of undress, she had been meeting a lover before she returned to the palace and was killed.

"Secure the stairs," Nick ordered. "No one is to be admitted except the Queen. Round up any witnesses, and take them to the Guard House. I want to talk to the person who found the body. Separate the others so they can't talk with one another." Conversation between witnesses would only muddy their recollections even more. Even kept apart, Nick knew that eyewitnesses were notoriously unreliable, that two people who saw the same thing would nonetheless have different stories to relate. It was a curious trick of the mind that people only saw what they wanted to see. Eli had told him that the human mind could only interpret events according to the experience of the viewer, that anything outside that experience was altered and made to fit accordingly. And the amazing thing, he said, was that it was done in complete innocence with no thought of deception. "We can tell ourselves anything," he said, "and believe it." That was why Nick did not hold with torture. In his experience, a man would say anything to stop the pain, believing that every word he uttered was gospel.

The soldiers silently moved to do his bidding, leaving Nick a lantern. A stub of candle lay near the body, its wick extinguished in the pool of blood and wine. Perhaps Mary had taken it from one of the nearby storerooms, the way he had seen Codpiece do, in order to light her way. He had noticed a lantern missing from the hook beside the cellar door when he arrived; now he wondered if the killer had taken it. Searching for it in other parts of the palace would be hopeless, as all the lanterns were of the same design. Sadly, Nick looked at the pathetic heap of clothes and humanity that had once been a living girl who, only a short while ago, had wept tears of grief as her friend's coffin was carried from the palace. Soon Mary would make the same journey home. As if sharing his grief, Hector gave a single, mournful howl and then padded to the steps, where he silently lay down, his ears pricked, his immense body still, but coiled for action.

Holding up the lantern, Nick crouched by the body, careful not to disturb it. The first thing he noticed was that, unlike with Cecily, there was a lot of blood, a pool of it spreading in a circle around Mary's head like a crimson halo. Her face was undamaged, but when he gently turned her head to the side, he saw that halfway between the nape of the neck and the crown, the back of her skull was caved in, splinters of bone poking through the matted hair and torn flesh. Someone had hit her with a heavy object, using enormous force. A large mallet used for hammering in the bungs in the casks lay in full sight beside the body, casually discarded after it had done its gruesome work. He used one himself at The Black Sheep and knew just how lethal it could be if swung with force. An empty flagon lay, partially concealed, beneath the tap of the cask. From the smell of the wine, Mary had been in the process of siphoning some off into a jug when the killer came upon her. Crouched down with her back to the stairs, perhaps too intent on her task, she would not have noticed another light descending the stairs behind her, especially if the killer shuttered it, and would have had no chance to defend herself. A tremendous blow to the back of the head with a weapon that was conveniently to hand would have rendered her immediately unconscious. She would have fallen forward in an untidy heap, her eyes still open. Not content with dealing her a deathblow, the murderer had then taken time to lay Mary on her back, with her arms crossed over her breast like an effigy on a tomb. The exact same positioning as Cecily's body. The murderer had also taken the time to turn off the tap in the cask so that the entire contents did not flood the floor. Even so, the back of Mary's shift from the hips down was soaked with wine, and her upper back was red with blood from the terrible head wound.

The great quantity of blood beneath her head told Nick that Mary had not died right away. After the blow had felled her, she had lain bleeding on the floor until her heart stopped. Probably, Nick decided, she had been unaware of what was happening to her and would not have known she was dying. *A small mercy,* he thought. Nick frowned: this was a completely different type of killing than the murder of Cecily, but the body was laid out in the same way. Generally, a murderer stuck to the same method of killing; Nick knew that some professional killers swore by the garrote, whereas others favored the stiletto. The difference in the method of the murders of Cecily and Mary suggested two separate men, but the way the body was posed suggested that the killer was the same. Nick touched her eyelids; there was a slight sign of stiffening, but her arms were still limp. From Eli he knew that rigor mortis began between two and six hours after death in the eyelids, neck, and jaw and slowly progressed down the body. She had been killed a few hours ago while he slept. On the right side of her neck, he noticed bruising, as if she had been grabbed in an attempt to subdue her. This could not have happened in the cellar, because there was no sign of a struggle, no overturned table, no bloody handprints; besides, she would have been unconscious as soon as she was struck. And it could not have happened immediately before she was struck because she would hardly turn her back on a man she had just fended off violently enough for her to have sustained injuries. So the fight and Mary's death, Nick reasoned, must be two discrete events and have occurred in two separate locations. The motive, however, looked the same—an argument with a jealous lover ending in a crime of passion.

He noted that the linen of her shift was ripped in several places at the neck and stained with tiny spots of blood. When Nick moved aside the fabric, he saw several scratches on her chest, as if someone had grasped the collar in a struggle. Next Nick examined Mary's nails: they were torn and bloody, underscoring his theory about the argument. Mary had put up a valiant fight. Nick swallowed. He remembered her cheeky face, the humor in her eyes, and her passionate grief for her friend.

Nick noticed that the soles of Mary's slippers were wet and grass-stained. She had clearly been outside just prior to her death, but her cloak was missing. He went to the bottom of the cellar steps and called the guard, instructing him to tell his captain to dispatch some men to search the palace grounds for a woman's cloak. Given the cold, Mary would not have ventured outside without one, especially as the deep hood would have served to disguise her identity as she made her way to the rendezvous.

Nick returned to the body and hunkered down beside it again. Like the chapel, the cellar was a perfect location in which to kill and escape undetected. Both places stood empty at night; above all, both places were hidden from the gaze of nighttime servants and guards who patrolled the corridors and grounds. It was possible that one of the kitchen staff might have seen either Mary or the killer entering the cellar, but Nick was not very hopeful. Despite being located off the same corridor, the entrance to the kitchens was around a dogleg bend, with no direct line of sight to the cellar door. Only someone making a delivery from a cart drawn up outside might have witnessed something, as they would have had to walk past the cellar and make a right turn to get to the kitchens.

A warning growl from Hector drew Nick out of his reverie; he became aware of someone standing next to him. Glancing up, he saw the Queen looking as if she had come straight from bed, with a fur-lined cloak thrown over what looked like a nightdress and a deep, ermine-trimmed hood pulled over her head so that her face was in shadow. The countess was with her and, unlike the Queen, had taken time to fling on her clothes for propriety's sake. When it came to the sudden death of one her ladies, the Queen, Nick knew, did not give a fig for propriety. Nick made as if to rise, but Elizabeth waved him down.

"No ceremony, man," she said in a gruff voice. She sounded as if she were fighting back tears. "The same killer," she said, indicating Mary's pose.

Nick did not reply, as the Queen had not asked a question. Personally, he was not sure—the method used to kill Mary was completely different from that used to kill Cecily, despite the identical staging of the bodies. And the emotion behind each murder felt completely at odds: Cecily had been killed with surgical detachment; Mary, in a fit of hot rage. If Mary's murderer had been present in the chapel when Cecily's body was found, then he would have seen how Cecily was laid out. Posing Mary in the same way could be a ploy to throw Nick off the scent, make him believe that the same man had murdered both women. Nick kept his mouth shut; it was too soon to voice his doubts out loud.

Hector was still growling. "Quiet," Nick ordered.

The Queen stood motionless, looking down at Mary. "Her cloak is missing," she said.

"I have asked the guards to search for it in the grounds."

Elizabeth nodded approvingly. "She was outside." So the Queen had noticed the wet slippers. "She must have left the palace to meet someone."

"She was always a loose one," the countess muttered.

"Now, now, Eleanor," the Queen said. "Let us not speak ill of the dead."

"She was stealing your wine, Majesty. A thief as well as a whore."

"Enough!" the Queen barked. "Leave us!"

Nick saw the countess redden as if she knew she had gone too far. Then she curtsied and made her way back up the steps. Not for the first time, Nick wondered how the Queen could abide the company of such a miserable old bat.

"She's getting worse," the Queen muttered to herself. Then to Nick: "Remove the body. We can't leave the poor girl lying here for all and sundry to gape at."

Nick marveled that even at a time like this, Elizabeth's mind continued to work: Both Cecily and Mary had been killed in the heart of the palace, near to the royal apartments, and both had been displayed for the court to see. The death of yet another of the Queen's ladies-in-waiting, coming only five days on the heels of the first, would not remain a secret. News of the murders would be the only topic of conversation in the taverns that night and in the inns along the London roads. For all its size, London was like a large village when it came to rumor and gossip. What happened one day was known the next, and the news flowed outward into the countryside beyond the city walls in an ever increasing circle like the ripples on a pond when a stone is thrown in.

"Majesty," Nick said. "I need you to order a complete lock-down of the palace. No one is to enter or leave."

Elizabeth nodded.

"I also need you to order every male between the age of eighteen and forty to assemble in the Great Hall. I will need parchment, ink, and quills." This was something he should have done before—test everyone's writing, see if he could match it to the note found on Cecily's body. Despite the difference in the way the murders were committed, if the killer was the same, then Mary would have received a similar note, and Nick was determined to find it. He had already ascertained that such a note was not on the body. "I'll come as soon as I can."

The Queen glanced at the corpse, then back at Nick. Her comprehension was instant. "I will so order it," she said. Then continuing, "Find him, Nick." Taking one of the lanterns, Elizabeth walked toward the steps, her back erect as always, the only clue to her sorrow the slowness of her steps.

Nick ordered the remains lifted on boards and carried to the crypt of the same chapel where, only a few days before, Cecily's body had been found. Before he left the cellar, he steeled himself to search the pool of blood on the flagstones where Mary had lain, but discovered nothing. Wiping his bloody hands on a rag he found on one of the cellar tables, he summoned a guard from the top of the steps and ordered him to sluice down the floor. By nightfall the cellar would be lit by candles and adorned by sprigs of holly left in lieu of flowers, their bloodred berries an unintended and ironic reminder of Mary's violent death.

The Queen was right to be worried: people would now be whispering that the devil roamed the court, meting out retribution for its excesses, its licentiousness, its extravagant wealth. If not superstition, then envy masquerading as moral outrage would fan the flames of discontent, and with it would come sedition. In England, the Puritans were the most vociferous in their condemnation of the Queen, claiming she was idolatrous in her religious practice, that as an inveterate dancer of the sexually charged volta, she was on the path to perdition, that she was too lax when it came to all manner of satanic revelries such as the theater and masques. And they held as proof of her degeneracy her lack of an heir to succeed her, saying that in the fullness of time God would wipe the ungodly Tudors from the face of the earth.

This last troubled the Queen the most, for it was true: she was now too old to bear a child even if she married. Mary, Queen of Scots, was next in line to the throne, yet Elizabeth feared the power of Rome, feared its support for Spain and its willingness to use the Jesuits to foment treason. She had seen what her sister had done; from her prison in the Tower, she had smelled the greasy pall of charred flesh that had hung over London like a shroud, so many did Bloody Mary consign to the flames. Next in line after the imprisoned Scottish Queen was her young son, James. Taken from his mother when a baby and raised in the new religion by Calvinist lords, he was the messiah for whom the Puritans longed. In the meantime, they used any excuse to pillory the Queen, and the murders of her ladies-in-waiting would be ideal fodder for their seditious pamphlets, published on underground presses or smuggled illegally from Holland. What better proof that Elizabeth was a Jezebel than to show her ladies as such?

★ ★ ★

His head in his hands, Hector at his feet, Nick sat beside the body in the crypt, on the lid of a cracked sarcophagus of a long-forgotten minor royal. He was responsible for Mary's death. He should have seen something, heard something during the night. If only he hadn't let Hector sleep beside him under the covers, the dog's acute sense of hearing would have picked up the sound of Mary's footsteps as she sped along the corridors, down the stairs, and out into the night. The thing that puzzled Nick the most was why she had been killed in the cellar instead of outside. Under cover of darkness, the pleasure gardens and tiltyard empty of witnesses, the killer would have gone undetected. Had Mary escaped his clutches and run back to the palace seeking help? But then why was she killed in the act of stealing a flagon of wine? This was not something she would do if she was in fear for her life. Most likely Mary had either allowed the killer to escort her back to the palace, as any gentleman should have done despite the argument, or he had secretly followed her and then murdered her.

Most of all, Nick blamed himself for not insisting the Queen send her ladies back to their country homes immediately after Cecily's death. Mary would be alive now if not for his criminal incompetence. It was freezing in the crypt, but even so, the body was beginning to give off a disturbingly meaty odor like the smell of a butcher's stall in the market.

Nick heard footsteps and looked up. He was startled to see Rivkah instead of Eli. The Queen must have sent for Eli by royal barge, by far the fastest way to travel as it was law that any wherries or shipping on the Thames were to give way as soon as the royal pennant could be seen flying, the golden oars of the bargemen flashing in the sun. At full stretch and with a favorable tide, the barge could travel as fast, if not faster, than a galloping horse. He had to restrain himself from jumping up and crushing her in his arms, burying his face in her hair so he could breathe in the living scent of her so great was his relief at seeing her alive after the terror of his dream.

Nick got to his feet. "What are you doing here?" he said, his tone harsher than he had intended.

"Eli couldn't come," she said. "He's performing a Caesarian on one of Kat's women."

"It's not safe," Nick said, grasping her by the arm. "Didn't John warn you?" He was appalled, as if his dream were about to come true. As if it had been a terrifying prophecy and they were fated to act it out.

Rivkah looked down at Nick's hand, and he let go. "Sorry," he said, stepping back, trying to beat down his panic.

"John came by last night," Rivkah said.

"You shouldn't be here."

"It's what I do," Rivkah replied. Then she turned to the body. She stood looking down at Mary for what seemed a long time. "Eli told me the details of the other girl," Rivkah murmured, as if to herself, "but seeing . . ."

Nick knew what she meant. There was a world of difference between hearing about it and seeing it firsthand. The colors, the smell, but most of all the sad diminishment of a body bereft of its vital spark, a child's doll discarded and forgotten, limbs twisted, skirts awry, its frozen smile a sad parody of life.

Lightly, Rivkah touched Mary's face, an oddly moving gesture of one woman to another, a sort of farewell; then she gently closed Mary's eyes.

"What is your opinion of what caused these?" Nick gestured to the scratches on Mary's chest.

"Fingernails," Rivkah said. "See how they are parallel to one another?" She picked up a hand and examined it, then the other. "She fought back," she said, and her voice shook slightly.

Next, Rivkah bent to examine the bruising on the neck.

"Not strangled," she said. "The neck was only gripped on one side. It would take two hands to choke someone to death."

Nick nodded.

"And the killer is left-handed," Rivkah added.

Nick looked at her quickly. "Are you sure?"

"Yes," she said. "Look here. The bruising is predominantly on the right side of the neck." She indicated where lateral marks clearly showed the outline of fingers now that the blood was beginning to settle and darken. "But this round mark here," she touched the front of the neck, "was made by the thumb, the strongest finger in gripping."

Before Nick could react, Rivkah turned toward him and grabbed him by the neck with her left hand. "Note where my fingers are placed," she instructed, "on the right side of your neck. It is the only way the fingers can encircle the throat. And if I could squeeze hard enough, you would have the exact same pattern of bruising as Mary."

She released him and stood back. Nick touched his neck, not because Rivkah had hurt him—her hands were too small, her grip too weak—but because his flesh burned where she had touched him. He forced himself to turn his mind to the implications of what Rivkah had just demonstrated.

He now had a clue to the man who had argued with Mary violently enough to have left the marks of his hand on her. To be left-handed was relatively rare; it was also considered a sign of ill omen as the left was traditionally regarded as the evil side, from the Latin *sinistra*; children in the schoolroom were forced to write with their right hand by having their left arm tied to their sides. Nick wasn't remotely superstitious, but in this case he had to own that it was strangely apt.

Grateful as Nick was to have something to go on, he was acutely conscious that it was not enough to prove that the man who had fought with Mary was the same man who had killed her.

"Will you help me turn her over?" Rivkah asked.

Gently they rolled Mary over and placed her facedown on the slab. As Eli had done with Cecily, Rivkah took a quill from her medical bag and poked at the wound on the back of Mary's head. Nick looked away.

When she finished examining the wound, Nick handed her the mallet. Covered in hair and what looked like bits of brain, there was no doubt it was the murder weapon; nonetheless, Rivkah held the head of it above the wound.

"The width is the same," she confirmed.

"Could she have fought with her assailant after receiving the blow?" Nick asked.

Rivkah shook her head. "Not a chance. She would have been unconscious before she hit the ground. Her eyes were still open, although the orbs have rolled upward. A classic sign of deep unconsciousness." She wiped the quill and put it back in her bag. "We need to turn the body again," she said.

Together they rolled Mary onto her back. Like Nick, Rivkah manipulated Mary's limbs one by one to check for rigor mortis. She confirmed Nick's timeline for the murder.

"Sometime between one and five this morning. I can't be more exact than that, I'm afraid." She covered Mary's face with a white cloth she took from her satchel. Nick helped her put on her cloak.

"You must find whoever is doing this, Nick," Rivkah said urgently. "If you don't, he will surely do it again."

Nick remembered Kat saying the same thing after Cecily's death, yet he had been unable to prevent Mary's murder.

As if reading his thoughts, Rivkah patted his arm. "You will find him. That's what you're good at."

"Not good enough," he replied, looking at Mary's body lying so still and forlorn on the cold slab.

CHAPTER 12

The Palace of Whitehall

After her examination of the body, Rivkah caught a wherry from Whitehall Stairs. Nick tried to insist on an escort, but she refused.

"I can take care of myself," she told him.

As Nick handed her down into the boat, she paused and looked up at him.

"Mary's death is not your fault," she said. "You know that, don't you?"

Nick shrugged. He could not so easily absolve himself. She squeezed his hand briefly, then stepped into the gently rocking boat. He watched as they pulled away, Rivkah a small, shrouded figure in the stern, cloak wrapped tightly about her, hood up. It seemed to Nick as if he were always watching her leave, and he had to resist an overwhelming impulse to call the boatman back and climb in himself so he could leave the palace behind, this place of intrigue and death. He would have liked nothing better than to stroll along the bank with Rivkah, watching the river come to life in the wintry light, to measure his longer steps to her smaller ones,

note how she walked with head erect, eyes taking in her sur-
roundings with a kind of fascination as if she were still amazed by
this strange country she and Eli had fetched up in, orphans and
exiles, members of a persecuted race. Perhaps that accounted for
the quietness of her demeanor when she was in public, her impen-
etrable reserve and the way she always covered herself from head
to toe in a cloak as if to hide from curious eyes. He raised his
hand briefly in farewell, but she did not turn around. Soon she
was lost to him in the misty murk rising from the river, the only
sound the chop of the oars rising and falling until they too fell
silent.

An enormous sense of relief that the river now separated her
from the killer roaming Whitehall overcame him. And Kat was
safe too. But Nick couldn't shake the vision of Rivkah being lit-
erally torn to pieces by a baying mob. He cursed himself for not
accompanying her, at the very least sending Hector with her, but
she had been adamant.

"I know how to be anonymous," she had once told him. "I
learned that in Salamanca during the persecutions." Then she had
given a smile of such sorrow, it had torn at Nick's heart. "Haven't
you ever wondered why Eli calls me 'Mouse'?"

★   ★   ★

With great reluctance, Nick turned back to the looming warren
of the palace and headed straight for the Queen's apartments. The
only women in danger were the remaining ladies-in-waiting, and
he intended to do now what he should have done immediately
after Cecily's body was discovered.

When he was admitted to the Queen's sitting room, he was
surprised to find her gone.

"A meeting with the Dutch ambassador concerning the Puritan communities there," Codpiece informed him. "Apparently they're inciting the Puritans here to produce scurrilous pamphlets denouncing the Queen as a Jezebel. Good Queen Bess is even now tearing a strip off the ambassador." The Fool was sitting at his ease in a child-sized chair by the fire, an open book in his lap, his finger marking a page. His voice was the voice of Richard, not Codpiece. Glancing around, Nick saw that the rest of the apartment was empty.

"She didn't want you along to make fun of the Puritans?" Nick asked, sitting down opposite Richard. "I'm surprised you could pass up the opportunity."

"I wish." A brief flash of humor before his face grew somber. "She knew you'd come here first. She wanted me to tell you that she's sending home the rest of her ladies."

"Thank God," Nick said.

"Except for one," Richard added. "The countess." He pulled a face. "She refused to go, said someone should be here to take care of the Queen. They had a bit of a barney about it. Courageous, I suppose, considering there's a killer on the loose. Or foolish."

"A row about sending the ladies home?" Nick asked, surprised.

The Fool shrugged. "Seems so. All she cares about is the Queen. But when the countess left, she looked like she'd just discovered a turd at the bottom of her porridge pot."

"She always looks like that," Nick said.

"How true."

Nick then told Richard of Mary's murder, of his interpretation of the scene and Rivkah's examination of the body.

"I'm left-handed," Richard said.

"I think I can safely rule you out," Nick said, getting to his feet.

"Because I'm a short-arse?"

"Something like that," Nick said, grinning. "Where are the other ladies?"

"Packing." Richard lifted his chin to indicate a floor above. "The countess is supervising."

"Right," Nick said. "I'll go talk to them now." He instructed Hector to remain with Codpiece. "Don't want to frighten the ladies," Nick said when the Fool raised an eyebrow.

"Ask them about Hugh Danby," Richard called after him. "There's a rumor he and Mary were lovers. He's the eldest son of Sir Edgar. You'll have to get the Gorgon out of the room first," he added, pulling a face. "They'll clam up with the countess present."

★ ★ ★

After instructing a guard to find Hugh Danby, bring him to his room in the palace, and stay with him until he got there, Nick took the stairs to the floor above, eager to catch the women before they left. Multiple times he had to flatten himself against the wall so an endless stream of servants, carrying chests and leather bags, could pass him on the stairs like a file of ants carrying away a picnic. He noted the panic on the servants' faces, especially the women, eyes looking at him askance, the way the servant girls avoided even the slightest physical contact with him by drawing their skirts aside as they passed. Nick cursed silently: servants were the weathervanes of their masters, and their mood told him that fear and suspicion now stalked the corridors of the palace. Cecily's death had been bad enough but might still have been an isolated event. Tragic, they reasoned, but an anomaly. With Mary's death, everything had changed: a madman was on the loose, bent on carrying out whatever mission he had set himself. No woman, high or low, was safe. The urgency of finding the killer was like an iron hoop around his chest, squeezing the breath out of him. Soon there would be wholescale panic spreading out into the city like a contagion. And when people were afraid, they sought someone to blame. The Jewish race was the ancient whipping boy of Christendom and, more recently, the Spanish. Eli and Rivkah were both. The Queen might fear civil unrest—it was why she had commissioned him—but Nick's fears were much more personal. Now more than ever, he could not afford to fail. In addition, he couldn't help but feel as if he were being tested by the Queen, as if his own loyalty, as a member of a prominent recusant family suspected of practicing the old religion, was under scrutiny. If the murders turned out to be related to a Catholic conspiracy to undermine the throne—Walsingham was even now on the trail of the members of such a conspiracy—then Nick's failure to bring the killer to justice would jeopardize not only himself but his whole family. If the murders were connected to a Puritan plot and he failed to arrest the killer, then he would be accused of Catholic bias. Either way, he felt himself to be in a cleft stick.

The chamber he entered was chaotic, women frantically packing, others sitting on their beds staring into space, clothes strewn about them as if they couldn't decide what to take and what to leave. Several of them were in a state of undress, hair loose as if just arisen from their beds. Nick surmised that some of them had been attending the Queen while the others were still asleep. He knew they worked in shifts. There was no conversation, just the strident voice of the countess giving orders and chivvying them, with servants dodging in and out. Nick saw a young woman standing by a small casement window, the bleak wash of light lending her face an unnatural pallor.

The activity in the room stopped when he entered, women freezing in different attitudes like so many statues—one putting up her hair, pins in her mouth; another shaking out a long linen garment in readiness for folding; yet another fumbling with a buckle on a shoe. He sent the servants out.

"The Honorable Nicholas Holt," the countess proclaimed, as if she were announcing him at a ball.

Two of the women curtsied out of reflex, but the rest just looked at him.

"Countess," Nick said, giving a small bow. "If you could wait outside while I speak to your ladies." He indicated the door and gave her his most winning smile.

The countess puffed out her bosom like a pouter pigeon. "I insist on remaining," she said. "It's not decent."

Sick at heart as he was, Nick almost laughed. A murderer was running around the court killing her ladies-in-waiting, and the old harridan was actually worried he might lay siege to their virtue. "Nevertheless," he said.

The countess glared. "Most irregular," she said, sailing past him. "I shall inform Her Majesty immediately."

Nick shut the door firmly behind her. Immediately the tension in the room relaxed like a crossbow released. He sat down on one of the beds, signaling that he was the opposite of the bossy, inquisitorial countess and that they could now speak their minds.

"The Queen has tasked me to find the man who murdered Mary and Cecily," he said. At the bald naming of the crime, several women flinched and covered their mouths with their hands. Only the girl by the window did not react.

"I need you to tell me if you saw or heard anything out of the ordinary last night. Anything at all." Nick waited for his words to sink in, for the women to collect themselves. One plucked up a cloak and threw it about her as if she suddenly realized she was half naked. Another smoothed back her hair and pinched her cheeks as if she were about to step through a door into a public reception room and wanted to look her best.

Unlike Elizabeth, these women had not been tempered to unbreakable steel by a life spent negotiating the treacherous currents of the court. Of noble birth, they had spent their childhoods on pleasant country estates, shielded from the worst of human nature, their soft rounded faces bespeaking lives of relative ease and happiness, their main tribulations putting up with the countess and finding a suitable husband. All except for one. Nick's eyes kept going to the girl by the window. Only she seemed to be feeling the weight of grief; the others were more concerned for their own safety. He would speak to the others as a group, he decided, then speak to the girl alone. He seemed to recall from his previous interviews that her name was Lady Alice de Montfort.

The women could only tell him what he had already worked out for himself: that Mary was "easygoing" and full of life. He correctly identified this as code for a good-time girl who was relatively free with her sexual favors. He asked if there was a particular man, and the room fell silent, but five pairs of eyes slid to the silent figure at the window, then returned to Nick almost as quickly. He filed this away and changed the subject. What had Mary's day been like yesterday? When had she retired for the night?

One girl snorted. "Mary seldom 'retired' for the night," she said. Then, appalled, covered her mouth with her hand. "I didn't mean . . ." She began to cry.

"It's all right," Nick said gently. "So Mary used to see men at night?"

The women nodded mutely.

"And last night?"

"She was going to meet someone," a wan-looking girl said. She looked to the others for confirmation. They nodded. "But she wouldn't say who."

"She said she'd bring back some wine," one girl chimed in.

"Did she often do that?" Nick asked. "Raid the cellar?"

"Yes."

"And the pantry," the same girl added.

So stealing wine would have been a regular thing, and the killer might have known that, Nick thought.

"Did she receive a note?" he asked.

"She wasn't one for book learning," another girl said.

Nick took that to mean Mary could hardly read or write. "But she did receive a note?" he pressed.

"Yes."

So whoever it was knew that Mary was barely literate. Interesting, Nick thought. Yet another confirmation the killer was someone who moved in the Queen's inner circle or knew someone who did.

"Through a servant or in person?" Nick asked.

They shrugged.

"Do you know when she was approached?"

"Must have been after chapel yesterday," the girl who had been pinning up her hair said. "We were busy all day after that."

"Repairing dresses," someone chimed in irrelevantly. "It took forever. The countess kept making us unpick everything and start again." There was a general muttering and rolling of eyes at this.

But Nick was thinking of the chapel. A logical gathering place of the inner court before the day's duties scattered everyone, the only place the killer could be sure all the ladies-in-waiting on duty would be present. Did he sit there during the service and watch them, deciding who was going to live and who would die? Or was his choice more haphazard, based more on whom he could safely approach without being noticed? But the difference between the murders kept niggling at him. The kind of man who would coolly sit in a holy place of worship and select a victim, who was not afraid of either being detected by the authorities or struck down by the Almighty, was a far different character from the man who had savagely bludgeoned Mary to death. Mary's murder was opportunistic, Nick was sure, whereas Cecily's had been meticulously planned. Nick couldn't shake the uneasy feeling that he had missed something crucial, that he had made a fundamental error somewhere in his line of reasoning, but for the life of him, he couldn't figure out what it was.

"Everyone knows who she was meeting," the girl at the window said in a low, hard voice, which nevertheless seemed to echo around the room, so vehement and charged with emotion were her words. For the first time she turned around, and Nick saw that her face was not pale from grief, but from jealousy.

"Mary was a whore," the girl said. There was a collective gasp from the others. The girl shot them a withering look. "She was," she said. "We all knew it. No point in pretending otherwise." The others looked at the floor as if the sight of the girl's suffering was too much to bear. Interestingly, none of them contradicted her.

"Lady Alice, isn't it?" Nick said. The girl nodded. He turned to the others. "Finish your packing," he said, "then you can go. You stay," he informed the girl.

The women finished dressing and packed quickly now that the countess wasn't there to get in their way by criticizing and making them refold things. They threw garments into chests willy-nilly and gathered up armfuls of trinkets and scarves and stockings, stuffing them into bags.

While they were doing this, Nick searched through Mary's belongings, picking up each item of clothing and running his hands over it to see if it concealed hidden notes in the seams. When he slit the bodice of her two dresses to search between the velvet and the silk lining, there was a collective moan of horror as if he had committed blasphemy. He ignored it. Aside from a goblet under the bed, sticky with old wine lees—proof of Mary's habitual pilfering from the cellars—he found nothing of interest, so he stripped the sheets back from the bed she had shared with Cecily, down to the straw-stuffed mattress slung on ropes. Again, nothing. He was about to give up when he noticed a tiny slit in the ticking of the mattress, too neat to be a tear, more like a cut with a sharp knife. He widened it with his own knife and poked around inside. His fingers met the crackle of paper and he carefully withdrew a small rolled piece of parchment. With his back to the room, he unfurled it and saw a picture of a heart and a crude outline of a large oblong with a cross marked along one of the short sides next to a circle with a triangle in the middle of it. The Roman numeral II was written on the outer edge of the circle.

Nick crossed the room and stuck his head outside the door. "Find the captain of the Guard and tell him to search the Privy Garden," he said. "Then return here." The guard looked puzzled but hurried off.

* * *

Nick sat down on the bed and looked at the note again. It was signed with the letter *H*. The formation of the letter was bold, confident, and gave no indication whether penned by a right or left hand, aside from a slight smudging at the top of each upright stroke as if the wet ink had been brushed by a hand moving from left to right. The slant of the handwriting looked similar to the writing on Cecily's note, but Nick thought it disappointingly inconclusive; the method used in the schoolroom to teach handwriting was fairly standard, the resulting script reasonably uniform. Besides, children were taught to write with their right hands even if they were naturally left-handed. In addition, a single letter was impossible to use for comparison with the other, more extensive, note to Cecily. What he could deduce was that the man who had sent the note knew very well that Mary could not read well and so had drawn a diagram as if for a child. Even the use of Roman numerals was like tally marks on a stick used by illiterate farmers when counting cattle or sheep or barrels of apples. Total illiteracy among nobles was rare, even for a woman. Most could read or write in English; they were expected to keep an eagle eye on their steward's accounting of household goods and expenses. Whoever had drawn this came from the court very close to the Queen. More than ever, Nick was convinced the killer came from her inner circle. It made his skin crawl to think that someone he saw every day was laughing over Nick's bungling, gloating over his own successes with Cecily and Mary, and—worst of all—selecting his next victim and planning her murder. Thank God he had now ordered the ladies-in-waiting to be sent away from court.

At last the room was empty except for Nick and Alice. She had not moved from the window, but stood facing him, backlit so it was difficult to make out her face. Nick motioned for her to come sit down on the bed beside him. She did so reluctantly, perching on the end near the wall, as far from him as possible, and folding her hands in her lap, a model of a well-bred young lady except for the way her fingers whitened at the knuckles with the force of her grip.

He studied her in silence for a moment, letting her know that he meant to have the truth and was prepared to wait till Dooms-day to get it. If she had been happier, she would have been pretty, but her face was pinched with misery, and two unhealthy spots of color burned in her cheeks. Her fair hair was severely scraped back, and he could see it pulling at her scalp. A pulse in her throat raced. She looked at him defiantly, her chin tipped up.

"Alice," he said, "tell me about Mary and Sir Hugh."

She flinched at her lover's name, then regained her composure and sat up straighter. "She was a whore and he's a whoreson," she said, her words all the more shocking for the quiet matter-of-fact way in which they were uttered, as if her anger and jealousy had burned out, and only the ashes of despair and disillusionment remained. If she had dreamed of Mary's death, she was now learning that revenge was not sweet at all, but sad and oddly disappointing. He felt a sudden deep pity for her.

"You and Sir Hugh were engaged," he pressed gently.

Alice looked surprised that he didn't phrase it as a question, then nodded and lowered her head, but not before Nick saw the glint of tears, the first he had seen.

"We were going to be married after Christmas." She swiped at her eyes with her sleeve and raised her head. The tears were gone: she had successfully regained control of herself, and Nick could not help admiring her strength. He rather liked Lady Alice. Plenty of pluck, his mother would have said.

"We were betrothed when we were children. We were always meant for each other." This last said with utter forlornness.

Nick looked down so she would not see his anger and think it was directed at her. He understood why most marriages were arranged, especially between noble families. A marriage was not just a private agreement between two lovers, but a complicated, far-reaching treaty between two families and their respective dynasties, often with huge sums of money and vast swathes of land at stake. He understood that. What he could not stomach was the still common practice of betrothing minor children to each other, children not only too young to give their consent, which was, the last time he checked, an absolute prerequisite for a valid marriage, but too young to even understand what marriage was, let alone sex. He had heard of infants in the cradle being pledged to each other by their ambitious fathers. There was something deeply distasteful about two men bartering and selling their children like chattel, especially girls. In Bankside, men and women were not sentimental about marriage—plenty of people married as a way of cementing a business partnership—but it was an arrangement agreed upon by the parties involved, the man and woman themselves, with the understanding that it was for mutual benefit. Master Baker, Nick knew, had married his wife because she was reputed to be the best pastry-maker in all of Southwark. Mistress Baker had known this and consented. As far as Nick could tell, and if the quality of their confections and bread was anything to go by, they were as happy as any married couple could expect to be. Sir Edmund Spenser, Sir Philip Sidney, and the rest of their poetic, Platonic ilk might witter on about fairie queenes, nymphs, and pining swains and shepherdesses, but he for one preferred a real flesh-and-blood woman who could give as good as she got, both in witty conversation as well as in bed. Rivkah and Kat flashed into his mind—uneasy bedfellows. His metaphor made him wince, and he guiltily banished the image that had risen unbidden in his head.

"When did you suspect Sir Hugh was having an affair with Mary?"

"On Accession Day," Alice said. "I saw Mary flirting with him in the stands at the jousting. Cecily and I had just come back from getting some ale. They didn't see us. I saw Mary whisper something to him that made him blush."

As well he might, Nick thought. He could all too plainly imagine what Mary had whispered in Hugh's ear.

"He didn't stand a chance," Alice blurted out passionately. "He's a complete innocent."

Nick noted her use of the present tense as if, even now, she thought her fiancé unsullied by lust and infidelity. He thought of his own escapades with willing milkmaids in the barn at home and strongly doubted Hugh had been a virgin before succumbing to Mary's charms. He suddenly remembered seeing Sir Hugh at the Accession Day Ball, flirting and chatting with Mary; Nick had even seen him dance once with Cecily. He kicked himself for not remembering this before.

"Mary was a whore," Alice repeated. "Always giving the glad eye to men. She was a terrible influence on Cecily too; they were always giggling about something. Cecily was so *naïve*."

As were you, Nick thought to himself, *once upon a time.*

There was a difference between a tease and a whore, but Nick suspected Alice was right. Like a dog instinctively alerting to a bitch in heat, he himself had not been insensible to Mary's come-hither sexuality, especially as it suggested tangible benefits and not just the promise of them, endlessly postponed.

It was odd, he had always thought, how a scorned woman always shifted the blame to the "other woman" instead of the man who had betrayed her. Men also blamed women, of course, citing the shopworn frailty-of-Eve argument, but this was just spinelessness. His mother was fond of pointing out that not only did Adam eagerly eat of the apple, but then he had the unmitigated gall to blame Eve for it when God came calling.

Nick had always been puzzled when women used the same argument. He expected them to stand by their own sex, and was amazed they could not see they were endorsing a belief in the very assumptions they railed against in other circumstances. Kat had always complained that women were the worst critics of other women.

"Not men?" he had asked, surprised.

Her lips had curved upward in a slow, lazy smile. "Men," she'd said with a fondness she reserved for Hector and all dumb beasts. "Women can handle men. Like lambs to wolves by comparison."

But Hugh was no lamb, Nick thought. Lady Alice's betrothed showed every sign of being a predatory wolf when it came to women.

Mary had realized this too. Did that make her dangerous? Given time, would she have worked out who had killed her friend? Was she murdered to silence her or for some other reason?

"Hugh started acting differently," Alice was saying, "kept making excuses not to meet, said he was too busy. Hah!" she exclaimed bitterly. "He was busy all right! Fucking Mary!"

The coarseness of her comment struck him as out of character. Before her betrayal, Alice must have been much like Cecily, dreaming of Hugh in her virginal bed as if he were a celestial being and not some randy youth. Now she deliberately used the language of the gutter in order to conceal the deep disillusionment that her intended was composed of no more or less than frail human flesh. Every gesture, every expression that passed over her face bespoke a profound and crippling embarrassment at having been made such a fool of. How to tell her that although it didn't excuse his faithlessness, Hugh was like any other man—willing to enjoy a woman's body without giving her his soul. Guiltily, Nick thought of Kat. But Alice was in no state to receive such advice, much less from him. Let her mother sort her out when she returned home.

"I prayed she would die," Alice said. "But I didn't really mean . . ." And all at once her brittle composure cracked, and she fell into a storm of weeping, bending over at the waist with arms clasped tightly around her as if she were trying to hold herself in, to stop herself bursting asunder with the weight of her guilt.

Nick took her in his arms, shushing her as he had often done with his nieces when they had a minor childhood mishap, a scraped knee or the loss of a treasured toy, the smallness of the event dwarfed by their huge grief. But Mary's death was no small thing that could be remedied with a sweetmeat and a few soothing words, nor was Alice a child. Perhaps for the first time in her young privileged life, she was faced with genuine tragedy, with something that could not be remedied. It would mark her for life, of this Nick was sure, but whether that scar would become a sign of strength, a token of a battle survived if not won, or a tragic and irredeemable disfigurement, only time would tell.

She wept inconsolably, babbling torrents of words into the front of his damp shirt. Nick could make no sense of what she said but was certain it was a confession, a vomiting out of her hatred and jealousy and hurt, a cleansing of the poison that had infected her for so long. At last she fell silent.

"Stay here awhile," Nick said, releasing her gently. "There's a guard on the door, so you'll be quite safe."

She nodded, face averted, mortified to have stripped herself bare in front of a stranger.

Nick handed her a handkerchief, gave her a final pat on the shoulder, and left, shutting the door quietly behind him.

⋆ ⋆ ⋆

After collecting Hector from Codpiece, who, he discovered, had made friends with the dog by feeding him what looked like the Queen's mid-morning snack of bread and cheese, he returned to his room to find a guard lounging against the wall, picking his teeth with a dirty fingernail and looking bored. A young man was sitting in a chair, slumped over, his head in his hands. Nick nodded at the door and the guard left. The young man did not stir, did not even seem aware that anyone else was in the room.

"Sir Hugh," Nick said, approaching him.

For the first time the youth looked up. "Is it true Mary is dead?" he asked.

"I'm afraid so."

"Oh God!" he moaned, dropping his head into his hands again, retreating back into either shock or self-pity, like a hermit to his cave. Alternatively, he could just be a very good actor.

Nick felt a surge of anger. His lover was lying on a cold slab in the crypt, battered to death, and Hugh was concerned only about himself. What he had briefly glimpsed of Sir Hugh's face had shown him a pointed chin; a weak mouth; and delicate, almost pretty, features. A shock of corn-colored hair lay over his forehead and curled over his collar. He was dressed in the latest fashion, his peapod doublet barely covered the tops of his thighs, revealing long, muscular legs sheathed in tights. A dandy, Nick thought. Fancies himself a ladies' man. Nick remembered watching Hugh at the Accession Day Ball, how the lad had swaggered in front of the ladies, bowed a little too low, laughed a little too loudly. No wonder Mary had been able to lead him a merry dance. Despite appearances—and Nick had not seen any blood on his clothes—Nick knew he could be looking at a killer, knew that beneath the self-pity and vanity could reside a soul capable of monstrous evil.

Nick pulled up a chair, scraping it noisily over the floorboards, and placed it with a bang in front of the youth. When he sat down, he was so close that their knees were touching. Sir Hugh's head shot up, and Nick saw fear in his eyes, but whether it was from Nick's haggard appearance from lack of sleep and the whiteness of his scar highlighted by the dark stubble on his chin, or from guilt, he didn't know. He supposed he looked pretty disreputable, sinister even. Perhaps Hugh thought Nick was the Royal Torturer. All to the good, Nick thought. He wanted the lad in fear for his life. And poor besotted Alice was mistaken in thinking him an innocent—the sensuality of his mouth and general air of spoiled indolence belied that. If Hugh could leave bruises on the neck of his lover, God only knew what he was capable of doing to a wife he grew tired of.

"How long had you been fucking Mary?" Nick said. Sick at heart at what he had just witnessed in the cellar and determined to come at the truth, he made his words deliberately coarse, an echo of Alice's own description of Hugh's behavior. He knew the answer, of course—since Accession Day—but he wanted to see Hugh's reaction. He wasn't disappointed. The lad almost leapt out of his chair with terror, his eyes darting around the room as if looking for an escape. Hector was sitting by the door, his usual spot during interviews, to discourage the foolhardy from thinking they could leave before his master was done with them.

"And don't bother lying to me," Nick warned.

"I . . . she . . ." The boy swallowed. "Since November seventeenth."

"And last night?"

Nick thought the boy was going to pass out, so pale had his face become, his eyes all but rolling back in his skull.

"I didn't kill her," he croaked. "You must believe me."

"But you met her last night." Nick did not make this a question. The boy looked away and did not answer. But he did not deny it either. Nick folded his arms, content to let the silence draw out.

Then, just as Hugh was off his guard: "Catch," Nick said, tossing him the topaz he had found at the site of Cecily's murder. The boy instinctively caught it, looked down in amazement as if it had magically appeared in his palm, then up again at Nick, his expression puzzled.

"Is this yours?" Nick said, holding up the handkerchief he had found on the floor of the chapel. Hugh just looked at it.

"I'll take that for a no. Had a cold recently?"

"Hasn't everyone?" Then, seeing the look in Nick's eyes, "No."

Next Nick handed him the note he had found in Mary's bed,

watching Hugh's reaction carefully. The boy covered his mouth as if he were about to vomit. "I've never seen this before," he said, returning the scrap of paper with a trembling hand.

Nick stood up abruptly and, taking Hugh by the arm, roughly hauled him out of his chair. The lad came unresisting, a dead weight stumbling on his feet. Nick pulled him over to a table by the window and pointed to an inkwell, quill, and sheets of parchment.

Nick unrolled the parchment on the table, weighting it down. He dipped the quill in ink and handed it to Hugh. "Write," he commanded.

"Write what?"

"Your name."

Hugh took the pen with his right hand. It was trembling so much he blotted his first attempt.

"Again," Nick said. In the end, he had the lad write his name half a dozen times. "Now write your name again with your left hand," Nick said. When he had tossed the stone to Hugh, the boy had instinctively caught it with his left hand.

This time there was a faint smudge over the letter H on the upward strokes in exactly the same place as the ones in the note. Nick placed the note and the parchment side by side.

"Identical," he said. He took out the note that Cecily had received and compared it to Hugh's handwriting. Again, there were similarities, but they weren't conclusive enough to say for sure. Certainly there were no smudge marks where the hand holding the quill had passed over the letters. As evidence that Hugh had written both notes, it was weak. "Sit," Nick said, pointing back to the chair in the middle of the room.

Hugh shambled over and sat down heavily, looking at Nick

with dull eyes, as if he had resigned himself to arrest, torture, a brief stint in prison, and the hideous death of being hung, drawn and quartered.

"Better confess," Nick said. "It will go easier for you." The lad put up no resistance, answering in a flat monotone. Yes, he had been seeing Mary since Accession Day; yes, he had sent the note to meet at two at the sundial in the Privy Garden.

"Bit cold to do it outside, wasn't it?" Nick said.

"We usually just met up there and then went to a storeroom near the kitchens."

Nick raised an eyebrow.

"I share a room with two other lads," Hugh explained. "No privacy." That made sense; rooms were at a premium in the teeming palace, so only the very highest courtiers were given the luxury of a room to themselves. Someone as low on the pecking order as Hugh would be forced to share.

"Romantic."

"But not last night," Hugh said. "She didn't want to. Said she was off to the cellar to filch some wine and then she was going back to bed." If the lad was telling the truth, then that explained why Mary had been in the cellar, and if stealing from the kitchens was a habit, then someone else could have known her movements. Hugh would have known that instead of entering the palace off the Stone Gallery—the quickest way back to her room—she would have turned left toward The Court and entered by the door near the wine cellar and the kitchens.

"So you argued with her," Nick said, "followed her back to the palace, saw her go down the steps into the cellar, and killed her."

"No!" The boy clasped his hands in supplication. "You must believe me. She was very much alive when she left."

"What happened to her cloak?"

Hugh's eyes flicked away and then back again. "She dropped it," he mumbled.

"And ran back across the garden in her shift?" Nick said. "On a freezing night?" He shook his head. "You'll have to do better than that, Hugh. A three-year-old child wouldn't believe you. Only a woman who was in fear for her life would run away nearly naked, leaving her nice, warm cloak behind."

When the boy didn't answer, Nick shrugged. "Guard," he called. The man stuck his head in the door. "Take Sir Hugh to the Tower." Nick began to get up, as if he couldn't bear to waste any more time on the boy.

"No," Hugh cried, suddenly coming to life. "Please."

Nick sat down again.

"We had a fight," Hugh admitted. "She told me she had found someone else. We argued."

"Is that where you got those scratches?" Nick said, pointing to the base of Hugh's neck near his collarbone. He had not spotted them at first because Hugh's starched collar had covered them, but the more agitated Hugh had become, the more he had pulled at the material around his neck. Now the scratches were on full display—two red welts running down the side of his neck. Hugh fingered them uneasily.

"I was angry. When she tried to leave, I grabbed at her and that's when she gave me these," he said. "I only succeeded in ripping off her cloak. She ran in without it."

Nick remembered what Rivkah had told him about the bruises on Mary's neck. "You're lying," he said. "You took her by the neck and shook her. Somehow she twisted away, and you ripped off her cloak, tearing her shift and leaving scratch marks."

He leaned forward until his face was inches from Hugh's. "I've seen Mary's body," he said. "Your handiwork is all over her."

The boy began to weep. "All right. I did take her by the neck. It's as you say. I was angry." He wiped his nose on his sleeve. "Wouldn't you be? She had just told me she was seeing someone else. Said I was a boy, that she had found herself a real man." This last was said as if Nick, being a man himself, would agree that this slur on Hugh's virility justified his violence. Faced with his own inadequacy as a lover, Hugh comforted himself that all women were faithless whores.

"The way you were faithless to Alice, you mean?"

Hugh reared back as if Nick had struck him.

Nick sat looking at him. He didn't like the boy, but he had to admit that what Hugh had told him was plausible. But he also knew that the best lies were always based on a grain of truth. What better cover for murder than to admit to a part, but not the whole? Nick could easily see the sequence of events: a violent argument ensuing after Mary told Hugh she had tired of him; Hugh grabbing her by the neck—as he admitted; Mary twisting out of his grip, getting away; the cloak falling; Hugh pursuing Mary in a rage and seeing her disappear down the cellar steps; Hugh following and murdering her.

"What about Cecily?" Nick asked.

Hugh looked confused. "What about her?" Then comprehension dawned. "You think I killed her too?" He began to laugh, rocking back and forth on his chair, the sound manic, verging on hysteria. Again the guard stuck his head through the door, but Nick waved him away.

"Why not?" Hugh cried, flinging his arms wide as if to include the whole palace, the whole of London. "The more the merrier. You've obviously made up your mind that I killed Mary. Why not Cecily too?"

"Did Mary mention the name of her new lover?"

Startled at this abrupt change of subject, Hugh calmed. He considered the question and shook his head.

"About a week ago," Hugh said. "Mary started acting differently. Seemed distracted when we were . . ." He glanced at Nick, clearly embarrassed, though whether from delicacy or wounded vanity, Nick couldn't tell. "You know . . ."

"Making the beast with two backs?"

Hugh nodded, color flooding his face. "I began to suspect she was losing interest." He said this sadly. Clearly wounded vanity rather than a broken heart like Alice's. Nick gritted his teeth to prevent himself from pounding Hugh to a pulp.

"Then I saw her talking to someone in a corridor."

"Who?" Nick said.

Hugh shook his head. "I couldn't see. She was leaning against the wall near a staircase, her face turned up like he was standing on one of the steps above her. I never saw him."

"Him?" Nick said. "I thought you couldn't see who it was?"

"Think I don't know how she was when she was flirting?" he said, his face twisting in a sneer. "Coming onto him, thrusting her tits in his face. Giving him a good old look." Hugh's obvious fury at being discarded was easily a motive for murder, Nick thought. And he could be lying about the man he claimed he saw Mary talking to as a way of throwing suspicion off himself. Nick would have to try and find this other man. As for Hugh: Although Matty hadn't seen who was in the chapel talking to Cecily, she had heard him. There was a slim chance she would recognize Hugh's voice. If she did, then Nick was looking at the killer.

Chilled at the prospect that two young girls might have lost their lives over nothing more than thwarted adolescent lust, Nick summoned the guard and instructed him to accompany Hugh to the Tower. At this, the boy's legs seemed to give way, and the guard had to hold him up. Hugh began to weep again.

"You will not be harmed," Nick said, not unkindly. Then, hardening his voice: "Unless, of course, you are guilty."

CHAPTER 13

The Palace of Whitehall

Nick left the room intending to head straight to the Privy Garden, where he was certain the guards had now discovered Mary's cloak. The witnesses being held in the Guard House would have to wait. They had already been kicking their heels for hours and would, no doubt, be none too pleased considering most had been on their way to market when the body was found. The markets had been open at least that long, and they would have missed the early morning housewives intent on getting the freshest produce. He felt guilty about keeping them waiting, knowing their livelihood depended on selling what little they could grow, especially meager in the winter months. He hoped no children would go hungry this night because of him.

On his way out the main doors, he bumped into John. Rivkah had gone straight to The Black Sheep, John explained, and told him what had happened. He was carrying a burlap sack with a change of clothes for Nick.

"Rivkah said you needed them," he told him. "Said you could do with a wash and a shave as well. So I brought your razor."

"Thanks," Nick said, relieved to see his friend and to have a clean shirt, although it didn't please him that Rivkah had noticed his stench.

Nick quickly filled John in on Mary's murder and what he had found out by talking to the ladies-in-waiting, Alice, and Hugh.

"So you think the lad did in Mary?" John asked. "The Lady Cecily too?"

"I can see him killing Mary, but I just can't picture him killing Cecily. The murders are too different."

"But if Mary was laid out the same way as Cecily, then he must have," John said.

"Except that most of the court saw Cecily laid out on the altar," Nick replied. "And Hugh was present that day."

John looked appalled. "You mean there are two murderers?"

Nick gave him a tired smile. "It's possible." He scrubbed at his face with his hands. His eyes felt gritty from lack of sleep, his mind dull from lack of food. "Ah, John, I don't know. This whole case is more tangled than a basketful of eels. What if Hugh is telling the truth?"

"He's lying," John said. "I'll take Hector and search his rooms for the stiletto, talk to his roommates about his whereabouts the night Lady Cecily was killed."

"Look for blood on his clothes," Nick said. "Whoever moved Mary in order to pose her would have gotten blood on them and then changed."

John nodded. "After that, I'll see if Matty can identify Hugh's voice as the man she heard talking to Cecily in the chapel. If she does, he's cooked."

"I'm not holding my breath on that," Nick said. "Remember,

she only heard whispers." He then reminded John that he had ordered Hugh to be taken to the Tower. If he hurried, he might be able to catch them before they left the Guard House. Both John and Nick knew how slovenly the palace guards were; there was a chance Hugh would be sitting in a room while his escorts finished a pot of ale and a game of dice.

John clicked his tongue at Hector, and they headed toward the kitchens, the place where Matty was most likely to sleep during the day. Nick hadn't seen her among the servants clustered at the door of the cellar earlier.

Grateful that his friend could take some of the burden of the investigation off him, Nick carried on to the Privy Garden. Laid down by Henry VIII for Anne Boleyn after he took over the palace from Cardinal Wolsey—King Harry was an insatiable grabber of prime real estate—it was only a short distance from the royal apartments. Intended as the Queen's private pleasure garden, it was here that Elizabeth would walk with her ladies, perhaps listening for the laughter of her mother from happier times before her failure to produce a male heir soured Henry's devotion. Mary would be very familiar with this place and, even in darkness, would have felt safe meeting her lover here.

Nick was met at the entrance to the gardens by the captain of the Guard, a bearded, thickset man in his forties who was good at his job but continually hampered by the gormless farm boys who had come to London to make their fortunes, and then signed up to keep from starving. After a bout of drinking in The Black Sheep one night—he was a great frequenter of the Bear Garden close by—he had described himself to Nick as more of a nursemaid than a soldier.

"Bleeding babies missing their mummies," he opined. "Or their favorite goat."

Today he was stone-cold sober and all business. "You were right," he said. "We found the cloak lying near the sundial." He indicated a gravel path that led into the garden, at the end of which was a tall stone plinth with a sundial mounted on top. In the middle of the dial was a large brass gnomon, or shadow-caster—the triangle on Hugh's diagram that Nick had recognized the moment he saw it.

A midnight-blue cloak lay beside the plinth, muddied as if trampled during a scuffle. Nick examined it where it lay, noting that the chain fastening the cloak was broken, and the hood ripped where Hugh had said he grabbed at Mary.

Nick paced the area, picturing it in his head. Here, at the sundial, they had fought, and she had lost her cloak. The gravel near the base was scuffed as if by several feet—the gardeners raked the gravel every day, even in winter, so Nick knew the marks were recent—and a patch of grass near the path bore the distinct impression of a man's boot heel. Nick noticed a tiny spot of blood on the edge of the stone base that was surmounted by the brass shadow-caster, probably transferred by Hugh's fingers after he had scratched Mary. Perhaps Mary had pushed him in her attempt to get free and he had stumbled, instinctively putting his hand out for support.

Hugh's demeanor during the interview, his shocked disbelief when he had described the argument, made it clear that Hugh had not expected Mary to resist, a common mistake of serial philanderers who could not believe that any woman could reject their advances. Their contempt for women caused them to assume each woman was identical, much as one cow in a field was the same as another. From what Nick had seen of Hugh, he was certainly vain enough to have been enraged when Mary told him it was over between them. So far the evidence he was seeing at the scene corresponded with Hugh's account, although he was probably lying about the rest. His claim that he had simply let Mary go after the fight was hardly believable; it seemed obvious to Nick that Hugh, still wounded by Mary's rejection and enraged by her defiance, would have pursued her. Finding her in the cellar with her back to him, the mallet lying conveniently to hand, the opportunity for revenge must have been simply too great.

But Nick was still troubled. Though Hugh was certainly vain and self-centered, Nick wondered if the man possessed the kind of overweening arrogance that treated the world as if it were populated by dead things, not living human beings. Once, in Portugal, he had come across a shark thrashing on a beach, cast up by a storm. When he squatted beside it to take a closer look, its eyes regarded him wholly without fear, but with the single-minded hunger of a born predator. Even in its death throes, it longed to tear and rend him, reduce him to gobbets of flesh and bone and gristle. Such eyes he had seen in killers—a blank opacity, a kind of weary boredom—confirming his theory that it was a fatal lack of imagination that ultimately delivered the murderer to the executioner, not Nick's own skill. By contrast, Hugh's eyes had been filled with fear and, when he was taken away by the guard, despair. Nick could picture the spoiled youth lashing out in anger, but a stiletto through the heart was an entirely different kind of evil. Unless, of course, the posing of the body was an attempt to shift the blame onto Cecily's murderer, a dangerous gambit as that would not necessarily remove all suspicion from Hugh.

"I'd like you to set a guard on the garden. I want no sightse-
ers trampling the ground or overzealous gardeners neatening
things up."

"Already done," the captain said.

Convinced that the cloak and the spot of blood were all there
was to find, Nick did not bother to order a wider search. Everything he had seen in the garden so far tallied with Hugh's story.
Even now John would be searching the boy's room. If he found
nothing to link Hugh to Mary's death—no bloody clothes—and
if no one saw Hugh enter or leave the cellar, then the case against
him would be purely circumstantial. But Nick knew that prisoners were condemned on flimsier evidence every day. A swift trial
and execution would do much to calm the court and the populace at large. Hugh's fate was virtually sealed, especially if he
could also be condemned for Cecily's murder. For this, Matty's
testimony would be crucial. In the meantime, Nick wanted to
continue his investigation, at least into Cecily's murder. To do
this, he must keep his unease about Hugh's guilt to himself, even
from the Queen. When it came out he had done so, he would
be in very hot water indeed, but this was a risk he was willing
to take. As much as he disliked Hugh, his conscience would not
allow an innocent man to mount the scaffold for a crime he had
not committed.

"Nobody is to leave the palace," Nick said to the captain. "I
don't care how high and mighty they are. And I want the palace
searched; that means rooms, cupboards, under beds, chests, personal belongings—you name it. If anyone complains, tell them
it's by order of the Queen. You are looking for a stiletto with a
small yellow stone missing from the pommel."

The captain grinned and started bawling orders to his men,

clearly cheered by the prospect of humiliating some of the higher-ups who treated him and his men as if they were hired thugs. Nick could imagine the guards' glee as they rifled through chests and rummaged in saddlebags, no doubt pocketing a few coins that would be spent on ale that night. The irate occupants of the rooms would already be waiting for him in the Great Hall.

Nick picked up Mary's cloak and walked back to the palace the way he believed Mary had gone, eerily retracing her steps past the cellar where she had died not many hours before.

★   ★   ★

Expecting to hear a hubbub of outraged voices as he approached the Great Hall—after all, it had been a very long time since most of the illustrious men present had been in the schoolroom—Nick was astonished to walk into complete silence. At first he thought it was out of respect for Mary, but the real reason soon became apparent. The Queen was sitting on a throne on a raised dais at the far end of the room, staring stonily at her subjects, the rings on her right hand drumming on the arm of the chair, a look of barely contained fury on her face. That she felt betrayed, Nick had no doubt. Through the deaths of two of her ladies-in-waiting, the killer was striking at Elizabeth and her court. He had not told her that he had arrested Hugh so, for Elizabeth, the killer could be any one of them standing before her, his face schooled into an expression of meekness and mock horror. Behind a mask of grief, he could be laughing at them all. That the Queen had been venting her suspicions and outrage on her subjects prior to Nick's arrival, he had little doubt. The room was thick with fear, and there was not a man present who did not see the shadow of the ax-man in his monarch's flinty gaze. Even the venerable Baron

Burghley, above suspicion by virtue of his advanced age, if not his long devotion to the Queen, was looking at the ground, his face gray with apprehension. Sir Francis Walsingham, chief spymaster, was looking as dour as ever, but Nick thought he caught a flicker of approval in his eyes when he glanced Nick's way. Cecil gave him a look that was as inscrutable as always. The guards lining the walls and positioned at the doors made it plain that Elizabeth meant business. On this occasion, the "off with his head" joke that courtiers used to describe Elizabeth in certain moods was not amusing in the slightest.

Nick approached the throne. "Majesty," he said, bowing. Now, Nick knew, was the moment to inform the Queen he had a possible suspect, but he kept silent. If there was even the slightest chance that Cecily's murderer was still at large—despite the almost unbelievable coincidence that both men were left-handed—he had to go through with it.

"Get on with it, man," the Queen said, flicking her hand to indicate a trestle table on which were laid parchment, ink, and quills.

Codpiece was perched on the edge of the dais at his mistress's feet. Even he looked unusually somber. The countess, standing stiffly to the right of the Queen, shot Nick a poisonous look. Despite her shock at the murders, he suspected that what had really disturbed her was the sudden overturning of all the social and court protocols she held so dear. The spectacle of the cream of England's aristocracy lining up at the table like so many commoners queuing for tickets at The Theatre in Shoreditch must have made her nearly apoplectic.

He turned to face the crowd. "Lords, gentlemen," he said. "Thank you all for coming." *As if they had a choice,* he thought, but to suggest they had come voluntarily was a salve to their wounded pride. Nick would need their relative good will if he were to make headway in his investigation, even though, as soon as they heard about the arrest of Hugh, they would clamor that the case was solved, that Nick had humiliated them for nothing. He asked them all to write their names on a piece of parchment with the hand they naturally favored—he stressed that—and a sentence of their choosing directly beneath.

"How about 'Long live the Queen'?" Codpiece suggested.

Nick swung around, irritated. So much for his attempt to smooth ruffled feathers. The Fool raised an eyebrow, and Nick realized that his suggestion was actually rather clever: the phrase might provoke a sneer or a look of irony, which Nick might catch. He gave Richard a small nod of appreciation.

"Fitting," the Queen said. "I'm sure you correctly anticipate the sentiments of my *loyal* subjects, Fool." There was a flurry of insincere agreement as those present noted her worrying emphasis on the word *loyal*. "Proceed," she commanded.

Nick watched as, one by one, each man dipped a nib in ink, signed his name, and wrote "Long live the Queen." The phrase did not provoke anything out of the ordinary. Out of fifty-five, three men were left-handed, with only the handwriting of Sir Thomas Brighton even remotely similar to the handwriting on the first note to Cecily. Nick tapped each of them on the shoulder and asked them to remain behind, noting that while they looked uneasy, they did not seem unduly worried. In itself, this meant nothing. The killer moved freely among the court during the day, smiling, laughing at jokes, playing "hail fellow, well met" with impunity. He was bound to be a consummate actor.

Nick was also checking for blood as the men came forward.

Once he saw a dark stain on the front of a doublet, but when he took the man aside to ask him about it, he was told huffily that it was wine accidentally spilt the night before. To Sir Digby's mortification, Nick sniffed it to confirm it was indeed what he said it was. Its fruity aroma was unmistakable. "You can go," he told him.

"Much obliged, I'm sure," that gentleman said with heavy irony, and then he nervously glanced over his shoulder to see if the Queen had heard.

When all had signed, Nick told them they could go, but not before informing them that their rooms were even now being searched, and they were in no way to interfere. He didn't need to add that it was by express order of the Queen.

"No one is to leave the palace," the Queen added.

It was a significant sign of the Queen's authority and the glacial effect of her displeasure that the men did not even speak once they had filed out of the Great Hall, but hurried off, heads down, no doubt glad to have them still resting on their shoulders.

★   ★   ★

Nick quickly ascertained that two out of the three left-handed men had alibis. He sent them off under guard until these could be checked, then turned his attention to Sir Thomas Brighton. The Queen had been sitting silently, but now she stirred.

"Step forward, Sir Thomas. You say you have no explanation for your whereabouts last night?"

For the first time, Sir Thomas looked discomforted. "I do have an alibi, Your Majesty," he replied, "but alas, I am sworn to secrecy."

The Queen's face hardened. "Come, come, Sir Thomas. No

one has any secrets from their monarch." Her voice was deceptively gentle.

"Nevertheless, Your Majesty, I took an oath."

"You also took an oath to me," the Queen said. Something in
her tone made two of the guards step forward. Although he kept
his eyes firmly on his Queen, Sir Thomas had seen their movement. His face set. Either he was a very brave man or he was stupid beyond belief, Nick thought.

"Even so," Sir Thomas replied.

Stupid, then.

About his brother Robert's age, Thomas Brighton was of
stocky build and dressed fashionably in a tight-fitting doublet of
dove gray with moderately padded shoulders, tapering to a peapod point low over the belly; short gray and black striped breeches;
and white hose that revealed legs that were a touch bandy; but he
was no court dandy. Instead of a plate-size ruff, like Nick he
favored only a moderate collar with a plain cambric shirt beneath
the doublet. Taciturn and serious, he was reputed to be a man of
great courage, commanding cavalry in the Netherlands under the
Queen's favorite, Robert Dudley, Earl of Leicester, who spoke
highly of him. He was also said to be stubborn, and judging from
the set of his jaw as he stood before the Queen, Nick thought the
rumors true. An admirable quality in a soldier, disastrous in a
courtier. Recently returned to court and in reward for his bravery, he had been granted permission to marry a distant cousin of
the Queen's, the former Lady Wakefield, a rich widow and older
than him by ten years. Court rumor said they didn't get on.
Hardly likely to admit to being unfaithful to the Queen's relative,
however distant, he was just the sort of mulish, honorable fool to
go to the block before revealing the name of a lover. Irritated at

Elizabeth's obtuseness at not realizing this, Nick nevertheless held his tongue.

"I insist," the Queen said, her eyes glittering dangerously.

Sir Thomas looked at the floor.

"Do you not owe fealty to me and to me alone?"

Say yes, man! Nick prayed silently.

"Majesty," Sir Thomas said, bowing stiffly, "my sword is yours to command, but my conscience is my own."

Nick winced. It didn't do to throw the Queen's own words back in her face. On her accession to the throne, she had famously declared that she didn't intend to make windows into men's souls, signaling that, unlike her sister Bloody Mary, she would not persecute those of the old or reformed religion as long as their actions were not treasonable. Given the many Catholic plots to assassinate her, Nick suspected she had long regretted that statement. Sir Thomas was just the sort of man, Nick thought, to confuse matters of the soul with matters of the heart. Either way, he had just put his head into the Tudor lion's mouth, for not only had he reminded the Queen of her famous promise, he had also struck at her even more infamous vanity.

Elizabeth delighted in flirting with her male courtiers, choreographing an elaborate dance of mock courtship that, it was tacitly agreed, could never, *ever* be consummated. Only once had a man been so deluded by his own charms to think his wooing of the Queen was real and not illusion. Her childhood friend, Robert Dudley, had foolishly thought she might marry him. It was widely rumored—with much tittering and smirking—that he had got down on his knees in the middle of St. James's Park—a rather soggy stage for his romantic drama seeing as most of the park was unclaimed marshland—when he and the Queen had been out hunting with falcons. Here, with stagnant water creeping unpleasantly into his hose, he had popped the question. Her answer had been to wheel her horse about, snatch up the reins of his mount, and gallop off, leaving him to slog back to the palace on foot—a miserable three miles, with his prize falcon, Jezebel, flapping fractiously on his wrist. It was said that he arrived soaking wet and covered in foul-smelling mud, only to learn he had been banished from court until his ardor cooled.

As Elizabeth aged, the game of courtship had grown grotesque; her suitors were often young enough to be her sons. Nevertheless, a man who dared imply the Queen was not his heart's desire and goddess of his dreams was either an honest man or a suicidal one. Nick suspected Sir Thomas was both. He watched him carefully. There was something about his brooding silence, the way he kept his eyes carefully shuttered, the curious lack of expression on his face that made Nick think he could be looking at a killer.

Elizabeth snapped her fingers, and the guards, who had been inching ever closer, stepped forward and drew to attention. "Convey Sir Thomas to the Tower. Let us see if a few nights' rumination will reveal to him his proper fealty."

"Majesty," Nick pleaded as Sir Thomas was led away under guard. As he had done with Hugh, he would rather have interviewed Sir Thomas in his own room. If he had judged the man correctly, Sir Thomas would immediately clam up in a prison cell; he would regard his silence as a trial of courage. Immediately, Nick knew he had made a mistake. Vanity had ever been Elizabeth's gravest fault, and in this instance, it had clearly overruled her razor-sharp mind. Her harsh and peremptory treatment of Sir Thomas had not exhausted her ire at his unintended snub.

Nick had visited the Tower often enough to interview prisoners to know that even a day cloistered within their damp, rat-infested walls was sufficient to instill terror if not consumption. Nick fervently hoped he wasn't the next recipient of Her Majesty's displeasure.

"One week," Elizabeth said. She held up a be-ringed finger. "You have one week. The mayor tells me that Londoners are blaming the Jews. In some parts the bailiffs have had to break up mobs. The moneylenders have all gone into hiding; merchants have shut up shop. It's bad for business, Nick," Elizabeth said grimly. "What's worse, it's bad for my reputation."

Pretty bad for the Jews too, Nick thought.

"I want this murderer caught before the Christmas festivities," Elizabeth said, staring hard at him.

"Yes, Majesty."

"Glad to hear it." Then Elizabeth stood and swept off the dais, with the countess following in her wake like a squat tugboat nosing behind a gorgeous barge.

The Fool jumped down from his perch on the dais. "Well, that went tits up."

"It could have gone better," Nick admitted. "I notice you didn't put your oar in."

"I'm not a fool."

"Very funny," Nick said sourly. No doubt he'd soon be spending Christmas sharing a cell with Sir Thomas, bored senseless by endless anecdotes about the difficulty of watering horses in a country as flat as a dinner plate and below sea level. After he checked in with John, he'd better get himself to the Tower and interview the man, see if he couldn't winkle out an alibi or, alternatively, put him in the frame for murder. At this point, with time running out before the Queen's impossible deadline, the prospect of framing someone for the crime was beginning to look tempting. And there was something about Sir Thomas that made Nick suspicious, something odd about his guardedness, as if he had something dangerous to hide, something for which he was willing to risk his freedom and perhaps his very life.

Or perhaps the reason Sir Thomas couldn't answer was that he was caught between a rock and a hard place—either admit to betraying his wife, the Queen's cousin, or betray his mistress, who could very well be highborn herself and the wife of a powerful lord. Not to mention the offense he would give his sovereign, yet another woman, whichever answer he gave. *Poor sod,* Nick thought. Sir Thomas was beginning to look like Orestes, pursued by the Furies for killing his mother in order to avenge his father; or Oedipus, who killed his father and married his mother and was likewise pursued by the weird sisters. Aeschylus and Sophocles, those ancient Greek playwrights, sadists both, loved to stack the odds against their heroes. They must have had spectacularly unhappy childhoods to have such serious parent issues, Nick had always thought. Whatever the reason, he would have to get to the bottom of it, and that meant a long walk across London to the Tower.

He ran his hand over his chin. Rivkah was right: he needed a shave and a wash. Briefly he entertained the notion of returning to Bankside and dropping in on Kat. She had had a bathhouse installed in the garden behind the house—this despite Henry VIII making them illegal, given his belief that they were breeding grounds for the French pox. Nick longed to submerge himself in hot water, let her run a soapy sponge over his back and other more hard-to-reach parts. And a shave: Kat was the only woman he trusted to hold a sharp blade to his throat. Rivkah he didn't dare ask, having seen her wield a scalpel on some poor unfortunate to excise a cyst on his groin. Just the thought of it made him shudder. He could have had heated water brought up to his room in the palace, but he didn't have time to wait for a surly laggard to show up with a half-empty bucket after spilling most of its contents on the stairs.

"I didn't see puce pants poncing about," Nick said, referring to the absence of Sir Christopher in the Great Hall.

"Ooh, alliteration!" the Fool said, clasping his hands and looking dreamy. "Positively poetic."

"Cut it out, Richard," Nick said crossly. "I'm trying to solve a murder here."

"Sorry," the Fool said. "It's a hard habit to break. Anyway, I overheard the countess telling the Queen that her precious nephew left for Dover the day before yesterday. Something to do with a shipment, apparently."

That ruled out Sir Christopher as a suspect for Mary's death. Even so, seeing as he had to go through Cheapside on his way to the Tower, he would drop by the house and talk to Perkin. He wanted to double-check that the times Sir Christopher had given for his visit to the Custom House stood up, despite the corroboration of Master Summers. Although illogical and most likely a waste of time, Nick felt that Perkin might have something important to tell him. Nick remembered he had also intended to check in with Wat, Master Hogg's apprentice. This too was probably a dead end—he hadn't held out much hope about the Guinea spice—but he could afford to leave no stone unturned now that the Queen had given him an ultimatum. When called to account for his progress or lack thereof, he must be able to report that he had assiduously followed every lead.

First he decided to check in with John to see if Hector had discovered anything damning in Hugh's room and if Matty had been able to identify Hugh as the man she heard. Then he had to hurry to the Guard House to interview possible witnesses, although he was not hopeful.

Next he would walk to the Tower. On the way he would drop in on the apothecary and see if Wat was in. After the Tower, he resolved to cross back to Bankside on London Bridge and check in on Rivkah and Eli. Perhaps visit Kat afterward for that longed-for bath and a spot of dalliance. Feeling a little more cheerful, Nick said goodbye to Richard and left the Great Hall.

CHAPTER 14

The City of London

On his way out of the main Court Gate, Nick stopped to talk to John, whom he spotted leaving the Guard House. Only one man, a pig farmer on his way to the meat market in Newgate Street—Nick recalled the crates of squealers he had heard—had anything interesting to report. He had parked his cart next to the kitchen door about half past two—"Five hours before sunup, any road," was how he described the time—to deliver his load. When John commented on how early that seemed, Farmer Trotter explained that the palace was only his first delivery, that he had several other locations to go to before he could continue on to the market to sell the rest.

"I'm surprised you do any business in Advent," John said, "seeing as meat is banned."

"People are already preparing for Christmas," the farmer explained. "Salting, curing, and such. Advent and Lent are my busiest times. Good job I live over by Westminster way," he continued chattily. "Not far from home, see. Only have the one horse, Petunia. Getting a bit long in the tooth now, of course."

After he had suppressed a smile at the mare's name, a clapped-out nag of dubious temper, John had to patiently steer Farmer Trotter—"I swear to God," John said when Nick raised his eyebrows at the aptness of the farmer's name—from his beloved horse back to the subject at hand. As he drove past the buildings that separated the wide expanse of The Court from the Privy Garden, he heard voices.

"Going at it hammer and tongs," he said. "Man and a woman, before you ask. Must have been married," he added thoughtfully.

When John asked if he could overhear any words, he said only the word "bitch," frequently repeated.

"Definitely married," the farmer concluded.

Asked if he had seen anyone or heard anything when he unloaded his crates and carried them past the cellar door to the kitchens, he shook his head. "Only the cellar door was open," he said. "And the lantern on the hook, missing. I noticed that because it was dark, and I nearly tripped over one of those uneven flagstones. Wouldn't do to drop a crate in the palace," he said, grinning as he imagined the chaos that would ensue, piglets racing about, servants falling over one another, the cook brandishing his ladle like a general directing his troops.

"Where were you when the body was found?" John asked.

At the mention of Mary, the farmer lost his amused look. "I was leaving the kitchens after taking in the last crate," he said. "While I was chatting with the cook—we're old mates, you know," he added irrelevantly—"he sent one of the kitchen maids to fetch some small beer from the cellar. We like a bit of a drink on a cold morning, him and me. Keeps out the chill."

"The body?" John reminded him, thinking that, never mind

piglets running around the corridors, it was harder to keep Farmer Trotter on track.

"We heard the maid screaming, and we all rushed down the cellar to see what was amiss. Then we saw her. The dead lass, I mean. Horrible, it was." He took off his battered hat as if out of respect and twisted it in his hands. "After that, one of the guards came and shooed us all up the stairs. Then the scruffy cove with the massive dog arrived and started giving orders. Friend of yours, is he?" the farmer asked. When John nodded, the farmer scowled. "Then tell him from me that thanks to him, me and Petunia's lost a day's trade."

John questioned him further, but he'd had no more to tell him aside from the fact that the farmer had seen no guard on duty in The Court. When John asked the guards about this, a jug-eared northern lad whose uniform hung loosely on a lanky frame shamefully admitted he had gone into the guard house for "a bit of a warm-up seeing as it were right parky outside."

"Bit of a kip, you mean," the captain said, advancing on him with clear intent to cause grievous bodily harm.

John had left them to it.

"Can I go now?" the farmer asked, clapping on his cap of worn fustian, which smelled suspiciously of pig shit. "Petunia's been standing outside for hours, poor luv. Feels the cold something horrible."

John also broke the depressing news to Nick that none of the other kitchen staff or tradespeople had seen or heard anything.

"At least Farmer Trotter gave us a time," Nick said. "Half past two. The killer must have slipped down to the cellar when he was in the kitchens. Very risky. Farmer Trotter was in and out of that corridor between the kitchens and the cart. The killer would have had to wait his chance and then slip down unseen. Speaking of which," Nick said, "turn up anything on Hugh?"

John shook his head. "Not a thing," he said. "No bloody clothes, no stiletto."

"Matty?" Nick asked.

"Even when I made Hugh whisper, she still couldn't tell."

Nick sighed. He hadn't been very hopeful, but he was desperate for some hard evidence. He then told John about Sir Thomas Brighton and asked him to search his room.

"Check his clothes, John," he said. "Take the place apart."

Nick told John he was intending to return to The Black Sheep after his interview with Sir Thomas at the Tower but that he would return to Whitehall the next morning.

"I need you to remain here in case the search of the rooms turns up anything. Talk to the captain and organize a patrol of the palace tonight and every night until I say so. And get some shut-eye while you can. Neither of us is going to sleep until this is over."

"And, John?" he said as his friend turned to go back to the palace. "The place is going to be abuzz about Hugh's arrest. People are going to be saying that the murderer is caught; they are sure to ask why they are still being kept in the palace. It's probably going to get ugly."

"Not to worry," John grinned. "I'll just blame you."

★ ★ ★

Whistling up Hector, Nick set off north along King's Street.

At St. Pauls' Cross he looked for the beggar girl but didn't see her. Instead, a meat pie-seller, touting his illegal wares from a tray slung around his shoulders, caught his eye. Steaming in the cold air and swimming in rich gravy, the pies' aroma was heavenly, and the growling of his stomach reminded Nick that he hadn't broken his fast since the day before. He bought four for a farthing each and sat on the steps of the Cross to eat them; two for him, two for Hector. If he was lucky, the meat inside would be rabbit trapped that morning near Smithfield; if unlucky, it could be pigeon or even rat. The city bailiffs kept a stern eye on butchers and pie-sellers in Advent and Lent to make sure the ban on meat was being observed, but there was always a thriving under-the-counter trade with country poachers. Nick didn't care; he thought the Almighty had better things to worry about, and he'd eaten worse on a voyage to the Continent where the ship had run straight into a storm in the English Channel that had blown them so far off course it had taken a month to beat back. By the time they'd limped into port, Nick and the crew had been down to hard tack and weevils, with rain water to drink, foul and bilgy. His hatred for rats stemmed from this voyage, where he and the ship's crew had had to battle the vermin for food and keep a watch at night for fear they would be bitten. After letting Hector lick his fingers clean and wiping them dry on his cloak, something Rivkah would have told him was woefully unhygienic, he continued toward Cheapside, dodging plump matrons with cowed maids in tow, staggering under huge baskets, and sweethearts strolling arm in arm, taking up the entire sidewalk in such a romantic fog that they were oblivious to other pedestrians and the irritated glances from people in a hurry, unable to pass them.

"Gardez loo," a voice yelled suddenly from a window over-hanging the street. Nick ducked smartly inside a doorway as the contents of a chamber pot splashed revoltingly into the gutter. A man with his sweetheart on his arm wasn't so lucky; his

218 ~ Suzanne M. Wolfe

plum-colored stockings would never be the same. His lady love wrinkled a pert nose and glared at him as if it were his fault. Safely on the inside, closest to the houses, her sky-blue skirts had been gallantly shielded from just such a mishap by her considerate lover. As far as Nick could tell, he didn't seem to mind; judging from his moony expression when he looked at her, he was too far gone to fret over a ruined pair of hose.

The sound of a woman's voice raised in anger issued from the upstairs room where the chamber pot had been dumped. Nick caught the words "You'll get us fined, you lazy slattern—" before the window banged shut. The angry tirade continued, muted by the glass. In an upscale neighborhood like Cheapside, the emptying of chamber pots into the street was frowned upon by the authorities. A hefty fine was imposed if a neighbor reported it, and judging from the disgusted look on the face of the haberdasher who rented the ground floor, the upstairs household would soon be visited by the bailiff.

Nick had shelled out over a pound to have an indoor water closet installed in The Black Sheep; intended solely for use by the family—patrons had to use a jakes in the back, although most staggered out the front door and pissed in the Thames. He had also convinced Robert to install water closets at Binsey House; the abundance of streams providing flowing water on the property made this a lot easier to do, but no cheaper, alas. Even the Queen had had a flushing privy installed at Richmond Palace. In his travels on the Continent, Nick had been impressed by the sanitation in several Spanish cities, had thought it much more advanced and efficient than in England, owing to the influence of the Moors and Jews, who considered hygiene and sanitation an indispensable adjunct to the practice of their faith. In addition, the Continent retained the historical memory of ancient Roman baths and sewer systems. Nick had always found England woefully backward in this regard, suspicious as it had ever been of foreign influences.

When the coast was clear, and with a quick glance upward to see if the contents of another chamber pot were imminent, Nick stepped back out into the street, only to be stalled by a nursemaid herding a gaggle of small children in front of her like so many errant goslings, cluttering up the walkway and slowing down to a complete wide-eyed halt at the sight of Hector. One of the children, a boy of about four, his nephew Nicky's age, jumped into the road and started stamping gleefully on icy puddles, splintering them into starbursts. Nick lunged just in time to pull him to safety before he was run over by a cart.

"Watch out, lad," Nick said.

The boy giggled as if being rescued from sudden death were a lark. Nick's heart beat painfully. The child's blithe unconcern for a world full of danger reminded him of Cecily and Mary.

"Oy," the nurse shouted. "Leave him be." She had been too busy trading flirtatious looks with a shop apprentice to have noticed the near demise of one of her charges.

"Mind the young 'uns, Mistress," the driver of the cart bellowed.

"You mind your own business," she yelled back.

The children petted Hector and waved shyly. Nick waved back. The nurse scowled and shooed the children on, scolding them as she went, the words "Nasty man; nasty dog" drifting back to him.

As he neared Sir Christopher's house, he saw a stout middle-aged woman, wearing an apron, on the front step, talking loudly with another woman leaning on a broom. Both looked to be domestics; Nick guessed the woman with the apron was Sir Christopher's cook, judging from the proprietary way she was leaning on the doorpost. The other woman, younger and thinner, looked like a maid from next door. Nick pretended to be interested in the front window display of the wigmaker's shop a few doors down and listened in.

"Done a bunk, hasn't he," the cook said. "Nary a word to me nor the master neither."

"Where's he gone then?" the maid asked.

"Dunno." The cook folded her arms on her wide chest. "He has family out Shoreditch way. Maybe gone there." She frowned. "Odd though. Perkin hated his dad, said he were an evil bastard, used to beat him something awful when he were in his cups. And his mam's dead."

"Maybe he has a sweetheart?" This last said with a definite note of wistful longing. Nick guessed she harbored secret hopes.

The cook guffawed. "Perkin? A sweetheart? You must be joking."

"Ain't you worried?" the maid asked.

"I'm more worried about who's going to keep the kitchen fire lit, that's what," the cook said. "It were stone cold. Couldn't get me bread in, could I? At least the master's not home. That's a blessing and no mistake. He would have had me guts for garters if there were no fresh bread. Evil sod."

Nick sauntered up. "Morning, ladies," he said, bowing.

The maid tittered and gave an awkward curtsey, her broom almost taking out Nick's eye. The cook gave him a shrewd once-over and frowned. Nick knew he looked a fright: his clothes were rumpled; he needed a shave; and, as Rivkah had pointed out to John, he stank.

"Who might you be then?" she asked. Nick noticed that she was an experienced servant who had dropped her London dialect in case he was someone of note.

"The Honorable Nicholas Holt at your service, madam," Nick said, laying on the formality with a trowel. In his experience, servants were far greater sticklers for protocol than their masters, believing their own worth to be in direct proportion to their master's social standing; the more important the visitor, the more important the master, and hence the servant. "I was here a few days ago to speak to Sir Christopher and his aunt, the countess."

At the stating of his credentials—the reference to her master and his formidable aunt—in a clearly upper-class accent, the cook's face assumed a helpful and servile expression.

The maid continued to gape. "What kind of dog is he?" she asked, indicating Hector with the end of her broom. Hector was busily snuffling around the steps, probably catching the scent of Sir Christopher's dog. Which reminded Nick: he couldn't hear it yapping.

The cook gave the maid a glare. "Off you go, Lucy," she said, "while I see to his *lordship*." She gave the girl a none-too-gentle nudge off the steps to speed her on her way. "Won't you come in?" she said, addressing Nick with a curtsey. She looked dubiously at Hector. "I've just cleaned the floors."

"Sit," Nick told Hector.

The maid giggled and half-heartedly resumed sweeping the steps of the house next door.

Once Nick was ensconced in the cook's domain at the back of the house and he had encouraged her to take a load off by sitting opposite him at the kitchen table, her stiffness and habitual guardedness with her superiors began to diminish. The air of cozy informality was heightened by a roaring fire and the fact that Nick, after courteously asking permission, liberally helped himself to a plate of freshly baked scones. Mistress Plunkett, as he had learned, was like cooks the world over—she loved to see the fruit of her labor consumed with gusto.

"You managed to get the fire going, I see," Nick said.

"Boy next door brought in the wood," the cook replied. "Here." She pushed a jar of blackcurrant jam toward him. "Try some of this. Put it up last summer."

Nick slathered it on and tasted it. "Delicious," he complimented her. "Better than my mother's."

The cook beamed. "The secret's in the lemon juice," she said. "Can't always get lemons, but Sir Christopher got some from a Swiss merchant he knows."

"I'll be sure to tell my mother." He eyed the last scone.

"Go on, then," the cook said, pushing the plate toward him. "Ain't no one else here to eat them."

"I couldn't help overhearing that Perkin seems to have run off," Nick said seizing the opening she had unwittingly given him.

"Seems like," she said.

"Did he take anything?"

Her eyes darted to the kitchen door, then returned to Nick. "Not exactly." She played with some crumbs on the table, moving them into a little pile. She was clearly debating whether or not to tell him something. Nick waited. He didn't want to jeopardize her trust by pressing her, by revealing he was here to pry into the life of the household and not just pass a pleasant morning in gossip.

At last she sighed, heaved herself to her feet, and walked over to the kitchen door. Opening it, she pointed to a white object lying by the side of the kitchen path. It was Sir Christopher's dog.

"I found him this morning in his basket. At first I thought he were asleep, but he usually barks and runs around when I come in, so I went to check. Dead as a doornail."

Nick squatted by the side of the dog and felt it. Already beginning to stiffen and freeze in the cold, its neck was twisted at an unnatural angle, its eyes partially open as if watching him, its liver-colored lips drawn back over tiny needle-sharp teeth. Even in death it looked as if its last thought on earth had been to bite.

"The neck's broken," he said. They left the pathetic little bundle and returned to the kitchen table.

"I reckon Perkin killed him and scarpered because of what the master would do when he got back," the cook said. "Thought the world of that dog, he did. I kept it so he could bury it proper."

It made sense. Not only would Perkin have feared a beating, but he would have also feared being taken up by the bailiff and thrown into prison. Bred specially as companions for rich and idle women, lapdogs were expensive things to own, a sign of status and wealth. If Sir Christopher had pressed charges, and Nick thought he was vindictive enough to do so, Perkin could hang or, at the very least, be fined and publically whipped. No wonder the lad had done a bunk.

"Did Perkin take anything?" Nick asked again.

"Steal, you mean?"

Nick nodded.

"Not that I can see," she said.

"Was he unhappy here?"

"He hated that dog," she said, nodding at the door.

Nick recalled the tear in Perkin's hose that had been clumsily

sewn up. Ankle height. Perkin and the dog had been mortal enemies. The dog's death might even have been an accident; under
all that fur Nick had felt how small and brittle its bones were,
more like a rabbit's than a dog's. Nick could see Perkin grabbing
the dog to stop it biting him, accidentally squeezing too hard, and
breaking its neck. Then he had panicked and done a runner. But
if so, then Nick thought it odd that Perkin had not helped himself
to something before leaving. If he was going to be pursued by a
vengeful master for having killed his dog—theft in the eyes of the
law—he might as well be taken up for palming a few coins or a
silver candlestick. Not only would he need money to fund his
escape, but it was a case of "in for a penny, in for a pound."

Mistress Plunkett didn't seem to have realized this and was
still ruminating on the dog. "Horrible little beast. Still," she said,
"I didn't want it dead. There'll be hell to pay when the master
returns."

When questioned, she confirmed what Nick already knew,
that Sir Christopher had left for the south coast the day before
yesterday. Nothing unusual about that, she said. He was always
going to Dover to check on his merchandise.

"Sometimes, he even goes to them foreign places across the
sea," she added. From her expression, Nick could tell that she didn't
understand why anyone would want to leave Merry Olde England.

When asked about Sir Christopher, Mistress Plunkett was
more than forthcoming. As usual, servants knew far more about
their employers' business than any of their so-called betters
dreamed. She told him that Sir Christopher was the only son of a
"right evil bastard," if the countess was to be believed. Against
the wishes of her family, the countess's younger sister had married
a country squire—miles beneath her station, the cook informed

him with withering disapproval, as if she too was of aristocratic stock and horrified at such a sin against the social order. An early death in childbed had done little to rehabilitate the sister in her family's eyes, but the countess, childless and widowed, had taken an interest in the boy.

"Sir Christopher was raised by his father," she said. "Mad as a hatter, he were, if her ladyship can be credited."

"In what way?" Nick asked.

"About God and such," Mistress Plunkett replied, waving a hand as if to dispel the fog of theology. "Dunno the ins and outs, but the father beat the boy black and blue, that I do know. Claimed the mother were unfaithful and the boy were a cuckoo in the nest. Called the lad a 'limb of Satan.'" She frowned. "Strange thing, though. Apparently the lad worshipped his dad, hated his mother. Seems like us women always get the blame, don't it?"

Nick couldn't deny it: Cecily and Mary had been treated like so much rubbish. And it was clear that Hugh considered Mary a whore as a way of justifying his act. He refilled Mistress Plunkett's beaker with ale, and she took a deep draft before resuming her account. After the father's death—"keeled over in mid-rant," she said with great satisfaction. "Apoplexy. Serve him right, I say. Off his bleeding rocker, he were, pardon me French"—the countess had taken in the boy.

"Sir Christopher's her heir, I assume," Nick said, remembering what Codpiece had told him about the countess threatening to leave everything to the Crown.

"That's right. Brought him to London when she became chief lady-in-waiting to the Queen, God bless her. Bought him this house, set him up in business. Dotes on him," the cook said, "although she can be right sharp when she feels like it. Couldn't stand his dog for one thing, nor the clothes he wears. Must be because he were never allowed to wear nothing but rags when he were a tyke."

"When did you last see Perkin?"

"Both him and that rat dog were in the kitchen. Perkin was supposed to be plucking chickens. Made a right mess." Nick had already spotted a few droplets of blood on the corner of the large dresser that held crockery.

"So you don't live on the premises?"

Mistress Plunkett gave him a look as if he'd gone daft. "Live over in Shoe Lane. Me hubby's head turnkey at the Fleet, like his dad and granddad afore him," she said proudly. "I come in every-day to cook and mop the floors."

"Surely there's a maid and housekeeper to see to the clean-ing?" Nick said, catching her tone of grievance at the mention of the floors.

Mistress Plunkett sniffed. "You would think so," she said, "in a place as grand as this, but His Nibs's too mean to employ a full staff. Just me and Perkin, if you can believe that. Only me now. Dunno how I'm going to manage."

For the first time, her air of solid competence faltered, and Nick saw a tired, middle-aged woman trying, like the rest of working London, to make ends meet. Perhaps she had managed to save a little money to see her and her husband into old age? Perhaps not. Infirmity and old age were terrifying prospects for most. Without grown children to take care of them, the elderly were often reduced to penury. Nick had noticed the joints of Mistress Plunkett's hands were swollen, her fingers twisted—a crippling malady common in female domestics who spent their lives immersing their hands in cold water. He could imagine that kneading out dough was painful for her now. How long until she was unable to work? He couldn't imagine Sir Christopher pensioning her off with a generous stipend.

It was an odd state of affairs to have only a half-grown boy and a cook running a household such as Sir Christopher's. Mistress Plunkett said her master was parsimonious, but maybe he had money problems. The import business was particularly fickle, depending as it did on the elements, and ships making it safely to port. Many a merchant had gone bankrupt after his ship was lost at sea.

Nick stood up. The cook started to rise, but Nick waved her down. "I can see myself out." He bowed. "Thank you, Mistress Plunkett. You've been most helpful. And your scones are the best I've ever tasted. I'll be sure to pass on your tip for the jam to my mother."

The cook beamed.

"Let me know if Perkin shows up," Nick said. "I'm at Whitehall until Christmas."

"Right-o."

Hector was still sitting obediently on the front step when Nick pulled the front door to. Nick took the scone he had secreted in his jerkin and tossed it to the dog, who caught it in midair and gulped it down whole.

"Come on," Nick said. "Next stop, the Tower."

CHAPTER 15

The Tower of London

Nick approached the Tower from Thames Street after stopping off at the apothecary's on Candlewick to see if the apprentice, Wat, was around. He wasn't. Master Hogg told him the boy was off delivering cold remedies to sick customers, and he couldn't be sure when he'd be back.

"Knowing him," he said sourly, "he's in a tavern somewhere, swilling ale and ogling strumpets."

Nick wished he were so lucky. He thought longingly of The Black Sheep and hot spiced wine. It seemed an age since he'd been home. After days of bitter, glittering cold, the sky had turned leaden while he had been sitting in Mistress Plunkett's kitchen, gray clouds rolling in from the east, massing overhead. There was a coppery taste to the air, a sure harbinger of snow, accompanied by a damp chill that was slowly seeping into his bones. The pedestrian traffic had thinned as people wisely hurried home after their morning errands.

A jubilant din of church bells greeted Nick as he left the shop and stepped back onto the street. Midday. A throwback to medieval times, when bells reminded the faithful of the liturgy of the hours, they now served as Londoners' timepieces, telling them when to rise, when to eat, when to sleep. And in the event of fire, an ever-present specter in a predominantly timber-built city, where houses stood cheek by jowl, when to rush out into the streets with buckets of water or sand. This great discordant music with its myriad chimes of high and low, long and short, flat and true, was the voice of London. Nick loved it with a passion.

★   ★   ★

He came to the region by the western side of the outer curtain of the Tower wall, known as Petty Wales. Turning right toward the river, he entered the Tower by the Bulwark Gate and walked up a path that bisected a small garden where the Keeper planted herbs and summer vegetables. Sometimes the sound of the Keeper's children could be heard coming from this garden. Nick had always thought that if he had been a prisoner here, the sound of innocent laughter floating through the bars of his cell would have tormented him more than the rack, serving as a cruel reminder of the sweetness of the life he was about to forfeit. Surprisingly, prisoners had told him that the sound had been a comfort to them, a pledge that after the flash of the headsman's ax lay a paradise where such voices would forever ring.

Now the garden was bedded down for the winter, its beds covered in straw. The raspberry canes tied up against the inner wall were a sickly bundle of sticks, and even the evergreen rosemary looked blackened and frost-burned. In summer, Nick had always thought this a strangely domestic welcome for visitors to a place as sinister as the Tower. Now its barrenness looked the part, a fitting antechamber to the dank echoing walls within.

He left the garden by the Lion Gate and walked down a short corridor, past the Lion Tower set into the southwestern tip of the wall. Hector growled at the pungent scent of the lions, the fur along his neck and back standing on end.

In truth, the lions were mangy brutes who were too old and too long in captivity to be fearsome. They mostly sat around looking bored, lazily tracking gawkers and occasionally washing their faces with plate-sized paws, looking for all the world like extremely large tabby cats. The Tower guards had names for them—Blossom, Alf, Harry—and when a fourth, Cedrick, died of old age in the autumn, it was said the guards—the hard cases who put the screws to prisoners—had wept like babies and had had a whip-round for a proper funeral.

A left turn took him to Middle Gate Tower, where a guard admitted him to yet another stone-walled walkway that led across Wet Ditch, the deep, marshy hollow dug between the inner and outer walls, to yet another tower—the Byward Tower Gate. Traitors' Gate lay farther to the east, abutting the river, roughly in the center of the south wall. The mossy stones of the tunnel led to the steps of the tower, and the dank drip of water was the last sound of freedom for many a royal and highborn prisoner. Once through the Cross Walls and Gates—the numerous tunnels bisecting the curtain walls of the Outer and Inner Wards—Nick emerged inside the Bailey of the Tower, the heart of the castle complex. He had to admire the ingenuity of the defense system of the Tower, with its many gates and its intricate system of passages and walkways, its double walls, moat, and ditch. In all its long history, the castle had never been stormed, but had stood impregnable for half a thousand years, deliberately built to face west toward the Anglo-Saxon city as a vaunting reminder of the Conqueror's prowess in arms and his determination to rule with an iron fist. Rising to the north was Tower Hill, where public executions were held. Inside the Bailey on Tower Green was the site of the block and scaffold where private executions were held if civic unrest and mob violence were feared—Lady Jane Grey, Anne Boleyn, and Catherine Howard being the most famous prisoners to be beheaded there in recent memory. William the Conqueror's palace, the White Tower, stood in the center of this formidable ring of stone. Now woefully fallen into disrepair, with several towers uninhabitable, and hopelessly outdated as a royal palace, last used by the Queen the night before her coronation nearly thirty years before, the Tower remained a place of brute power, a reminder of the almost limitless scope of the sovereign, the conqueror over the conquered. The Queen's precipitate order to have Sir Thomas imprisoned there illustrated the point, and given the recent murders of her ladies-in-waiting, Parliament, that supposed curb on royal hegemony, was unlikely to protest.

After inquiring at the Lieutenant's Lodgings hard by Bloody Tower Gate, where river prisoners were brought before being taken to their cells, he was told Sir Thomas was being "housed" in Beauchamp Tower, set in the middle of the western side of the inner wall. Nick blinked at the word as if the Lieutenant were mine host of a particularly luxurious inn on the London road.

Sir John Avery was a tall man of thin, stooping build, who looked more like a schoolmaster than a jailer; it was easy to overlook the hard, shrewd eyes in his pale, scholarly looking face. But the Queen had a reputation for picking her subordinates well. Sir John might have been soft-spoken and courteous, but he did not shrink from doing whatever was required. Nick had seen him watch a prisoner being tortured with an impassive face and pose questions between screams with the utmost civility, never failing to use honorifics such as, "my lord" or "sir." Nick had no quibble with him. He had had dealings with Sir John before and found him reliable and honest. For one thing, he took no bribes, an almost unheard of rectitude in a servant of the Crown especially in view of the staggering wealth of many of the Tower's inmates. For another, he oversaw the Yeoman Warders, or Beefeaters as they were called (for their weekly ration of beef gratis from the Crown), with an eagle eye for corruption and bullying. It was said he'd had one of his men locked in a dungeon for a week, on bread and water, after he had caught him stealing food from one of the prisoners.

Nick asked to see Sir Thomas's belongings, taken from him as a matter of procedure. They would be returned to him if he were lucky enough to walk out of the Tower, or given to his family as part of his effects if he was unlucky enough to be executed. As expected, there was no stiletto, nor was there any item, jewelry or otherwise, inlaid with topaz. In fact, there was no jewelry of any kind, quite unusual for courtiers, who usually loved to adorn themselves with earrings, chains, and rings. There wasn't even a handkerchief. Only a scrap of paper caught Nick's attention; it had been torn off a larger sheet, and the ink had smudged, as if the paper had been frequently handled and had become greasy with use. Nick made out random numbers in two neat columns. It looked like a fragment of a ledger.

The ink had bled at the edges of the numerals so that they ran into one another, making them even harder to decipher. Nick pocketed it.

He followed one of the Beefeaters past the Queen's House

to the left of the Bloody Tower and across the Inner Bailey to Beauchamp.

The guard turned a key in the lock of a studded oak door with an iron sally port set at head height in the middle. "Here you go. I'll be outside. Just knock when you're done."

* * *

Sir Thomas's highborn status, his bulging purse, and the fact that he hadn't actually been convicted of any crime other than pissing off his sovereign, had secured him a swanky room. Perfectly circular and comprised of the entire circumference of the tower, it featured a stone fireplace with a crackling fire and a bed with a thick mattress and a sheepskin coverlet to keep off the chill. A desk and chair stood under a barred window that looked down on the Inner Bailey; another window looked west over the city. Both windows had heavy wooden shutters—glass being thought too much of a temptation for the condemned before the headsman got his chance—thus forcing the occupant of the room to choose between warmth and light: Sir Thomas had chosen the latter. He stood with his back to Nick, looking out at the city spread before him.

"It's snowing," he said.

So it was: fat, feathery flakes drifted past the window with a falling hush, as if the world had lowered its voice.

Sir Thomas turned to face him, and Nick was shocked by how haggard the man's face had become in the few hours since Nick had last seen him. A room in the Tower could have that effect, comfortable as this one might be. Sir Thomas must have known, as Nick did, that the farther down in the Tower you went, the more cramped, lightless, and ominous the rooms became. In underground chambers lay the torturer's dungeons, where the rack and the Scavenger's Daughter, an A-shaped metal frame that compressed the body rather than stretched it—a hideous counterpart to the rack invented by Sir Leonard Skeffington—resided, awaiting the unlucky few. It took a cold-blooded, heartless bastard to dream up such a device on his day off, Nick had always thought.

"I regret that it had to come to this," Nick said. "I would have much preferred to have had this conversation at the palace."

What he didn't say and what Sir Thomas immediately understood was that the Queen had been too hasty in having him arrested. Both men knew that it was wise not to criticize the Queen out loud.

"I have to ask where you were last night," Nick said. No point beating about the bush; they both knew why he was there.

Sir Thomas shook his head. He walked to the bed and sat down.

"All right," Nick said. "Try this: Where were you the night Cecily was murdered?"

"Can't remember."

Nick pulled up the chair from the desk and sat facing him. "Silence won't help you," he said. "This is a murder inquiry. The Queen is taking a personal interest." Again, this was code for the Queen being prepared to compel cooperation by any means necessary.

Sir Thomas gave a small smile. Nick couldn't tell if it was the word *murder* or *Queen* that had elicited it, or, perversely, the none-too-subtle threat of torture. Was Sir Thomas that rare type of man who loved violence for its own sake and not simply as a means to an end, as some soldiers did? Or was he just supremely confident in his own physical courage to withstand the rack?

The thought of torture made Nick queasy; it was a last resort but one he would not balk at if it was the only way to get at the truth. Torture was technically illegal in England, but all it took was the merest whiff of treason and it was employed with impunity. And the definition of treason was on a conveniently sliding scale that could encompass almost any act that put the Queen's person or her reputation at risk.

Abruptly Nick stood and crossed to the window. The snow was falling more thickly now, blurring the hard outline of rooftops and spires, smothering muddy lanes and byways, erasing the boot prints in the gravel of the Privy Garden. It was as if all the clues to the identity of the killer of Cecily and Mary, however tenuous, were disappearing before his eyes. The landscape that remained was featureless and led nowhere.

A raven, hunched on one of the stone parapets of the tower, its inky feathers stark against the swirling white, cawed harshly and then swooped down, a slashing black line against a blank page.

Nick turned back to the room. Sir Thomas was still sitting motionless on the bed, elbows resting on his knees, hands dangling between his legs, staring at nothing. He might have been alone for all the attention he gave Nick, as if he had retreated deep inside himself. Was this a result of the shock at finding himself summarily arrested and brought to the Tower, or did it suggest a capacity for detachment that Nick had already observed in the planning and carrying out of Cecily's murder. Perhaps Sir Thomas was one of those men who did not feel fear. Nick had met a few in his line of work, men who exhibited complete unconcern for their physical well-being. Reckless and dangerous, careless with their own lives, they were also careless with the lives of others. Was this the reason why Sir Thomas was considered brave? In Nick's opinion, courage without fear was no virtue at all.

Nick studied him. Sir Thomas was of average height; he was easily strong enough to have overpowered Cecily and lifted her body onto the altar. Cecily had been slender and small-boned; she would have weighed barely more than a well-nourished child.

"Take off your shirt," Nick said.

Sir Thomas glanced at him and Nick saw a momentary flicker of fear, as if he thought the torture was going to start now. Then a shutter came down over his eyes, and he shrugged. Nick watched as he peeled off his shirt. He must have been cold, but he showed no signs of it. A livid scar curved down from his breastbone to below his ribcage, puckered at the edges like an imperfectly sewn hem. Sir Thomas pointed to it.

"Sword slash," he said. "My horse was killed beneath me, so I was fighting on foot." He twisted around so Nick could see his back. Three round hollows to the right of his spine. "Musket balls," he said. "Different battle."

Nick was impressed. Judging from his wounds, Sir Thomas was no tin soldier content to sit safely behind the lines and issue commands. It was obvious he led the charge himself; the wounds in his back clinched it. In order to have taken a round in the back, he must have been in the front lines with the enemy behind him. One of the deadliest and most effective battlefield maneuvers, the pincer movement first encircled and then squeezed, moving ever inward, bringing death from all sides. It was a miracle Sir Thomas had survived. Again, Nick felt, if not liking, a kind of respect for the man.

He indicated Sir Thomas should put his shirt back on. Then he stepped forward and held out the scrap of paper taken from his belongings. "Explain this."

Nick saw a flare of recognition in Sir Thomas's eyes before they went blank again. "Never seen it before," he said. Nick knew he was lying. He got up and hammered on the door for the guard to open it. While the key was jangling in the lock, he turned back. "Did you know Mary?" he asked. Again that brief flicker of something in Sir Thomas's eyes, quickly extinguished.

"Can't say that I did."

Again, Nick knew he was lying. He had seen Sir Thomas dancing with Mary and Cecily both at the Accession Day Ball.

★ ★ ★

Before leaving the Tower, Nick decided to look in on Sir Hugh, hoping that the youth would confess to the murder of Mary and save himself needless suffering before his inevitable trial. Despite his misgivings, Nick had to own that Hugh was the only one he knew of with a motive. Although the evidence against him was purely circumstantial, if Nick could not find unimpeachable evidence that Mary had been killed by someone else, Hugh would die on the scaffold. He was not expecting to learn anything new from the boy, but Nick felt an obscure responsibility for him; after all, it was he who had sent him to this terrible place.

Nick found him in a cell at the bottom of Bell Tower, a room completely different from the one Sir Thomas was housed in, but at least above ground. Small and dark, it had a low ceiling that dripped with damp, the only light a narrow arrow slit high in the wall. As Nick's eyes adjusted to the gloom, he saw Sir Hugh crouched on the floor in a corner, knees drawn up, arms tightly gripping them for warmth. A faint keening came from him. The boy did not look up when Nick entered, seemed not even to be aware of his presence. Nick had seen this same withdrawal before in prisoners condemned to die, as if they had already left the world of men so that what remained was purely animal. Hugh reminded Nick of a young falcon he had caught when he was a boy; it had broken his heart when it preferred to starve to death rather than be kept in captivity.

"Fetch a blanket and some food," he ordered the guard, and then, squatting in front of Hugh, he said his name. No response.

"Hugh," Nick repeated.

Still the boy did not lift his head, but Nick realized the keening was not just inarticulate sounds, but words, spoken over and over. He leaned in closer.

"I didn't do it. I didn't do it."

CHAPTER 16

Bankside

Nick left the Tower after leaving instructions that Sir Thomas was to be held in strict, though comfortable, confinement and not to be molested in any way. He gave the same orders about Hugh but doubted the boy would even notice. He shrank from ordering torture, something he must oversee so as to pose the right questions. Interrogating suspects under physical duress was a fine art: too much and the suspect would say anything to make it stop; too little and the suspect would make up convincing lies that would take time to check. Hugh, he suspected, would say whatever he thought Nick wanted him to say. Sir Thomas would hold out until the end.

Nick suspected that anyone who could survive such terrible wounds as Sir Thomas was a man who could withstand a lot of punishment. Not convinced of the efficacy of physical pain, which could send the subject into shock or render him unconscious, and troubled by its inhumanity, Nick preferred to exert emotional and mental pressure. To do this, he had to know something of his subject, know whom he loved, what he held dear.

He had once extracted vital information from a man who not only was preparing to betray his country but also was on the point of abandoning his family by fleeing to the Continent. Clearly a man of no conscience or ordinary human affections, he confessed when Nick threatened to kill his horse. Shortly before he had captured him, Nick had watched from a dark alley as the man rubbed down his horse and talked to it as one would to a lover. When asked what his last wish was on the day before his execution, the man had asked to say goodbye to his horse.

Nick emerged from Bulwark Gate into a changed world, a world of drifting gossamer, of dazzling light. He stood motionless for a moment, blinking. So thickly was the snow falling, so still the air, he fancied he could hear the sound of each snowflake as it landed. He crossed Petty Wales into Thames Street, his footsteps muffled by the more than three inches that had accumulated since he had arrived. Hector placed his feet hesitantly and snapped at the snowflakes swirling past his nose as if at pesky flies, puzzled when his jaws clamped on nothing. Nick realized this was the first snowfall his dog had seen. He bent, scooped up a handful of snow, shaped it into a ball, and let fly. Hector lolloped after it, snuffling and circling around where it had fallen, then prancing about, tail wagging, tongue lolling, ready for Nick to throw another. He obliged a couple more times before calling Hector to heel. He must hurry if he was to reach The Black Sheep before nightfall. The snow, if anything, was falling faster and thicker.

He continued west on Thames Street. The fish market at Billingsgate had closed early and lay deserted except for a few lads pretending to sweep up, but hampered in their task by the constant need to dodge snowballs thrown by other boys not so industriously minded, ones whose masters had either gone home or had adjourned to The Saucy Salmon on the corner of Fish Street and Thames. The windows were lit, and muffled by the closed door came the sound of raucous singing, the fishmongers clearly celebrating their early release. A black cat with a fish head in its mouth streaked across Nick's path.

London Bridge was quiet, the shops having taken in their wares and put up their shutters, only the faint creaking of cart wheels and the muffled clink-clink of a horse's harness breaking the silence. A carter, a gray shape hunched over the reins, with a piece of sacking cowling his head and shoulders, raised a hand in greeting. Ghostly in the falling snow, he reminded Nick of the somber passing of the death carts during times of plague, when those who took away the dead covered their faces and did not speak for fear of contagion.

As he made his solitary way across the silent bridge so changed from the boisterous clamor of his walk with Rivkah only a few days before, Nick pondered his interview with Sir Thomas. He was protecting someone—of that Nick was certain. A highborn mistress? But someone's embarrassment, even public disgrace, was still not a weighty enough reason for him to risk torture. And if it were not some adulterous tryst he was covering up, why not admit it?

Nick knew Cecily's murderer to be capable of great detachment. Hugh, Nick was now certain, did not possess this quality, but Sir Thomas had certainly struck him as not only intelligent enough to have planned the murder but also self-controlled enough to have carried it out. Could it be that the Queen's fit of pique had inadvertently delivered Cecily's killer into Nick's hands? Sir Thomas was clearly a hard man, battle-seasoned and no stranger to bloodshed and appalling violence, like Nick himself, but there was also a sense of deliberation about him, as if he weighed every word before he uttered it; and he had a curious trick of closing off his mind to those who would seek access to his thoughts, as completely as the shops on London Bridge had now closed their shutters. Now that he thought about it, the notion that Sir Thomas was protecting a lover struck Nick as ludicrous. After taking the measure of the man, Nick couldn't picture Sir Thomas mooning over some woman not his wife; he struck Nick as more likely to seek solace for an unhappy and perhaps sexless marriage in a brothel, where he could walk away without emotional complications or engage in a casual dalliance. But give his heart? Never.

Nick could clearly hear the roar of the water beneath him, a sound usually drowned out by the noise of shoppers and foot traffic, as the river rushed between the starlings of the bridge. It was an odd juxtaposition, the almost magical stillness of the bridge above, the ferocious turbulence below. It reminded him of the Windrush River back home, when it would ice over in winter; yet beneath that apparently solid surface, the river flowed on. As a boy, Nick had once been foolish enough to walk on it and had fallen in. Lucky for him, John had been with him and was able to pull him out before he froze to death or drowned.

This case felt a lot like that to Nick: superficially solid but with hidden, treacherous depths. He couldn't shake the feeling he was on the wrong track, that he had ventured out too far on the ice and that, sooner or later, cracks were going to appear. He prayed that there wouldn't be another murder.

Although it was only late afternoon, Nick glimpsed a woman dressed in a nightgown and sleeping cap lighting a candle in an upstairs window above a leather and saddlery shop. He wondered how those who lived on the bridge could sleep at night, knowing they were suspended over a raging torrent, a few planks of wood all that separated them from a watery grave, much like birds huddled in a nest above a swift-flowing river. Much like his predicament with only one week to catch the killer. His friend Will would be proud of him for coming up with such a poetic analogy, he thought ruefully.

Having experienced his share of storms at sea, Nick marveled anew at how changed the world could become by a simple act of weather, how blind and helpless nature could make man, how puny his will and aspirations. He could barely see five yards in front of him, and the snow had seeped into his boots, turning his feet into blocks of ice. The wind blowing down the river and finding its way between the gaps in the houses buffeted him and drove the snow into his eyes. Looking down, he saw Hector trudging along with his head down, his shaggy coat rapidly turning white along his back.

"Soon be home," he told him.

Bankside was a ghost town when they turned off the bridge, past the Great Stone Gate. There was just enough light to make out the spire of St. Mary Overie and the squat huddle of the Clink Prison on his left as Nick made his way west along the south bank of the river. Sensing home, Hector gave a grateful whine and quickened his pace.

Did the killer move in such a world? Nick wondered. A world emptied of people; a world made silent, ominous, and cold by his smothering hatred of women? Perhaps the blankness of Sir Thomas's gaze was not merely deliberate concealment, but a true reflection of the landscape of an empty and featureless soul. When asked where he had been the night of Cecily's murder, he had said he couldn't remember. Not for an instant did Nick think

244 ⌐ Suzanne M. Wolfe

that was true. On the contrary, Sir Thomas struck him as a man who could account for every waking moment of his life.

Approaching The Black Sheep, Nick saw threads of light around the edges of the shutters and heard a low hum of voices coming from within. Tomorrow he would have to return to the Tower and begin a more strenuous interrogation. For now, he was only looking forward to being indoors, among friends, where he could blot out, if only for one night, the vision of Cecily and Mary's bodies.

As he crossed the road in front of The Black Sheep, Nick bumped into some children building a snowman in the middle of the road.

"Wotcha, Nick!" one of them called out, a runt of a lad with a long-stemmed pipe clamped between his teeth and a slouchy hat pulled rakishly over one eye.

It was Johnnie, the cheeky and felonious ten-year-old grand-son of Black Jack Sims, Bankside's most powerful crime boss. Despite being the heir apparent after his father, John Jr., had been shanked by a rival four years before, Johnnie was popular among the local kids. Impressed by his ever-present bodyguard, Ralph, and as grateful recipients of tobacco and grog filched from the docks, the other boys had elected him their leader.

Johnnie was definitely a chip off the old block when it came to criminal enterprise; his gang swarmed the docklands like an infestation of rats, nicking anything not nailed down. He was the bane of every merchant and captain who docked at the Bankside wharves and who could do nothing about the thieving owing to Black Jack Sims's protection. The grandfather doted on the boy and was pleased as punch that Johnnie showed such criminal apti-tude at so young an age.

Nick was surprised and heartened to see that Johnnie and his gang of diminutive toughs were engaged in something as childishly innocent as building a snowman, even if said snowman was holding a knife in his twiggy hand and was smoking a pipe.

A huge black shadow materialized from under the eaves of the tavern. A hand, which had been hovering over a dagger, dropped to its side when the owner recognized Nick.

"Ralph," Nick said, opening the door to the tavern. "You and the lads come inside and get warm." He had long ago given up trying to refuse to sell Johnnie and his underage crew ale after Black Jack had sent one of his heavies around to "have a little word," as he euphemistically put the threat of retribution if Nick refused to "let the lad wet his whistle once in a while." The rate he was going, Johnnie was on his way to becoming a full-blown toper by the time his voice broke.

Ralph didn't reply. Now that Nick posed no threat to his charge, he had lost interest in him. Nick didn't take it personally. Everyone knew Ralph was dumb both in speech and in wits. Built like the side of a proverbial barn and reputed to be the best knife-man in Bankside—no mean feat in an area filled with violent criminals—Ralph had the mental age of a five-year-old but also the pure devotion of a young child. He shambled behind Johnnie like a trained bear and meekly did whatever he was told as long as it was Johnnie who was giving the orders. Everyone else he either ignored or murdered. Nick would have felt sorry for him had Ralph's habitual expression not been one of blissful contentment, admittedly a little unnerving when he was coming at you with a knife.

Nick walked into a warm fug and tremendous noise. He stood blinking on the threshold. Packed with bodies in varying stages of thaw, cloaks steaming before the fire, puddles collecting around the boots of those newly arrived, the taproom of The Black Sheep was a startling contrast to the ghostly world he had just left, as if he had been rudely awakened from an enchantment.

A man staggered over and clapped him on the shoulder. "If ale be the food of life, drink up," he slurred, raising his beaker and spilling most of it down his front.

"Hello, Will," Nick said. "Bit early to be pissed as a newt, isn't it?"

Will grinned blearily. "I'm celebrating," he said.

"I can see that."

"Phil Henslowe's just told me he's going to build a playhouse in Bankside the year after next," Will said. "He's calling it The Rose." His enormous, lustrous, almost feminine brown eyes shone with delight. "I wanted him to call it The Globe," he said, opening his arms wide and spilling the rest of his drink, "seeing as all the world's a stage. But Phil's a philistine." He paused, swaying, a small frown puckering his hugely domed forehead.
Then he laughed. "*Phil*istine. Get it?"

Nick nodded wearily. He was cold, tired, hungry, dirty, and perplexed. Tomorrow, if Sir Thomas continued to refuse to talk, he would have to put the man to torture. The last thing he wanted tonight was to trade witty puns with a bladdered playwright.

"Congratulations," Nick said. He deposited his inebriated friend on a stool before Will could fall over, then pushed his way through the crowd to the bar, where Maggie and Henry were filling beakers from two large barrels set on the back counter, as fast as they could. Jane, the baby, was sleeping peacefully in a large laundry basket behind the counter. Nick envied her ability to sleep through such a racket, but then the tavern was all she had ever known. She would probably wake up screaming if the tavern suddenly fell silent. In between orders, her mother was taking money, mopping spills off the bar, and fielding wandering hands. Maggie's cheeks were rosy from exertion, and her hair was plastered to her face. Henry merely looked sullen, his usual adolescent expression.

"Tell John we could do with a hand," she said, peering around the row of shoulders hunched along the bar, looking for her husband.

Nick broke the unwelcome news that John was still at Whitehall.

"We need him here," she said crossly. "It's bedlam. Lucky we got in a delivery of barrels before the snow started. Even so, if it goes on like this, we'll run out by the end of the evening."

Nick unbuckled his sword belt and vaulted over the bar. He hadn't planned on helping out—he would have preferred to bunk off to Kat's for a bath, preferably with her in it—but he couldn't, in all conscience, leave Maggie and Henry to cope alone on a night like this. His only hope was that the tavern wouldn't become a doss house if they were snowed in overnight. He didn't fancy a bunch of rowdy drunks sleeping it off, then waking to pounding hangovers the following morning. And with John absent, he didn't like to leave Maggie to the less than chivalrous propositions of the tavern's clientele. The drunker they became, the more amorously inclined and the less likely to take no for an answer, even if Maggie's version was a swift knee in the groin. Oddly, this only seemed to inflame them further, perhaps because they were used to being bullied by their wives at home.

Later in the evening, three hours after nightfall, the snow stopped falling, and much to Nick's relief, the tavern began to empty out. The snow was over a foot high by that time, but as most of the customers lived locally, they opted to walk home. Some of the less fortunate were fetched by irate wives, who glared at Nick and Maggie as if they were the ones responsible for stealing food out of their children's mouths, rather than the shamefaced sot they now held firmly by the collar.

At last the tavern was empty except for Will, who was passed out in the rushes in front of the fire, his head on Hector's flank. Nick draped a cloak over him after banking down the fire for the night.

"Henry and I can manage now," Maggie said, collecting empties and stacking them on a huge tray she held expertly with one hand and balanced on her hip. "You look done in."

Nick kissed her on the cheek, punched Henry playfully on the arm, which elicited a grudging smile, and staggered up the back stairs to his bedchamber. He was stone-cold sober, but weaving with fatigue, so exhausted he might well have been in his cups. He had managed to stuff a few handfuls of bread into his mouth in between shouts for more ale but was too tired to eat more and too tired to wash. He kicked his door shut and fell facedown on the bed with his clothes on.

He was woken by the sound of shouts and smell of burning. Instantly, he was on his feet. Thanking God he had not undressed, nor even taken off his boots, Nick snatched up his sword. Fire was every Londoner's nightmare. In the distance he heard the first clang of the bell from St. Mary Overie, rousing the neighborhood and bidding them come fight a common enemy. Hector was baying, an eerie, mournful sound. Nick's first thought was that the tavern was on fire, but when he careened down the stairs into the taproom, there was no sign of burning. Indeed, there was no sign of

Will, Maggie, Henry, or Hector. The front door to the tavern stood open, letting in the chill night air.

Grabbing a bucket from beside the fireplace, Nick rushed out. He turned left, following the sounds past the Bear Garden, now deserted. Just beyond he saw a seething mass of bodies luridly lit from behind by the burning roof of a house.

"Rivkah!" he cried and broke into a run. As he neared, he was able to make out the shouts coming from the mob.

"Filthy Jews!" one man shouted, a burning brand raining sparks down over the heads of the crowd as he waved it to and fro in the air.

"Burn the vermin!" another man bellowed. There was an ugly cheer.

Elbowing his way through the crowd, he saw Rivkah's face at the window, a white terrified mask. Nick drew his sword and, standing on the front step, pointed it at the crowd. Hector leapt up on the step next to him, baring his teeth. "Stand back," he yelled. "The first man to come any closer is a dead man."

There were a few jeers, but some of the men in the back began to slink away. To his relief, Nick didn't recognize any of them. It would have broken his heart if Eli and Rivkah's neighbors and patients had turned on them. Judging from their clothes and advanced state of inebriation, he reckoned they were sailors come ashore from a ship docked at St. Mary's Queen Dock hard by the Great Stone Gate of London Bridge. The question was: How had they known where Eli and Rivkah lived? Nick filed that away for another time. Right now, all he could think of was how to get Rivkah and Eli out of their home alive.

Feeling for the door behind him, his sword still pointed in front of him, he opened it. "Stay," he commanded Hector, and backed inside, covering his face with the edge of his cloak. He could hear Hector scrabbling and whining at the door.

The tiny, neat kitchen was full of smoke, but no flames that he could see. He could just make out Rivkah in the gray murk. Her hair was wild about her face, and she was dressed in a long linen nightdress. She had a cloth held against her nose and mouth.

"Where's Eli?" Nick shouted.

Rivkah pointed up the ladder leading to the attic. "The roof is burning," she said. Her face was streaked with soot, her mouth trembling, but it was her eyes that stopped Nick cold—they were the eyes of an animal caught in a trap, rolling, white-orbed, crazed with fear.

Now Nick understood. Her home in Salamanca had burned down, torched by such a mob as this. She had tried to save her baby sister and failed.

Wanting nothing more than to gather her in his arms, instead he took her roughly by the wrist and dragged her toward the back door. "Out," he said.

She struggled to break free. "Eli!" she screamed. "I'm not leaving him."

"OUT!" Then, relenting: "I'll get him, Rivkah. I swear." He pushed her through the back door and locked it to prevent her from reentering. He heard her beating on it, cursing him in Spanish.

At that moment there were shouts from outside. Someone howled in pain. The sound of footsteps running away. Risking a quick glance through the window, he saw one of Black Jack Sims's bullyboys laying about him with a cudgel. Kat's man Joseph was wading through the crowd, lifting men up above his head and tossing them farther back into the street as if they were so much firewood. It was the first time Nick had seen him in action as the Terror of Lambeth, and he was impressed. One sailor was lying in the snow, a dark pool spreading around his head; the others were backing off, eyeing the crime lord's ruffians warily, recognizing professionals when they saw them. Hector had a sailor by the leg and was shaking him back and forth as if he were a rag doll. One brave soul darted forward, took the prone man by the ankles, and dragged him back toward the docks. Hector let go of the leg, and its owner limped away, whimpering.

"Let them go," Black Jack ordered. Despite his advanced age, he was propping a ladder up against the house. Nick heard Maggie's voice calling for buckets and a human chain to be made from the river. He glimpsed her holding Jane tightly against her shoulder. Scanning the crowd, he recognized Kat and some of her girls, Master Baker and his wife, Harry the Tinker, Will, and Henry, all carrying buckets.

"Use the snow," Black Jack bellowed from the top of the ladder. "The river will take too long." People hurried to fill their buckets from the drifts in the street and began to pass them up the ladder.

Wasting no more time, Nick climbed to the loft. He could just make out Eli pulling down great hanks of smoldering thatch with a fire hook and stamping on them. *Thank Christ for the snow,* Nick thought as he joined him.

"Mouse?" Eli shouted.

"She's safe."

"Blessed be He," Eli muttered.

★   ★   ★

In the end, it was the snow that saved the house and Eli and Rivkah's lives. The thatch was so sodden that the firebrand that had been tossed onto the roof had failed to spread. As it was, the house was uninhabitable until a new thatch could be put on, and Harry the Tinker said he had a mate—Tom the Thatcher, inevitably—who would do it.

They were gathered in the taproom of The Black Sheep, he and Eli and Rivkah coughing from the smoke, all cold and dirty. Henry had made up the fire and Maggie had set a big cauldron of wine on it. She was ladling the hot wine into pewter tankards and passing them around. Rivkah was crouched on a stool near the fire, wrapped in a sheepskin coverlet from Maggie's bed; her face was white and still and blank. She had not said a word since Nick had reunited her with Eli after they had put out the fire. Eli had his arm around her shoulders, holding her close. Nick caught his eye, and he shook his head minutely as if to say, *She'll be all right. Just give her time.*

"You must come back to the house with me," Kat was saying to them. "We've got plenty of room."

"Thank you," Eli said. Rivkah did not respond, but just sat staring dully into the fire.

To take his mind off his anxiety for her, Nick turned to Black Jack Sims. "Thanks for lending a hand." The man's quick thinking about using the snow had probably saved the rest of the house from going up.

Black Jack almost smiled but then caught himself just in time. "Think nothing of it," he said grandly. "I was just protecting my investment. I own the house."

"That explains it then," Nick said, playing along. He happened to know that Black Jack thought the world of Eli and Rivkah, which was only partly due to the fact that he was a martyr to gout and swore that only their physic gave him any relief. But Nick also knew that Black Jack regarded them as kindred spirits—both he and they being exiles from the law. That he had probably broken all Ten Commandments numerous times had never seemed to occur to him.

A milky dawn was breaking when people began to drift off to their homes. Nick watched as Kat took charge of Rivkah and, arm about her, guided her out the door. Kat glanced back at him over her shoulder and shrugged. Nick could see she was as worried as he was.

"I'm going back to bed," Nick said, stretching.

"Me too," Henry said, yawning ostentatiously.

Maggie announced that, since she was already up, she might as well stay up, and that went for Henry as well. His face fell. Nick winked at him as he made his way to the stairs.

CHAPTER 17

Bankside

Nick slept hard and woke much later than he had intended. At first he was confused as to where he was, the eerie white light and strange silence outside so alien to the usual gloom of a winter's morning and ear-splitting racket of Bankside going about its business just below his window. He threw back the covers, then immediately regretted it and almost dove back under again. He had forgotten to close the shutters the night before, and the room was freezing. Hopping from foot to foot, he dragged on his clothes, which stank of smoke from the night before; stuffed a clean shirt and hose into a leather satchel; grabbed his sword belt and boots; and stumbled down the stairs.

"I'm off to Kat's," he told Maggie as he pulled on his boots.

Maggie gave him a sidelong glance as she poured warm ale into a cup and handed it to him. "You'll need your strength, then," she said, cutting him a wedge of cheese and pushing it and a small loaf of bread toward him.

"For your information, I'm going for a long, hot soak," Nick said, buckling on his sword, downing the ale in one gulp, and grabbing the food to eat on the way. "Be back in an hour if anyone wants me."

"Make sure Kat washes all the naughty bits," Maggie called after him as he left.

★   ★   ★

In addition to the peevishness provoked by Maggie's comment, the events of the night before had dampened Nick's ardor and hopes that Kat would join him in the bathhouse. Just as well, as Kat gave him a chaste peck on the cheek, thrust a towel and bar of soap at him, and left him to it. Kat seemed distracted, Nick thought, as he submerged himself in blessedly hot water and shut his eyes.

He found out the reason when, fully dressed in clean clothes, newly shaved, and smelling pleasantly of the lemon oil he had poured liberally into the bath water, he sauntered into Kat's bedroom. He found Kat and Lizbeth, one of the girls from the brothel, tending a woman who was lying in Kat's bed, looking more dead than alive if the parchment of her face and the unnatural stillness of her repose were anything to go by. The room was stiflingly hot and close, like the bathhouse he had just left. A cauldron of boiling water was steaming over the fire, and rags with blood on them were soaking in a bowl. From an old wooden cradle with a carved hood, next to the bed, came snuffling sounds and a faint mewling. Nick peered in and saw a tiny scrap of a baby with a newborn's red, scrunched-up face, impossibly small fists bunched up under its chin, its scrawny little limbs tightly bound in linen swaddling bands. He leaned down and offered the baby his pinkie and was astonished anew, as he had been with each of his newborn nephews and nieces, at how strongly the infant gripped his finger.

"How is she?" Nick asked, understanding now that the corpse-like figure in the bed, little more than a girl now that he had moved closer and could see better, must be the poor woman on whom Eli had performed the Caesarian the day before.

"She's alive," Kat replied. "Just."

"And the baby?" Nick asked, rocking the cradle with his toe.

"Surprisingly robust, considering the poor little mite was breeched and taken untimely from the womb," Kat said, looking down at him, her face briefly softening. "Poor little mite," she repeated quietly to herself. "If he survives, it looks like he'll be motherless."

"He'll have you," Nick said. Kat had never given birth as far as he knew, had never even fallen pregnant, very unusual for a woman of her profession. He knew that Rivkah was her personal physician and would never discuss her patients' ailments with anyone, except perhaps her brother if she needed advice. And although she had never said anything directly, Nick knew, from a few things Kat had let slip over the years, that the way she had been violently and repeatedly raped in the brothel when she was a girl had somehow damaged her inside. Now she was past child-bearing age. From the way she allowed her girls to keep their babies when they fell pregnant—most madams would employ a wise woman to get rid of them with potions and other, more hideous, means—Nick was certain the lack of a child of her own was one of her greatest sorrows.

"What's his name?" Nick asked.

"He hasn't got one yet. If Emily recovers, she can christen him. Otherwise. . . ." Kat shrugged and turned back to the woman on the bed and began wiping her forehead with a cloth she dipped in cold water from a bowl on the bedside table.

The baby was squalling with a vengeance now, its face screwed up and almost purple. Nick picked it up and jigged it up and down in his arms, pacing the floor.

Kat looked over and smiled. "I didn't know you were a nurse-maid," she said. "You have hidden talents."

"Plenty of practice with my brother's brood," Nick said. He stuck his little finger in the baby's mouth, and immediately the baby started sucking vigorously. "This little fellow is hungry," Nick said. "He's not going to be fooled long."

The girl called Lizbeth took the baby from Nick, sat down in a low nursing rocker by the fire, and with a complete lack of self-consciousness, unbuttoned her chemise and offered a large, blue-veined breast to the child. He gave a last tiny mew, then latched on and started gulping greedily. Lizbeth bent her head over him, murmuring endearments. Her bare rounded shoulders, falling curtain of hair, and curved arms enfolded the babe in an inviola-ble circle from which the world in general and in particular he, as a man, was excluded.

Nick remembered that Lizbeth had recently lost her own infant son to whooping cough. Now, watching how tenderly the girl gave the child suck, how protectively she held him, Nick felt a lump forming in his throat. Two souls, one bereaved and one soon to be bereaved, had found each other. That was a rare thing in a world in which innocent girls were murdered and women were forced to sell their bodies so they wouldn't starve. He turned away before he became unmanned in front of Kat, but it was too late; she was regarding him with an expression he would have called love in any other woman.

At that moment, the door opened, and Eli and Rivkah came in. Nick scanned Rivkah's face surreptitiously and was relieved to see her usual air of unflappable composure had returned. Gone the blank-eyed stare of the night before. Her dark eyes took in Nick, and something flashed there, but then they quickly sought the woman lying on the bed. She nodded to Eli as if silently communicating a diagnosis, and they immediately crossed to their respective patients, Eli to Emily on the bed, Rivkah to the baby in Lizbeth's arms. The relief Nick felt at the return of the Rivkah he knew was quickly replaced by mortification. Bad enough that Kat and Rivkah and he were together in the same room, but that the room was Kat's bedroom made it infinitely worse. He felt himself blushing furiously. Chagrined, he made for the door.

"I'll be off then," he called over his shoulder.

"Let's call the baby Nicholas," he heard Lizbeth say. "Nicky for short."

Nick fled. He didn't want to see the expressions on Kat and Rivkah's faces, let alone have to protest that he wasn't the child's father. He doubted whether either of them would believe him. At the bottom step he heard someone call his name. Looking up, he saw Rivkah leaning over the balustrade. "Thank you," she said. "For last night." She was gone before Nick could think of a reply.

★   ★   ★

Feeling less burdened than he had felt in a long time, despite the fact that he felt in his bones that a murderer was still on the loose, Nick nipped back to The Black Sheep to pick up a few things and told Maggie of the Queen's ultimatum about solving the murder before Christmas. His fear that he was being tested for his loyalty, he kept to himself.

"I suppose that means I won't see hide nor hair of the pair of you for the week," she said; then, putting a hand on his arm, "You and John be careful, Nick. This man is a devil."

"I need Hector with me," Nick said. "Sorry." Ordinarily, he would have left the dog to guard Maggie, Henry, and Jane if both he and John were not there, but he had a feeling Hector's nose was going to come in useful.

"I'll send over to Kat and borrow Joseph if things go pear-shaped. Don't worry."

"Black Jack Sims owes me a favor or two," Nick said. "He said his lads would be patrolling the waterfront until the murderer is caught."

"I'll not have that riffraff in my tavern," Maggie replied, eyes flashing. She made no secret of despising Black Jack, but for all that, he had always treated her with gallantry. Privately, Nick thought Black Jack admired her spirit. If the man had been a couple of decades younger, Nick would have been worried for John's health.

Nick set off for the Tower back the way he had come the previous evening. As he trudged across the bridge, he wondered how the sailors had known which house to burn. Perhaps someone from the court had talked about the murders in one of Bankside's many taverns or the Bear Garden or even Kat's brothel. But they still couldn't have known Eli and Rivkah were Jews unless whoever it was knew Nick and who his friends were. It made him profoundly uneasy, as if there was a spy in their midst. Then he gave an ironic and slightly despairing laugh: He could name one: Himself.

Shaking off this futile train of thought, he considered how best to approach Sir Thomas. By the time he entered the Tower

Gate again, he had decided that the direct approach was the best: he would take him down to the dungeon where the instruments of torture were kept and let him feast his eyes on them while he questioned him. If that didn't work, he would, reluctantly, be forced to use them.

Shivering more from the thought of deliberately and cold-bloodedly inflicting pain on another human being than from the cold, Nick approached Sir John.

"I'm here to see Sir Thomas," Nick informed him.

Sir John looked at him with surprise. "He's not here," he said. "An order came from the Queen this morning to release him. I thought you knew."

Without saying a word, Nick turned on his heel and left.

★   ★   ★

The city of London was struggling to emerge from the smothering cocoon of snow that had temporarily immobilized it. Household servants and shop apprentices were busily shoveling their doorsteps and the street directly in front of their premises. Delivery carts were scarce, for most people had thrown the snow into the middle of the street, making it all but impassable. Nick was forced to stop only once when a stray shovelful of snow landed squarely on his boots. The grin on the shop-boy's face faded when he saw Nick's expression.

"Sorry, mister," he said, pulling at his cap.

Nick grunted and moved on, Hector keeping pace at his side, sensing his master's mood of cold fury.

On reaching Whitehall, Nick pushed past the soldiers at the front entrance, ignoring their protests, and took the stairs two at a time.

"Let me pass," he ordered the guards at the door of the Queen's apartments. When they refused to uncross their pikes, Nick hammered on the door. Behind it he could hear the Queen's voice pause in full rant and then the bellow, "Let him in, you dolts!"

Glancing nervously at each other, the guards stepped aside. Nick gave them an evil grin and entered the room.

"Where the hell have you been?" were the first words out of his sovereign's mouth.

Nick opened his mouth to reply, but the Queen had already lost interest, turning instead to her primary victim, Cecil, who, Nick was pleased to see, was standing in the middle of the floor, cap in hand, misshapen shoulders slumped, like a naughty schoolboy receiving a tongue-lashing from his tutor. John was standing near the window, keeping well out of it. Sir Thomas was standing next to Cecil, looking as stoic as ever under the hail of imprecations raining down on their heads. As soon as Nick had learned Sir Thomas had been sprung from the Tower, Nick had put two and two together. Sir Thomas was one of the Spider's London agents, the domestic equivalent of Nick himself.

Only Codpiece looked relaxed. He was perched on a footstool in front of the fire, paring his nails with a dagger and looking bored. Briefly his eyes sought Nick's and flashed a message: "If you know what's good for you, you'll keep a sock in it."

Injecting himself into the conversation—if a one-way royal bollocking could even be called such—was tantamount to standing in front of a charging rhino. Nick wasn't stupid or suicidal, so he crossed his arms and prepared to enjoy the spectacle in silence.

"Just when were you going to inform me that Sir Thomas was one of your spies?" the Queen was saying. She had been pacing in front of the hapless Spider but now halted directly in front of him, close enough no doubt for him to feel her breath on his face. Given that Elizabeth's teeth were black with tooth decay from the sweetmeats she loved, Nick didn't envy him that experience.

Cecil waited a heartbeat in order to ascertain whether the question was rhetorical or not, then plunged in.

"I was intending to inform Your Majesty when Sir Thomas had got sufficient proof of a plot to defraud you."

"*Proof!*" Elizabeth shouted. "And when would that be? When I was reduced to receiving foreign dignitaries in my shift? Perhaps begging in the street?"

Nick winced.

"I didn't want to worry you," Cecil said.

"I'll be the judge of that!" the Queen bellowed. She stabbed a finger into his chest. Cecil flinched but stood his ground. "Do you think I need a nursemaid?" Stab. "Do you think I'm a puling weakling who gets a fit of the vapors if she breaks a nail?" Another stab. "Perhaps you think," she went on in a deceptively gentle tone, "I'm a weak woman who needs protecting from unpalatable realities by the likes of you?"

Definitely rhetorical, Nick thought, hoping the Spider would be foolish enough to offer a reply. Disappointingly, Cecil kept his mouth shut.

The Queen resumed pacing. "You've made me look a fool, Spider," she said quietly. "I arrested my own spy in front of the entire court."

The Queen had never used Cecil's nickname in public before, and for the first time, Cecil looked afraid. She had never humiliated him like this, and more than anything else she had said, her willingness to do so now was the truest measure of her fury.

Despite himself, Nick felt a twinge of sympathy. The Queen in full apoplectic spate was infinitely preferable to this deceptive softness of tone, this apparent world-weariness.

"Get out," she said to Cecil, turning her back on him.

Cecil opened his mouth to speak and then wisely thought better of it. Giving a more than usually low obeisance, he backed out of the royal presence and left the room.

Nick had no doubt he would receive a summons from the Spider later, a summons he was intending to avoid if he could. He had no desire to be on the receiving end of the Spider's wounded pride after being so publically dressed down in front of two of his most trusted spies. Nick was well aware that shit always flowed downhill.

The Queen sat down in a chair by the fire but did not invite the others to do likewise. Without a word, the Fool filled a goblet with wine and handed it to her. She quaffed it off and held it out for a refill.

"So," she said after a long pause, regarding Nick and Sir Thomas over the rim of her goblet. "Let me see if I've got this straight. A murderer is running around my court, killing my ladies in an effort to discredit me." She turned her eyes on Nick and then on Sir Thomas, who had not moved a muscle during the entire time Nick had been in the room. "And unbeknownst to me, Cecil tells me that you, Sir Thomas, are his spy and are close to having evidence of some kind of tax fiddle going on at the docks. Have I got that right, gentlemen?"

Both Nick and Sir Thomas nodded.

Nick risked a glance over the Queen's shoulder at John and saw him shrug as if to tell him he was on his own with this one.

"What do you think, Fool?" the Queen asked Codpiece.

"I think Your Majesty is surrounded by fools," he replied, completing his manicure and buffing his nails on his jerkin. "Perhaps Your Majesty should employ me as a spy?"

The Queen looked at him sharply before laughing. "Perhaps, Fool. Perhaps."

Nick saw Sir Thomas's mouth twist with contempt. Nick was careful to hide his own admiration of the Fool's acting ability, although for a panicky moment, he had thought Codpiece had been too clever by half and had almost given away his true role. In reality, Codpiece had been testing Sir Thomas. The Queen, Nick saw, had been just as startled until she realized what the Fool was up to. She was smiling now, and Nick saw that the Fool had also intended to cheer her up with a veiled reminder that, through him, she had a secret weapon at court. Clever, clever Richard.

Elizabeth sighed. "Right," she said. "Let's have it then." She pointed a finger at Sir Thomas. "You start."

Drawing himself up to military attention, Sir Thomas began. He told the Queen that when he was stationed in the Netherlands, he had been recruited into the spy network by Sir Robert Dudley, his commander, who had recommended him to the Spider.

At the name, the Queen's face softened slightly. Nick silently applauded Sir Thomas for throwing in her favorite's name. Behind the soldier's stoic demeanor was a sharp mind and not a little cunning. Nick was starting to like the man.

"When I returned to England, Cecil contacted me," Sir Thomas was saying. "He already had a chief spy on the Continent." Here Sir Thomas glanced at Nick. "Although I didn't know his identity."

And I didn't know yours, Nick thought with an irritation directed more at the Spider than at Sir Thomas. For the first time, Nick saw that the Spider's insistence that each spy in his network should be ignorant of the identity of his fellow spies could be a weakness rather than a strength. It was true that if one were caught, he could not name others under torture. But it was also true that sometimes they operated blind and at cross-purposes as had happened in the fiasco of the day before. Nick suspected that the Spider's need to be the only one who knew everyone was more to do with a love of power than a need for security. He and Sir Thomas needed to have a nice long chat.

Sir Thomas continued detailing his investigation into widespread fraud on the docks, where luxury items like wine, spices, glass, and precious stones and metals were recorded as much humbler commodities.

"Such as?" the Queen asked.

"Dried peas, horn, barley, tallow," Sir Thomas said. "Anything, as long as it is cheap and common enough for the tax to be low."

"How long has it been going on?" The Queen was obviously totting up how much she had been bilked, and she did not look pleased.

"Five years," Sir Thomas said.

"*Five years!* And you have only just discovered this?"

"Yes, Your Majesty." Sir Thomas turned to Nick and held out his hand. "If I may?"

Nick gaped at him for a moment. Then the penny dropped. He withdrew the scrap of paper he had confiscated the day before from among Sir Thomas's personal effects at the Tower and handed it over.

Elizabeth held out her hand, and Sir Thomas passed it to her. She squinted at it for a few minutes before returning it. "What is it?"

"Part of a secret ledger kept by Master Summers. One of my agents is embedded as a scribe in the Custom House; he managed to tear off a small piece before he was interrupted. Fortunately, he was able to maintain his cover. Now we have proof, we are planning on raiding the place shortly."

Elizabeth studied him. "Well," she said, "at least you're making progress. Albeit five years too late. Perhaps I should demand that you repay me the monies lost in taxes, Sir Thomas? That would be a pretty incentive to harder work, don't you think?"

"Yes, Your Majesty."

"And you," Elizabeth said, turning a flinty gaze on Nick. "Speaking of hard work. I see you have caught the murderer. Just when were you planning on informing me of this, might I ask?"

Oh, bollocks, Nick thought. *Here it comes.* Out loud, he said, "I have doubts about Sir Hugh's guilt, Majesty."

Nick could have added that her monumental cock-up in having an innocent man, one of her own spies to boot, put in the Tower had wasted an entire day, but he refrained. He was in enough hot water as it was.

"Doubts?" the Queen said. "Hear that, Fool?" she informed Codpiece with a sarcasm so profound, Nick shuddered. "He says he has doubts. Well, fancy that!"

"Perhaps, Majesty, you should hear him out?" the Fool suggested. For once his tone was completely serious.

Elizabeth held her Fool's gaze for a moment and then turned again to Nick. "Go on then," she said. "Astonish me. And make it good."

Nick detailed the events surrounding Mary's death, her assignation with Hugh in the Privy Garden, their argument, the approximate time Rivkah had determined that Mary had died.

At the mention of Rivkah, Sir Thomas glanced at him, obviously intrigued.

"So far I am not hearing anything but a motive for Sir Hugh to kill Mary," the Queen said.

Nick then explained that the difference in the way the two girls had been killed made him suspect that there might be two different murderers.

"*Two?*" The Queen's expression darkened.

"Yes, Majesty," Nick said. "I can see Hugh killing Mary in the heat of passion but I cannot picture him planning and carrying out Cecily's murder. I believe that whoever killed Cecily is still at large and is extremely dangerous." He decided that now was not the time to add that Hugh's hopeless repetition of denial in his cell the previous day had begun to make Nick wonder if he were innocent after all.

After he finished, the Queen sat silent for a long time. No one moved a muscle, not even Hector, who, sensing squalls ahead, had taken refuge with John as soon as Nick had entered the room. Even the Fool kept his peace. Nick could hear doors slamming in the corridors, voices shouting, a dog barking—even, he fancied, the shriek of seagulls skimming over the river.

A log collapsed on the fire, sending up a shower of sparks, and the Queen roused herself. She looked from Nick to Sir Thomas and then back again, as if assessing them. "Cecil speaks highly of your abilities," she said at last.

First I've heard, thought Nick.

"So I will be patient a little while longer." She stood up. "I want results, gentlemen." She pointed to Nick. "Now that Sir Hugh is in custody, I cannot hold the court off much longer. They are baying for his blood. People are frightened; they want answers. And so do I." The way she said it made it clear this was a royal command. "Therefore, find me a murderer. Or two murderers," she added. "I don't care as long as you do it. And you," she said, pointing to Sir Thomas, "find me those cozeners."

Nick and Sir Thomas bowed, and along with John, who sidled past the Queen as if she had the plague, left the room.

It wasn't until they had entered Nick's room in the palace and were seated in front of the fire, with a cup of ale in their hands, that they allowed themselves to relax.

"Bloody hell," Nick said.

"I'd rather face the rack," Sir Thomas said, running his hand over his face. It was the first time Nick had seen his composure crack.

"I don't think so," Nick said.

Sir Thomas looked at him. "Would you have tortured me?"

Nick shrugged. "Probably. No offense."

Sir Thomas gave a weak grin. "None taken."

Nick briefly told John about the fire. At first it was all he could do to stop him returning to Bankside. John kept asking about Maggie and the children.

"They're fine," Nick said for the umpteenth time. "Henry rather enjoyed himself," he added then regretted it when he saw John's jaw tense. "Black Jack's boys are keeping an eye on things until we get this sorted." When his friend still looked unhappy, Nick said, "I need you here, John. Maggie and the children are safe."

"All right," John said eventually. "So what happens now?"

"Now," Nick said, putting down his cup and getting to his feet, "I'm off to interview an apothecary's apprentice." With no other leads to go on, Nick thought he might as well satisfy his curiosity about the mysterious servant who had purchased Guinea spice for his master. A waste of a morning, he suspected, but he couldn't just sit in his room and wait for his deadline to expire or, worse, the murderer to strike again. "You?" he asked Sir Thomas.

"I'm going to stay right here by this comfy fire," he said.

"Avoid the Spider, you mean?" Nick said.

"And my wife," Sir Thomas agreed.

"By the way," Nick said, "seeing as you're being so affable all of a sudden, what's the name of this mystery woman you're seeing?"

"Who says I have a mistress?"

"I do."

Sir Thomas looked at Nick for a moment, then shrugged. "She wasn't my mistress," he said. "A dalliance, no more."

Nick waited. He had noticed the use of the past tense.

"It was Mary."

Nick nodded. Hugh had told him that Mary had taunted him by saying that she was sleeping with a man and not a boy. She must have been drawn to Sir Thomas's hard-bitten air of experience, his quiet self-confidence, so different from Hugh's vain posturing. He had also been right in his assessment of Sir Thomas's character; he would never dishonor his wife by taking a permanent mistress but, like many men—like Nick himself—would find temporary assuagement of his lust with someone known to be promiscuous. He wondered if Mary had known this or if she had thought she had found true love. The thought made Nick sad. But Sir Thomas could not have been with Mary the night before. Almost every moment of her last hours were accounted for. Even so, he could understand why Sir Thomas had been reluctant to name his lover to the Queen the day before in such a public place as the Great Hall. Coming so soon on the heels of Mary's violent death, he might have been torn to pieces by the mob.

"You were investigating the custom fraud the night Mary was murdered," Nick guessed, another piece of the puzzle falling into place.

"That's correct," Sir Thomas said. "So you see, I couldn't very well blurt that out in front of everyone, could I?"

"You could have told me when I talked to you in the Tower."

"I didn't know about you and Cecil then, did I? I had no idea I could trust you."

Before Nick could reply with a scathing comment about the Spider, there was a knock on the door.

"Come in," he shouted.

A page in the Queen's livery entered. Behind his shoulder, standing in the doorway, Nick glimpsed a woman who looked familiar.

"Someone to see you, Your Honor," the page announced with ridiculous formality. He was young, Nick noted, perhaps only eight, the minimum age for a page, and new at his job, judging from the pristine nature of his uniform. Give him a few months and he would be as slapdash, scruffy, and insolent as the rest of the Royal Pages.

Nick beckoned for the woman to enter, and when she stepped into the light, he recognized Mistress Plunkett, Sir Christopher's cook.

"I'm sorry to disturb you, Your Honor," she said, bobbing a

curtsey and glancing nervously around the room as if she expected to see the Queen sitting there.

"Not at all," Nick said. "Come in and sit down."

"I'll stand if you don't mind, sir," she replied.

Nick noticed that she was doing her best to erase her London accent, but she was nervous, even distraught, and it kept creeping back into her speech. It would have amused him if he had not picked up on her distress. He introduced her briefly to John and Sir Thomas. "Now, Mistress Plunkett," he said. "What can I do for you?"

"It's Perkin," she said. "He's gone and fetched up dead."

CHAPTER 18

The Fleet Ditch

Nick stood on Ludgate Bridge on the corner of Bridewell and Fleet Streets, staring down into the ditch. Formally a wide river, the word *fleet* being a derivation of the Saxon *flod*, meaning "flood," the Fleet was anything but a flood now. Originating from a spring on Hampstead Heath in Caen Wood and emptying into the Thames, it had once been Roman Londinium's main source of sweet water. As the city grew, it had been used by Londoners as a convenient repository for their household waste, despite numerous royal edicts banning such a practice. A succession of kings had vowed to have it cleared of debris and offal, to reinstate its former swift-running glory when it was said that ten ships could sail up the river side by side, but it had filled up with rubbish almost as fast as it had been dredged, its water undrinkable for centuries. One of Nick's classics tutors at Oxford had told him he had found Roman coins on the bank; Nick hadn't asked him what he had been doing rummaging around ankle-deep in shit with his moth-eaten robe hoicked up about bony knees, but that image had given him much solace as he sat in his tutor's stuffy rooms, translating endless passages of Livy and Cicero.

Now he watched as the two guards he had commandeered from the palace, strips of cloth tied over the lower half of their faces to stop them keeling over from the noxious vapors emanating from the great sewer, dragged the body of Perkin out from under the stone balustrade of the bridge nearest to the bank and laid him flat on his back. If the weather had not been so cold, the sewer all but frozen solid, the body would have washed into the Thames and might never have been found. Nick was not sure why he had come to view the body except that Mistress Plunkett had reached out to him in her distress and the Fleet was on his way to the apothecary's.

On the walk over, he learned from Mistress Plunkett that a servant from the Fleet Prison, emptying the piss pots that morning, had seen a foot sticking out from under the bridge. He had alerted the turnkey, Master Plunkett, and he in turn had recognized the lad and sent for his wife.

Nick crossed the bridge and clambered down the slick sides of the embankment to the Fleet, trying not to inhale nor look at the mountain of filth below, even though it was covered in snow. John and Sir Thomas prudently opted to remain on the bridge. Despite her husband's objections, Mistress Plunkett had returned to Sir Christopher's house, saying she had to prepare a meal in readiness for her master's return that afternoon.

Shuddering with horror at the thought of falling into the ditch, Nick gingerly approached the body. Perkin lay as if asleep, eyes closed, face relaxed. Nick sighed. He didn't think he could stand looking at the premature death of the young one more time.

He had ordered a bucket of water to be brought from the prison well and now signaled to one of the guards, making sure to stand well back. The guard sluiced the body down, washing the muck off the face and front of the body, and Nick crouched beside it to get a closer look. He had already sent for Eli and had asked him to meet him at the Fleet Prison on the bank above them, but he found that studying a corpse in situ was often helpful. The body was in pretty good shape considering it had lain in a sewer for several days. The cold and snow had kept the rats at bay and prevented the body from sinking into the morass or being carried to the Thames.

Perkin's right arm lay at an odd angle, partly under the body, and straightening it, Nick realized it was broken at the elbow. He glanced up at the bridge, judging the distance. If the body had been tipped over the balustrade, the arm could have broken on impact. From his conversation with Mistress Plunkett the day before, Nick estimated that the boy had been murdered the night before last—the same night Mary had been killed—after running away from Sir Christopher's house. But for the absence of bruising to the face and grazed knuckles, Nick would have thought the most likely cause of death was a tavern brawl turned deadly. After witnessing the boy's hatred of the dog and his master, Nick thought Perkin just the sort to pick a fight after downing a few pints of ale.

Nick ran a finger over the crude stitching in the boy's hose near his ankle and felt a sudden stab of pity. The boy had not lived long enough to get a new pair of hose, let alone shave every day. His short life had been dominated by the whims of a foolish master and a canine nemesis who nipped perpetually at his ankles.

Mistress Plunkett had said that Perkin's mother was dead and his father had been a violent drunk. Slowly Nick got to his feet. Not for the first time, he wondered at the benevolence of a God who had ordained that this boy should have such a brief and miserable life when his so-called betters lived long, luxurious existences before dying peacefully in their beds.

At a sign from Nick, the guards lifted the body onto a makeshift stretcher and, slipping and sliding, carried it up the bank. Nick followed. Perkin's broken arm fell over the edge of the stretcher and flopped toward the ground, jolting with each ungainly step the guards took. When they reached level ground at the top of the bank, Nick lifted it and placed it gently across the boy's chest. The body was then carried into the prison and laid on a table that had been brought into an empty cell.

Again, it was Rivkah who arrived instead of Eli. "Emily's taken a turn for the worse," she said. And then to Nick's unspoken question: "The baby is thriving."

He took her aside. "Are you up for this?" he asked in a low voice. "After last night, I mean." He could still smell the smoke in her hair.

"I'm fine." She turned away, but not before Nick had seen a look of gratitude in her eyes.

Sir Thomas raised an eyebrow at a woman's presence in the death chamber but wisely held his tongue. When Rivkah began to strip the body, he looked away, as if embarrassed.

"No wounds on chest or belly," Rivkah said. "But look here." She pointed to a crust of blood in the corner of Perkin's mouth that Nick had missed. "It looks like he coughed up blood. Help me turn him."

When Perkin was facedown on the table, Nick could clearly see what had killed him. One stab wound in the lower back over the right kidney and one stab wound higher up between the shoulder blades, slightly to the left of the spine. There was extensive dark bruising on the back, where the blood had settled. "This accounts for the aspirated blood," Rivkah said, pointing to the higher wound. "The knife punctured a lung. And it looks as if it also punctured the aorta. And this," she said, indicating the wound in the lower back, "tore through the kidney."

Nick shuddered. "How long would it have taken Perkin to die?"

"If the first blow was to the aorta, then moments."

"Weapon?" John asked.

"Long, wide blade, I'd say."

"Not a stiletto?"

Rivkah placed her index finger and thumb on either side of one of the wounds. "See for yourself." Her fingers were almost two inches apart. "And he was already dead when he broke his arm." She had rolled up Perkin's sleeve and was pointing to the elbow joint where a sliver of white showed through the flesh. "No bleeding."

So Perkin was dead when he went over the bridge. He hadn't been the first dead body to be disposed of that way.

"No sign of a struggle," Rivkah said, wiping her hands on a cloth. "That's why I think the first stab was to the aorta. He would have bled internally so fast that he would have quickly lost consciousness. The stab to the kidneys was to make sure."

That tallied with what Nick had seen for himself. Either Perkin had known his attacker, enough to have felt safe turning his back on him, or he had been taken completely by surprise from behind, say, in a dark alley.

If Rivkah was correct about the aorta, then Perkin would have dropped where he stood, mortally injured. The killer had then carried his body to the bridge over the Fleet and tipped him in, hoping the body would go undiscovered. And if December had been its usual wet month and not one of unseasonable cold, his plan would have worked. Either the rats would have destroyed Perkin's identity, and he would have ended up in a pauper's grave with *Nemo* chalked on a crude wooden cross, or he would have been carried out to the river and eventually drawn out to sea by the tidal flow.

Nick walked over to the barred window that looked out onto Shoe Lane. The sun had come out and was melting the snow on the rooftops. The steady drip, drip, drip from the eaves was like the deadline for solving the murders, counting down.

"What time did your wife say she was expecting Sir Christopher's return?" Nick asked, turning back into the room. Master Plunkett was standing by the door, turning his great ring of keys around and around in his hands, his eyes going everywhere except to the body in the middle of the room. He had known the lad, Nick remembered.

"Sometime this afternoon," the turnkey replied.

"Right," Nick said, making up his mind. "We'd better inform him his servant's been murdered." He let John and Sir Thomas precede him from the room. Master Plunkett followed. Rivkah was covering Perkin with a blanket. Nick saw how gently she laid it over him, smoothing it down like a mother tucking a child into a bed.

"Sorry to keep dragging you across the river," he said.

Rivkah shrugged. "If a physician cannot keep someone alive, then the next best thing is to find out how he died."

"Perkin wasn't your patient," Nick said.

Rivkah smiled. "To a physician, everyone is a patient."

Unconsciously, Nick touched a finger to his scar.

They split up outside the prison, Sir Thomas gallantly offering to escort Rivkah to Temple Stairs, where she could catch a wherry back to Bankside. He offered her his arm, and with a quick glance at Nick, she took it. Nick watched as they turned right on Shoe Lane toward Fleet Street and the Strand. Sir Thomas was saying something to her, his head close to hers, and Nick could see her profile beneath the habitual hood she wore as she lifted her face up to his, laughing.

Accompanied by John and Hector, Nick reluctantly turned in the opposite direction to Holborn, then right toward Cheapside. John was headed to Sir Christopher's to await the nephew's return; after seeing Rivkah onto a wherry, Sir Thomas said he had business elsewhere. Nick guessed that it was to do with the fraud case and asked no questions. Nick himself was going to beard Master Hogg, the apothecary, in his den on Candlewick Street, a short walk east from Cheapside. If Wat was out running errands, then Nick was determined to get a list of his customers and track him down. They arranged to meet up again at Sir Christopher's afterward.

"Think this death is connected with the ones at the palace?" John asked.

"I don't know," Nick said. "The type of killing is completely different from Cecily's and Mary's murders."

"Three killers?" John stopped in the road to stare at Nick.

Nick shrugged.

They walked in silence for a few streets. "The knife is bothering me," Nick said eventually. "It seems too big for street use. More like a carving knife than a dagger."

John pulled a face. "This case is getting me down. It seems like everywhere we look, we find a new murderer."

Nick clapped him on the back. "Be patient. We'll get there."

Despite his words, Nick was deeply frustrated by the anomalies in all the murders, not least in this latest murder. Why, for instance, did Perkin's killer not just leave him where he dropped and make his escape? Why risk discovery by carrying him to the bridge and tossing him over? Even that late at night, there was seldom a time when the streets were completely empty. Filled as it was with the destitute, London was alive with silent watchers. His guess was that the killer lived in the vicinity and did not want a body cluttering up his doorstep or the local watch asking awkward questions. The Fleet was just far enough away to serve as a convenient dumping ground.

As they came to the Cross at St. Paul's, Nick saw a small bundle of rags hunched on the lowest step, rocking back and forth in an effort to keep warm. He walked over and hunkered down in front of her.

"Hello," he said. "Remember me? Did you see anyone come this way last night? A man? Perhaps carrying something?"

The girl stared at him. Her skin was chalk-white, her lips blue. Her thin body shuddered as if with fever. Nick couldn't tell if she recognized him from before or if she had even understood his question. Coming to a decision, he reached into his money pouch and, bringing out a shilling, held it in front of her face. A spark came into her eyes, and she reached out a dirty claw.

"You can have it if you come with me," he said.

Immediately she took his hand. Nick wondered how many men had offered her money but for very different reasons. Nick heard the pie-seller on the corner mutter, "Filthy bastard!" before spitting on the ground; the man was obviously thinking the same thing.

"She can get warm by Mistress Plunkett's fire while I go talk to Wat," he explained to John. "She'll die if she stays outdoors. Perhaps we can talk to her when she's recovered."

John nodded and looked away. Nick knew he was thinking of his own daughter, Jane.

They proceeded more slowly, matching their steps to the child's. Instead of shoes, her feet were wrapped in rags, and she walked with a stumbling, stiff-legged gate. Nick feared frostbite. Perhaps he would ask Rivkah to take a look at her, even though he was loath to drag her back across the river twice in one day. Suddenly his promise of a shilling didn't seem enough. Not even close. He realized he didn't even know the girl's name. Scooping her up, ostensibly to lift her over a pile of snow, he kept hold of her. She weighed almost nothing. After a while she gave a little sigh and laid her head on his shoulder. By the time they arrived at Sir Christopher's house in Cheapside, she seemed to be asleep.

Carefully transferring the girl into John's arms without waking her, Nick continued on to Candlewick Street with Hector loping beside him. He had toyed with leaving the dog with John but figured that he might get less of Wat's cheek if Hector was with him. Innumerable times in the past he had found that the unblinking gaze of his monstrous pet could unnerve even the most reluctant witness, encouraging them toward garrulity if not truthfulness. Nick didn't tell them that what Hector was probably thinking about was not tearing them limb from limb, but taking a nice long nap in front of a roaring fire at The Black Sheep.

On the way, Nick went over Perkin's murder. If Perkin had been killed by a thief, why had a lad who obviously didn't have two farthings to rub together been chosen? Mistress Plunkett had said that nothing seemed to be missing from the house when he had talked to her in the kitchen the other day. And if a drunk in a tavern, then why did Perkin's body have no signs of a fight. It was possible, of course, that Perkin's natural insolence had rubbed someone the wrong way, and he had been set upon after leaving a tavern. But that didn't explain the location of the body. Why would a stranger go to all that trouble to dispose of the body? Perhaps a tapster had discovered the body on the premises of his tavern and decided to get rid of it quietly.

It was possible the killer could have been someone Perkin knew from the neighborhood, but this was unlikely. Despite its name, Cheapside was far from cheap, populated as it was by wealthy merchants and shopkeepers selling luxury goods; not the type of neighborhood frequented by either drunks or vagabonds. The nearest tavern was The Mermaid, which catered to respectable business types in the heart of the Guild district. If Perkin had been found in Bankside, Nick would not have been nearly as troubled.

It looked as if Perkin's death was a completely random event, but the more Nick thought about it, the more he had a feeling that there was a connection between the killings. This vague unease— not even a hunch, but more like a pricking of his thumbs—was why he needed to find Wat. Nick pushed open the door of the apothecary, in no mood to trade banter with either Master Hogg or his apprentice.

"Can I help you, sir?" Master Hogg asked. He was writing something in the ledger and had not looked up when the bell rang above the door.

"I'm here to speak to Wat," Nick said.

The apothecary raised his eyes. "You," he said. Then his gaze shifted to Hector, who was sniffing at the floor. The dog let out a tremendous sneeze, and Master Hogg jumped, spilling ink from his quill.

"You've blotted your copybook," Nick pointed out.

"And you've just missed Wat," the apothecary said with some satisfaction.

"I need a list of his deliveries."

"That's confidential."

"Fine," Nick replied. "I'll just wait here until he returns." He walked behind the counter into the back room of the shop and sat down, crossing his legs. A flagon of ale and a cup stood on the table. Nick cleaned the cup with his sleeve and, filling it, drank. "Not bad," he said. "Not as good as The Black Sheep's, though."

At a signal from Nick, Hector lay down in the middle of the floor. A customer came to the door but, when he saw the dog, decided his purchase was not so urgent and went away.

Master Hogg tore off a corner of the ledger and started scribbling. "This is harassment," he grumbled, handing the list to Nick. "I've a good mind to lodge a complaint."

"Make sure you ask for an audience with the Queen in advance," Nick said, taking the paper. "She's a bit busy at the moment."

He left Master Hogg standing behind the counter with his mouth open—it was getting to be a habitual expression—and left the shop. Glancing at the list, he saw that Wat's first delivery was on the same street as The Mermaid, just around the corner. He smiled to himself. He knew exactly where to find him.

Just as he'd thought, Nick found Wat slouched on a stool in the corner of the tavern, a tankard of ale on the table in front of him. Surrounded by wealthy merchants in velvet doublets and cambric shirts, Wat's fustian made him as conspicuous as a nun in a whorehouse. Nick plonked himself down on a stool opposite. Hector sat down next to Wat, effectively boxing him in.

"Time for a chat?" Nick asked pleasantly.

"I suppose," Wat mumbled, eyeing Hector warily.

Nick waved over the woman making the rounds, with a tray balanced on her hip to collect the empties, white breasts pushing up out of her bodice so far Nick doubted she could safely lean over. Nick noticed Wat getting an eyeful.

"What'll it be, sir?" the barmaid asked, quickly sussing that Nick was the one with the money. She had pointedly turned her back on Wat who, Nick suspected, was one of those cursed tavern patrons who nursed a beaker of ale for hours, taking up valuable space where those more frequently imbibing might sit. He had a few of those in The Black Sheep. Harry the Tinker came to mind, a malodorous lump forever cadging drinks from the other customers and trying to pinch Maggie's bottom whenever she passed. She only tolerated him because he seemed to have nowhere else to go.

"Mulled wine, I think," Nick replied. He nodded at Wat's tankard. "And the same again for him." He ordered bread and vegetable soup for himself and beef bones for Hector. "Make that two soups," he said, seeing the wistful look on Wat's face. The boy brightened.

"Ta," he said. Then his face darkened with suspicion again. "What do you want?"

"You're not as thick as you look," Nick said.

As they ate, Nick regarded the apprentice over the top of his bowl. He ate like a starveling, hunched over his bowl, spooning in the broth as fast as he could, and cramming large pieces of bread into his mouth. Nick remembered what is was like, as a growing lad, to be perpetually famished, and Wat could not be much older than sixteen if his gangly frame, huge hands and feet, and the unattractive bloom of acne on his chin and forehead were any-thing to go by. Nick waited until the boy had finished, partly out of kindness, partly because he had no desire to view the masticated contents of Wat's mouth as he ate and talked at the same time.

"That hit the spot," Wat said at last, belching hugely. Like a full-fed baby, his eyes were already beginning to droop. In a few minutes he would be nodding off.

"Tell me about the servant who purchased Guinea spice for his master on November third," Nick said.

"No livery," Wat said drowsily. "Which was strange, come to think of it, because he had a full purse of gold on him. So his master must have been stinking."

"Anything else?"

"He were a scruffy cove."

"Did you talk about anything?"

Wat gave him a look as if Nick had lost his senses. "Master Pig-Face were there, weren't he?" he said, as if this explained everything.

Nick smiled at the nickname.

"He usually serves the posh customers. Leaves me to serve the riffraff. Even so, he doesn't like me passing the time of day with any of them," Wat concluded. "Miserable sod," he added by way of punctuation.

"Would you recognize the servant if you saw him again?"

"Might do." Wat sat up. "What's this about then?" he asked, showing interest for the first time.

Nick stood up. "Murder," he said. "Get your cloak. We're going for a little stroll."

Once Nick had popped his head into the apothecary's and informed Master Hogg that he was borrowing his apprentice for the afternoon on the Queen's business, Wat cheered up considerably and regaled Nick with the names of all the barmaids in the taverns from Cheapside to as far away as Shoreditch.

"That piece in The Curtain is a right strumpet," he said, as if this were a compliment. "I go out there quite a bit to see the plays. Have a drink after."

"Like the theater, then?" Nick asked.

"Nah," Wat replied. "I only go to feel up the prossies."

"Charming," Nick muttered.

★ ★ ★

They stopped off at Sir Christopher's house on their way to the Fleet. Nick told Hector to guard the front door—he didn't want to risk Mistress Plunkett's wrath by decorating her gleaming floors with muddy paw prints. Hector gave him an accusatory look but did as he was told.

"Good boy," Nick said.

Wat gave him a sidelong glance as if he thought him mad to be talking to a dog.

"At least he listens," Nick said, pushing open the door. "Unlike some I know."

Wat grumbled something that sounded suspiciously like "off his bleeding rocker" and followed Nick inside the house.

A leather saddlebag was lying on the floor by the stairs. Nick heard voices and followed them to a back room on the ground floor. Judging by the look of it, Sir Christopher used it as his study. It was small and cramped, with only enough room for a table strewn with papers by the casement window, which looked out on the long, narrow strip of garden and the path where Nick had found Sir Christopher's dog. A chest, lid open to reveal a tumble of parchment rolls, was pushed against the wall opposite, and a chair at the desk at which Sir Christopher was seated were the only other items of furniture. Nick leaned against the door-jamb, as the room was already crowded by the presence of John standing just inside the door to the right. Wat hovered irritatingly over Nick's shoulder, his beery breath and toxic body odor enveloping him in a noxious fug. Nick was beginning to regret bringing him along.

"It's terrible," Sir Christopher was saying to John, blowing his nose loudly on a white cambric handkerchief. "Poor little thing. And Perkin, of course," he added, seeing Nick in the doorway. "Do you need me to formally identify the body?"

"No need to trouble yourself," Nick said with heavy irony. It was clear Sir Christopher didn't give a monkey's about Perkin except, perhaps, to be irritated that he would now have to find another servant and also possibly because, with Perkin being dead, he couldn't prosecute him for the death of his beloved pet. "Mistress Plunkett identified the lad."

"Terrible," Sir Christopher repeated, fiddling with a quill and inkpot on the table, as if he were eager to get back to work and the news of his servant's death was but a trivial interruption in his busy schedule.

Nick waited to see if Sir Christopher would ask how Perkin

had died, but he did not. Nor did he show any sympathy for his longtime cook who'd had to see the body. Nick thought that there was hardly a man he had come to loathe more than this foppish, self-centered man, and found it incredible that the countess had taken in the likes of Sir Christopher and made him her heir. Just another reason to rail at Fate, in Nick's opinion. Or God.

"I'm assuming you'll want to see to the arrangements for the burial," Nick said in a hard voice.

"Eh?" Sir Christopher looked momentarily puzzled and made a faint gesture toward the window and the garden beyond.

"Not the bloody dog," Nick said. "Perkin." The boy's father had sounded as if he were too poor or too indifferent to see to a proper church burial for his son. If Sir Christopher did not shell out a few shillings, then Perkin's body would end up in a pauper's grave, tipped into a shallow pit in the corner of the graveyard where beggars, prostitutes, and other unfortunates ended up.

Sir Christopher blinked. "Oh," he said. "Quite."

Nick turned away in disgust. John followed him along the passageway and back into the hall.

"So," Wat said. "Master Fancy Pants needs another servant, does he?" He cast an appreciative glance around the hall and snuffled the air where the aroma of cooking meat and fresh baked bread was emanating from the kitchen.

"Forget it," Nick said brusquely. "You're better off with Master Pig-Face, believe me." Wat looked crestfallen, but he nodded. He too had taken Sir Christopher's measure.

Nick turned to John. "Where did he say he'd been?"

"Dover. To check on a cargo of wine that had been held up at Customs." John shrugged. "We can confirm that, but it will take a week."

"At least," Nick said. It was two days hard riding to the south coast, and that was only if the freeze continued. Rain would turn the roads into rivers of mud.

"Pity we can't arrest him for being a heartless bastard," John growled. He nodded at Wat. "This the apothecary's dogsbody then?"

"Hey," Wat said with a hurt expression.

"I want him to take a look at Perkin's body." Nick shrugged. "Probably a dead end."

Wat smirked. "Dead end," he said. "Nice one."

"Shut up," Nick and John said in unison.

Nick and Wat left the house. John said he would wait for Sir Thomas to show up.

Before leaving the Fleet, Nick had requested that Perkin's body remain in the cell.

"What if I have to use it?" Master Plunkett complained. "We're full to bursting as it is."

"I'm sure the presence of a corpse would be salutary on the criminal mind," Nick said. "*Tempus fugit*, and all that."

"Eh?"

Once there, Nick led Wat toward the cell. The lad hung back at the door, perhaps thinking that Nick had tricked him and he was about to be arrested.

"Come forward," Nick said. "Do you recognize him?"

Nick drew back the covering from Perkin's face.

"Blimey," Wat said. "That's him." Now he had plucked up courage, he seemed fascinated by the corpse, touching Perkin's face with his finger, as if to make sure he was really dead. He didn't seem upset, merely curious.

Nick didn't reply. He now knew that the same person who had murdered Cecily had killed Perkin.

"Come with me," he said.

Nick ran back through the streets to Cheapside, dodging carts and pedestrians and being liberally cursed for his pains until those shouting glimpsed Hector; then their invectives subsided into low mutterings. Wat followed close behind.

On the way over to the Fleet, the puzzle of how Perkin had ended up dead began to make sense. Wat's identification had been the final piece. And Nick was furious with himself for not seeing it before, would always blame himself.

Arriving breathless at the door to Sir Christopher Stokes's house, Nick hammered on the door with his fist until John opened it.

"What the—?" he said as Nick and Wat pushed past him.

"Where's Sir Christopher?" Nick shouted, running down the passageway and glancing into the study. Empty. Returning to the hall, he took the stairs two at a time. The leather bag that had been lying at the foot of the stairs was gone. Hector began sniffing the floor, a low growl vibrating in his throat. If only he had brought his dog into the house the first time he had visited, Nick thought. Another thing he would never forgive himself for.

Reaching the landing, he looked into the room where he had questioned the countess, but it was empty, as were two of the bedrooms. Hector had followed him up the stairs and was now ranging all over the upper floor, tracking. He ran into one of the sleeping chambers, a large, ornate room at the front of the house with a casement window overlooking the street. Women's clothing lay neatly folded on the bed; a jewel casket was open on a small table. It was obviously the countess's room. The dog put his forepaws on a stool in front of the table and nosed at the casket, upsetting it and scattering necklaces, rings, hairpins, and brooches.

"Get out of there," Nick ordered, gathering up the jewels and trinkets and shoveling them back into the casket. The last thing he needed was for the countess to complain to the Queen that he had been going through her things.

Nick ran out onto the landing and tried a fourth door. It was locked. Nick kicked it in, the jamb splintering around the lock. At the sound of the door breaking, John appeared. Together they entered the room. It was Stokes's bedchamber, judging by the yellow doublet lying untidily on the bed and a strong scent of something that irritated Nick's nose. On a table by the bed, Nick saw a twist of paper. When he opened it, red granules spilled onto the floor. He sneezed. Guinea spice. He recalled Sir Christopher's dog sneezing when his master had been holding him, the hand-kerchief that Sir Christopher had blown his nose on in the study. Nick had thought he had been upset by the death of his dog, but now it appeared it was from a reaction to his dog. When he first visited the house, Nick had noticed how liberally coated Sir Christopher's doublet had been with dog hair; his whole house must be full of it. Eli had told him that many people sneezed around dogs and cats, even horses, he said. Matty had heard someone sneeze in the chapel and all this time Nick had been assuming it had been caused by a cold.

"Sir Christopher left just after you," John said. "What's going on?"

"I need to find him," Nick said. "Wat identified Perkin as the servant who paid for the Guinea spice."

John swore softy. "I'm sorry, Nick," he said. "I didn't have anything to hold him on."

"Not your fault," Nick said. He jerked his head back downstairs. "I'm going to take Mistress Plunkett and the girl away from here. When I've done that, I want you to find the location where Perkin was killed, starting with the kitchen. And search this room. You're looking for a will. And John?"

His friend looked up from going through the contents of a chest.

"Arm yourself."

At that moment, Sir Thomas appeared at the top of the stairs. He was red in the face and panting as if he had run all the way from the river. "We need to find Sir Christopher," he said. "He's involved in the tax fiddle. I just arrested Summers, who confessed before I'd even laid a hand on him. Apparently, the reason why Sir Christopher has to go down to the docks to personally supervise the unloading of a shipment is so that he and Summers could fiddle the dockets. I also found out that Sir Christopher's been stirring up trouble at the docks about the Jews. Seems it was he who told the sailors where to find your friends."

Nick grunted. Now it made sense why he had harbored suspicions about Sir Christopher all along, although he had put it down to his intense dislike of the man. Nick was certain that Matty would identify Sir Christopher's voice as the man's voice she had overheard in the chapel.

"We have another problem," Nick said, pushing past Sir Thomas and descending the stairs, heading for the kitchen. "Take Wat and get a deployment of guards from the palace. Bring them back here."

"What's going on?" Sir Thomas asked, running down the stairs behind him.

"No time," Nick said. "Just do it."

Looking uneasy, but without saying another word, Sir Thomas left the house, followed by Wat. Nick suspected that this was the most exciting day of the lad's life. It could have been the most exciting day of Perkin's life too except that Nick suspected that he'd somehow found out about Cecily and had had to die. Nick could not yet account for the time that had elapsed between Cecily's and Perkin's deaths, but speculated that the servant could have been blackmailing the killer—Perkin was certainly bright and cocky enough to have thought he could get away with it. The fact that Sir Christopher said he had been in Dover did not signify; he could easily have lied and remained in London, staying perhaps at one of its myriad inns, only coming to the house after dark. Nick believed that the dog had been strangled to prevent its yapping from alerting the neighbors to Perkin's murder. In fact, the more he thought about it, the more it seemed to make sense.

Ordering Hector to guard the front door, Nick barreled into the kitchen. Mistress Plunkett was cutting into a pie at the table. He glanced around for the girl, but there was no sign of her.

Mistress Plunkett nodded at the pantry door. "She's in there," she said. "Sir Christopher came to ask when his dinner would be ready, and she started screaming the place down. Then she hid." She gave a sad smile. "Reckon she's had her fill of men, seen things no child should ever see."

Nick believed the girl had witnessed Sir Christopher dumping Perkin's body. Yet another thing Nick had royally ballsed up. St. Paul's Cross was equidistant between Sir Christopher's house and the Fleet River. Anyone coming from Cheapside to the Fleet would have been noticed so late at night, especially if they were carrying something heavy or even wheeling a small handcart. Even if the girl had been invisible, curled up in a dark doorway, her terrified reaction at seeing him and Mistress Plunkett's explanation of where the girl had come from put them both in grave danger. Confronted by the accusing eyes of the girl, he had fled. This was now the endgame because the killer now had nothing left to lose.

"I need you to take the girl and go to your husband at the Fleet Prison," Nick said.

Mistress Plunkett's brow furrowed. "The master'll be wanting his dinner."

Nick shook his head. "Sir Christopher left. There's no time to explain," Nick said, seeing a look of puzzlement, then alarm, on her face "I need you to trust me. Can you do that?"

Mistress Plunkett looked at Nick for what seemed like a long time. Nick was desperate to get them off the premises, but he didn't want to frighten her or the girl.

At last, Mistress Plunkett nodded. "Reckon I can," she said. She went over to the pantry and gently opened the door. Nick saw the girl crouched in the farthest corner, wedged between a barrel of flour and the wall.

"Come on, love," the cook said. "This nice gent's going to take us someplace safe." She held out her hand to the girl, and after a moment, the girl took it and allowed herself to be drawn out into the kitchen.

Nick grabbed a piece of pie off the table and, crouching down, handed it to her. "Mind if I carry you?" he asked.

The girl solemnly regarded the pie, then looked up at the cook. Mistress Plunkett gave her an encouraging nod.

"Has he gone?" the girl asked, the first words Nick had heard her utter.

"He's gone," Nick replied, his heart twisting at the terror and misery of her short life, her utter friendlessness. "I won't let him hurt you."

"All right," the child said in a small voice as she held her sticklike arms out to him.

"Brave girl," he said, lifting her and resting his cheek briefly on her matted hair. "Brave little girl."

She looked at him with great serious eyes. Then she put her head on his shoulder, arms clasped tightly around his neck, almost strangling him. Once they had left the house, Nick fretted at Mistress Plunkett's slowness. Even now, the killer might be getting away. It was all Nick could do to force himself to maintain a moderate pace.

"What's this about?" Mistress Plunkett asked.

"Have you seen the countess recently?" Nick asked, ignoring her question.

Puffing and panting at his side, the cook shook her head. "She usually stays at her manor in Convent Garden when her nevvy's away."

Nick stopped in the middle of crossing a road. "I thought she owned the Cheapside house?"

"That belongs to Sir Christopher," Mistress Plunkett said. She gave him an appalled look and put a hand over her mouth. "Oh my God," she said. "To think I've been living in the same house as a killer all this time."

"Watch yourself," a carter shouted.

Nick put a hand under the cook's elbow and moved her out of the middle of the street. "Tell me where the manor is," he ordered, deliberately brusque in order to snap her out of her panic. He could not afford to have a hysterical woman and a vulnerable child on his hands right now.

After dropping Mistress Plunkett and the girl off at the Fleet, Nick began to run, Hector loping by his side. He had told Master Plunkett to send a message to Sir Christopher's house so that when Sir Thomas arrived with the guards, he would know to go to the countess's house on Cockspur Street.

"By order of the Queen," Nick shouted back over his shoulder.

CHAPTER 19

Cockspur Street

Fortunately, Convent Garden was a little closer to the Fleet than to Whitehall, situated as it was north of the Strand and Charing Cross. But the area was huge and abutted an even bigger space—St. James's Park. Without the address the cook had given him—Cockspur Street was the road that divided Convent Garden to the east and the park to the west—Nick would have had to cover acres of land, some of it densely wooded. An impossible task, even with the help of Hector.

He found the countess's manor set in a garden so large it was like a small park, the huge oaks and elms surrounding the house black against a pewter sky. Winded from his run, Nick leaned against a tree for a moment until his breathing slowed to normal, then followed the driveway to a large graveled forecourt. Rooks cawed at him from the trees. A single horse, still saddled, stood quietly nosing at the grass through the snow. It lifted its head, stepping nervously when it saw the dog, but when Hector ignored it, it lowered its head again and went on cropping.

The manor was ancient, a huge rambling two-story structure

of whitewashed timber and plaster. Like parts of Binsey House, it probably dated back to the time of Edward Longshanks. A deep covered porch at the front led to a vast oak door, black with age and the grime from generations of hands. The door stood ajar. Quietly removing his sword from the scabbard on his hip and slipping his cloak off his shoulders for greater ease of movement, Nick pushed it and entered. Immediately, Hector's hackles rose along his back, and he gave a low, rumbling growl.

Putting his finger to his lips for silence, Nick made the signal for "seek." Immediately, the dog moved to the bottom of the staircase and alerted.

Stepping as quietly as he could on the polished oak floor-boards, Nick mounted the stairs to a wide upper gallery with doors leading off it. Hearing raised voices, he stopped and, keeping to the wall, inched forward toward the room and chanced a quick glance inside.

Sir Christopher and the countess were standing on either side of a wide fireplace, facing each other. Nick ducked back out of sight, but not before he had seen a knife in Sir Christopher's hand.

"The girl recognized me," Sir Christopher was saying.

"What girl? Make sense, man."

"A beggar girl. The one who always sits on the steps of St. Paul's Cross. Somehow Holt found her and brought her to the house. When I walked into the kitchen, she recognized me and started jabbering, said she'd seen me, knew what I'd done."

"You're a fool," the countess spat. "A puling, lily-livered fool. I curse the day I ever took you in."

"And you're an evil old witch!" Sir Christopher shouted back. "My father was right about you. He hated you and so do I. So did my mother."

"How dare you?" the countess said. "My sister loved me. It was your father she hated. He made her life a misery with his rants and his jealousy. Drove her to an early grave."

"Shut your filthy mouth about my father."

Nick chanced another look. Sir Christopher was advancing toward the countess, blade raised in his left hand. She seemed unaware of the danger.

"I gave you a home and property and a place at court. I treated you as if you were my own son. And this is how you repay me?"

Sir Christopher tugged his forelock in a sneering parody of a servant doing obeisance to his master. "I thank you for your money and property, Aunt, but the price is too high. Putting up with your unreasonable commands, your absurd whims. 'Yes, Aunt, no Aunt, three bags bloody full, Aunt.'"

Nick flinched at Sir Christopher's quote from the nursery rhyme "Baa, Baa, Black Sheep." It was the tune Rivkah had hummed and the reason why he had changed the name of his tavern. It reminded him that it had been Sir Christopher who had set the mob on Eli and Rivkah.

"As for your loyalty to that Tudor whore . . ." Sir Christopher said.

The countess's eyes flashed. Maligning her sister was bad enough, but attacking the Queen herself was not to be borne. Nick tightened his grip on his sword and prayed the countess would not do something stupid.

She did. No sooner were the words out of her nephew's mouth than she took a step forward and delivered an open-palmed crack to his cheek.

"Traitor!" she bellowed. "Ungrateful, misbegotten wretch!"

It was so fast, Sir Christopher did not see the blow coming, and delivered with the full force of the countess's considerable bulk behind it, it rocked him back on his heels. "You fat bitch," he screamed, raising the dagger.

Nick was through the door in a flash, sword raised. The countess's eyes widened and Sir Christopher whirled around, grabbing the countess as he did so and holding the dagger to her throat.

"Drop your weapon," Nick commanded.

"You don't understand." The hand that held the knife was shaking. A trickle of blood ran down the countess's neck, and she gave a low moan.

"I do, you know," Nick said, keeping his voice calm. "I understand everything. I understand why you did what you did."

Sir Christopher had spotted Hector and didn't seem to have heard. "Call off your brute," he implored.

Hector was circling Sir Christopher and the countess, his lips peeled back in a snarl.

"Down," Nick ordered. Immediately the dog sank into a crouch.

"Talking of dogs," Nick said, "it was a pity about yours."

For the first time, something human flickered in Sir Christopher's eyes. "I don't want to talk about it," he said in a low voice.

"Always the coward," the countess sneered.

Sir Christopher's arm tightened about her throat.

"When Perkin was killed," Nick said, "the dog wouldn't stop barking. Am I right?"

Sir Christopher nodded.

Nick recalled the spots of blood on the dresser in the kitchen. Not made from plucking chickens as Mistress Plunkett had thought, but from a stab wound, much like the drop of blood left in the pew where Cecily was killed. "Must have been a nuisance having to get rid of the body," Nick said. "Perkin's, I mean." He inched a fraction closer as he was speaking. "Couldn't have it cluttering up the kitchen for Mistress Plunkett to find."

"He was heavy," Sir Christopher said. "Surprisingly so, considering how thin he was."

Nick inched a little closer. "Thin because you were too mean to pay him enough."

Despite the knife to her throat, the countess nodded. "Blood tells," she said, addressing Nick. "His father was common as muck."

At the mention of his father, Sir Christopher's hand holding the dagger jerked and a fresh trail of blood snaked down his aunt's neck. "I said, shut up about my father, you bitch." Nick kept his eyes on Sir Christopher's knife hand. It had begun to tremble violently.

Another step. He was only two feet away from Sir Christopher now. The countess was watching him. Nick silently willed her not to move.

"Give me the knife," Nick repeated, holding out his hand. "Killing your aunt is not going to help you."

"I'm already lost," Sir Christopher whispered. "He will never forgive me."

"Who?" Nick asked.

Sir Christopher jerked his chin toward the ceiling.

"You mean, the Big Man *up*stairs?"

At the word "up" Hector sprang, Nick lunging forward at the same time. Dropping his sword, he grabbed the hand holding the dagger with both hands, preventing Sir Christopher from pushing it home. The dog fastened his jaws around Sir Christopher's leg and hung on. Sir Christopher staggered but remained upright. Nick was surprised at how strong he was. They struggled for control of the knife, their faces only inches apart, the countess's bulk in between them, hampering Nick's movements. When Nick looked in Sir Christopher's eyes, he saw nothing. No fear, no triumph, no pain, no hope. The strain of fighting Nick for the knife was beginning to show. A bead of sweat rolled down from Sir Christopher's hairline. Perhaps the countess felt this momentary weakness, for it was in that instant that she jabbed her elbow into her nephew's stomach. His grip on her loosened, and she tore herself free. Nick bent at the knees and, using all his strength, came up and forward, bringing Sir Christopher down and landing on top of him, both hands still locked around the other man's wrist. Hector immediately transferred his grip to Sir Christopher's throat. Nick banged Sir Christopher's hand down hard on the edge of the fireplace, and the dagger came free, skittering across the floor.

"I recommend you don't move a muscle," Nick said. He stood, dusting down his clothes. He felt contaminated and suddenly immensely weary.

"Guard," he told Hector. The dog was slow to obey, and Nick didn't blame him one bit. He made a mental note to reward Hector with the largest bone he could find. Nick had trained him to go into a crouch at the command of "down." The word "up" was the signal to attack. Simple, really. But it was amazing how many villains mistakenly thought a crouching dog was a quiescent dog.

Sir Christopher lay rigid, almost catatonic with shock, unaware that Nick had no intention of allowing Hector to rip his throat out. Nick wanted him alive.

Out of the corner of his eye, he saw the countess pick up the knife. The look she gave her nephew was one of pure hatred.

"You are a monster," she said to him. "I see that now. I thought I could save you from the taint of your blood, raise you from your low birth. I was wrong. Now you will die for your crimes." She spat on him. "I curse you as I cursed your father."

"Countess," Nick said.

She looked at him and drew herself up. A small part of Nick could not help but be awed at her self-control. "I commend you, young man," she said. "You have caught the fiend who butchered those young girls, who took the life of his own servant, even his own dog. Rest assured, I shall inform the Queen of your bravery."

"Give me the knife, Countess."

Out of the corner of his eye, he saw Sir Christopher raise his arm, and Nick half-turned toward him; seizing her chance, the countess threw herself toward her nephew, dagger upraised. Nick tackled her in mid-strike. Snarling, she turned, the blade grazing his shoulder as he twisted away. Clamping one hand around her wrist, he spun her toward him and punched her in the face with the other, sending her staggering back toward the fireplace. A loud crack as the back of her head struck the mantel, and she sank to the floor, unconscious.

A horse whinnied outside and there was the sound of hooves. Stepping over the prone form of the countess, Nick looked through the casement window and saw a troop of horsemen riding into the forecourt below. At the head of the troop was the captain of the Palace Guard, with John and Sir Thomas directly behind, followed by four soldiers. Nick opened the window.

"Up here," he called.

CHAPTER 20

The Tower of London

Nick entered the Tower and, accompanied by a guard and one of Cecil's secretaries, made his way once again to the Bell Tower.

"This is the one," the guard said, halting at a heavy oak door banded with iron with a sally port set in the center. Two stools had been placed in readiness beside the door for Nick and the scribe. Normally, the prisoner would have been brought to another room to be interrogated, a room designed to give more comfort and light to the interrogators rather than the prisoner. But the Queen had forbidden this: the last glimpse of daylight the prisoner would ever see, she averred, was to be from the scaffold, a cruel taste of the dawn before the fall of the ax sent the soul spinning into everlasting night.

Handing the lanterns to Nick and the scribe, the guard unhooked a huge ring of keys from his belt, selected one, and fitted it into the lock. "I'll have to lock you in, I'm afraid," he told them. "Orders."

Ducking his head under the low lintel, Nick entered the cell.

The first thing that met him was the noisome stench from an overflowing bucket in the corner that served as the prisoner's privy. Holding the lantern higher, Nick made out a shape in the corner, which, as his eyes grew accustomed to the dim light, gradually resolved itself into a human form.

The Countess of Berwick was hunched on a low stool next to a filthy straw pallet—the stool and primitive bed the extent of the luxury the Queen was prepared to concede to the age of such a despised felon. Behind him, Nick heard the scribe quietly setting up his writing equipment, followed by a soft scraping as he sharpened his quill. Nick placed his own stool a short distance from the countess, sat down, and put the lantern on the floor between them. The countess blinked at the unaccustomed brightness, the first sign of life she had given. Then she spoke.

"You," she said.

Nick had been prepared to see a change in the countess's appearance since he had apprehended her at the house on Cockspur Street two days ago, but nothing as radical as this. Dressed in the gray, coarse dress given to female prisoners to preserve a modicum of decency, her hair tangled and matted, her face begrimed and with a livid swelling under one eye from the blow he had given her, he hardly recognized her for the great lady she had once been. Gone the rich brocades and jewels, the haughty carriage of the head, the air of authority; gone the veneer of the court with its meaningless courtesies and the semblance, at least, of goodwill.

The countess drew herself up, her manner as imperious as if she were receiving him at court instead of in a reeking, squalid cell deep within the bowels of the Tower. "You can be sure the Queen will hear of this, young man. The way I am being treated is an outrage. Conduct me to her at once." She made as if to rise.

"Sit down," Nick said. "You are here by express order of the Queen."

The countess sank back on her stool. Then, visibly rallying, she said, "There must be some mistake."

"No mistake." A quick glance over his shoulder told Nick the scribe was ready with quill poised. A small, taciturn man, he looked completely at ease, as if he took notes every day in squalid cells thick with the choking miasma of human suffering. Perhaps he did, Nick reflected.

"I don't understand," the countess said. "You have arrested my nephew for the crimes. Why am I here?"

"You know why."

The countess just looked at him.

"I know everything, Countess," Nick said. "I know how you planned the murders; I know how you carried them out. I know that you forced your nephew to be your unwilling accomplice in covering up Perkin's murder. I even know it was you who killed Sir Christopher's dog. I have made my report to the Queen, and she is satisfied that you are guilty. As am I. So let's not beat about the bush, shall we? All I want to know is why. Why did Cecily and Mary have to die? Perkin, I understand; somehow he found out and had to be silenced. But the ladies?"

"The first mistake you made," said the countess, ignoring his question, "was to assume that Cecily and Mary had been killed by a man." She smiled. "Like most men, you underestimate women. You think us weak, but that is because you are afraid of us. Compared to us, men are as weak as ditch water is to wine."

Nick had to own that, generally speaking, he agreed with her, but did not give her the satisfaction of saying so out loud.

"I was right about one thing," Nick said. "The note Cecily received was written by a man. A left-handed man. Your nephew, Sir Christopher." He had seen Sir Christopher holding the dagger in his left hand.

"He fancied himself in love with Cecily," the countess sneered. "After only one dance. Infatuated fool. I was watching from the dais and saw how repulsed she was, how she shrank from those clammy hands of his. The dance was barely over, the last notes of the lute still hanging in the air, when she made good her escape. She forgot all about him, I can tell you."

Not so Sir Christopher. Nick could picture him walking home to Cheapside in a daze of romantic longing, convinced he had found his one true love, penning his pathetic note as soon as he reached the house, thinking it a masterpiece of passionate prose instead of a chilly and peremptory summons.

"It was you who slipped Cecily the note," Nick said.

"Of course. I put it in Cecily's pocket that morning in chapel after service. It was easy."

"If you disapproved of your nephew and Cecily so much, Countess, why did you pass on the note?"

She gave him a pitying look, as if to a village idiot. "To test her, of course. If she had not gone to the chapel that night, I would have let her live." She shrugged. "It was her own fault."

Nick wanted to fasten his fingers around her fat neck and squeeze until her face turned black and her eyes bulged in their sockets. He looked away until he got himself under control. He felt a contagion of evil and unhappiness leeching into his bones, wrapping itself around his heart and squeezing. His sudden, over-whelming rage, he fancied, was a sickness caught from the very stones of this place, a plague that ate away at all that was good and true and beautiful.

"Evil must be purged," the countess said, drawing herself up with a dignity that was grotesque; it was as if they were having a chat in one of the sumptuous palace parlors. "The court must be cleansed."

"By you?"

The countess looked surprised. "Of course," she said. "I am the Queen's protector."

Nick laughed. He couldn't help it.

"A slur against me is a slur against the Queen," the countess said. "It is rank treason. You would do well to remember that, young man, before you mock me again."

"Why Cecily?"

"I would have thought that was obvious."

"Humor me."

"I have been with Her Majesty a long time," she said. "The ladies who wait on the Queen have come and gone; only I have remained." Smugly, the countess folded her hands in her lap. "Over time, I have noticed a marked deterioration in the morals of the court."

As if Henry VIII was such an upstanding character.

"Adultery. Fornication. Immodesty of dress. Coarse language. Lasciviousness of all kinds," the countess said.

Nick watched with fascination as this woman, dressed in rags and living in her own filth, capable of plotting and carrying out cold-blooded murder, prated about the world going to hell in a handbasket.

"When Cecily came to court, I thought, 'Now here is some-one unsullied, someone pure. Here is a girl I can train to one day take my place.'" The countess peered at Nick. "I am not deluded, young man. I know I will grow old and infirm. The Queen will need someone young when that day comes."

The countess was talking as if the Queen were immortal, exempt from the ravages of time. In reality, Elizabeth and the countess were the same age. Like a Catholic's devotion to Our Lady, the countess had adored and worshipped the Virgin Queen, her royal person the shrine she dressed each morning and put to bed each night. Nick remembered how he had dismissed the countess as a fussy old woman, a battle-ax, a mere stage nurse, fit only to be derided and then ignored. He had failed to see the fatal obsession in her behavior, had been blind to the insanity of her hero-worship, a worship that bordered on religious mania.

"It was at the Accession Day Ball that I realized Cecily was like all the rest," the countess said. "She had become friendly with that little whore."

"Mary."

The countess had a faraway look in her eyes, as if reliving the moment. "Always giggling together. Running instead of walking. Sneaking off when there was work to be done. Her clumsiness I could have mended," the countess said. "Her soul I could not. Then I saw her dancing with my nephew." Her eyes narrowed. "She ensnared him, caught him in her wiles. And when my nephew told me he was in love with her and gave me the note, I knew what I had to do."

"Sir Christopher said he was with you around midnight that night," Nick said. "That was true. You were together, but I did not consider to ask where."

"The chapel," the countess confirmed. "I knew he would be there mooning about, waiting for that slut to arrive. I gave Cecily some extra work to do to delay her and I came myself."

"Matty overheard you."

"Who?"

"Matty, the cinders at the palace," Nick said.

The countess shrugged as if the idea of a lowly servant testifying against her was too outlandish to entertain.

"How did you persuade Sir Christopher to leave before Cecily arrived?"

"I told him the girl was not coming, that I had overheard her telling Mary he was pigeon-livered and lacked gall. I told him he made her sick to look on."

The cruelty of it took Nick's breath away. He could imagine Sir Christopher's heartbreak, his shame and terrible sense of betrayal. His dreams in ruins. Never mind that he might have discovered his aunt was lying if only he had remembered that Cecily had not known who wrote the note because it bore no signature. A lifetime of doing exactly what the countess told him to do had overridden his judgment. If Sir Christopher had been weak and foolish, the countess had made him so.

"So you were waiting for Cecily when she arrived," Nick said. "Somehow you got close to her without her suspecting."

"When I revealed the identity of her precious suitor, she burst into tears," the countess said. "When I approached her, she thought I was going to offer comfort."

Swallowing down his revulsion and aware that the scribe was recording every word, Nick forced himself to continue. "You stabbed her through the heart and then lifted her body onto the altar."

"Light as a feather," the countess confirmed.

"Why pose her?" Nick asked. This was one of the aspects of the murders that had puzzled him the most and led him and the Queen to suspect a religious and political motive. In a sense they had been correct; the countess saw herself as a holy scourge driving out the evil of the court.

"She was an offering to the Queen, of course. A sacrifice."

Hearing a soft gasp behind him, Nick saw the scribe sitting white-faced, pen poised motionless above the page. Up to now, the man had been writing with the impassive face of a bored bureaucrat, as if the appalling confession entered his ears and flowed straight to his hand, bypassing his soul on the way. But even he, it seemed, had reached the limit of his endurance.

"We'll take a break," Nick said.

Ignoring the countess's protests, Nick banged on the door for the guard to let them out.

Both Nick and the scribe instinctively made for the stairs and the daylight above. Once outside, Nick leaned against the Bell Tower's outer wall and drew in great cleansing breaths of cold air. He felt like Lazarus newly emerged from the tomb, the memory of the countess's words the winding cloths that bound him still.

"You all right?" the guard asked. He had followed them out after locking the cell door.

Nick managed to nod. The scribe came out and scuttled past, making for the guards' privy on the other side of the inner court.

★ ★ ★

Returning to the dungeon was one of the hardest things Nick could remember ever having to do. He had to force his feet to take the stairs down into the darkness, as if he knew that, once there, he would never reemerge into the light.

The countess was sitting on her stool in exactly the same position, as though no time had elapsed at all.

"Mary," Nick said without preamble. "You saw her leave the palace to keep her assignation with Sir Hugh."

"She was regular as clockwork in her sluttish ways," the countess admitted. "I'll give her that."

"You saw her come back into the palace and go down into the cellar."

The countess nodded. "Regular in her thieving too."

The rest Nick knew from the state of Mary's body. He had been right about the difference between Mary's murder and Cecily's but wrong about assuming there were two killers. Mary's death had not been a crime of passion so much as a crime of opportunity. The countess confirmed this. "I had marked her out to die the same way Cecily had. In the chapel. But God put her in my way as a sign."

"A sign?"

"That I was doing His holy work, of course."

"And you would have continued to kill?"

The countess wagged a finger at him. "Except you sent all the others away."

Thank Christ for that, Nick thought. It was the only wise thing he had done in this whole tragic business.

"I had words with the Queen about that, told her not to send her ladies home, that it was not fitting for her to be left untended. She insisted."

Nick recalled Codpiece telling him that he had overheard the Queen and the countess quarreling after Mary's death. The countess might delude herself that her objection was based on concern for the Queen's state, but the countess had obviously been enraged at being deprived of further victims.

Nick was now desperate to bring the interview to a close. He had long since abandoned his stool and was pacing up and down, unable to keep still, the lanterns throwing lurid shadows on the walls, a restless demon mimicking his every move.

"And then there was Perkin; he found out somehow and was blackmailing you."

"He was always loitering outside doors, eavesdropping," the countess said. "He overheard my nephew accusing me of murdering Cecily the same day you came to the house to interview us. At first I paid him off, but I knew, of course, that he would never stop, that he would have to be silenced. I asked him to reach something down for me from the dresser in the kitchen, and when he turned his back, I stabbed him with one of the kitchen knives." The countess shrugged. "It was easy. The hard part was shifting the body and shutting up that bloody dog."

Nick had maligned Sir Christopher, thinking he had killed his own dog. Until Sir Christopher had met Cecily, the dog was probably the only living thing that he had ever truly loved. But, like Cecily, even his own dog had not loved him in return. Nick recalled the hatred in its eyes when Sir Christopher had been holding it. Nick may have intensely disliked Sir Christopher, but the loveless sterility of the man's existence almost made him weep. So too Perkin's brief, miserable life, untimely taken.

"That lack-wit of a nephew couldn't even get rid of the body properly," the countess said. "I told him to throw it in the Thames, where the currents would have taken it away. Instead, he chose the Fleet and was seen by that urchin. Useless." Then she looked at Nick, and a cunning look came into her eyes. "What we have been talking about is all speculation, you know. A pretty fiction. There is no proof. Without that, you have no case." She rose to her feet, smoothing down the rags of her skirts as if she were about to parade into the Great Hall of Whitehall Palace behind the Queen. "Escort me hence," she said imperiously, holding out her hand in order to lean on Nick's arm. "The Queen must hear of how her loyal subjects are treated."

"A moment," Nick said, taking something out of the inside of his doublet. He held it up. "Do you recognize this?"

The countess squinted in the gloom. "Never seen it before."

But Nick had seen her face change in recognition. In his hand was the long hairpin he had found in the countess's jewel casket in the house in Cheapside the day he had gone in pursuit of Sir Christopher, after Wat had identified Perkin's body. Putting back the jewels, he had found the wickedly sharp needle. It had reminded him of similar hairpins his mother owned, now considered old-fashioned. No longer did women wear headdresses made of boxlike frames draped with veils, a Spanish fashion that Henry's first wife, Katherine of Aragon, had brought to England. The countess's hairpin had been designed to hold a precious stone at its tip, but the stone was missing. When Nick had fitted the topaz into the hole, he had found it to be a perfect fit.

As soon as he saw it, he realized that he'd found the weapon used to kill Cecily. Not an assassin's stiletto but a woman's hairpin. When he had run to Cockspur Street, he had known the countess was Cecily's killer. After Sir Christopher confessed that same night, Nick knew that the countess was also responsible for Mary's and Perkin's deaths.

★   ★   ★

Dusk had fallen by the time Nick left the Tower and trudged back through the streets of Petty Wales toward London Bridge. A great cloud of starlings swooped above the rooftops, making their harsh calls as they gathered and settled for the night in the ancient elms hard by Tower Green.

The Queen was expecting him to make his report on the interview, but he didn't have the heart. Let the scribe give her the official verbatim account to read. After Nick's arrest of the countess in Cockspur Street, he had given the Queen an initial briefing, but he had decided to delay making his official report until after the countess's execution. That was to take place two days hence. If this irritated Good Queen Bess, so be it.

He had caught a killer, but at what cost? Cecily's death could not have been prevented, but he would always blame himself for the deaths of Mary and Perkin. At least he had been able to save Sir Christopher.

If Nick had not brought the beggar girl to the Cheapside house, Sir Christopher would not have panicked and fled to Cockspur Street. Up to this point, Sir Christopher had been prepared to keep silent in return for possession of the countess's will, which named him as her sole heir. When John searched Sir Christopher's house the day of the arrest, he had discovered the document hidden behind a panel in the walls of Sir Christopher's study. The name of the Queen had been crossed out and the nephew's written in. If not for Sir Christopher's hold over his aunt, he would have inherited nothing.

As soon as she set eyes on him at the house on Cockspur Street, the countess would have known her nephew had to die; he was too dangerous to be allowed to live. A bare hour later and Nick was certain he would have found Sir Christopher's body, a dagger clutched in his hand as if he had killed himself out of remorse. A confession of his crimes would have been found conveniently to hand. But for Nick's discovery of the hairpin and his prevention of Sir Christopher's murder, the countess would have escaped justice.

Turning onto London Bridge, Nick slowly made his way to the opposite bank and home. Far beneath his feet, the mighty river flowed inexorably to the sea; tomorrow it would return. Nick wished his heart were tidal, for then all that he had witnessed, all that he had heard, could be washed clean. Instead, his heart was a fortress moated by blood, and he, both gaoler and condemned, forever doomed to live within its walls.

CHAPTER 21

The Black Sheep Tavern

The annual Christmas bash at The Black Sheep was in full swing. Well, if Nick were honest, it had started out as a party, but as the evening wore on and regular patrons drifted in, it had turned into a right knees-up. It was Nick's fault, and judging from the looks Maggie had been sending him, she thought so too. He was stationed by the door and hadn't had the heart to turn anyone away. Earlier in the evening, it had been a much quieter affair with just a few friends: Maggie, John, and the children; Rivkah and Eli; Kat and Joseph; Richard, aka Codpiece, currently sitting on the floor and entertaining Jane, the baby, by pulling faces that should have terrified her but somehow sent her into paroxysms of giggles; Sir Thomas who had put back a fair bit of ale and was looking at Rivkah in a way that made Nick want to throw him through the wall; Black Jack Sims; his grandson, Johnnie, clutching the inevitable tankard of ale in his grubby fist, with Ralph lurking in the background; Will Shakespeare, legless as usual. And Kit Marlowe, even more sloshed. Any minute now their debate concerning the use of masque would come to blows, Kit maintaining that it lent an elegant symbolism to drama, Will saying it "buggered up the realism."

"Now a play within a play," Will slurred. "That's something else. Comic subplot and all that."

"Bawcocks!" shrieked Bess the parrot. Kit saluted her with his tankard; Will raised two fingers. As elegant a summary of their opposing aesthetics as anything Nick had witnessed.

Now the gathering had swelled in numbers: Harry the Tinker was slouched in a corner, trying to grope any woman within reach; Mistress Baker was in earnest conversation with Maggie about how to make sure a pie crust didn't burn; numerous neighbors, sailors from the wharves, and punters just let out from the Bear Garden and the Bull Baiting Ring were in full cry, laying odds on the Garden's latest acquisition, Bardolph the bear, said to have been captured in Epping Forest. And there was a shy newcomer in their midst, sitting on the floor with Codpiece and holding Jane on her lap. Matty, the cinders from Whitehall, who had not stopped eating since Nick had brought her from the palace and told her The Black Sheep was now her new home.

The little beggar girl from the steps of St. Paul's Cross had been taken in by Mistress Plunkett and her husband. It turned out the child's name was Allison. "Our own are all growed up and moved away," Mistress Plunkett said. "Allie's family were carried off in last summer's pestilence. How she survived on the streets, only the good Lord knows." The little girl standing next to the cook had been wholly unrecognizable as the small heap of rags Nick had first encountered. Washed and dressed in a plain but good-quality frock, her hair combed and plaited, her cheeks beginning to show a little color from plentiful food, Allison now looked like a human being rather than a death's head. She had been too shy to speak, but when Nick crouched down to say goodbye, she had thrown her arms around his neck and clung to him. Over her shoulder he saw Mistress Plunkett surreptitiously dab her eyes with a corner of her apron. "She says you saved her," she told Nick.

"I think it's you who is her savior," he replied.

Nick sat nursing his drink, content for the moment to be a spectator, to drink in the noise, feast his eyes on people he called friends, people who seemed to bear more substance in the world than he did himself. The investigation had worn him down, left him feeling like a counterfeit coin passed from hand to hand for too long, the base metal beneath the gold beginning to show.

★ ★ ★

On the day of the execution, Nick had gone to see the Queen. She was in her private suite, and there was no sign of Codpiece. Expecting to be dragged over the carpet for having delayed making his report, Nick was pleasantly surprised to find Elizabeth in a good mood.

"Well, Nick," she said, waving him forward and indicating he should sit, "you've done well."

"Thank you, Your Grace," he said, eyeing the flagon of wine and the extra goblet.

"Go on, then," Elizabeth said. "And give me a top-up. We've much to celebrate."

The problem was, Nick didn't really feel like celebrating. That morning he had stood on Tower Hill with Sir Edward Carew, Cecily's father. Mary's parents had declined to come.

The countess had mounted the scaffold with grotesque dignity, seemingly oblivious to the hail of filth, rotten vegetables, and stones pelted by an angry mob. The ugliness of the crowd's mood now that the countess—dubbed the "Court Killer"—was herself caught (a pun the Londoners relished) was in direct proportion to their fear when she had been at large. Denying the countess a private death on Tower Green within the walls was a sign that the Queen would show no mercy or favoritism when it came to the meting out of justice. Nor would she allow the countess any final words from the scaffold. But she had refused to order the commoner's death of hanging, drawing and quartering; instead, she granted what mercy the countess's exalted rank entitled her to— the headsman's ax.

As the executioner's blade had flashed on its downward descent, Nick had turned away. He had had enough of death, had no stomach for more, however richly deserved. He pushed his way through the crowd, sickened by the bloodlust he saw in peoples' eyes, in his friend's eyes. At the meaty thump of the ax, the crowd had sighed with almost orgasmic release, then cheered itself hoarse as the executioner held the severed head aloft.

He waited on the edge of the crowd until Edward joined him. Slowly they walked back toward the city.

"I thought I'd feel better," Edward said after a long silence. "But Cecily is still gone."

Nick drew his cloak more tightly about him and quickened his pace, Hector loping at his heels. He didn't know what to say except that he had often found this to be true, that any death, even the justified death of an enemy, was so much ashes in the mouth. He clapped his friend on the back and left it at that.

The countess had destroyed much more than the three lives she had deliberately taken. Lady Carew, Edward told him, had never completely regained her wits after the murder of her eldest child.

"She blames herself," Edward said. "She was the one who put Cecily forward to the Queen."

★   ★   ★

When he had returned to The Black Sheep from his interview with the countess in the Tower, the first thing Nick had done was strip and wash himself in the icy water from the well. Then he busied himself helping John and Maggie prepare for the Christmas rush, serving behind the bar until closing time, sitting in a corner by the fire during lulls, silently sipping wine and trying to ignore the concerned looks of his friends.

That same night, Rivkah stopped by—unusual for her, as she seldom frequented the tavern when it was open—and, after a few low words with Maggie, came over to where Nick was sitting in his usual place.

"Here," she said, handing him a little packet. And when Nick didn't open it, she added: "St. John's Wort."

"Thanks," Nick replied.

She sighed and sat down beside him. "You don't know what it is, do you?"

"Not a clue."

Rivkah looked as if she was going to explain, then changed her mind. Instead, she took the packet from him and tipped some of its contents into his wine, stirring it with her finger.

"Hey," Nick said.

"Drink," she instructed.

"Yes, Doctor."

She looked at him for a few seconds, then rose. "I'll be going, then."

Nick put a hand on her arm. "Stay."

She smiled and shook her head. Giving a pat to Hector who was sleeping at Nick's feet, she left. Nick sat looking at the door for a long time.

★ ★ ★

The Queen was speaking, and Nick hadn't heard a word. He tried desperately to pick up the thread. It didn't do for a subject's mind to wander when their monarch was holding forth.

"You've no idea what I was saying, have you?" Elizabeth said.

"Er . . ."

She gave him a shrewd look. "That bad, eh?"

Not for the first time, Nick was convinced she could read minds. He lifted his hands palm upward in a helpless gesture.

"No time to go all mopey on me," the Queen said. "I need you."

"Thank you, Your Majesty."

"Don't thank me yet, Nick. The next job may be worse."

Elizabeth was looking into the fire as if lost in thought. Then suddenly she laughed, but when she turned back to Nick, her eyes were hard and bright. "Do you know what the Puritans call me?"

If Nick was startled by this abrupt change of subject, he was careful not to show it. "No, Your Majesty."

"'Mother of Harlots and Abominations,'" Elizabeth said. "It has a certain ring to it, don't you think?"

Nick wisely said nothing. For all her toughness, he could tell Elizabeth was wounded by being called a harlot. It hurt her to find that there were subjects who still plotted against her, still longed to see her dead. It was as if she were a mother reviled by her own children. And no matter how many subversives and traitors she sentenced to death, like the many-headed Hydra, more sprang up to replace them. Nick knew that he and Sir Thomas would be busy for many years to come. Which made him remember: he still hadn't gotten around to reporting in to the Spider yet after his mission to the Continent.

"Then there are those who believe I am the Virgin Queen," she said. "Indeed, I have encouraged them to do so." Her face darkened. "The countess certainly believed it." Suddenly she leaned forward in her chair. "Do you think I am responsible for creating such a monster, Nick? Is it I who have the blood of Cecily and Mary on my hands?"

It was as if Nick were suddenly looking at the Queen in her shift before she put on her gorgeous robes of office, and what he saw was a woman, alone and beset by doubt. "No," he said. "You have always known the limits of your state; the countess never did. She styled herself your servant and used it to justify her actions, when all along it was herself she served."

Elizabeth searched his face. "Thank you," she said at last. "That is a comfort to know." Then, smoothing down her skirts, she rose to signal the audience was over.

"You must be eager to return to your den of iniquity," the Queen said.

Nick thought that he would vastly prefer the iniquity of Bankside to that of the court. South of the river, evil did not wear a disguise, but walked openly. Nevertheless, out of politeness, he started to protest, but the Queen waved him to silence. "No, no, don't start lying to me now. You were doing so well. Off you go," she said. "And take this." She handed him a heavy leather purse. "Give this to the Jewish doctors with my thanks. I might have a use for them again."

Nick bowed to hide a grin. He couldn't wait to tell Rivkah the Queen had used a plural noun to describe Rivkah and her brother. She would value that far more than the gold.

"And what about you?" Elizabeth asked.

"Majesty?"

"A reward, you dolt. And don't give me any guff about service to your Queen being its own reward."

So Nick had asked the Queen if he could bring Matty from the palace to The Black Sheep. She looked thoughtful. "Not going soft on me again, are you Nick?"

He knew she was referring to the clemency he had bade her show Sir Christopher despite being an accessory after the fact to the deaths of Cecily and Mary by keeping silent, and Perkin by disposing of the body. Not to mention the tax fiddle he and Master Summers at the Custom House had been involved in. She had satisfied justice by imposing a huge fine on them both and stripping them of their trading licenses. Then she had banished Sir Christopher from court but had allowed him to inherit part of his aunt's fortune; the rest had reverted to the Crown. The last Nick had heard, Sir Christopher had retired to the most remote of the countess's estates on the far northern border with Scotland. Master Summers had gone to live with his sister in Bristol.

"Sir Christopher's suffered enough, Majesty," Nick had said. "The countess tormented him for years, made him her lapdog, broke his spirit utterly. Let him find whatever peace he can."

The Queen had harrumphed but had taken his advice.

Sir Hugh had been released from the Tower the same day as

the countess's arrest. Much chastened by his experience, he had left the court and returned home to his father's manor near Bath. It was rumored that he had since amended his promiscuous ways and become unusually devout; he and Lady Alice were to be married as planned in the New Year. Perhaps love could conquer all, Nick mused when he'd heard the news.

The Queen had granted her permission about Matty.

"Thank you, Your Grace. Happy Christmas."

"Happy Christmas to you too, Nick."

As he closed the door behind him, his last glimpse of the Queen was of an aging woman sitting alone, staring into the flames.

★   ★   ★

Much as Nick was doing at the Christmas party. Will Shakespeare staggered over and put a heavy arm across Nick's shoulders, whether out of friendship or to prop himself up Nick wasn't certain. "Thou must be patient; we came crying hither," he intoned. "Thou knowst, the first time we smell the air, we waul and cry." He hiccupped.

"Thanks, Will. That really cheers me up."

"All's well that ends well," Will said, raising his tankard.

Nick looked affectionately at his friend and chinked tankards. "To thine own self be true," he said.

Will squinted at him, blearily, and then his face lit up. "That's bloody brilliant," he said. "Mind if I pinch it for one of my plays?"

Author's Note

The Australian novelist and journalist Geraldine Brooks said that historical fiction is "taking the factual record as far as it is known, using that as scaffolding, and then letting imagination build the structure that fills in those things we can never find out for sure." Choosing to set a mystery in the Elizabethan era is a daunting task because the period is already crowded with historical events, from the Babington plot to the invasion of the Spanish Armada and beyond.

It is also dominated by two figures who cast very long shadows—Elizabeth I and William Shakespeare. As Brooks notes, the historical novelist's challenge is to find the spaces between these known facts in which to create a believable fictional world. I have done this, in part, by mixing historical figures in with fictional characters. The fictional Nick Holt is drinking buddies with Will Shakespeare and Christopher Marlowe in The Black Sheep Tavern, and frequents a court populated by the fictional Codpiece and Countess of Berwick and the real-life Cecil and Sir Francis Walsingham.

A sharp-eyed historian will spot that I have placed the young Shakespeare in London in 1585, which is almost three years earlier than the historical record attests. I just could not envision a novel about Elizabethan London without his presence. I hope purists can forgive this liberty.

I have also taken liberties with the character of Cecil. In 1585 he was only twenty-two and a student at Cambridge University, but I wanted

326 ~ AUTHOR'S NOTE

to establish him as an antagonist to Nick from the outset of the series. I believe that, as the son of Baron Burghley, one of the most powerful of Elizabeth's courtiers, it is not too much of a stretch to believe he obtained an influential position for his son. The playwright Christopher Marlowe serves as a precedent: as a young man he was on the books as a student at Cambridge while in reality he was spying for the realm abroad. The nickname I've given Robert Cecil—the Spider—is entirely fictional.

Another indulgence relates to the character of Codpiece, who is entirely fictional. Unlike her father, Henry VIII, Elizabeth did not have a Fool. I have also given Elizabeth more ladies-in-waiting than we know she had: I did this to allow myself plenty of scope in killing two of them off. All are fictional.

For the record, Elizabeth was probably not as unwashed as I make her out to be. In fact, her father, Henry VIII, had a "bathing room" installed in Whitehall Palace in the 1540s which Elizabeth updated. References to her lack of hygiene in the prologue are for comedic purposes and are given from the point of view of a naïve character. Forgive me, Gloriana.

Language poses an especially difficult challenge. I have tried, wherever possible, to employ words that were in use during the Elizabethan era, but to do so exclusively would have made my characters sound like they were spouting a pastiche of Shakespeare's worst lines. So I have occasionally employed later British usage for the sake of readability.

Incidentally, the quotes from Shakespeare are intentionally garbled. I figured the Bard had the right to misquote lines he hadn't set down in writing yet, especially when in his cups.

One final note: in Elizabethan England there was no such thing as the separation of Church and State. Everything political had religious overtones, and vice versa. To be a practicing Catholic was treason. This explains why Nick is haunted by his family's status as suspected secret Catholics or "recusants," forcing him to tread a very fine line at court.

For all other discrepancies and inaccuracies, I humbly say, along with Shakespeare's Puck: "Gentles, do not reprehend: / If you pardon, we will mend."

ACKNOWLEDGMENTS

Many thanks to my agent, Carol Mann, for her unflagging support over the years.

A huge shout-out to Faith Black Ross, my editor at Crooked Lane Books, and the entire editorial, production and marketing team.

Thanks to Naomi Hirahara for her advice and encouragement during the writing process.

Magdalen, Logan, and Esther; Helena; Charles, Sarah, and Penny; Benedict: You are the best.

And Greg. Always and forever.